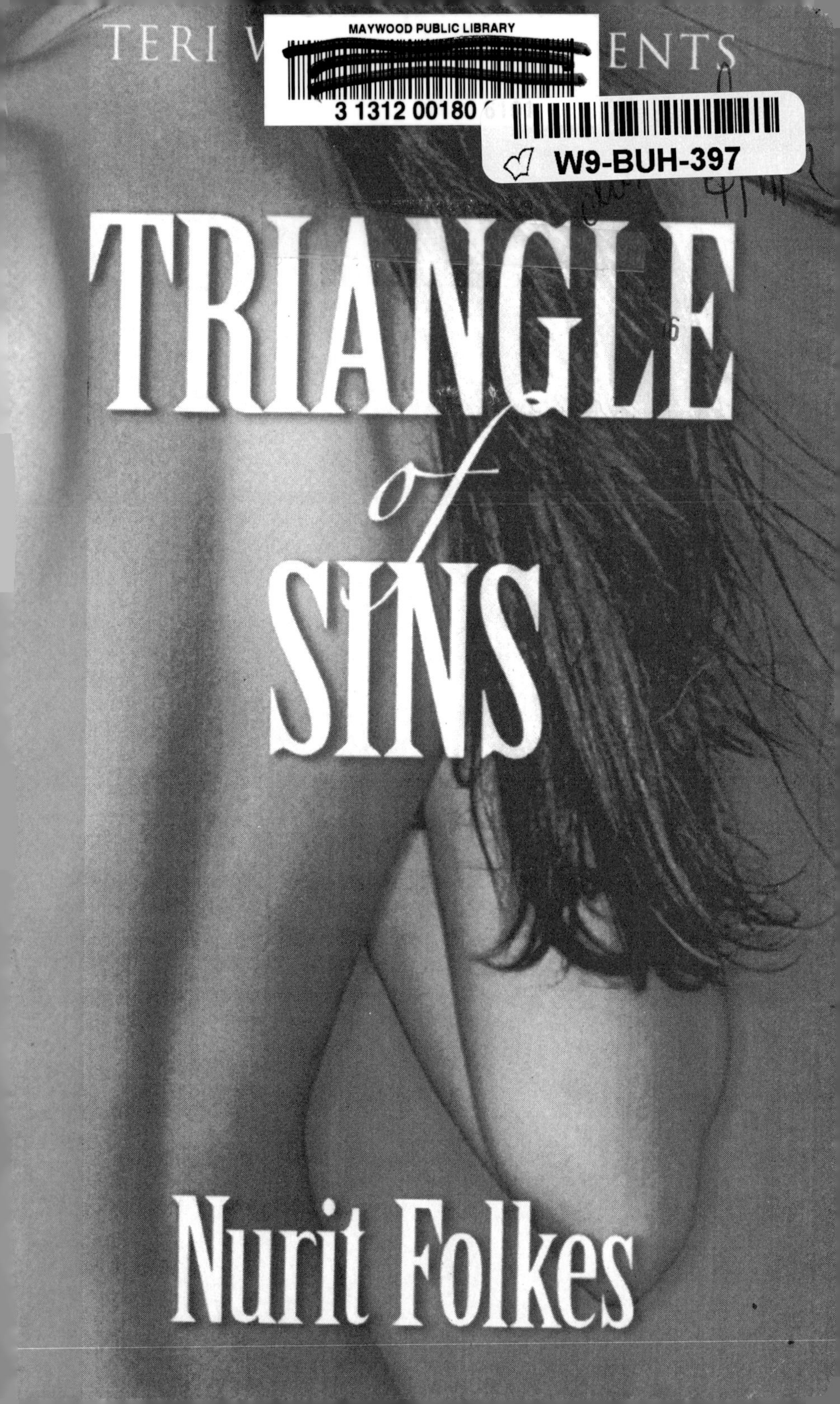
TERI W ENTS
MAYWOOD PUBLIC LIBRARY
3 1312 00180
W9-BUH-397
TRIANGLE
of
SINS
Nurit Folkes

For information on how individual consumers can place orders, please write to Teri Woods Publishing, Greeley Square Station, P.O. Box 20069, New York, New York, 10001-0005.

For orders other than individual consumers, Teri Woods Publishing grants a discount on the purchase of 10 or more copies of a single title order for special markets or premium use.

For orders purchased through the World Wide Web and/or P.O. Box, Teri Woods Publishing offers a 25% discount off the sale price for orders being shipped to prisons, including but not limited to federal, state and county.

PUBLISHED BY TERI WOODS PUBLISHING

TERI WOODS PRESENTS

TRIANGLE *of* SINS

Nurit Folkes

This novel is a work of fiction. Any resemblances to real people, living or dead, actual events, establishments, organizations and/or locales are intended to give the fiction a sense of reality and authenticity. Other names, characters, places, and incidents are either products of the author's imagination or are used fictitiously, as are those fictionalized events & incidents that involve real person and did not occur or are set in the future.

Published by Teri Woods Publishing
Greeley Square Station
P.O. Box 20069
New York, NY 10001-0005
www.teriwoods.com

Library of Congress Catalog Card No: 2003100731
ISBN: 0-9672249-3-4

Triangle of Sins Credits:
Written by Nurit Folkes
Edited by Barbara Colasuonno
Manufactured by Malloy Lithographing
Text formation by Group 33
Cover design created by Group 33 and Lucas Riggins
Cover graphics by Group 33

PRINTED IN THE U.S.A.

ACKNOWLEDGEMENTS

I have to thank God who has put up with a lot of my transgressions. Yet, he still keeps blessing me. I thank my parents, Neville Folkes and Avery Folkes, for staying together long enough for me to grow up having them both in my life. Thank you Daddy for being a good father back then. I love you. I give special thanks to my mother for being there for me every single time I need her. Mommy, you need to know that you are appreciated even after all the headaches I've given you. I love you. Thank you Nico, my rambunctious son, for keeping mommy sane, for loving me unconditionally and wholeheartedly, for the unexpected kisses, hugs, "I love you mommy", for provoking the drive in me to succeed, for making me laugh, and for just being so darn adorable. Mommy loves you infinitely. I have to thank my sisters and brothers, Funny-as-hell David, "Evil-ann" Patti-ann, "Sweetine" Nadine, Ras Judea, Mikey and Pat for the life lessons, for having my back and for the family gatherings that make me appreciate having so many damn siblings. You all make me laugh and love me unconditionally. I wouldn't give that up for anything. There is nothing like family.

I must thank Paula Harris for pushing me to read a book that disappointed me. I thought to myself, "I could've done better than this!" Then out poured TRIANGLE OF SINS.

I have to thank Teri Woods for giving me an opportunity to see years of my creativity come to fruition. You hooked a sister up, and you did it fast! I am truly grateful. Thanks to Teri's secretary, Latoya, who took on the challenge of reading my big ass manuscript. I'm glad you didn't let its size scare you off, and you took the time to pick up that heavy thing and read it! I must thank my attorney and pal, Lorin Lewis, for being the first to read Triangle of Sins straight to the end and giving me the kind of review and response that really made me get on my P's and Q's to get this novel out. Thanks Lorin for being there for me by helping me out with my legal matters and for being such a cool person.

Thanks to my female friend, Erica "Sha-Sha AKA Shaqualla" Sheppard who is the only female who could bear that title for this damn long. You always encouraged my creative visions and ideals as well as feed my ego. Although we get on each other's nerves and we spit fire like no one else can, we've managed to remain friends for over a decade. Go figure. I love you, girl.

Finally, I thank whoever bought this book and those who believe in unconditional love. Even I give up on that notion from time to time, but I know that where there is a heart, there is love.

Live to love and love to live.

Nurit Folkes

TERI WOODS PRESENTS

Nurit Folkes

PUBLISHED BY TERI WOODS PUBLISHING

Chapter One

❤

REQUIEM FOR LOVE

Pop, pop, pop! *Gun shots?* Her thoughts raced. She hopped out of bed and ran down the long hallway to her parents' room.

"Oh God!" she gasped, her heart pounding fast. "Mommy!" she screamed.

The two figures standing over the bloody body looked in her direction. She was too stunned to move. But when she finally did, everything seemed in slow motion. By the time the smooth bottom of her slippers made her skid across the floor, a bullet whizzed by her head and hit the hallway mirror. The fragments of glass scattered over the floor.

"Damn! I ain't get the bitch!" One of the men shouted in frustration. He continued to aim. Luckily, her brain began to function, and her feet moved faster than she thought they could. When she reached the back door, she heard, "Run baby run!" It was her father's voice.

She ran out onto the deck, then through the backyard. She ran about a mile before reaching her neighbor's house. She squeezed her limber body under the wrought iron fence and ran to the front door, her adrenaline in overdrive. She banged on the door as hard as she could. A few minutes passed before it creaked open.

"What's going on?" a tall woman wearing a silk bonnet asked.

With tears rolling down her face, she screamed, "M-mommy is bleeding!"

Her mother died instantly. Her father lived for two days on a respirator before succumbing to the Grim Reaper. After the fact, Natalia learned that one of the murderers worked for her father. He was terminated just days before the murders because of his cocaine addiction. She was nine years old.

Natalia Fole's flashback caused her to shiver in New York City's sweltering ninety-degree weather. The memories of her parents' murders played often in her mind. They reminded her of why she had become an avid activist for non-violence. She was a motivational speaker and self-appointed advocate for victims of violence. Educational institutions, local politicians, and charities regularly requested her.

Impatiently, she waited for Principal Gaines. *If he doesn't hurry up,* she thought, *I'm going into that office to drag his fat ass out here.* She giggled aloud at the image. She uncrossed her moist thighs, slid out of the chair and, with legs apart, stood to smooth the wrinkles from her powder blue skirt. All eyes were on her, including those belonging to the secretary and school nurse. They had whispered about her since she walked in. Her curvaceous body was the epitome of sexy. She was used to the envy of other women. Her full C cups always commanded attention, and her clear, honey-brown face was angelic. Perfectly arched eyebrows complemented her innocent doe eyes. Soft, dark hair flowed to the middle of her back.

Although she looked like eye candy and lit up a room with her infectious smile, she was a fully loaded package. Well educated, she had earned her master's degree in sociology from New York University.

When Natalia turned twenty-one, she inherited land on both Jamaica and St. Croix which included tourist shops, restaurants and motels. She also inherited the remaining available units in a ten-story condominium complex in Brooklyn Heights that she rented out, two thriving McDonald's restaurants in Manhattan, and the posh Westchester home in which her parents had died. After her aunt, her legal guardian, had died, she couldn't bear to live in the house all alone with its tragic memories so she sold it, furniture included, for a whopping 1.4 million dollars.

Principal Gaines finally emerged from his office to greet her. They returned to his office, and she pleaded with him to postpone the lecture she was scheduled to deliver the next morning. After ogling her he finally gave in. She thanked him and gladly hurried out of his ice-cold office. Because he was overweight, he needed to refrigerate his office. His thick, creased neck was always slick with sweat.

Natalia sighed as she stepped outside into the thick humidity. The day had been a trying one. She had gone from one business meeting to another. At times, her responsibilities were tiring and overwhelming, but she was afraid to let another step in to oversee things. Her father never needed help so she figured she didn't either. But now that her work was finished for the day, she set out for her final destination — home.

Aaah!" She settled into the beige and gold marble tub. Her bathroom was regal, fit for a queen. Equipped with gold fixtures and a private toilet enclosed in frosted beveled glass, there was also a forty-five inch television with surround sound built into the wall facing the whirlpool. All her life she had been spoiled. In the beginning, it was her parents. After their deaths, it was her aunt. Then soon after she graduated college, her aunt died from cervical cancer and left her on her own with no family in America.

It was nine-thirty at night, and as her fiancé rang the bell, he peered into the hidden security camera. He looked around at the house and smiled at its beauty. Building the house in Manorville was her vision. She had helped design and develop the plans for it. She liked the seclusion Manorville offered and felt safe there. Even when the foreman strongly suggested that she enclose her estate with a stone wall and security gates, she refused. Instead she chose fruit trees.

Natalia cracked open the front door and peered out. Badly attempting a Chinese accent, she shouted, "We no-uh wan whut you-ah selluh!"

"Well, I ain't selling nothing," he shouted back, laughing. She flung open the door and walked away.

"Nat, don't be angry", he said as he reached for her, but she pulled away from him.

"I tried to get here as fast as I could, but traffic from Midtown was crazy! You know how it is."

"You know what Mark? This is the umpteenth time you've made me re-schedule to spend time with you, and you show up hours late!" she huffed.

"I'm sorry, honey." Mark knew how to make the situation right. Kiss her on the forehead, tenderly run his hands through her hair, look into her eyes as if this was their last time together and plant a wet, lingering kiss on her soft lips. Natalia would always become putty in his hands. But not this time. She folded her arms and glared at him.

"You're gonna get it you spoiled brat!" he quipped.

"Don't fuck with me!" she growled. She plopped down on the edge of a frilly chaise lounge and crossed her legs. "There are going to be a lot of lonely nights for you if you don't make me a priority in your life," she grumbled. Yes, spoiled was an understatement.

"Natalia, I'm not going to drop to my knees and kiss your feet every time you throw a tantrum. You need to change your attitude, or I'll find other ways to fill my lonely nights!" Mark turned from her to hide the smile at the corners of his mouth. He just wanted to get a rise out of her. He loved her, spoiled and all. Natalia, on the other hand, thought of him as a loyal puppy dog.

Mark was a stockbroker and a damned good one. He was partner potential. Last year, he had made three billion dollars for one client alone. But there were times when Natalia craved excitement, and Mark just couldn't deliver anymore. Even still, there was something about him that kept her interested. Besides, he had proposed to her on one knee in the middle of Newark Airport, presenting her with a five-carat Marquis-cut diamond ring. How could she have said no?

"I have to give a lecture at Shore High tomorrow at eleven-thirty. I want you there with a suitcase filled with shorts and t-shirts. We're going to Hawaii," she said matter-of-factly. She had been dying for Mark to whisk her away like he used to. When they first met, he flew her to Miami just for dinner. On her birthday, he pulled major strings to rent out the Museum of Modern Art and had it decorated like a ballroom. He even had a wardrobe woman dress her up like Cinderella, complete with a pair of clear acrylic pumps with Lucite heels. Afterwards, they trotted down Fifth Avenue in a horse-drawn carriage pulled by two beautiful white horses to The Waldorf Astoria Hotel. That night was hotter than hell. It took two weeks for her to come down off of cloud nine.

Mark knelt in front of her and slowly rubbed his hands up her thighs. His fingertips gently pressed into her smooth skin. "I didn't know that I had a master." He pulled his hands back, "Are you asking me to attend the lecture or are you ordering me to?"

"You figure it out," she spat. This trip would be an ultimatum. Mark looked up into her eyes, his face serious. "If I can make it, I'll be there," he sprang to his feet, backed away and muttered, "I'll come back when you're in a better mood." He thought she would ask him to stay. She didn't. He strolled out the door and down the path, pausing to give her a chance to stop him. Natalia got up and closed the door. As she watched him, she thought, "Why'd he have to be so damned cute!" His soft dark hair gleamed under the lights. His ocean blue eyes sparkled when he turned back to look at her longingly. Mark wasn't black but his olive complexion was dark enough for her. His six-foot-one frame was toned and muscular. He was a white girl's dream, but he belonged to her.

Mark flopped down into his car. He stuck the key into the ignition and looked out the passenger's window towards the house. He reached for the knob on the radio and turned it on, "She'll get over it," he sighed. His cell phone rang its distinctive ring.

Y*ep, here she is now, begging for her Italian stud,* he assumed. "Hi baby," he sweetly answered. But instead of Natalia's voice, he heard the ramblings of Mr. Pagachi, a new client. He spat some stockbroker mumbo jumbo at him and hung up. Mark was worried about Natalia; she hadn't been the same lately. He didn't know what was making her so moody. But what he did know was that he already missed her. Beep, beep! An angry driver behind him pounded on the horn. Mark quickly switched lanes and turned up the volume on the radio. Whitney Houston's version of 'I Will Always Love You' was playing. The song calmed him. *Yeah, she'll get over it,* he thought as he mouthed the words out of sync with Whitney.

So many of our urban youths have died because of guns. I know all of you feel that you must protect yourselves, but protection does not mean genocidal extinction."

Natalia was boring the hell out of the teenagers. They were restless and had stopped paying attention a half hour ago. The girls were busy gossiping, giggling and flirting. Most of the boys just stared at Natalia, fantasizing and comparing graphic descriptions of what they'd like to do to her.

"Yo, that bitch is buggin'. I keep the nine close," a pimpled, light skinned boy bragged to his friend.

His friend, who looked older than high school age, stared intently at Natalia. He had seen her before but just couldn't remember where. "Yo, she look mad familiar," he finally informed pimple face.

"You wish you knew her. She sexier than Janet Jackson's fake ass," he chuckled. His friend didn't respond and continued to stare.

Yo, Dray, we goin' to Flatbush to get that shit B-Blaze got or what?" pimple face asked, ignoring the far-off look on Dray's face.

Dray snapped his fingers, "I knew I saw that lady before. She was at Tymeek's trial", he said excitedly. Tymeek Wilson allegedly killed the son of a woman renting a condo in Natalia's building. The charges were dropped, however, due to a technicality. The woman tried to have the case re-opened but couldn't. Then she learned of Natalia's work in victim services and begged her for help. Natalia did just that. She helped the District Attorney apprehend Tymeek by calling in favors from the 67th precinct in Flatbush where she regularly sponsored the Police Athletic League programs. And by wisely allocating a portion of Natalia's contributions to paying for information, the police were able to tap a few of their street resources. In no time, a snitch came forward. The police learned Tymeek's whereabouts. He was an infamous drug and weapons dealer, and his supplier, Lou D'Agostino, was a despicable ex-mob low life. Natalia hired expensive detectives to tail both D'Agostino and Wilson. She was even bold enough to testify about her part in their capture at Tymeek's trial. She had her cake and ate it too when both were convicted. Tymeek awaited an appeal on Riker's Island while Lou D'Agostino was shipped off to a cushy federal holding center upstate New York.

"Yo, I gotta make a call", Dray announced as he hopped up and squeezed past knobby adolescent knees.

"And where do you think you're going?" one of the teachers asked.

"I gotta take a leak," he said with an attitude and brushed past the teacher who seemed afraid of the six-foot teenager. Dray ran into the bathroom and pulled out his cell phone. He dialed quickly. As soon as he heard the other answer, he asked, "Who dis?" Then without waiting for the answer, he blurted, "Ay, yo, tell Shawn I gotta tell him something important."

"Who da fuck is you, Niggah?"

Dray recognized the voice and chuckled, "Yo Ramel, it's me, Dray."

"Oh, whut up punk ass?" Ramel chuckled.

"Whatever niggah. But yo on da real, I got some info for Shawn. Something I know he wanna hear."

"Aiight, hold on." Ramel said.

"What?" Shawn sounded annoyed.

"Whut da deal, pretty boy?"

"That's P.B. to you niggah. Now what you got to tell me?"

"Aiight, check dis out, I'm in school and..."

"In school? Your delinquent ass went to school today?" Shawn laughed hard.

"Ha, ha, whateva. Anyway there's a lady here givin' a speech, and it's the same lady that got Tymeek knocked!"

Shawn wasn't in court the day Natalia testified. Tymeek always schooled him that he, of all people, should never show up if any of them got caught. He told him to send an unknown rookie in his place because eyes and ears were always needed in the courtroom.

"Say word?" Shawn contemplated. He remembered his big brother saying, "Somebody need to stick a dick in the bitch's mouth to shut her up!" He, in turn, asked his brother, "You want me to take care of that for you?" But Tymeek turned down the offer, mumbling "I don't want you in here like me. I need you out there."

Shawn always wanted to be like his brother. His mother pressured him into going to college. So he caved in and went to La Guardia College. But after a year, he dropped out and stepped in for his brother during his 'hiatus'. Now out on the streets, he was The Man. Shawn knew that he wanted to make the bitch pay. "She still up there?" he asked, trying to organize his thoughts.

"Yeah, she talkin' a whole lot of stop the violence bullshit, too." Dray chuckled, "But she fine as hell!"

Shawn didn't hear anything after "Yeah." He was too busy thinking of how he would avenge his brother. "Aiight Dray. Follow her. If she's driving, get her license plate number for me. If she taking the train follow her ass all the way to wherever she rest at. I want the address. And Dray don't fuck this up!" Shawn commanded.

"No doubt," Dray answered.

Natalia was angry. Mark was nowhere in sight. She finally gave up on him and left the empty auditorium. When she reached the teacher's parking lot, she realized someone was behind her. Thinking it was Mark, she turned around with a huge smile on her face only to find a tall, dark skinned boy smiling back.

"Hey, miss, you driving this?"

"Yes," she sighed.

"I thought you'd be in a Benz," Dray said as he kept his eyes on the vehicle. He walked around the back of it, trying to memorize her license plate.

Natalia was unpleasantly surprised, and it showed. She quickly changed her expression to an inquisitive one. "Did you listen to my lecture?"

"Yeah, um, I had to take a leak though so I left in the middle," he lied.

She looked at him suspiciously. "Well, basically, I was trying to get you to understand that I want all of you to make it to the ripe old age of a hundred. I mean, there's so much out there for you if you can just stay away from the negative and stay alive."

Dray felt like telling her to shut up, but he knew he couldn't botch his mission. "Yeah, but if you live where we at, you'd know why it's survival of the fittest out dis mutha...I mean...out here", he replied.

"All I'm saying is something's got to change, boo," she said, attempting to be hip. She heard that word many times in the various high schools she lectured at and couldn't resist using it. "I know that it gets hectic out there, but a black man is a terrible thing to waste," she smiled.

Dray chuckled and nodded in agreement while repeating the letters and numbers from her license plate over and over in his head. "Got it," he said under his breath. "Well, you take care miss. I gotta get back inside." He ran off. Natalia climbed into her SUV, suspecting her speech was in vain.

Dray rushed out of the parking lot and down the block. He flipped open his Startac and dialed Shawn's number. Shawn answered on the first ring and said, "Speak."

"Yeah, I got it. You ready?" Dray asked, pleased with the completion of his mission.

Shawn was eager to get started with 'Operation Payback' and pulled out his Palm Pilot electronic organizer. With the cursor, he pressed one of the icons on the color screen and said, "Go ahead."

Dray told him the numbers and letters quickly.

"Good lookin' out, yo. Come check me after five. I got something for you."

"Aiight, so I'ma see you." Dray checked the time on his fake Tag Heuer watch and smiled to himself.

Shawn had a lot of running around to do so he decided to hold off putting Operation Payback into effect right away.

Natalia needed to vent, so she drove to see her best friend André. She met him her first year in college. André owned two upscale beauty salons in Manhattan. Everyone who was anyone in the entertainment world knew him. He was a consultant on photo shoots, music videos and movies.

She strolled into the extravagant salon armed with a smile. "Oh my goodness. Is that my honey bunny?" André cooed. Natalia giggled. Only "Andy" — as she endearingly called him — could make her forget her anger. "Uh-uh gurl, you are looking fierce today!"

"You think so?" she asked bashfully.

"No, you didn't ask me something crazy. You know damned well that you are too hot to handle," he smirked. Natalia noticed a client sitting in the shampoo chair giving her the once over. The client smiled at her sheepishly. Natalia waved to Jean Claude who was blow-drying a client with hair as red as fire. "To what do I owe the pleasure of your company, missy?"

"I had a fight with you-know-who", she whispered.

"He fucked up again?" André asked loudly.

"I don't want the world to know!" she scolded him. He grabbed her by the hand and whisked her off to his office.

"Oh, please, Ms. Thang, I am so sick of you blasting that poor JFK Jr. wanna be." André grinned and shut the door behind him. Natalia couldn't stop herself from laughing.

"That was a good one Andy."

"Well, it's true," André giggled then asked, "So he didn't call you begging, please baby, baby please, yet?" he laughed.

"No," Natalia sighed and hung her head.

"You know shit is deep when he ain't ring your cell phone like a million times."

André was right. Usually when they argued, Mark would call her constantly until she finally gave in. Her phone hadn't made a sound since her personal assistant, Renée, called. "Do something with my hair, Andy. Make me desirable. I need a new man!" she giggled.

"Nat, you know you can get any man you want. Maybe you need something different," he stroked her back gently, batting his eyelashes at her.

"What do you suggest?" she grinned.

He twirled around and said, "Lets go bump and grind at some exotic club and dance your blues away, honey!"

"Why are you always so damn happy?" She pouted.

"Excuse me?"

"I'm just kidding, Andy, but you're always so damn happy."

"That's because I gets mine darling." They both giggled.

"So let's go shopping and you can pick out something for me to wear tonight."

"Okay! I want to go to the Chanel boutique. They have some fierce tube dresses that I know you'll look delicious in." André locked the door to his office and scanned the salon, checking each hair station carefully. "I want this place spic and span, do y'all understand?" he announced with attitude.

"Yes, master," his employees chimed.

Girl, you look fabu. Come on, turn around for me." André spun her around without waiting and said, "I am digging this outfit."

She stumbled over to the mirror to see how she looked in the Chanel creation André had selected. It was a long tube dress with a bolero jacket. She sighed before turning to André and said, "Andy, I don't like it. Let's go to Gucci."

"But honey bunny you look hot!"

"No, it's not me." In a flash she was out of the dressing room wearing her own clothes again.

André looked her up and down and said, "You are class all the way."

"Oh, you're so sweet," she said modestly. André flashed a smile and pointed toward the cash register.

"Look at that tall glass of champagne." He pointed to a tan Caucasian man holding a gold credit card in his hand.

"Sic im', Andy, sic im'," she instigated.

"Oh girl, I would make him do tricks! Mmm, mmm, mmm." They both laughed.

The Navigator swerved to avoid a yellow cab that cut in front of them. "Asshole!" Natalia yelled out the window. There were no parking spaces on the street so they ended up in a parking garage.

"You hungry, sweetie?" André asked after reaching for the handle on the glass door.

"No, but I do need a drink."

"You mean water, not liquor, right?" André looked at her with a raised brow.

"I mean like a smoothie, duh. It's so damned hot, my lips are burning. You know damned well that I don't drink," she sucked her teeth.

"Yeah, I know your boring prudish ass. When we leave here let's go to your restaurant. I'm in the mood for a free Big Mac." André laughed huskily. He was definitely a man. Trapped, maybe, but a man none-the-less. In fact, he never denied his masculinity. He dressed like a man and, for the most part, looked like one. His dark curly hair was faded on the sides, and his neatly trimmed goatee made it clear that he was a man. His features were almost Hispanic As he stroked his goatee, he said, "I don't want no Mickey Dee's, girl. I'm just playing."

After eating, they headed for André's place. Natalia had asked him to drive because she knew he could handle the bad driving cabbies. He drove fast to his Upper East Side condominium in a sky rise that seemed to go up forever.

"Damn, Nat, I'm gonna have to park this thing in the garage because once again there's no space out here," he said with his head halfway out the window, still searching for a spot.

"Whatever," she said blandly. André pressed the gas pedal hard, speeding down the slope leading into the building's underground garage. He drove in the tunnel like a maniac. When he pulled into a parking space, he looked over at Natalia. She seemed to be in another world. Even as they walked to the elevator, she was still drifting.

"Why are you frettin' over that man?" André asked as he pushed the elevator button.

"I'm not," she lied. She thought of the ultimatum she had given Mark and wondered if he was fed up with her demands.

André grabbed her chin, directing her to look into the mirrored elevator panel. "Now, that's a sexy bitch if I've ever seen one."

Natalia barely smiled. *What the hell is my problem?* she thought. *Why didn't I just leave well enough alone?* It worried her that Mark hadn't contacted her all day. *I guess he's really had it with me,* she thought. André opened his door and pulled Natalia inside his eclectic apartment. She perked up, ran into his bedroom and collapsed on his huge oval bed.

"I love your bed, Andy. I'm sleeping here tonight," she sounded like a little girl.

"You don't want to go out with me?" André asked.

"I don't feel like it. Don't go out tonight. Stay with me," she pleaded.

André thought about it for a moment. "Let's have a slumber party!" he announced as he pulled off his shirt.

"Wow! You are ripped, baby! Woo, look at that six pack!" she shouted and laughed.

"Don't do it to yourself, honey. You know I don't do fish," he snickered and went to his closet.

She reached for his phone. As soon as she picked up the receiver, her cell phone rang in her purse. She nearly broke her neck trying to get to it. "Hello," she breathed heavily.

"Nat, I'm really sorry that I couldn't make it to the lecture." Mark sounded sincere. Natalia was so happy to hear his voice, she didn't care anymore that he missed her lecture. Yet she remained silent.

"Honey, are you there?"

"Mm-hmn," she answered.

"Please don't be mad. I need to see you."

"Well, I'm in Manhattan...I'm with Andy and I promised to go out with him." She was distracted by André who was jumping up and down and waving his hands in the air. "Mark, I'll call you back and let you know," she finished.

"You promise?" Mark figured she would torture him before forgiving him.

"Yes, I promise," she smiled, satisfied with his late phone call.

"So you just gonna flat leave me, huh?" André asked after she hung up.

"What were you trying to tell me when I was on the phone?"

"Just go, Nat, 'cause I wanna get my party on, and I don't need you tagging along, stealing my men," he said, pushing her onto the bed.

"I'll go with you if you're not afraid of competition," she nudged him with her elbow.

"No, Miss Thang. You go get some nookie."

"I know that's right! I'm definitely running on empty," she squealed with laughter.

André fell on top of her and tickled her stomach with the tips of his fingers.

"He's a lucky man," he said looking into her face.

"Get off me before I rape you!" she hollered. Both of them laughed hysterically. André slapped her butt as she hopped off the bed.

"You're asking for it," she pointed a chastising finger at him. He just grinned.

She decided to go home and make Mark suffer. Since he made her wait, she'd go one better and make him wait longer. The drive made her weary. She wasn't sure if she could stay awake long enough to make it home without crashing. She turned up the volume on the radio loud enough to revive herself.

Tymeek was next in line for the phone. The guy on the phone finally said his good-byes and handed him the receiver. He dialed all the necessary numbers and said 'Ty' when the automated voice prompt asked for his name. One of Shawn's henchmen answered the phone. "Speak," he barked.

"Please hold. I have an important call," The pre-recorded voice said.

"Go ahead," the voice prompted.

"Yo, put Shawn on the phone," Tymeek ordered.

"Whut up Ty? It's me Spank," he said excitedly, avoiding the order.

"Sup, Spank? Put Shawn on the phone," Tymeek persisted.

"He on a mission, Ty. All I know is he said he gon' be right back but that was a long time ago," he chuckled.

"Who else is in my house?"

"Just me, Black, D.L. and Nut."

"Y'all better not be fuckin' up my house."

"Naw, never that man. We chillin', we ain't wildin' out."

Tymeek shook his head. He knew they were probably trudging dirt all over his wall to wall and sitting their dirty asses on his leather furniture. His friends always joked that he should be in the Rich and Famous magazine because his house was so stylish.

Shawn kept the house immaculate. He only allowed company to roam the finished basement — unless of course they were of the female persuasion.

"Where y'all at?" Tymeek asked.

"In da basement. Trust me, Shawn don't let us walk around in this house," Spank assured him.

"Damn, how long ago did he leave?"

"Like two hours ago. I told you he said he was gon' come right back, but he ain't been back since."

"So, what's goin on out there?" The first thing that came to Spank's mind was 'Operation Payback.' Shawn had already filled them in on what they had to do. It was all going down tomorrow night. But Shawn told them not to say anything to anyone. Not even to Tymeek.

"Ain't nothin' man. Just da same ol' shit."

"How's da store?"

"It's straight, no doubt." Spank was growing tired of talking to Tymeek so he asked, "Aiight, man. You wanna leave a message for Shawn?"

"Yeah, tell him I'm gonna call tomorrow around this same time, and he better be there."

"Aiight dog, one."

"One," Tymeek hung up. He missed his freedom.

Chapter Two

❤

TROUBLE IN PARADISE

As soon as Natalia stepped out of the shower, the aroma of oregano and garlic hit her. It was a sure sign that Mark was in her kitchen cooking some sort of Italian dish. Besides, he was the only person with a key to her house. She wrapped herself in a beige and gold monogrammed towel and removed her shower cap to free her hair. She crept downstairs and tiptoed into the kitchen. It was empty. Confused, she bumped into one of the glass columns decorating the hall and ran to the front door. There was no sign of forced entry. Before she could turn around, a warm hand cupped her toweled breast. She screamed and jumped simultaneously.

"I'm sorry." Mark's voice calmed her.

She slowly turned to face him. "I almost had a heart attack," she said, wiping away a droplet of water from her shoulder with her finger.

"I'm glad you didn't. I can't imagine wasting all of this," he said as he pulled her towel off. "You smell as good as you look, too," he smiled and kissed her forehead. She melted. She ran her fingers over his face, pulling it toward her. She kissed his lips and slid her tongue in his mouth. Desire overcame her. He hastily unbuttoned his shirt. She ran her hands over the soft hair on his chest, her breathing erratic. Grabbing her legs, he wrapped them around his waist and carried her to the kitchen. She clamped her feet around him. He placed her on the island counter. She was panting and passionately kissing his face and neck. The anticipation of him taking her right there in the kitchen excited her tremendously. As he stroked her back, shivers tingled up and down her spine. Then he backed away from her, licking his lips and went to the fridge. *He's going to use food. We're finally going to get wild and freaky!* Natalia thought. But as he turned around, she saw that he was holding a bottle of sparkling apple and raspberry cider and two chilled champagne glasses. The excitement fizzled and boredom once again crept in. She hopped off the counter and walked toward the stairs. "What the...Nat?" Mark was confused as he followed her. "Where are you going?"

"Upstairs," she answered blandly.

Sex with Mark had become so predictable and monotonous. He was romantic but in the typical way. At one time, he was spontaneous, but somewhere along the way, he lost it. Sex with Mark no longer excited Natalia. Always the same places and in the same positions. She ached for something different.

"Nat, what did I do now?" He followed her up the stairs still holding the two glasses and bottle of cider. "What did I do?" Mark asked again.

She wanted to say, "It's what you didn't do, now go home!" Instead she opted for, "Nothing."

"Are you okay, honey?"

"Yeah."

"So why did you run out of the kitchen like that?" He put the glasses down on the dresser and poured cider into one. He took a gulp, and waited for her to respond.

"No reason. Where's my glass?" she smiled, trying to hide her annoyance.

"Here." He tipped his glass toward her lips. She took a quick sip and went to her dresser. Out of a drawer, she pulled a lilac colored chemise and carefully slipped it over her head. Mark watched as she climbed into bed and curled up to a lavender silk pillow, more confused than before. "Nat, what's the problem? A couple of minutes ago you were hot and ready and now you're acting as if you're sick or something," he said, his anger barely suppressed.

"I just don't feel like moving now," she mumbled. She missed him all day but now wanted him to leave. He had turned her off.

"Do you want me to leave?"

"Markie, come here," she sat up and gestured with her index finger. *I might as well get this over with,* she thought. Moving her hands to her thighs, she began to rub herself. Mark sat next to her on the bed and whispered, "I want you to want it. Don't patronize me."

"I do want it, Marco," she whispered, sliding his unbuttoned shirt off his shoulders and unbuckling his belt. Staring at his bulging pecks, she became aroused again. She kissed him, licking his lips with her wet tongue each time she pulled away. Of course she forced herself into the mood as he began to journey downtown.

Mark's hands were warm as he slid them between her legs. He parted them and kissed the inside of her thighs while sliding his hands underneath her chemise. After a few minutes, he licked his way up to her stomach, circling her navel with his tongue. She trembled with every flick of his tongue. Grabbing the sides of his head, she pleaded, "Put it in me."

As he slid his pants down, he moved on top of her and gently positioned himself inside her. He slid one hand behind her head and one behind her back. He held her tight, pressing his body against hers, moving in slow, rhythmic movements. Minutes later, though it seemed like an eternity, he pulled out and sprayed her stomach with his semen — another thing that irked her. They both were tested for HIV regularly, and both received negative results each time. She made it a point to never miss getting her Depo Provera contraceptive shots. Yet Mark always pulled out before ejaculating, leaving a mess all over her. She felt like she was starring in a porno movie. As soon as he rolled off of her, she jumped up and headed for the bathroom. He fell back into the pillows, content. He decided not to quiz her about her behavior earlier and dozed while waiting for her to come out of the bathroom.

Natalia shook him awake. "Wh-what?" he slurred.

"I have to catch Andy before he leaves me." It was imperative for her to whine about her unhappiness to André tonight.

Mark checked his watch. "Nat, it's after ten."

"So?" she asked with an attitude.

"Are you serious? You're going to Manhattan now?" he asked, his voice raised.

"Yes. I promised Andy I would go with him, remember? I told you when we spoke earlier today. I said I'd call you later but...you just showed up."

"Should I go then?" He was ready to leave regardless of her answer.

"I'm going to spend the night over there so you should go home," she replied matter-of-factly. He ran his fingers through his shiny curls, frustrated by her cavalier attitude.

"You know what? You're really pissing me off. Why do you have to make things so difficult? What is more important? Shaking your ass with some fag or being with me?" he yelled.

"Well, well, well. How does it feel, now that the shoe is on the other foot?" She got dressed and continued. "I guess it's only okay for you to run off in the middle of being with me, huh? Mark, I'm bored. Maybe we both need some time away from each other." She stuffed some tanks, halters, jeans, skirts, dresses, nighties and a bunch of undergarments in a Louis Vuitton duffel bag.

"Are you kidding me? I didn't come over here for this bullshit," he dismissed her with a wave of his hand.

"Whatever," she said, avoiding looking directly at him, "We've been arguing way too much lately. I guess we should've seen this coming."

"Are you telling me it's over?" he asked, worried.

"No. I'm just saying that we need to re-evaluate our relationship. I'm not happy. I'm not sure what it is." She put her hair into an elegant upsweep while she bitched. "One day you're here and the next you're too busy. Then you expect me to just put up with it. I can't anymore. I need you to change. I'm willing to if need be, but it's really all you." She stood in the doorway dressed to kill. Mark was in pain. He didn't see this coming. He gathered his clothes and walked over to her naked. Natalia tried not to stare at his hard body. He stood directly in front of her, his blue eyes sad,

"I'll go. You probably want your house empty when you get back."

He's so pitiful, she thought. He stroked the side of her face and said, "I know that I fucked up a couple of times, but it's not all my fault that you're unhappy. I'm not a psychic. You need to tell me what you want." He paused. "I can try to change. But you need to communicate with me."

Natalia sighed, "I just communicated with you."

"So now you're giving me attitude," he sighed and shook his head. "All I'm going to say is have a good time tonight...and be safe." He eased past her, pulling on his pants and shirt before reaching the top of the stairs.

She watched him go, not quite sure of her feelings, only knowing that he didn't 'do it' for her anymore. She hurried back into the bathroom and grabbed her traveling toothbrush kit. She threw it in the bag. Checking herself in the full-length mirror, she whispered "Yeah, you're hot." Natalia grabbed a white Gucci clutch from her accessories closet and stuffed it with the rest of her toiletries. She heard the front door slam but didn't feel bad about it. She didn't feel a connection to him anymore.

When Natalia stepped off the elevator on the fifteenth floor in André's building, she spied an old man and a young brunette kissing in the hallway. "You go, grandpa," she said under her breath. At André's door, she heard R. Kelly's 'Keep It On The Down Low' blasting. After pressing the bell, she slipped to the side so that he couldn't see her.

"Who is it?" he shouted, looking through the peephole. "I said, who is it?" he shouted again.

Natalia knocked on the bottom of the door, keeping her head low. "What the hell?" André slowly opened the door trying to put the door chain in place. Natalia pushed her way in screaming, "Ta-da."

"You're a damn lunatic," André laughed loudly.

"I'm ready to go, darling," she said, posing like a model.

"I'm not going anywhere."

"Why not, Andy?"

"After you left me, I was listening to my music, and I just didn't feel like being bothered," he shrugged. He checked out Natalia's outfit.

"Ooh, baby you look so nice, though," he said, spinning her around.

Natalia cracked a weak smile, "Well, I guess I can just take this off now," she tugged at the side zipper of the dress.

"That dress is hot like fever, Miss Thang. I like that symmetrical thing happening right here." André ran his hands across the material barely covering her cleavage, "Don't take it off, Nat. I'll take you to the Spirit Lounge." Natalia had already pulled down the zipper.

"Make up your mind!" she screeched. André zipped the dress back up and spotted the bag on the floor.

"What's this? You running away?" He pointed to the bag.

"No. I can't go home tonight so I'm going to sleep here with you," she grinned.

"Ooh, I know something is up now. You want to go out and get you're groove on, and, to top it off, you're not going home. Humph, scandalous."

"Andy, I'm not marrying Mark," she sighed.

"Whaaat?" André screamed, his eyes nearly popping out of his head like a cartoon character. "What happened now?" He held his forehead like he was running a fever.

"Okay, first of all he came to my house unannounced. I was in the shower, and when I came downstairs, I was wearing only a towel. Anyway, he picked me up and brought me into the kitchen."

"Mm-hmn," André listened patiently.

"So I thought he was going to give it to me right there on the counter. But nooo, mister ordinary Joe leaves me there to get sparkling cider from the fridge. So I just went upstairs and then..."

André squinted and shook his head in disbelief.

"What's that look for Andy?"

"Nat, is that why you're not going to marry the man?"

"No, that's not all. He started to make love to me, but I didn't feel anything. I was bored out of my mind. We're always doing it the same old way. I want him to be daring and...freaky."

"What's wrong with you? It's always, I'm not happy, I'm bored, me, me, me," he mimicked her. "I suppose if the man slapped you around, pulled your hair, spanked your ass and treated you like shit you would be happy, huh?"

Natalia was shocked. She didn't expect this reaction from André. She sat on the edge of his bed in silence.

"Honey, I'm sorry if the truth hurts. But women have been fucking themselves over since the beginning of time," he went on, ignoring her glazed expression, "Y'all want a good man, yet when he does come along, y'all send him packing." He demonstrated by imitating a man running with luggage. Natalia couldn't help but chuckle. André chuckled, too. "Why? You know why...because what y'all really want is a man who's gonna dominate. Take control of you in the bedroom and treat you like shit from time to time to keep your asses in place. If he brings you roses and champagne, he's boring. But if he brings you trouble, oh he's so exciting. It's so sad." André was finished. He flopped down next to her on the bed and waited for her to say something. She was flabbergasted. He always took her side, but tonight he chastised her. She covered her face with her hands. She wasn't very nice to Mark, but he put up with her. By now, he was probably tired of her ways. André pulled her hands away from her face and gave her a stern look. "Nat, only you know what can make you happy. So, if it's not Mark, I don't know if you'll ever be happy. Personally, I think he's good for you," André said, rubbing his thumb across her cheek.

"You know what's really sad, Andy?" she turned to him.

"What honey bunny?" He asked. She liked when he called her that.

"All that stuff you said is true. I probably would get turned on if Mark roughed me up a little, pulled my hair, spanked me, robbed a bank, etc. etc.," she laughed at herself. André laughed with her.

"Don't feel bad, mommita. There are freakier people out there than you!" he chuckled and said, "Like me!" They both laughed so hard, their eyes watered.

"Let's go out. I don't want to be depressed."

"Missy after tonight, I suggest you give him one more chance and don't judge him too harshly. You may never find what you're looking for in someone else. But, you may be able to train Mark." They giggled.

Natalia left her Navigator in André's garage. They walked to the corner of 96th Street and 1st Avenue. André flagged down a cab and they got in. Natalia noticed the driver sneaking peeks at her through the rearview mirror. Her cleavage spilled over the top of her snug black and white mini tube dress. She rolled her eyes and ignored him the rest of the trip.

The line was long, but André walked directly to the entrance. The bouncer turned around just in time to see him coming and asked, "What up Dre? Mmm, who's this?"

"This is my best friend, Natalia. Ain't she fine?" André grinned. The bouncer nodded his head in agreement.

"Come on." The bouncer removed the barricade and led them through a steel door and down a pair of winding stairs. Each step was colorfully lit. As they made their way through the crowd at the bottom of the stairs, men pulled and tugged at Natalia's arm. The bouncer glared at one and warned, "Don't touch." Natalia smiled in appreciation. André took her to the bar where they thanked the bouncer. André then attracted the female bartender's attention, and she quickly produced a White Russian for him and a fruit punch for Natalia.

"A penny for your thoughts," he said, sipping his drink.

"I want to dance." She shook her shoulders up and down.

"Heeey, let's go baby," he put down his drink, took her hand, and they shimmied their way onto the dance floor. After gyrating, doing the hustle, the bump and every other old dance imaginable, André started to sweat and unbuttoned his shirt. Natalia pinched his nipples. He grabbed her hands and jumped back. "You're gonna get it, you keep it up," he giggled.

Natalia was attracted to him. Not being able to have him frustrated her. As he danced wildly, bobbing up and down, making suggestive movements while kneeling in front of her, Natalia became horny. "If only..." she sighed, and grabbed his hand pulling him towards the bar.

"What's wrong? You can't keep up?" He asked, fanning himself.

"Nuh-uh," she shook her head.

"You're a party pooper, girl," he frowned. She stuck her tongue out at him and sipped her drink.

Shawn looked at his watch nervously. He had a schedule to keep.

"Where they at?" he asked Nut.

"They comin', don't worry," Nut assured him. Minutes later, two jeeps pulled up in front of the house. The man driving the green Cherokee jeep pressed his hand down on the horn.

Shawn emerged from the house dressed in black. He demanded that everyone wear black for 'Operation Payback.' He pulled on a pair of black leather gloves.

"Y'all ready?" Nut shouted from behind Shawn

"No doubt," they shouted back. Shawn got into a gray, beat up Crown Victoria. Nut rushed to the passenger side. Shawn leaned out of the window and yelled to the others, "Follow me," and sped off down the street.

Once on the Long Island Expressway, Nut asked Shawn, "There's a safe in the house right?"

"I think so," he replied, not taking his eyes off the road.

"I hear she got mad expensive shit," Nut excitedly said.

"I don't know. Kamani at the DMV only gave me the address."

"I heard she pushin' a Navigator," Nut said lighting a cigarette.

"Yeah?" Shawn glanced over at him.

"So whatchu gon' do? You helping us or you just comin' to make sure shit get done right?" Nut asked.

"I'ma help. I'ma make that old bitch wish she never fucked wit Ty." Shawn turned onto Wading River Road leading into Manorville, a secluded, upper class neighborhood on Long Island.

"This is West Bubblefuck, yo!" Nut quipped.

"I hope we find our way back out this muhfucka," Shawn chuckled. He slowed down when he neared Natalia's house. A cluster of peach trees stood close to the road. An old-fashioned mailbox sat on top of what seemed to be a tree stump a few feet away. Shawn pulled up behind the peach trees, motioning to the others following in the jeeps to do the same. He put the car in park and stepped out onto the bright green grass. Nut slammed the car door after getting out.

"You stupid fuck! Just let everybody know we here," Shawn strained to keep his voice below a whisper.

Nut just grinned.

"Come on," Shawn ordered, shaking his head, "Y'all remember what to do right?"

"Yeah," everyone whispered in unison.

"Let's go." Shawn sprinted toward the house. The rest followed behind. The lights in front were bright but the side of the house was dark. Creeping up to the middle of three large arched windows, Shawn peered inside. All was dark. "Go!" he whispered to the others. They surrounded the house like a SWAT team. Nut and Shawn ran to the front and stepped up onto the veranda. They waited patiently. D.L. and Spank were in the back jimmying the locks on the patio doors. The rest were separated into groups of three at both sides of the house, using crowbars on the accessible windows.

D.L. and Spank were successful and entered cautiously. D.L. fell behind Spank who held a gun. With his free hand, Spank felt the wall for a light switch. When he found it, he tapped it slowly. They both looked at each other and grinned. They were in a huge kitchen with sleek and modern appliances. "This bitch got mad loot, son," Spank whispered.

"Damn!" D.L. exclaimed, looking around.

"Yo, we gotta open the door for Shawn," Spank whispered. They crept through the arched opening leading to the hallway and found the front door. Spank twisted the shiny brass handle and the door creaked open. Shawn and Nut both turned simultaneously. Shawn stepped inside while Nut went to the edge of the veranda and whistled. The others swarmed to the front of the house. Shawn went straight to the kitchen and looked around. *Rich fucks!* he thought as he peeked inside the dining room.

"D.L., go upstairs," Shawn commanded.

D.L. crept upstairs. When he reached the top step, he saw two huge white French doors open wide to an enormous bedroom. He quietly walked across the landing and leaned against the door frame. The room was empty. Then he tiptoed to a door on the left side of the room and peered in. As he switched on a light, he was blown away by the extravagant bathroom. After checking out the separate shower room, he proceeded to inspect the rest of the upstairs rooms.

"Ain't nobody here," he shouted to Shawn.

Shawn was furious. He came all this way for nothing. "Fuck," he muttered under his breath.

"Ay, they got some hot shit. Come up here," Spank shouted.

Everyone ran upstairs. Shawn inspected every room again. He became more pissed with every room he entered. "All this money and they try to stop us from gettin' some." He flew down the stairs to the living room, leaving the rest of the crew upstairs. What he really wanted was to kill the woman — now. He plopped down on a frilly chaise lounge, lowered his head into his hands and rubbed his eyes and forehead. When he opened his eyes, he did a double take. On the wall, was a life-sized, framed portrait of a woman perched on a velvet throne. She wore a thin strapped, white evening gown with a plunging neckline. Her hair was swept up but one curl cascaded down the side of her face. Shawn was mesmerized. *A black woman! A young black woman! A beautiful, young, sexy black woman!*

"Is that her?" he asked himself in disbelief. He was still gazing at her when he heard a stampede coming down the stairs.

"Yo, let's be out," Nut shouted at him from the hallway. Shawn ignored him for the portrait. "Niggah let's bounce!" Nut yelled.

Maybe I'll let them niggaz run a train on her, too, Shawn thought.

As he stood up and walked towards the hallway, he looked at her portrait again. "Aiight y'all. We gon' come back tomorrow night."

Shawn pulled over when he neared the parking lot at Parsons Boulevard. "Aiight, you know where to dump this shit right?"

"Yeah," Nut replied, and they gave each other a pound. As Shawn got out, Nut scooted over into the driver's seat and drove off. Shawn hurried to the parking lot and got into his own car.

The parking attendant's eyes lit up when he saw Shawn coming. "How are you tonight, man?" he asked.

Shawn barely acknowledged him. "You took care of my baby?"

"Yeah man, you know I always do." The parking attendant grabbed a bunch of keys from a hook behind him and rushed out to a pearl colored Lexus. He drove it right up to Shawn. "Thanks." Shawn slapped some bills into the man's hand.

He couldn't get the painting out of his head. He imagined ripping off the white dress and rubbing his hands all over her. "I need some ass," he chuckled to himself. He reached inside the glove compartment and pulled out an unopened box of condoms. Shawn accelerated out of the parking lot and drove straight down Hillside Avenue until he hit Guy Brewer Boulevard. He drove about a half-mile and stopped in front of a brick house with a yellow and white awning. He pulled out his cell phone and called the woman who lived there.

"Hello," a raspy voice answered.

"Tina, I'm downstairs. Come open the door."

Natalia found André standing next to the men's room talking to a dark-skinned man with a stud in his eyebrow. "Andy, I'm ready to go," she twirled a strand of hair around her index finger.

"Here we go..." André sighed, "Go to the bar. I'm coming."

When he finally showed up at the bar, he waved goodbye to the bartender and said, "Come on, little girl, let's go." He held out his hand, and she took it, squeezing as hard as she could. "Ow, girl, what's your malfunction?"

"Oh nothing, you slut."

André playfully nudged her. They caught a cab and once settled, André started gossiping. "Did you see that guy I was talking to?"

"Yeah?"

"Girl he is flaming! I'm like a magnet even in that straight club. He wanted me to go home with him."

"Really? He was good looking."

"Yeah, but I don't go home with someone I just met. You know me. I'm finicky like Morris the Cat. So right then and there, he was out of the balls game."

"You are too funny."

"I mean he was nice, but that come home with me shit turned me off. I was like, damn, get to know me before you screw me!"

The cab pulled up to André's building, and Natalia paid the driver. The doorman opened the door for them, and André playfully jumped on the security guard's desk. "Hey, Charles you see anything suspicious lately?" Charles tried to ignore André by staring at the security monitors.

"You better keep me safe," André said and rolled his eyes.

"Oh, leave him alone," Natalia smiled at the guard and attempted to pull André away from the desk.

André got up slowly and said, "I'm going now, but for the amount of money I paid for my place, you should guard me to the elevator."

The security guard chuckled and replied, "Have a good evening Mr. Howard, Ms. Foles."

"Bye-eee," André waved before the elevator doors closed.

"Do you know I saw your neighbor earlier. You know the old one with the poodle? He had another young girl up here today."

"Uh-uh, he about to catch a heart attack," André cackled and walked to his door. Once inside, they raced to the kitchen. "Get the ice cream," André demanded. Natalia opened the freezer and pulled out a box of ice cream.

After reading the word on the box, she frowned. "Peach? Who pigs out on peach ice cream? You're supposed to have chocolate ripple or chocolate chip cookie dough."

"If I had known that princess Natalia was going to grace me with her presence maybe I would've gotten a different flavor." He grabbed the ice cream from her and tried to stick a spoon in it. "That's the thing I hate about ice cream. It's always so damn hard. You can't get the spoon in." He tried to scoop some out.

"Humph, I thought you liked it hard," she laughed.

"You damn right!" André retorted.

She took out her toothbrush and went into the bathroom. André stood in the bathroom doorway, watching her.

"What?" she asked after wiping her mouth.

"Nothing," he lay across the bed.

"Let's watch a movie Andy. But first take a shower with me," she grinned, hopeful.

"Oh, stop it."

"Stop what? Just take a shower with me. This way we can both get out at the same time, and we can watch the movie together."

"Please, Miss Thang you ain't slick. I can wait for you to finish your shower," André sighed, knowing what she was up to. He grabbed the remote and turned on the television.

"Oh well, suit yourself. But when you can't wake up tomorrow, don't blame me. I was just trying to help you out." She slammed the bathroom door.

After her shower, she came out of the bathroom naked and dripping wet. André turned to look at her, his eyes opened wide.

"What's wrong with you? You're getting the floor all wet."

"I need a towel," she said innocently.

"You know where they are. You are something else, girl." He turned back to the TV, shaking his head in disbelief. She went to the linen closet next to the bathroom and pulled out a dark purple towel. After wrapping herself in it, she went to the bed and lay next to him.

"Did you find a towel, missy?" he asked without looking at her.

"Mmm-hmn," she replied.

"So go dry your ass."

"I want you to do it."

"You are too damned spoiled," he said as he snatched the towel from her and hastily rubbed it over her back and legs.

"All done," he handed her the towel.

"Andy you didn't do the front," she whined, trying to put the towel in his hand again.

"Stop it." He pushed the towel away.

"Where's my bag?" She found it and pulled out a satin nightie. Standing in front of the TV, she slipped it on over her head.

André sucked his teeth and rubbed his hands over his face. "Come here," he said and patted the spot next to him on the bed. On her hands and knees, she crawled to him.

"You're sick, you know that?" André shook his head. "Really. What's with you? You think I'm bisexual or something?"

Natalia blushed.

"I am very sure about who I am, sweetie. I love you like a sister. You're my best friend. And I am not attracted to you like you want me to be."

She sighed and hugged him. "Oh, I was just testing you, André. I have to keep you on your toes."

"Oh, whatever. Just call Mark."

André put his arm around her and played with her hair. They cuddled up tight, and he put his arm around her waist. "I love you, honey bunny."

"I love you, too," she sighed. "Why couldn't you be straight? You'd be perfect for me."

"Mark is perfect for you," André said as he twirled a lock of her hair between his fingers. "You just have to give him the chance to prove it. Did you ever tell him what you want in bed?"

"No."

"So, how the hell is he supposed to change when he doesn't even know what's up?" he sighed and rolled his eyes.

"I don't know. But I shouldn't have to tell him how to have sex. He should know," she shrugged.

"Girl, I could never be your man. I would've strangled you by now."

"Would you want to teach your lover? Wouldn't you rather that he be experienced?"

"I would want someone experienced, but for my pleasure, I would be willing to teach him," André replied.

Natalia grew quiet as the idea sank in. She never did tell Mark what she wants. She just expected him to come around. "Thank you, Andy," she pulled his arm tighter around her .

And with that, they fell asleep.

Chapter Three

❤

THE ICEMAN COMETH

The bright morning sun annoyed Shawn. And in the light, he didn't like what he saw laying next to him. Tina looked horrible, her light brown skin blotchy and her dry hair a frizzy mess. Shawn watched her in disgust as she struggled to open her eyes. He definitely preferred her with make-up. She was far from good-looking right now.

"W-where you going, Shawn? You can stay — my mother is gone for the week." Her voice sounded like she swallowed a frog.

"I got some things to take care of," he said as he pulled on his shirt.

"So you just came to get some and that's it?"

"Don't act stupid. You knew what the fuck I came for. I don't have time for this shit." He buttoned his shirt and stepped into his pants. Then he checked his beeper and took out his car keys.

"I need some money till I get paid on Thursday."

"Here," he reached into his pocket and threw a couple of twenties at her. Tina scrambled to pick them up. Shawn considered her a sneaker whore. All he had to do was buy her a pair of sneakers or give her a few dollars to make her happy. Once in a while, he'd take her to a dusty old movie theater far away from his usual hangouts. And if she wasn't on speaking terms with her mother, he'd get her a room at a cheap motel. She really believed he gave a damn about her. She didn't have a clue.

He watched as she picked up the money. Shaking his head, he decided not to see her anymore.

As he pressed the alarm deactivator on his key ring, the car doors unlocked automatically. He climbed in and closed his eyes. He was back in the big beautiful house with her. She smiled seductively at him and whispered in his ear, "Fuck me." His penis stiffened at the daydream. And then, just as Shawn gave in to the vision, one of his crew called his name and walked over to the car window.

"Whut up?" he offered his fist.

"Whut up?" Shawn replied, returning the pound.

"You was wit sexy ass Tina?"

"Yeah," Shawn checked his watch for the time.

"Where you goin' now?"

"Home, I need a shower." Shawn said nonchalantly.

"When I grow up, I wanna be like you, cat daddy," he chuckled.

"I'ma start giving mackin' lessons on the weekends for nineteen-ninety-five nahmean?" Shawn joked.

"I feel you. Just don't forget to hook a niggah up," he laughed.

"You need to re-up?" Shawn asked, getting serious. "Cuz I only got a couple left."

Shawn pulled out his cell phone and dialed Nut, "Hold up." When the answering machine picked up, Shawn yelled, "Pick up niggah!"

"Whut up?" asked Nut.

"Trev need work."

"Aiight, tell him to come in an hour."

"Don't have this cat waiting for you all fuckin' morning. Make sure..." he looked at his watch then said, "I'm just gonna drop him off by you now."

"Damn, I can't even brush my teeth and shit?" Nut whined.

Shawn laughed loud, "I'm about to go home, and I gotta pass by you. So I'ma drop him off on my way."

"Whateva," Nut sucked his teeth.

"Get in," Shawn motioned. Trev hopped in the back seat right behind him. "I'm not a fuckin' cab," Shawn barked.

Trevor got out chuckling and moved to the front seat.

After Shawn dropped Trevor off, fatigue set in. He hurried into his bathroom to brush his teeth and take a long shower. After he toweled off, he pulled a pair of silk boxers from the dresser draw. As he stepped into them, he wondered what to do about 'Operation Payback'. He already told his crew that it was on for tonight, but he was beginning to have second thoughts. After seeing her portrait, he no longer felt hostile towards her. He tried not to but kept seeing her innocent eyes. "Maybe I'll just send Nut and have 'im to do it," he said out loud. Just one problem with that — he wanted to see her in person. He couldn't get her out of his head. But after thinking a while, he realized that he had to no choice but to stick to the plan.

He dressed quickly then called Nut. "I'm on my way."

After stopping at a diner for breakfast, Shawn headed to Nut's house. Nut was waiting on the steps. "Whut up, niggah?"

"Whut up."

"Did you give Trev work?"

"Yeah."

"So why he ain't call me like I told him to."

"We was calling you and beeping you. Where was you at?"

"Damn, I was in the shower. I forgot to check if anyone called. So where's Trev?"

"He went back to Baisley."

"It's aiight, I'ma leave him there. I'll just call D.L. and send him to Brooklyn." He beeped D.L. with his call back numbers.

"So what's the schedule? We still goin' to that lady's crib?" Nut asked.

"Yeah, but I gotta get us some ski masks for tonight. Right now I'ma go uptown to see Jigg. We gon' negotiate on us getting that park Tymeek wanted. You see how Tymeek just be using the gift of gab and taking shit from muhfuckas?" he chuckled.

Nut laughed then said, "We get that park, it's over. That's where all them smoked out crackers be going."

"I know. That's yuppie central right there."

"Mo' cheddar no doubt. So you want me to come wit you?"

"I ain't afraid to go by myself. That niggah know better than to fuck wit me."

Nut sucked his teeth and twisted his mouth to the side, "Aiight Schwarzenigger. Lemme ride wit your Terminator ass anyway."

Shawn stuck the key in the ignition and started the car. Nut searched through Shawn's CD collection, stuck one in the CD player and turned up the volume loud.

"Why you always have to blast that shit?" Shawn scolded.

"Stop bitchin' and drive," Nut chuckled.

Shawn's cell phone rang. It was D.L. "Go to the E. lane spot. Them niggaz need guidance, feel me?" he chuckled.

"Aiight. One," D.L. chuckled.

"One."

The bright sun exposed every graffiti-ridden wall and urine-encrusted crevice on the deteriorating Harlem buildings. When Shawn pulled up in front of Jigg's place, he told Nut to stay in the car and disappeared into the newly renovated building adjoining a schoolyard on 113th Street. He pressed Jigg's bell and heard a gruff voice over the intercom ask, "Who is it?"

"Shawn." The buzzer sounded, and Shawn pushed the heavy glass door open. The elevator was waiting for him. He got on and pressed five. When he stepped off the elevator, he saw Jigg waiting for him in the hall.

"Hey young blood, how ya doin'?"" Jigg asked.

"Hangin' in there, you know?" Shawn gave him a pound.

"I hear ya. Come on in."

"You don't look like Tymeek." Jigg observed.

"I know."

"Sit down. You want something to drink?" Jigg offered.

"Naw, man, I'm aiight."

It was obvious that Jigg was a bachelor. Besides a worn brown corduroy couch, the only other thing Shawn saw in the apartment was a 60-inch television surrounded by a full theatre system. Jigg was at least 50 — old for the drug game. The mere fact that he had lasted as long as he had was a miracle. In every line on his face, the stress showed. Shawn was not impressed. But Tymeek had told stories of Jigg's ruthlessness,. of the things he had learned from Jigg and of how Jigg had earned respect — even from Colombians. To Shawn, the man was nothing but sick and old. HIV wreaked havoc on his immune system. And Shawn knew that the back-stabbing Jigg had done in his day now haunted him. Allies had turned into enemies, and the very ruthlessness that had carried him thus far was now ruining him. The man was biding his time until he left New York for Mexico. The park kept him in the city. But once he sold it and got his cut, he would take off. Tymeek was Jigg's only remaining ally, still loyal after all these years. So who better to inherit the park?

"Tell me, what kind of numbers you talkin' bout?" Shawn got right to the business at hand.

"Well, young blood, I see you don't play."

"I've got other things to take care of. You know how it is."

"I can dig it. I spoke wit your brother and he tells me you're a real good businessman. So I'ma give y'all the park. I expect my forty-percent and I don't care if y'all don't make nothing. I still want mine. I know I have to wait a couple months more before your brother can pay me the full amount he promised, but I still gotta live you know?" Jigg said matter-of-factly while scratching a razor bump on his neck. "So watchu say, young blood?"

"That'll work. No doubt." Shawn replied. They shook hands and Shawn left. The simplicity of it all didn't surprise him. He knew that whatever his brother wanted, he would get.

"We got it," Shawn said once back in the car.

Nut yawned, "Was there any doubt? You know he only giving it to you cuz of Tymeek."

On the way back to Queens, Shawn and Nut stopped at an army surplus store and picked up four black ski masks. The rest of the afternoon, Shawn was on the phone setting up a new selling spot and giving orders to his crew. It was already dark when he realized that he hadn't eaten all day. He drove Nut to his favorite restaurant and ordered a seafood platter. Nut ordered a porterhouse steak. Shawn had forgotten all about 'Operation Payback', but Nut reminded him. "We going to Crackerville tonight or what?" he asked and gobbled a piece of steak.

"Oh yeah. I'll call D.L. and 'em when we leave."

Nut sang under his breath, "Here come the men in black."

Natalia spent the day at André's condo. She lounged and watched talk shows and soap operas. She drew a bath and relaxed in his tub. When she finally pulled on a pair of jeans, André was just turning the doorknob. She slid a crocheted halter over her head before he came through the door.

"Hey, how's my baby?" he asked.

"I'm fine. I did absolutely nothing all day."

"You? I don't believe it!"

"Well, believe it."

"I guess you really needed a break. Did you think about Mark at all?"

"Yes. I called his office, but he was at lunch with a client so I just left a message."

"Nat, you know he's rarely ever in the office. Why didn't you call his cell?"

Natalia didn't respond. She purposely called his office so that she wouldn't have to speak to him. She wasn't ready yet.

"You think you're slick, don't you?" he asked and went into the bathroom to wash his hands. "So are you gonna cook or are we going out?"

"Let's go out. I have to admit I feel a bit claustrophobic after staying in all day."

"That was your choice, Miss Thang. But I guess we must oblige her highness." André sighed and unbuttoned his pants, "I'm gonna take a shower first then we can leave. Is that alright, princess?"

"No, peasant!" she quipped.

"Well that's too damn bad. Princess Natalia will just have to wait for Queen André," he laughed and closed the bathroom door.

Natalia stared at the television, and when one of the character's cell phones rang, it reminded her to check her own voice mail. She picked up her cell phone and dialed. Nothing but messages pertaining to business, lectures and requests. She then called her house to check the messages there. None. "I really don't have a life," she sighed.

"Hurry up, Andy."

"I'm moving as fast as I can," he spat. She put her clutch, phone and clothes in the Louis Vuitton bag. "Here, give me your bag." André held out his hand. Natalia gave him the bag.

"You sure you wanna go home tonight?"

"I'm sure. I miss my house."

"I'd miss that gorgeous house, too."

"Well then, Andy, why don't come home with me?"

"I can't. Remember, Dionne is on vacation, and I have to open the Madison salon for another week and a half."

"Oh, I forgot."

Natalia's phone rang. "I'm not going to answer it. Let's just go."

"Answer it Nat. It might be you-know-who."

She gave in. "Hello?"

"Are you still leaving me?" Mark asked.

"No, silly," she smiled.

"Nat, whatever I have to do to make you to love me again, I'll do."

"Then meet me and Andy at the Riverway Cafe."

"Done. What time?"

"We're leaving now. We'll probably be there in fifteen minutes. Where are you?"

"I'm close enough to be there in twenty."

"Okay, I'll see you there," she swallowed hard and said, "Oh and Mark, I'm sorry about last night."

"It's okay. We'll talk."

"Bye," she said feeling more alive than she had all day.

"Mmm-hmn. I guess you do love him after all," André smirked.

"I guess so," she grinned.

"He's a sucker for you, mommita."

Natalia drove to the Riverway Café and were seated at a window table overlooking the water. Mark arrived a few minutes later.

"Hi Mark, how are you?" André held out his hand.

"I'm fine thanks, and yourself?" He shook André's hand firmly.

"I'm okay," André smiled.

Mark leaned over and kissed Natalia's cheek. "Hi," he smiled seductively.

"Hi," she returned the naughty smile. He sat next to her and took her hand. André stood up and said, "I'm going to the bar for a while. Okay, kiddies, you play nice."

"Alright," Mark said, happy to be alone with Natalia.

"You behave, too," Natalia giggled.

As soon as André was out of view, Mark turned to her and said, "Natalia, I love you, and I understand you need space...but I can't lose you. I went crazy all day wondering what to do."

"I called you at the office and left a message with Allison."

"Why didn't you call my cell?" he asked but got no reply. "Nat, please let's get to the bottom of this. What's the problem?"

"Alright," she said with a sigh. "I am bored...with us. We aren't spontaneous anymore. Our sex life isn't as exciting as it used to be. That's really the problem, Mark. I am bored with the missionary position and the occasional doggy style. It may sound crazy to you, but sometimes I want us to get a little, um, freaky. Lately, I feel like we're in a rut...like there's no life in our life. We do the same old thing every time. I need some excitement." It felt good to finally admit what was bothering her.

"Nat, why didn't you just say so before?"

"I don't know. I felt like I shouldn't have had to tell you...you should have been more in tune with me and the relationship."

"Wow, Natalia. Please just give me a chance. Give us a chance. I will give you what you want." He pulled her chin toward his face and kissed her lips, "I love you."

"I love you more," she grinned.

Natalia decided that it would be better to leave Mark to think about what she had told him. After collecting André from the bar where he ate dinner alone, she said to her fiancé, "I'm going home. I need to unpack, review tomorrow's itinerary, and edit my speeches. It's going to be a full day. Is that okay, sweetie?"

Mark nodded. "Sure, I understand." He kissed her goodnight and watched her climb into the Navigator.

"I'll call you when I get home," she waved.

Once in the car, André said, "So I see we're back to normal. You're not as confused now, are you?"

"Counselor, I've taken your advice. You were absolutely right about me, him, everything," she admitted.

"Why didn't you take him home with you then? You might fall asleep at the wheel girl."

"No I won't. I'm too rested and happy right now. But I do have to get up early tomorrow for a lecture first thing in the morning. Then I have to meet with the co-op board."

"You are always busy, busy, busy."

"Don't I know it!" she said.

Natalia pulled up to Andy's building.

"Well? Get out and open my door, garçon," he joked. "I love you, honey bunny. I'll give you a wake up call bright and early at five," he grinned.

"No, six o'clock! Six, six, six!" she shouted.

André laughed and pecked her on the cheek, "Buh-bye," he slammed the door shut and hopped down onto the sidewalk.

"Bye, Andy. I love you, too!" she shouted out the window.

Shawn pulled up behind the familiar cluster of peach trees in a black Ford Taurus. The crew scattered then met up at the back entrance. D.L. went for the crow bar, but Spank stopped him. "Look, the door's still open from last night."

Nut sighed, "That mean ain't nobody home."

"You don't know that," Spank whispered, sneaking a peek inside.

"Man, do you see any lights on?" Nut snapped.

Shawn pushed past them and walked into the kitchen. He pulled on his gloves and looked around cautiously. Judging from the quiet, he realized that once again no one was home. D.L. followed. Spank and Nut were joking with each other and missed their cue. Already upset with the fact that the plan was once again not working out, Shawn shouted at them, "Get inside!"

"You fuckin' crazy? They could be calling the cops right now," D.L. warned.

"You know ain't no fuckin' body in here," Shawn barked. No one moved but Shawn. He sprinted up the stairs to Natalia's bedroom. It was as they left it. No one had been there since yesterday.

"Shit!" he yelled.

Nut ran up the stairs. "What? What happened?"

Shawn turned to him and said, "Nobody's been here."

"I knew it. Now what?"

"We wait." He sat on the edge of the bed. "The woman's got expensive taste." He ran his hands over the silk sheets. From behind a pillow, he pulled her lace chemise to his face and sniffed it.

"What the fuck you doing?" Nut asked.

Shawn ignored him.

"Oh, so now you're a pervert? Sniffing some bitch's nightgown and shit. You's a sick fuck." Nut laughed.

"You're the Nut," Shawn quipped.

"But yo, seriously, what if these people went on vacation?"

D.L. wandered around the room. "Yeah what if these rich muh-fuckas on vacation chillin' and we here waitin' on em'?"

What if his beauty was far away? Did it make sense to wait for her? "We're gonna wait," Shawn finally ordered and pulled off his ski mask.

Nut sighed. "Shit! I might as well get my rest on," he hopped on the king size bed.

"Get off, stupid!" Shawn yelled.

"What? Ain't nobody gon' know."

"Are you wearing gloves?"

"No?"

"Then get your dumb ass off the bed. And don't touch nothing."

"Aiight." Nut jumped off the bed and began wandering around.

"Niggah, do you have something else to do?"

"Shawn, we waiting around on some bullshit."

"You ain't saying shit. It ain't like you got bitches waiting on your lurch-looking ass." Shawn chuckled.

"You keep thinking you the only niggah gettin' pussy. I got mad bitches, son." Spank sucked his teeth and wiped away the beads of sweat from his forehead.

Tired of standing around wearing a ski mask in the middle of summer, Nut ripped it off and asked, "How come you can sit on the bed and I can't?"

"Cuz I'm the niggah in charge," Shawn grinned.

"Fuck that. I'm sitting down too," he plopped down on the bed next to Shawn. Shawn sighed. The evening was nothing like Christmas Eve, but he smiled to himself anyway, waiting like a child for morning to arrive so he could unwrap his presents.

The wheels of Natalia's Navigator hugged the barren road leading to her property. As she pulled into the driveway, she didn't notice the black car parked behind the peach trees. It was late, and she was sleepy. The truth was that she never imagined that she would become one of the victims she counselled and protected and thus, was relaxed when it came to her own security.

Hurrying from the car to her front door, she didn't remember to grab her overnight bag. She fished her house keys from her clutch, and fumbled to unlock the front door. Once inside, she noticed the kitchen light was on. "Damn! Doesn't that man understand English?" she grumbled, assuming Mark had ignored her request to go home alone. She shut the front door, went into the kitchen and looked around. There were no tempting aromas from steaming pots on the stove and no sign of Mark. She was certain, however, that Mark was somewhere in the house. She checked the dining room. She checked the living room. Both empty.

"I told you that I wanted to be alone!" she shouted as she ran upstairs into the darkness.

She entered her bedroom and was about to flip on a light when, from behind, a strong hand suddenly grabbed her arm. In an instant, the arm belonging to the hand was around her throat. A muffled voice whispered in her ear, "Don't scream, bitch."

Natalia's heart raced. A different voice from across the dark room shouted, "Where's the safe?"

"I-I..." she stuttered.

"Where is it?" the voice commanded. "We know you got one."

"I-I don't have a safe," she stammered.

"Bitch, don't lie to me!" the same voice shouted. The man holding her yanked her hair. Natalia was petrified.

"I don't have a safe!" she screamed back, nervous tears streaming down her face.

"Shut up!" And then a swift punch pounded her cheek. The sound of the blow rang unbelievably loud in her head. The sting kept her from passing out.

"Take her out to the car," Shawn ordered.

"What?" Nut asked in disbelief.

"Just take her out to the fuckin' car," Shawn shouted again.

"What the fuck you talking about? That's not the plan."

"Just do it!" Shawn ordered.

"Aiight. Pick her up y'all," Nut commanded.

Spank and D.L. tried to pick her up together, but their heads collided, and Natalia fell to the floor.

"Forget it! I'ma get her. Y'all just go ahead!" Nut yelled. He scooped her up from the floor and headed for the door. When he was almost there, she reached up and grabbed his ski mask, pulling it off. Then she bit into his cheek, hard.

"You fuckin' bitch!" he yelled and dumped her onto the parquet foyer floor.

"You gon' get it now b..."

Natalia hopped to her feet and rammed into him like a bull. Nut slammed into the stair rail and slumped down, writhing in pain. She turned back to the kitchen and bolted to the patio doors. Old memories flooded her mind. She was nine again, running to her neighbor's house. But her closest neighbor was more than two miles away. She was trapped on her own property, but she ran anyway. She ran towards the gravel road. Just as she was within a few feet of the road, Spank tackled her to the ground. Shawn ran over and grabbed her by the arm, pulling her to her feet. He towered over her. She looked up into his masked face but could hardly see his eyes through the slits. She trembled in his tight grasp, and as he brought his face close to hers, she felt his warm breath seep through the mask onto her cheek.

Shawn pulled her close, pressing his chest against hers. Her breasts were heaving from terror and the exertion of her attempt to escape. Realizing that she was trapped, Natalia broke down and cried.

"Shhh. Just do as I say, and I promise we won't hurt you," he assured her.

She spit on him and shouted at the top of her lungs, "Go ahead and kill me, you bastard! That's what you're gonna do right? Just get it over with!"

Shawn calmly wiped the spit from his shirt. "I don't wanna hurt you, lady. But if you do some stupid shit like that again, I'ma have to."

Nut ran over to Shawn with a bloody piece of tissue balled up in his hand. He grabbed Natalia's long tresses, balled up his fist and swung at her. Shawn blocked the blow.

"No!" he shouted.

"The crazy bitch bit me," Nut complained.

Shawn chuckled. She had spunk. It made him want her more.

"Don't worry, she'll get hers." He patted Nut's shoulder.

"Now, are you gonna be a good girl?" he asked as her turned to Natalia.

"Get your hands off me!" she spat, trying to wriggle free.

"You better calm your ass down," he warned. "Go ahead to the car y'all. I got this." He twisted Natalia's arm behind her back and put her in a loose headlock. He didn't put any force into it, though. In fact, it was more playful than threatening.

"Don't push me. Be a good girl, and it'll all be over before you know it," he whispered in her ear.

In a shaky voice, she asked, "What will all be over?"

He turned her to face him and simply stared at her. She, in turn, glanced down at his crotch, raised her knee and began to strike. With a chuckle, Shawn blocked the blow with his right hand and off-balance, she fell down onto the grass. Shawn jumped on her, straddling her with his knees and effectively pinning her down. He held her wrists firmly against the dewy grass.

"You like to fight, huh?"

She ignored the question and continued to struggle.

"You really think you can get up? Go ahead get up then," he challenged. Realizing her efforts were in vain, she stopped struggling.

"Please, just take the money in my purse and leave. I won't report this...Please just go."

"I want more than that." His lustful eyes were hidden in the darkness.

"I don't have a safe, I swear."

"I know you got money stashed."

"I don't have a bank card. You can't get anything. All I have is a checkbook."

"Stop lying to me. I'm trying to be nice."

"I'm not lying. Check my purse. You'll see." Shawn stared at her for a couple of minutes. *Maybe she's telling the truth,* he thought. He looked over at the car. Spank, D.L. and Nut were watching and waiting for his next move. He got off her and pulled her up. Then he ran his gloved fingers across her lips. Leaning down, his face just inches from hers, he warned, "You better be telling the truth."

"Where's her purse?" Shawn shouted. Nut looked at Spank. Spank looked at D.L., and D.L. looked at Nut. None of them knew. Spank volunteered to go back in the house to get it. He rushed back outside a few moments later empty handed.

"I didn't see no purse," he shrugged.

Natalia panicked. *Where the hell is my purse?* Then it dawned on her that it was still in the Louis Vuitton bag in the Navigator. "It's in the car!" she shouted like a student in class with the right answer. Shawn looked over to where her SUV was parked.

"Where're the keys?" he asked.

"Duh! In the house."

He smiled under the ski mask at her sarcasm.

"You're something else, you know that? I guess I don't scare you, huh?"

He did. But she wouldn't let him know it.

"All I want is for you to leave," she looked him straight in the eyes. "Is this personal?"

Shawn couldn't believe his ears. She must have a lot of enemies to have asked such a question. He looked away.

Nut turned on the radio in the Navigator and strolled over, bopping to the sounds blasting from the jeep.

"Yo, that shit is mad nice," he smiled.

"What is wrong wit you?" Shawn yelled.

"What now niggah?" Nut asked.

"Go turn it off."

Nut sucked his teeth, "I found this bag," he threw the bag on the ground. It landed in front of Shawn. "I ain't see no purse."

Shawn looked at Natalia waiting for an explanation.

"It's in there. I swear," she said as she pointed to the bag.

Shawn unzipped the bag and rummaged through her clothes, depilatories and undergarments. He pulled out thongs, bras and cosmetics and threw them all to the ground. When he pulled out the white leather clutch, she shrieked, "That's it!"

He dropped the cumbersome overnight bag and opened the clutch. In it, he found a leather covered checkbook, a change purse, three one hundred dollar bills and two twenties. He looked at her suspiciously. "I thought you only use checks?"

"Well, I do go to the bank occasionally to get some cash. You do need cash every once in a while, you know," she rolled her eyes at him.

"You always leave the house with this much money?" he asked, throwing down the purse.

"Not really," she answered nonchalantly. She hoped that having some money would make him leave. "Take it and go. Please."

Shawn shook his head. "This is chump change, ma. This can't do nothing for me."

"It's all I have. Please take it and go. Just go!"

"Not without you."

Shawn shoved Natalia into the back seat of the car. She flailed her arms and scratched at his mask. To stop her, he slapped her hard on the cheek. Shocked by the blow, Natalia sat stone still.

As he climbed into the front seat, the same thought that ran through his mind a hundred times since last night flooded his mind again. *She is so beautiful.* He glanced in the rearview mirror and noticed that her cheek was an angry red and beginning to swell. Unexpectedly, he apologized. "I'm sorry I hit you. But you was acting crazy."

Natalia didn't answer.

Nut and the others returned to the car. As usual, Nut sat in front with Shawn. D.L. and Spank carefully climbed in the back seat on either side of Natalia.

As Shawn backed up onto the road, Spank complained, "Yo, shouldn't we tie her hands and blindfold her. I'm tired of wearing this hot ass mask."

"With what stupid?" D.L. laughed.

Shawn abruptly stopped the car. He jumped out and ran back toward the driveway. He returned with the Louis Vuitton bag. "Find something in there to blindfold her with. And use this for her hands." He handed Nut his leather belt.

"Be careful. She's a wild one," Nut said as he tossed the belt to D.L. He searched the bag for something to wrap around Natalia's head.

"Hold her hands!" D.L. yelled at Spank. Spank grabbed them and squeezed them together behind her back. She didn't fight. She knew that fighting back was pointless.

D.L. wrapped the belt around one wrist two times then did the same to the other. To finish, he pulled the end of the belt through a loop in the middle and tucked it through the buckle.

"Nice and tight," D.L. proudly mumbled.

"Check it, D.L.," Shawn ordered.

"She ain't going no where."

"Aiight, this'll work for her face," Nut said as he passed a pale blue cardigan to Spank.

"Try it out first," Shawn commanded.

"What?" Spank was confused.

"Tie it around your head and see if you can see through it," Shawn sighed.

"Oh," Spank dully replied. He rolled up the cardigan lengthwise and tied it around his eyes.

"I can't see shit," he muttered.

"Good," Shawn approved. Spank tied the cardigan around Natalia's head covering her eyes and waved his hands in front of her face. She didn't flinch. With a collective sigh, everyone then slipped off their masks.

"Whew! Now a niggah can breathe," Nut exclaimed. He pulled down the sun visor to check his face in the mirror. "Shit! Look at my face. Fuckin' bitch scarred my face!"

Natalia's teeth marks dominated his right cheek. She smiled with satisfaction. *He'll never forget the day he messed with me,* she thought.

Nut continued complaining, "I better get checked for rabies."

"Shut up, Nut," Shawn grumbled.

During the long ride, Natalia didn't speak or move. She expected not to live through this and was no longer afraid. *I'll see you soon mommy and daddy,* she thought. Then she thought about Mark. *And to think I passed up being with you one last time.*

With the remote control, the garage door opened, and Shawn pulled in. Not wanting to speak in the car, he motioned for Nut to get out with him. Several feet away, Shawn whispered, "Look I'ma give y'all a lil' sumpin' for tonight. D.L. and Spank can go. But I need you to help me get her inside."

Nut already didn't approve of kidnapping, and this detour from the original plan bothered him.

"What's happened to the plan, Shawn? We wasn't supposed to bring her here. We ain't even get nothin'. No money, no nothin'! Shit, we coulda took that phat ass Navi she got. What you doing man?"

"I need you to help me right now, aiight?"

Nut shrugged, "You my niggah. I can't leave you hanging. So what you gon' do wit her?" Nut rubbed his hand over his mouth and chin.

"I don't know yet," Shawn replied.

"I know what you gon' do wit her. You ain't slick. So what da deal, son? I gotta get my revenge too, nahmean?" Nut said, excited.

Shawn shook his head, "Nah, man. She's special, nahmean?"

Nut sucked his teeth. "Whateva. Let's get this over with. You selfish muhfucka."

They walked back to the car just in time to find D.L. with his hand over Natalia's mouth, and Spank's hand about to slide under her halter. She squirmed and wriggled and cursed them. Shawn was completely enraged. He reached in, grabbed Spank by the neck and yanked him out of the car.

"What the fu...," Spank screamed as he tried to escape the vice-like grip around his throat.

"Leave," Shawn growled. Spank stumbled, and Shawn slammed him against the car.

"What's wrong wit you man?" Spank asked, his eyes full of fear and confusion. He asked again, "What's wrong wit you, niggah?"

"Just go home," Nut interjected.

"I'ma have something for y'all later," Nut continued.

"You want me to leave, too?" D.L. asked, distancing himself from Shawn.

"Yeah, I'ma holla at y'all," Shawn said calmly.

"Aiight, Dr. Jekyll," Spank chuckled. Then he spun D.L. around, "Let's go."

Shawn slid into the back seat of the Ford. He straightened out her top, taking extra care not to touch her breasts in the process.

"I'm sorry that happened," he again apologized.

"What do you want with me? If you're going to kill me, then just get it over with," she spat.

"I promised you I wasn't going to hurt you. I don't break my promises."

He moved closer to her. She couldn't see what he was doing but she could feel his breath on her cheek. "Why are you doing this to me? What do you want?" she wailed.

"Lemme get you out this car," he evaded her question. He helped her out of the car slowly. She nearly tripped and fell, but he caught her. "Be careful," he warned, holding her in his arms like precious cargo. Nut went ahead and opened the door.

Shawn guided her downstairs to the basement and led her to the couch in the hangout room. "You'll be comfortable here," he said, gently pushing down on her shoulders. Then he left the room.

In the hallway, Shawn found a chair and wedged it underneath the doorknob. Nut was right next to him, "This ain't gon' stop her from getting out." Shawn hadn't really thought the thing through, but he knew he would have to make it work one way or another.

"How she gonna get out with her hands tied and a blindfold on, stupid?"

Nut shook his head and went upstairs to the kitchen. Shawn followed. Nut took out a carton of orange juice from the fridge and poured himself a glass. "You my dog and all that...but, I don't know what you gettin' into," he said between gulps.

"I've known you damn near all my life, right?" Shawn asked.

"True."

"You know me, man. You've seen how I am wit bitches, right?"

"Yeah, and?" Nut wanted to know where this was going.

"I was supposed to be getting revenge for Ty. She got my brother locked up, but I'm not mad at her. Instead I want her but not just for ass, nahmean? I don't know. It's just something about her," he sighed and folded his arms across his chest, "What the fuck is wrong wit me, yo?"

Nut set his glass down in the sink and sighed, "I'm not gon' front. Shorty is bangin'. She got a fat ass, big titties and real hair," he chuckled. "Plus she rich and got a baby mansion. I know you got mad bitches and all that. But I'm sure you ain't never run across a bad bitch like this one. Maybe that's all it is...your dick is playin' tricks on ya." He laughed then said seriously, "Stay focused brother. Cause' if they start missing her — no, when they start missing her, you gon' be on lock down wit Ty."

Shawn heard everything Nut said. But, still, he was determined to keep her prisoner.

Nut could see that his advice fell on deaf ears. "So what up? Am I staying or what?"

"What?" Shawn asked, dazed.

"Do you still need me?" Nut rearranged the question.
"Oh, naw, man. But I want you to call me as soon as you wake up. Don't forget to drop the car off."
"You better not try to get none from her while I'm gone. She'll probably kick your ass then I'ma hafta bail your ass out of jail," Nut joked.
"Never that man," Shawn chuckled. He walked Nut to the garage.
"Later." Nut took the keys from Shawn's hand and got in the car. Shawn watched as Nut backed out of the driveway. Then he raced back inside, ran upstairs and grabbed a flat sheet, a towel and a washcloth from the linen closet. He also picked out a sweet smelling soap from one of the many he kept and a pillow from his bed. Grabbing the ski mask, he took everything downstairs to the basement. He pulled the chair away from the door and peeked into the room. Natalia was still sitting where he had left her.
"Are you hot?" he asked. Natalia didn't answer him.
"I'll put on the air conditioner for you," he walked over to a metal contraption on wheels. He pressed a button and the air conditioner started to hum.
"Much better," he sighed.
Natalia remained quiet. Shawn sat next to her.
"Where did you take me?" she finally broke her silence.
"Nowhere."
"Look, if you're going to kill me, please do it already. I can't take the suspense any longer. Just do it!" she pleaded.
"Talkin' like that ain't gonna help your situation," he said calmly. "Why don't you be nice? I'm being nice," he said and inched closer to her.
"My wrists hurt," she whined.
"I can't untie you. You might scratch me again," he paused. "I can't trust you."
"I won't do that again. I promise. And I keep my promises," she mocked what he had said to her earlier.
"You got a sense of humor. I like that. But I'm not gonna untie you yet," he said and stood up. He put the ski-mask on top of the television and took the bottle of gel soap, the towel and the washcloth into the bathroom. He looked around. It had been a while since he had cleaned it. With a bottle of spray disinfectant and a sponge, he scrubbed the sink, toilet and shower stall. He washed the floor with clean rags he found under the sink. When all had been sanitized to his satisfaction, he neatly laid the towel and washcloth on top of the toilet tank and placed the gel soap container on the caddy in the shower stall.

Natalia smelled the pungent scent of cleaning chemicals. Crazy thoughts ran through her mind as she awaited her fate. *He's probably going to rape my dead body or cut me into tiny pieces.*

Shawn interrupted her thoughts. "Can I trust you?"

"What?"

"I wanna let you take a shower, but I need to know if I can trust you. Because if I can't, we're gonna have problems. So can I trust you?"

"Yes," she whispered, unsure of his intentions.

"If you try anything, I'ma hurt you, understand?"

She nodded.

Shawn helped Natalia up from the couch and unwound the belt from her wrists. Fierce red welts puckered her skin.

"Damn, I didn't mean to mess up your pretty skin." Shawn shook his head in remorse. Natalia remained quiet.

As she stood gently rubbing her wrists, Shawn grabbed the ski mask from the television and placed it over this head again. When finished, he gently turned her around, untied the cardigan and let it fall from her face.

As she turned around, she weakly muttered, "Th-thank you."

"See, I'm not a monster." He pointed toward the bathroom, "That's the bathroom. I cleaned it. You can take a shower. There's a clean towel and washcloth in there. And here's a clean sheet for you to lay on and a pillow."

What is this, a hotel? Natalia thought as she went into the bathroom and picked up the washcloth and towel. She sat down on the closed toilet. "I get it now. They're holding me for ransom. But who is going to give them the money?" She sprang up and opened the bathroom door. Her kidnapper was outstretched in a leather chair, his feet up on the matching ottoman, staring at the television.

"See? That's why I wasn't gon' untie you."

"No, no. I just wanted to tell you something."

He turned off the television and said, "What do you have to tell me?"

Natalia remained in the bathroom doorway as he walked over to her. "I know now that you're holding me for ransom. But no one can pay it but me. No one else has access to my money."

Shawn laughed. "Just go and take a shower."

"But I'm telling you the truth. There isn't anyone else who can pay. How much do you want anyway?" she frantically asked.

"What's your name?" Shawn ignored her question.

"Look, I will give you all the money I have if you would just let me go."

"I will let you go...for free."

Natalia was confused. "I don't understand."

"What's your name?" he asked again. Natalia looked down at the floor, frustrated at not having her questions answered, and again didn't reply.

"I said, what's your name."

She began to say, "Nuh-tah...but wait a minute. You know my name. Who doesn't know the name of the person they've kidnapped?" she asked sarcastically.

"I didn't kidnap you. This isn't what you think it is." He was truly unable to explain, because he, himself, didn't know what he was doing. He sat back down and turned on the television again.

"Natalia," she said.

"What?" He muted the volume.

"My name. It's Natalia."

"That's very pretty. I like it," Shawn said, pleased.

"So what is your name?" she asked innocently.

"Come on now, I can't tell you that," he grimaced under the mask.

"Then why did you ask me mine?"

"Because I wanted to know."

Natalia thought for a moment. "At least give me a nickname. I mean, what should I call you? Mr. Kidnapper? The masked man? Mr. Clean?" she managed to smile.

Shawn grinned under his mask, "You're funny. You should be a comedian. It's nice to see that beautiful smile though."

Natalia fiddled with her thumbs nervously.

"Call me Sha," he finally answered.

"Okay, Sha, what am I going to wear after I get clean?"

"True...wait. I'll be right back," he left the room and positioned the chair under the doorknob again. He ran upstairs and searched his closet and drawers, finally settling for a pair of basketball shorts and a jersey. He grabbed a bottle of baby oil, some shampoo, and a new hairbrush as well.

When he returned to the hangout room, Natalia was perched on the end of the chair. "Were you a good girl?" he asked.

She stared at the things cradled in his arms. "I got you this to wear and some other stuff."

"Thank you," she said as she grabbed the collection of "stuff" from his arms and went back into the bathroom. A few seconds later she opened the door, leaned out and said, "You are, by far, the most thoughtful kidnapper I've ever met." She flashed a quick smile

and closed the bathroom door.
He smiled to himself, sat back down and put his feet up again.

An hour later, Shawn became suspicious. He wondered whether or not he should bust into the bathroom. It couldn't possibly take her an entire hour to clean up in that small bathroom. Before he could get up out of the chair, Natalia opened the door. She was wearing the jersey. It reached well below her knees. And she held up the shorts. "They're way too big for me."
"Why don't you put your jeans back on then?"
"I can't sleep in those things. They're too binding. Not to mention dirty...thanks to you throwing me down on the ground." She went back in the bathroom and shut the door again.
"Oh what the hell," she mumbled to herself. She put the shorts on, tying the excess material into a big knot on the side. "There. I hope they don't fall down."
Shawn knocked on the door and said, "Goodnight."
"Goodnight?" she echoed from behind the door. She heard his footsteps on the stairs and heard the chair being shoved back into place.
Once upstairs, Shawn cleverly removed the kitchen phone from the wall. "Sleep tight, Natalia."

Chapter Four

❤

THE ULTIMATE BETRAYAL

Mark called Natalia on her cell phone. Her voicemail picked up on the fourth ring. *Where is she?* he wondered. He always called her at lunchtime. When the prompt ended, he left a brief, sarcastic message, "I need my wife-to-be to return my call. Oh, and uh...I still love you."

He was in his office for the first time in weeks. Today, he would catch up on his paperwork. As he sat at his desk staring at his computer monitor, he wondered if Natalia had truly forgiven him. He doubted it — she didn't want to spend the night with him, after all. On an impulse, he buzzed his secretary. She hurried to his office. "Yes, Mr. Delucchio?"

"Did I receive any calls earlier?"

"No, sir."

"Hmmm. Okay. If I get a call from a Ms. Foles and I'm not in, please forward her call to my cell phone."

"Yes, sir. Only Ms. Foles?" she asked as she turned to leave.

"Yes, only Ms. Foles. Thank you."

Mark continued with his paperwork. After jotting down a few notes and figures, he gathered his papers and folders, stacked them in his briefcase and checked his schedule. He had a meeting with Stanley Forsythe in an hour. After double-checking the contents of his briefcase, he gulped the rest of the water in the paper cup on his desk and threw it into the trash. After some last-minute organizing and reviews of the activity on the DOW and Japanese market, Mark realized that he was going to be late. He jumped up, grabbed his briefcase and ran out the door.

Thank you, Mr. Delucchio. We'll send everything you need by

Monday noon," Mr. Forsythe informed Mark while getting into a white Lincoln Town Car.

"Thank you very much for meeting with me, Mr. Forsythe. I look forward to making you an even richer man than Bill Gates," Mark said through yet another phony smile.

"Take care of my money." And with that, Mr. Forsythe's driver pulled away from the curb.

The meeting was a huge success, but through it all, Mark's thoughts were on Natalia. He was desperate to hear from her. Luckily, an available cab appeared just behind his new client's car, and he jumped in and instructed the driver to step on it.

His secretary was at her desk when he returned. "Sarah, did I get any calls?" He stopped in front of her cubicle impatiently waiting for the answer.

"Yes, sir. I left all of your messages on your desk."

"Thanks." The rushed to his office and grabbed the stack of pink message slips. He hurredly checked all of them, but none were from Natalia. The thought crossed his mind that she was playing a joke on him. But the truth was that Mark was worried.

"Sarah, call information for me and get the number for a day spa called Salondre."

"Yes, sir."

Minutes later, Sarah relayed the number to him over the intercom. Mark quickly tapped out the number on the phone with his pen. "Salondre," a seductive voice answered.

"May I please speak with André?" Mark asked in his most professional voice. "I'm sorry, sir. André is at our other location. Please hold while I connect you."

"Salondre," a peppy male voice answered this time.

"André?"

"Um, no. Hold, please," the man replied.

"Hello? This is André."

"André. Hi. It's Mark."

"Mark. What a surprise. How are you?"

"Fine. And yourself?"

"I'm fine. Is everything alright?"

"Actually, no. I haven't heard from our dream girl all day."

"Well, that's strange. I gave her a wake-up call this morning at six, but she didn't answer. And then I called her ten more times up until eight-thirty."

"So you haven't heard from her today?"

"No, Mark. Not a peep."

"Shit. Where the hell is she then?" Mark was worried.

André tried to console him. "She had a lot lined up for today. She's probably too busy to call anyone. Don't worry, I'm sure she's okay. She'll call one of us sooner or later."

Mark paused. "Maybe your right, André. Listen if you hear from her first, please tell her I need to speak to her, OK?"

André said that he would and hung up wondering what little game his honey bunny was playing now.

Shawn crept quietly into the room. Natalia was asleep, wrapped tightly in the sheet he had given her. Her beautiful face was smooth and clear, the redness from his hasty slap all but faded. Her hair flowed behind her like strands of silk with only a few out of place. He smiled. "She's perfect," he whispered to himself. He gently moved his hand over her hair to put the straying strands neatly in place.

He left a new toothbrush, still in its packaging, on the sink. Then he placed a new tube of Colgate next to it. He crept out of the room and tiptoed up the stairs to the kitchen. After looking in all the cabinets, he couldn't find anything suitable for her to eat.

He hastily threw his jacket on, found his car keys and drove to the International House of Pancakes. After ordering three different combination plates and half a gallon of orange juice, he rushed home.

When he returned, he poured the orange juice into a fancy champagne glass and placed the pancakes covered in apple and cinnamon compote on a fancy white plate with gold trimming. He slipped the ski mask over his head and brought the plate and glass downstairs. He rested them on the floor and removed the chair from under the knob. Then he picked everything up and tapped on the door three times with his foot. "I'm coming in, aiight?" Natalia didn't answer. "I said, I'm coming in, aiight?"

"Fine," she wearily answered. He pushed the door open with his foot. "Breakfast is served," he said, striding in confidently. She looked refreshed and unruffled, sitting with her legs crossed and her hair neatly resting on her chest.

"Did you find the toothpaste and toothbrush?"

"Yes," she answered.

"I know it must've felt really weird to sleep on a couch. I know you're not used to that. Tonight I'll have a bed for you."

He sat in the chair and stared at her, unaffected by his failed attempt to cut the tension. "Here you go. I know you're hungry." He handed her the glass of orange juice. She inspected the glass.

"It's clean. And, no, I didn't put drugs in it. Trust me." He smiled widely, stretching the material of the mask around his mouth.

For lack of a table, she placed the glass on the carpet. Shawn moved to sit next to her. "Do you like apples on your pancakes?" She nodded. He put the plate on her lap. She looked down at it suspiciously.

"Do I have to feed you?" he asked as he grabbed the fork.

"I-I'm not hungry. I just want to go home," she whined, her expression begging for sympathy.

"Soon," he said and lifted the fork with a piece of pancake on it to her mouth. She turned away. "Look, I got up early this morning just to get some damn food for you so you better eat."

"I am too nervous to eat," she said looking down at his clean white and blue sneakers. She glanced at the door and asked, "What time is it?"

"About ten," he answered and dropped the fork in the plate.

"I missed an important meeting with important people. I'm sure the police must be searching for me by now."

"Are you gonna eat this or not?"

Natalia looked into the ski-mask but could barely see his eyes. He was being nice to her, but what if he had poisoned the food? Then again, she was certain he was going to kill her anyway.

"I am hungry," she said. Shawn picked up the fork again and offered her the same piece of pancake. Slowly, he brought it to her open mouth. Then, impulsively, he detoured from her open mouth and dropped the pancake into his own. She managed a smile. He cut another piece and brought it to her mouth. She looked down at the fork in hesitation. "Should I be afraid?" she asked. Shawn shook his head and chuckled. She took the offered food.

"Now, did that hurt?" he smiled at her. She chewed slowly, trying to detect any foreign flavors. But the pancake tasted fine. In fact, to her empty stomach, it was delicious. Shawn stuck the fork into another piece, but Natalia grabbed the fork.

"I'm a big girl," she said.

"Okay, big girl. I'll leave you alone so you can eat. Be good." He patted her thigh and left.

Shawn felt exhilarated and proud of himself. She didn't claw at him, and she didn't' try to escape. He attributed her good behavior to the good care he was taking of her. And he knew just what to do next.

He jumped in his car and headed into the city.

Although it gave him a thrill to see Natalia in his jerseys, he desired to see her in a dress as elegant as the one she wore in her portrait. Barney's New York, where she most likely shopped, was his destination.

After nearly an hour of careful browsing, he selected a silky black mini dress with rhinestone straps. Size six was his guess, and he paid in cash. Then he strolled to the shoe department and found the perfect pair of stilettos to complete the outfit. The heels were rimmed with sparkling crystals. "I'll take a size eight," he told the salesclerk. Within minutes, the transaction was complete, and Shawn was out the door.

On his way to the parking lot, he passed a quaint florist shop and decided that flowers would seal the deal. He purchased two dozen long-stemmed yellow roses and had the florist arrange them in a long gold box with matching bow.

He drove back to Queens exceedingly pleased with himself. There was no way Natalia wouldn't feel like a queen when he presented her with these expensive gifts.

On the drive back to St. Albans, Shawn's pager went off. With his cell phone, he called the number displayed on his pager. "Hey, young blood. It's Jigg."

"Whut up?" Shawn frowned.

"I got somebody for you to put in the park. You gotta do me this one solid. He's a good guy, ya know?"

"Nah, Jigg. I got enough of my own people up there already."

"Young blood, do me this solid, he's family."

"Man, I'm busy right now. I'll call you later on that."

"Do me this favor, young blood. Think it through good."

"Yeah, aiight," Shawn hung up before Jigg could say another word. At the moment, he had no interest in Jigg at all.

Natalia heard noises coming from the kitchen overhead. Her kidnapper had obviously returned.

While he was gone, she tried desperately to get free of her basement prison. The doorknob turned, but she was unable to push the door open no matter how hard she shoved her body against it. The tiny window high up on the wall was glued shut with years of accumulated filth. She couldn't see much through it — only a flicker of sunlight and a tiny patch of gnarled grass. She pounded the walls hoping for weak panels to give way and crumble, but none did. With no other choice and with much of her energy spent, she collapsed on the couch. Her heart ached for Mark; she missed him so much. She fantasized that he would come and rescue her. But there would be no chance of that. With his crazy schedule, he wouldn't even notice she had gone missing for a week! So she would die in a basement, held captive by some masked man, and no one would ever hear from her again.

The heavy footsteps scared her. What did he have in store for her? Would it be painful? But then reason sank in. *If he wanted to kill me,* she thought, *I would already be dead.* And he could have raped me last night as I slept. Hope replaced fear. "Maybe I will survive after all," she whispered wistfully.

More hours passed and the sliver of sun had been replaced by a dull gray. The kitchen noises had stopped as well. With nothing better to do, she raised the volume on the television and scanned the channels using the remote control. As she settled on a Laurence Fishburne movie, the heavy footsteps returned. She also detected voices. She grabbed the remote to mute the volume and strained to hear what was being said. Everything was inaudible. Frustrated, she turned the volume back on.

Nut pushed open the front door. "Yo!" he called into the house.

"I'm up here," Shawn shouted back. Nut ran upstairs and met Shawn at the top of the stairs. "What you been up to all day, niggah?" Shawn inquired.

"I was asleep, man." Nut pushed past him. "Where shorty at?"

"Look in the room," Shawn replied pointing toward the guestroom. Nut went in and looked around. Small hills of dust covered most of the gray carpet. Curved white-painted iron bars covered the windows. Plastic covered the bed and all the rest of the furniture.

"What the fuck are you doing?"

"This is her room, now."

"You gone, son. You lost your mind!"

"There's no lock on the door downstairs so to be on the safe side I'ma keep her in here."

"You act like she's a pet. How long you planning on keeping her?"

"I'ma let her go like in another week."

"What the fuck? Niggah, are you crazy? What you keeping her for? Let her go before the shit hits the fan."

"I'm gonna let her go. I just want her to..." Shawn stopped himself before finishing the sentence.

"You want her to what?"

"You wouldn't understand. Shit, I don't even understand."

"Talk to me man."

"We been talking and you know I get a vibe from her. I feel like she's not afraid anymore. It's like she can sense what I feel and that I'm not out to hurt her. Nahmean?"

"You not making sense, kid. I'm tryna understand you. But you gotta start making some sense."

"I want her. I want her to want me. I know it sounds ill. But there's something about her..."

"Pussy? That's why you trippin'? Well if it's pussy you want, then just do your thing and dump her somewhere. Anywhere far from here."

"Nah. I'm not gon' take it. You know that's not how I do. I want her to give it to me."

"Yo, son, you stupid." Nut shook his head and sat on the plastic covered bed. He laughed then said, "You built a fuckin' prison in your house all for some pussy? I hope that shit is platinum wit a cape hanging out that muthafucka. 'Cause you act like she da bomb, and you ain't even sniff the cat yet."

Shawn laughed. Was he going insane? "You gon' help me or what?"

"I ain't gettin' none. So I ain't doing shit," Nut snapped. Shawn gave him a serious look.

"Aiight, aiight, what you want me to do?"

"All you gotta do is help me clean up and then stay here while I get her some food."

"Damn, you act like y'all married and shit."

"Just do that for me"

"Whateva, niggah. But, yo, that shit better be so fuckin' good that your dick explode!" They both laughed hard.

Nut finished vacuuming the guestroom then pulled the plug from the wall and wrapped the cord around the hook on the back of the appliance. He stuck it back in the hall closet, went back to the guestroom and laid down on the bed. Shawn stepped into the room.

"Get up!" he barked.

"Nah, I'm tired."

"All you did was vacuum and you tired?"

"Hell yeah! I ain't used to hard work." They both laughed.

"I'ma get cleaned up, so why don't you go get the food for me?"

"What I look like your slave?"

"Yeh, you is. Here," Shawn handed him three twenties, "Get the seafood and steak platters. And the barbecue chicken, too."

"What about me?"

"I'll let you have some of the leftovers."

"Thanks, Massa. I's gon' go kills dem dere chickens now."

"Ha, ha. Just hurry it up." Shawn handed him the keys to both the car and the house. Like a little boy, Nut ran from the house. Shawn was letting him drive the Lexus.

After Nut left, Shawn set the dining room table for two with fresh linens and four tapered candles. With that task finished, he ran upstairs into the guestroom. He removed the dress from the black Barney's box and laid it gently on the scented tissue it was wrapped in. The stilettos he placed on the floor next to the bed, toes pointing toward the wall. It would be easier for her to put them on as she sat on the bed. As a finishing touch, he sprayed the room with his cologne. He scanned the room, pleased with the way it looked yet nervous about his first romantic interlude with Natalia. He was usually so cool with women. But Natalia was special, and he didn't understand why. He had spent thousands of dollars on her for what? He had no idea if she would even let him touch her.

After inspecting the living room one last time, he went back upstairs to take a hot shower. His nervous excitement wreaked havoc on his usual sensibilities. Searching his closets for an outfit was torture. Annoyed with himself, he finally settled on a pair of beige slacks still in the plastic from the cleaners. He pulled them on over navy blue boxers. The brushed silk of his white shirt slipped from his fingertips as he fumbled with the tiny alabaster buttons. With much concentration, he finally managed to finish dressing. And when he looked at his reflection in the mirror, he was quite pleased. He looked good. Real good. The white shirt accented his caramel brown skin perfectly. *Now, if only she could like me,* he thought and prayed.

As he left his room, he grabbed a small plastic bag from the dresser. On the way downstairs, he slipped a pair of handcuffs from the bag into his pants pocket. Exhilarated, gliding on air, he waited in the living room for Nut to return with dinner.

Minutes later, Nut bounced through the door carrying four plastic bags. "Come help me, nigga."

Shawn grabbed two bags from Nut's hand. "Do me one last favor."

"What now?"

"I need you to take her upstairs to the room."

"Why you can't do it?"

"Cause' I gotta keep her in suspense," Shawn grinned.

"Niggah, you need serious help."

"I know. So help me," Shawn quipped.

"She gon' see my face," Nut reminded him.
"Go get my ski mask off the dresser."
"Oh, man, you sure pushin' it." Nut went to get the ski mask. While he was gone, Shawn spooned food out of containers and onto white plates. After placing the plates on the dining room table, he removed the box of yellow roses from the refrigerator and balanced them on the chair where Natalia would sit. Nut returned wearing the ski mask just as Shawn nudged the chair under the table. "I'ma ready, boss," Nut chuckled.
"Aiight, go downstairs and get her. And take these wit you," he tossed Nut the handcuffs. "Press this down and slide this to the right."
Nut looked at him as if he were crazy.
"Just in case," Shawn grinned. Nut shook his head and went down to the basement. After removing the chair, he opened the door. Natalia crouched on the couch, her knees tucked under her chin, her legs ready to strike. Nut smartly remained out of striking distance and commanded, "Let's go!"
Natalia didn't recognize the gruff voice. It wasn't Sha. With increasing apprehension, she managed to place her feet on the floor. "Hurry up!" the new voice ordered again. Slowly, she stood up and slipped her shoes on. Nut roughly spun her around and snapped the handcuffs in place around her wrists.
"Walk straight, then make a left and go up the stairs," he instructed. She did as she was told. Nut kept one step behind her. He hadn't forgotten what she had done to his face and swore to himself that he was going to pay her back.
"Wait! Stop!" Snatching the sweaty towel dangling from his back pocket, Nut snapped it open and tied it tightly around her head to cover her eyes. And as further payback, he misguided her up the stairs. "Stop. You gonna hafta listen to me real good. When you get through this door make a right then another right. Walk faster, too!" She increased speed, following his directions exactly, and slammed into the banister on the second right turn. She gasped sharply at the pain in her ribs.
"Payback's a bitch, ain't it?" he chuckled. "Now go straight." With extra caution, Natalia felt the door frame to the room that was her final destination. Her prison.
Nut pushed her into the room and unlocked the handcuffs. Quickly backing out of the room, he instructed her to get dressed and slammed the door shut.
The noises Natalia had heard earlier in the day were actually locksmiths installing new hardware on the outside of the gue-

stroom door and security bars on the window. Shawn had called the local hardware store on his way back from the city and had them do a rush installation. So after shoving the slick new bolt into place, Nut went back downstairs.

Natalia ripped the smelly towel from her head as the slide bolt hit home. After her eyes adjusted to the light, she saw that she was in an average sized bedroom. The walls were painted brick red and the indirect lighting cast long shadows up from the floor. A shiny black lacquered dresser and matching armoire were placed on opposite sides of the room, and a queen-sized bed against the far wall was made up with black satin sheets. On either side of the bed were matching night tables with heavy black porcelain lamps covered with red silk shantung shades.

As she approached the bed, she kicked something but ignored it for what was on the bed. A little black dress was neatly laid out on sheets of pink tissue paper. And on the floor next to her foot was one black stiletto sparkling with crystals. She bent down to retrieve its mate that she had inadvertently kicked under the bed.

"What the hell is going on?" she asked to thin air.

Curiosity gave way to confusion. She sunk to the bed. What was this all about? She shook her head. Was it a game, a test? Had Mark set this up? Of course...Mark was behind the kidnapping. He could afford to do it and had the motivation. Christ, in not so many words, she had asked for this. *Mark has an imagination after all!*

Natalia was giddy with joy and decided to get ready as fast as she could. "What a little devil!" she exclaimed to herself. *Changing his voice, scaring me half to death. Oh, I'll get him. Payback is most certainly a bitch. But for now,* she thought, *I will play along and give an Oscar-worthy performance of my own.*

She removed the jersey and slipped the dress over her head. It was tight at the top, but, luckily, the material had a bit of a stretch to it. The shoes were a size too big but not unwearable.

With nothing but her fingers, she combed her hair and pulled it back into a long ponytail. Using strands of her hair to secure it, she twisted the ponytail from the end up and twirled it around and around into a tight bun. The ends she tucked into the bun. Ready in five minutes flat!

Nut sat at the kitchen table and ate his steak. "You think she ready?"

"Calm down man or you're gonna make me the nut!" Shawn cried. "It took her an hour in the shower yesterday. She ain't ready yet." But to be prepared, Shawn threw Nut the ski mask. "When you finished?" Shawn asked nervously. He felt like a teenager on his first date.

"Aiight. I'ma done, massa." Nut dropped his fork on the empty plate.

Shawn instructed, "I'm gonna sit at the table, so you go get her and bring her down to me."

"When you went on your little shopping spree, you shoulda got her a blindfold. I'ma hafta use your ski-mask."

"Just put a plastic bag on right quick."

"Yo, you better get it together man, for real." Nut shook his head and wiped his mouth with a napkin. "You owe me big time." He grabbed one of the yellow plastic bags from the counter and put it over his head. "Can you see me?"

"Just go get her." Shawn smoothed his shirt, slipped the other ski mask over his head and went to wait in the dining room.

When Nut unlocked the door, Natalia jumped up from the bed wearing a smile from ear to ear. She was certain that Mark was behind this entire charade, and she was anxious to play her role in it. The yellow plastic bag over his head amused her even more, and she barely suppressed a giggle.

"What you so happy about?" Nut raised an eyebrow. Natalia didn't answer. She stood up, put her hands behind her back and waited compliantly. "Don't do nothing stupid," Nut warned her then cursed himself because he forgot the handcuffs. So he held her hands behind her back and squeezed her wrists hard. As they neared the hallway, he let her hands go free for a moment and wiped the sweat dripping into his eye under the plastic bag. Grumbling, he pushed her down the hall and nudged her into the dining room where Shawn was waiting at the table. Nut left them and returned to the kitchen.

Natalia stood in the entranceway and scanned the room. The only illumination was from candles flickering from the center of the dining table. She smiled. Mark loved candles. And there he sat at the head of the table with a mask on. *Who did he get to help him,* she thought. It didn't matter though. He had done all of this for her and even though she had been frightened, she was excited at the evening ahead of them.

Shawn stood and walked over to her. Gently taking her hand, he led her to her chair, and as she waited, he pulled it out for her. On it, she saw the long gold box. She gasped. *How like Mark,* she thought. *He's a walking cliché.* But she was prepared to forgive his inadequacies for this delicious masquerade.

Sliding into the chair, she lifted the box onto her lap. Slowly, she slipped off the gold bow and dropped it to the floor. Then she lifted the cover and tossed it aside as well. The perfume from the fresh roses was overwhelming. Taking one in her fingertips, she lifted it to her nose and drew in its sweet fragrance.

"Thank you," she said and winked at him seductively. Shawn smiled widely under the ski mask wanting to kiss her, wanting more for her to kiss him.

Natalia placed the box and the rest of the roses on the floor, and Shawn helped push her chair under the table the rest of the way. He then resumed his seat across from her.

"Wow, look at all this food!" She selected a shrimp from one of the plates, took a small bite and chewed it slowly, licking her lips seductively. Shawn was in heaven. Her behavior fed his already huge ego.

Natalia slid out of the chair and slinked over to him. Resting a hand on the table in front of him, she leaned forward. "You know, I'd rather be doing something else," she said as she swung a leg across his lap. Slowly descending onto his lap, she reached for his mask. Shawn reacted quickly and grabbed her hands before she could pull it off.

"Oh, I'm sorry Mr. Kidnapper. I forgot I'm not supposed to see you," she grinned. "But, then, how am I going to kiss you?" She rubbed her fingertips over Shawn's covered lips.

Impulsively, Natalia pushed herself off him, sidled up to the wall and pressed her back into it. She heard Mark's heavy breathing through the thick material of the mask, heard his excitement in every breath. Natalia closed her eyes and waited for him to come to her.

No sooner than she sensed his nearness, she felt the fabric of his shirt brush against her. Blindly raising her hands to his face, she whispered, "You don't need this anymore tonight." Natalia licked her lips and pushed the mask up just enough to expose his lips. Shawn pressed his body against hers and ran his hands down to her hips. Their lips touched, mouths opened, tongues explored. And Natalia opened her eyes and shrieked.

Shawn cupped her mouth with his hand. "What are you screaming for?" Natalia's legs could longer hold her, and she collapsed on the floor. She backed away from him into the corner.

"What's with you? You kissed me. Why you actin' crazy now?"

"Who are you?!" she screamed.

Shawn offered her his hand but she batted it away. He tried again and again she hit at him. She looked like a trapped wild animal with no option but to strike back.

Shawn was stunned at the dramatic change in her attitude but realized that she had every reason to behave the way she was behaving. He looked at her deeply, and in his most calm voice, said to her, "I ain't gonna hurt you. I haven't yet have I?"

Natalia considered the gentle and considerate ways in which he had treated her the past day and came to the realization that if he had wanted to, he would have already taken her by force. Her shoulders relaxed and her breathing slowed. Against all reason, she decided to trust him and reached up for his hand. He took it gently and guided her into the living room. "Here, sit on the couch. Um, are you okay?" he asked, genuinely concerned.

The brighter light in this room revealed a remarkably handsome face with features chiseled like a model's. He had a deep clef in his strong chin, and his brown eyes slanted upward at the corners exotically. His caramel brown skin was unblemished, and his lips were full and moist.

Shawn repeated his question, "Are you okay?"

"W-who are you?" she stuttered.

"How come you acting like this?"

"Excuse me? How should I act? Who are you?!"

"Why did you kiss me like that?" Shawn purposely gave no answers.

Color blossomed in her cheeks. Despite the insane circumstances, Natalia was uncharacteristically embarrassed. She turned her face to avoid his insistent stare.

"Well?" he persisted.

Natalia realized that he would not give up. "I thought...I thought you were my boyfri...I mean my fiancé."

"What made you think that?"

Panic assaulted her again, and she shouted at Shawn like a mad woman. "What are you gonna do to me? Why did you bring me here? Let me go!"

"Enough wit the 20 questions!" he shouted back. "Listen. I know you must be hungry, so let's eat. Just eat, okay?"

Shawn took her hand and led her back to the table. "Eat. No questions." He sat down and helped himself to some shrimp.

Natalia refused and instead, nervously tucked back into place a few strands of hair that had fallen out of her bun.

"Go ahead, starve yourself," he shrugged while now chewing a piece of steak.

Anger slowly replaced Natalia's terror. "I am so tired of this. I demand to know who you are. And why I am here!" she yelled.

Shawn threw his fork down on the table. "You know what? I

should've just beat your fuckin' ass like I was supposed to!" Natalia's angry expression turned to one of surprise.

Shawn shook his head. "Look, I'm supposed to hate you. But I don't." Then his temper flared again, "Oh fuck this, just fuck it!" He shoved his plate of unfinished steak across the table.

Natalia should have become more afraid at his outburst. Instead, she found herself strangely attracted to him. "Sha," she said coyly, "I thought you said you wouldn't hurt me."

Getting no response, she tried another line of questioning. "Why are you supposed to hate me?"

Disparate emotions flashed across his face so quickly that Natalia did not have enough time with any of them to be able to define them.

"Natalia," he began as he approached her. "I can't hate you. I'm supposed to but I just can't. And that's my damn problem," he sighed. He stared at her so longingly that she felt exposed and vulnerable in a way that she was not accustomed to.

"Do I have to lock you up again or can I trust you to hang out with me?" Shawn asked as bluntly as he could manage.

"I promise to be a good girl," she said as she tilted her head up to look at him. With soft fingers, he brushed her silky lips and then reached out to take her hand. With her fingers entwined with his, she voluntarily let him lead her upstairs. Somehow the kiss had bonded them, and she was curious to see what would happen next. And besides, she told herself, she didn't have a choice.

Shawn led her not to the room she had dressed in earlier but to his bedroom. Natalia looked around. A ridiculous leather sleigh bed and a huge television dominated the room. With a loud plop, Shawn fell onto the bed. He found the television remote under a pillow and aimed it at the forty-five inch wide-screen. "I got a satellite dish so I got something like 300 channels," he bragged like a little boy.

"Great," Natalia replied with more than a hint of sarcasm.

"Why don't you sit down?"

"I'm just fine standing."

"Ain't nobody gon' do nothing to you so just sit your ass down."

Natalia quickly sat at the edge of the bed. His temper sent sweet chills up and down her spine.

"I'm not gon hurt you. I like you, nahmean? So just be easy." He didn't even look in her direction.

"You wanna watch a movie?"

"No," she answered softly. He could be very intimidating.

Surprisingly, she was very turned on by his abrasiveness.

"What?" he asked harshly.

"I said, no."

"Did I get your sizes right?"

"Excuse me."

Shawn repeated slowly, "Did...I...get...your...sizes...right?"

"Well, no, not exactly. The dress is a bit too snug and the shoes are too big." She was worried about offending him so she added, "But they are nice."

Shawn smiled. "You can lay up here. Relax yourself." He patted the pillows next to him. Natalia looked at the pillows then at him. *Why should I go and snuggle up with this bratty man and his uneven temper?* she thought. *I should run out of here.*

"I promise I won't do anything you don't want me to. Trust me, aiight?"

Trust him? Natalia thought. *He kidnapped me to make me his sex slave, and just when I'm interested, he turns on the television and ignores me.* Natalia cracked half a smile. I must be out of my mind, she thought as the shoes fell to the ground.

"You comfortable?" Shawn asked as she propped herself up on the pillows.

"Yes, I am. It's a little chilly, though," she rubbed her hands over her bare arms. Without saying a word, Shawn got out of bed and adjusted the temperature of the air conditioner. Natalia watched his every move and wondered, *How old is he? What does he do? Where am I?* At a certain point, however, she stopped asking herself questions she really didn't care to have answered.

Shawn yawned and looked over at Natalia. She was fast asleep. He ran his fingers up one of her legs and smiled as goose bumps rose on her skin. "I respect you," he whispered near her ear as he covered her with the spread.

Shawn slowly pushed himself off the bed and quietly searched his room for his cell phone and beeper. He had neglected his duties long enough and knew there was a lot of catching up to do. Once he found them, he took the landline phone from its charger unit and left the room. He went downstairs to the kitchen. *Nut must be long gone,* Shawn thought. The car and house keys were on the counter. From the basement, Shawn heard the television. He ran downstairs. Nut was still there.

"You fucked her yet?" he asked, with his mouth full of potato chips.

"Shut up! Why you still here? And why you leave food and shit on the counter like that?"

"Why you leave food and shit on the table in the dining room like that?" Nut chuckled.

"Aiight, you got that," Shawn laughed and checked his pager. He called back the last page. "Whut up?"

"Yo, some kid just came up here saying Jigg sent him to work."

"What? Where he at?"

"He left. I ain't give him nothin' so he was actin' like he got beef."

"Yeah?"

"He was sayin' some dumb shit like you ain't gon' keep him from makin' money."

"Don't worry about that petty shit. That niggah don't know no better. I'ma talk to Jigg, that muthafucka must be gettin' senile. Other than that, everything aiight?"

"Yeah."

"Shit is straight?"

"No doubt."

"Check wit me later."

Nut was eavesdropping as usual. "What Jigg do?"

"Ain't nothing, Nut. He sent some punk up to the park on some bullshit."

"I knew that shit went too smooth. I thought that niggah was Ty's man though."

"I don't know what that niggah is on."

"But Ty don't need that park, on the real."

"Ty wanted it, so you know it had to be done. To Ty, this is like a corporation merger, nahmean?"

"That niggah gettin' greedy, that's all."

"True," Shawn agreed.

"So, why you ain't up there tearin' shorty back out?" Nut smirked.

"Don't worry about it," Shawn plopped down next to him on the couch.

"Ah-hah, you ain't get none. Man, you better drop that bitch back in West Bubblefuck where we found her. Just take a loss, son. You can't fuck every pretty bitch you see." Nut nearly choked he was laughing so hard.

"It's all good, though. I'm a playa, baby. I'm gon' make her beg for this, watch me," he grabbed his crotch.

"Yeah, aiight. Whateva," Nut said. "Listen, D.L. and em' called me to re-up so I told 'em to come check me here. They gon' come get me and then we gonna go to the spot."

"Yeah, good, good," Shawn rubbed his hands together.

"You know they want that money you owe em'?"

"Tell 'em to take it from that stack they collect from the Lane set up. I'ma be upstairs. Beep me later."

"Aiight, go get her tiger," Nut burst out laughing.

"You got jokes, niggah, but watch me. You know me. I'ma have that with no problem." Shawn went back upstairs. He lay down next to Natalia. She was still sleeping. He slid his arm around her waist and closed his eyes.

Natalia dreamt of Mark. In her dream, when the mask came off, Mark's face was revealed. They were not in a bedroom but floating naked in a lake. Mark playfully dunked her under the water. But when she came up for air, Shawn was there instead. He grabbed her and pulled her to him. Mark tried to separate them but Shawn hit him, and he fell under the water. Shawn grabbed her face and forced his tongue into her mouth. She struggled, but he wouldn't let her go. As their bodies merged into one messy lump of flesh and colors, Natalia opened her eyes. Shawn was sleeping behind her with his arm draped around her waist. Natalia tried to ease out from under it. She turned onto her stomach and stole a glance at him. His eyes were wide open. "Going somewhere?"

"Um, I just wanted to take a shower. I need one...to help me relax."

"Uh-huh, right. So you were going to take a shower? Even though you don't know where the bathroom is?"

"Well, when we came upstairs, I thought I saw one. So that's where I was going."

"Why didn't you wake me?"

"You are awake," she cleverly replied and hopped to her feet.

"You don't have anything to wear," Shawn grinned.

"What did you do with my bag?"

"I think it's still in the car. But I threw most of your stuff on the floor."

"It's okay. I'm sure I can find something that's clean."

"Aiight, come on," he got off the bed and reached for her hand.

"Why do I have to go with you?"

"Let's not play games. Just come with me."

"Are you gonna lock me up again?" she asked sweetly.

Shawn ignored her and guided her to the door.

"Sha, wait, haven't I been good? You can trust me. Besides where am I gonna go?" Shawn looked around and determined that he could hurry out to the car, get her bag and be back in no time. He released her.

"I'll be right back. And I do mean right back," he emphasized.

"Okay," she said jubilantly. Natalia batted her eyelashes, sat on the bed and crossed her legs. He smiled at her, pulled the door slowly toward him and watched her until the door was fully closed.

Natalia crept to the door and listened to his footsteps. When they became faint, she hurredly started searching the room for a phone, for a piece of identification, anything that might help her. She searched his dresser first. Nothing but an endless supply of name brand underwear and socks. So she raced to the night table and pulled open the drawers. Electronic gadgets, instruction manuals and boxes of condoms. Finally, she investigated the closet. A black pant leg hung halfway out of a hamper. She yanked the pants out and something hard fell from one of the front pockets onto the closet floor. She scrambled to find it among the collection of shoes and sneakers. A cordless phone! Yes! She quickly dialed Mark's cell phone number.

He answered on the first ring. "Hello? Hello?"

Natalia screamed into the phone, "Mark, it's me! It's me!!"

"Hell-ooo?!" he shouted.

"Help me, Mark!" She screamed into the receiver. He couldn't hear her! Damn! The battery light on the phone glowed only very weakly, and Natalia realized that the phone wasn't charged enough to do more than make static.

"Mark!!!!" she howled again. But he was gone. "Shit!" Natalia threw the phone down and ran out of the room. Without hesitation and as fast as she could, she flew down the stairs and threw herself at the door that would lead her to freedom. The lock was stuck! "No!" she wailed as she jiggled and fumbled with the lever for what felt like an eternity. Finally, the lock gave way and the door opened. Fresh air! All that stood in her way now was a locked screen door. The street was only yards away. She pinched the little knob on the lock with trembling fingers and managed to slip it into the unlocked position. Then Shawn's face appeared on the other side of the screen. Natalia screamed, slammed the inner door closed and retreated into the kitchen to find another way out.

Shawn dropped the bag and burst through the door in a rage. He followed her to the kitchen.

"Come here!" he shouted. His terrifying command stopped Natalia dead in her tracks. She turned slowly. "I'm sorry, Sha. I just couldn't stay cooped up any longer," she said with a sweet smile.

"Why you tryna play me?" The look in his eyes frightened Natalia.

"No, no, I wasn't..." she stammered.

Without hesitation, Shawn grabbed her and threw her over his shoulder. Carrying her like a sack of potatoes, he went back to the porch, grabbed the Louis Vuitton bag, slammed both doors and locked them. Then taking the stairs two at a time, he carried her to his bedroom and threw her and her bag on the bed.

He grabbed her by the neck with one hand. "What was you gonna do? Huh?" Natalia's eyes filled with tears. Shawn loosened his grip. Her face was so beautiful. He wiped away her tears.

"If you really wanna take a shower, the bathroom is out this door to your left. If you wanna run, run. Do what you want." He sat on the edge of the bed with his elbows resting on his knees. He couldn't hurt this woman and he saw that she wasn't going to want him. The reality of the situation made him give up.

As Natalia headed for the door clutching her bag, she paused to look at him. Unexpectedly, she found herself feeling sorry for him. She set the bag on the floor and sat next to him.

"What do you want from me?" she asked softly. Shawn didn't answer. "Please, Sha, just tell me."

He looked at her and said simply, "You."

"Me? What do you mean?"

"Never mind. Just do what you wanna do."

Natalia picked up her bag and closed the door behind her. But before heading down the stairs, she lingered on the landing. *What did he mean, you?* she thought. It was strange to feel flattered in spite of all that had happened but she did. A handsome stranger wanted her so much that he went to extremes to have her. At that moment, Natalia admitted to herself that the ordeal was exciting. As scared as she had been, she knew that what Sha provided was what had been lacking in her life.

Shawn lay back on his bed and sighed heavily. He knew he was going to find himself in big trouble, but he didn't care anymore. For the first time in his life he hadn't completed an assignment...and he hadn't scored either. He lost the one game he desperately wanted to win. He wanted to win so badly. He never knew that he could feel such strong desire for a woman.

Time passed. He didn't know how long. He remained on the bed, not moving, wondering what was going to happen to him. She had seen his face. What a mess. He felt like such an asshole for screwing up so miserably. "Shit," he muttered under his breath.

Just then, the door, and Natalia sauntered into the room wearing a black thong decorated with red appliqued lips.

"I couldn't find any clean clothes in my bag," she said.

The sound of her voice made Shawn jump up. When he saw her,

he was too shocked to speak or move.

Natalia said again, "I couldn't find anything to wear."

Shawn's eyes grew bigger than saucers. Natalia stood over him stunning, gorgeous. He closed his eyes and shook his head, hoping that when he opened them, she would really be there. She was.

Natalia reached up to release her hair from the bun she had made. Long tendrils fell down her back and across her breasts. She slid down on the bed next to him. Sweetly, she asked, "Do you really want me?"

Still in a stupor, Shawn nodded slowly.

"Then take me," she slid on top of him. Shawn rubbed his hands over her smooth skin. She was real. This was really happening. She whispered seductively, "Protect me."

"What?" he asked, dumbfounded. She rubbed her hand over the bulge in his pants.

"Cover him," she smiled.

Shawn slid his hand under him into his back pocket and pulled out his wallet. Natalia took the wallet from his hand and squeezed it to feel for the condoms. She slipped in her fingers and pulled out two Magnum-sized condoms. *Magnums? Well, aren't we ambitious,* she thought.

Shawn rolled over and gently placed his weight on top of her. He kissed her forehead first. Then her temples, eyelids, nose and cheeks. At each spot, his lips lingered, sending tingles down her spine and butterflies to her stomach. Not willing to wait a second more, Natalia threw her arms around his neck and pulled his lips to hers. She kissed him gently at first then opened her mouth to his. The tip of his tongue played with the tip of hers, but then in a great swell of hunger, he sucked on her mouth until her tongue was completely in his. He licked her tongue as she seductively thrust it in and out of his mouth. With his head in her hands, Natalia pulled him away and directed his mouth to her neck. He breathed in the natural scent of her body as he kissed her neck and let his tongue linger in the soft hollow behind her ear. Unable to restrain himself any longer, he lifted his body off of hers and licked his way from her neck across her collarbone down her full breasts to her brown nipples. They were hard with excitement under his tongue. Without touching her body with his hands, Shawn continued the exploration of her skin with his tongue. He licked her soft, flat stomach and at the fringes of her neatly manicured pubic hair. Then he licked his way down until he found the spot between her legs that caused her to moan in ecstasy. He tickled her with his tongue, expertly flicking it all around, before slipping it into her juicy pleasure center. Natalia released a high pitched moan. The feeling was exquisite — she swore she could see the stars. With both hands, she grabbed his head and pumped frantically, screaming her way to an explosive orgasm. He slid back on top of her and thrust his tongue in her open mouth to give her a taste of her own sweetness. He grabbed a handful of her hair, jerked her head backwards and shoved his tongue deep into her mouth. Her body shuddered. Shawn ripped her panties off with one tug. Natalia was beyond restraining herself, lost in intense pleasure. He undid his pants and pulled them and his boxers down. Using his teeth, he tore open one of the condom packets. Natalia watched him, panting wildly. He slid the condom onto his cock and rammed it into her. Now she knew why he had Magnum condoms. His long, thick penis squeezing it's way into her narrow opening made her feel like she would lose consciousness. After punishing her for a while, he slowly pulled out, keeping two fingers on the end of the condom. He flipped her over and propped her up on her elbows and knees. He entered her slowly at first, then quickened his pace. She screamed and arched her back. Shawn grabbed her hips and pulled her toward him, again and again. He pounded faster and faster, each time with more force, grunting louder and louder. He pulled out and rolled her over onto her back, grabbing her legs and wrapping them around his waist. He reached around her back and yanked her off the bed. He pressed her back up against the wall and put his heat back inside her. He watched her beautiful face as she gasped with every thrust of his pelvis. She bobbed up and down, moving faster and faster until he came so hard that his knees nearly buckled. He pressed his lips on hers and squeezed her tightly in his arms. She held onto him for dear life...certain that she had died and gone to heaven.

Why did you stay?" Shawn asked as he leaned back onto the rumpled sheets.

"I don't know," she propped herself up on her side using the pillows next to him. He turned to face her.

"I'm glad you did," he touched her face tenderly.

"So what happens now?" she asked innocently. She had just given her body to a total stranger, a man who had kidnapped her. Natalia was certain that that made her insane. Yet, she wanted him again.

"Don't worry you gon' get some more," he grinned.

"No, I mean do I get to go home?" she asked, knowing damn well that she had no intention of leaving just yet.

"Do you want to go home?"
"Of course I do."
"I'll take you home. But, you're mine now."
"Excuse me?"
"I'm saying, I like you and I know I can make you happy. I can take care of you in every way," he replied smugly.

Natalia gulped. It would be crazy to continue seeing him. He kidnapped her for God's sake! Mark was the right kind of man for her. And she knew that he loved her. There was no way she could dump her fiancé for a crazed, kidnapping teenager.

Shawn's hand gently nudged at her chin, forcing her to look up into his eyes. "I'm serious, I want you. I've never respected any woman, besides the ones in my family...and now you. That's a big step for me." His words struck a chord. Natalia realized that he spoke the truth from his heart. She pulled his face close enough for her to press her lips against his. Then he rolled on top of her and took her to heaven...again.

She woke up to the delicious aroma of food. As she sat up and looked down, she realized that she was still naked. It hadn't been a dream at all. Glancing at the alarm clock on the night table, she saw that it was eleven-thirty. *I'd better let Andy know I'm okay before he calls the FBI,* she thought as she hopped off the bed in search of her bag. She found it and pulled out a short, summery dress. She put it on and ran downstairs to find her Ghetto Fabio. He was in the kitchen fully dressed. Two plates with onion and cheese omelettes were on the counter. Natalia crept up behind him.

"Put your hands up! We've got you surrounded," she tried to deepen her voice.

He quickly turned around and grabbed her, squeezing her in his arms.

"Good morning, Natalie."
"Who?" she asked with a scowl on her face.
"You."
"My name is Nuh-tal-yah," she pronounced slowly.
"Oh aiight, Nuh-tal-yah. I hope you're hungry." He picked up one of the plates and held it in front of him, "For you princess."
"Mmmm," she licked her lips.
"Don't do that. You gon' start something," he grinned.
"You're a bad boy," she playfully scolded.
"I have a surprise for you."
"Oooh, I love surprises. What is it?"
"Look in that bag over there," he pointed to a Macy's shopping

bag on the floor.

She rummaged through it and pulled out a pair of Donna Karan blue jeans and a pair of Nike sneakers. She looked at him confused. "I know you're not used to that kind of stuff. But you need something to wear home!"

She smiled weakly. She had a lot of explaining to do when she did get home. But at the moment, she didn't care. Shawn had made the ordeal very much worth her while.

"When are we leaving?"

"As soon as you're ready. But, Natalia, you have to promise me that this isn't over," he said seriously. She didn't know what to say. She didn't want it to be over either, but then there was Mark. She couldn't bring herself to break his heart.

"Sha, I don't know..."

"My name is Shawn," he said smiling. "Look, I know we met in a weird way, but I'm feeling you, ma. I wanna make you mine, nahmean?" He smiled.

"But I'm engaged. It's complicated," Natalia confessed.

"I don't care," Shawn said waving his hand dismissively. "Just promise me I'll see you again."

Natalia told him what he wanted to hear. "You'll see me again. I promise."

Shawn smiled and lifted her up onto the counter. He sucked on her neck. It felt like he was biting her.

"Explain that to your man," he chuckled after wiping away saliva from the hickey he had just made on her neck. Natalia giggled. He made her feel like a schoolgirl.

Natalia dressed in her new jeans and sneakers. Shawn got her bag and waited at the door. "Ready?"

"Yes," she looked around the room. Although she had been held against her will, somehow she didn't feel like she had been abducted by a stranger. In fact, she felt as if she had known Shawn before and that she had merely taken a detour from her daily routine. The circumstances were far from normal, for sure, but being with him was exciting. He definitely did not give her the opportunity to be bored! She walked over to him and reached out her hand.

"It was nice meeting you, Mr. Kidnapper," she took his hand in hers and shook it firmly. He dropped her bag as he lifted her up and swung her around. She laughed so hard that she almost peed in her pants.

"Are you my angel?" he asked her with a glazed look.

"I bet you say that to all the girls," she giggled.

"I never said it to a woman...and I never meant it, until now," he said, mesmerizing her with his eyes. She couldn't get over how handsome he was.

"Can I trust you? You not gon' call the cops, are you?"

"Why would I?"

"Yeah, aiight. We'll see."

"Don't worry, I won't tell. I like you too much," she simpered.

Shawn picked up the bag and scooped her up in his arms again — to carry her down the steps this time.

"Oh, my, God. Fresh air! And look...the sun," Natalia pointed dramatically to the sky.

Shawn laughed as he watched her and thought, *Damn.*

"Where are we?" .

"Queens," he replied. He took her hand and led her to the garage. After throwing the bag on the back seat, he opened the car door for her. "After you, baby girl."

The music blared as Shawn started the car. As he backed out of the garage, he turned the volume up even louder.

Natalia scanned the neighborhood. The street was lined with trees on both sides and every yard was well kept. Some homes had elaborate sculpted hedges. All in all, it was a quiet suburban street.

As he drove, Shawn bobbed his head up and down to the beat of the rap song vibrating through the speakers. He glanced over at Natalia who seemed uncomfortable.

"You don't like this music, do you?"

"It's okay, I guess. It's just that I don't understand why these rappers feel compelled to use such profane language and call women such derogatory names."

"It's just slang."

"Calling a woman a bitch and hoe.... please!"

"You're neither," he grinned.

"I know that," she smugly replied.

"Seriously, though, not all rap is about that. They talk about a lot of other shit too."

"You curse a lot," she frowned with disapproval.

"Oh, now I curse a lot 'cause I said shit. Well, you talk like a valley girl."

"Whatever," she giggled and looked out the window again.

Reality. Natalia reluctantly shifted her thoughts to Mark. He had probably gone to the house to look for her. André had probably called her a thousand times by now. And her poor assistant was probably swamped with a hundred angry phone calls. A lot of people were going to be asking for explanations. What on earth was she going to tell them?

Shawn lowered the music. "You okay?"

"I'm fine."

"You look worried," he said concerned.

Natalia sighed. "I don't know how I'm going to explain my disappearance."

"You don't have to."

"I do. I missed a lot of important meetings. A lot of people were depending on me."

"Oh, so I fucked it up for you, huh?"

"Well, yes...in more ways than one," she smiled.

"I'm sorry about that, baby girl. Hey, can I call you Nay-Nay?"

Natalia cringed. "Why Nay-Nay? Try Nat."

"Is that what you want me to call you?"

"I'd prefer it."

"Nah, I like Nay-Nay better. All your seditty friends probably call you Nat." She laughed because he was exactly right. "So, Nay-Nay it is," he confirmed with satisfaction.

Nay-Nay leaned her head on the headrest. The exciting adventures of the past few days had left her exhausted. Eventually, she dozed.

When Shawn pulled up in front of her house, she was fast asleep. In the afternoon light, her face almost glowed and as he watched her breasts rise and fall with her breathing, he knew it was too late for him. She had him open.

He quietly climbed out of the car and opened the back door to retrieve her bag. He then walked around to the passenger side door, opened it and lifted her out of the car. Natalia stirred as he hurried into the house. He took her upstairs and gently laid her down on the bed. As he began to undress her, she woke up and sleepily asked, "What are you doing?"

"Hey, sleepy head," he smiled.

"I'm home!" she squealed with joy. "Home sweet home. Thank you. You've been such a gentleman."

"It's the least I could do considering...well you know."

Natalia sparkled as a devilish grin played on her lips.

Shawn knew what she wanted. "You need a fix? You want some of this?" he grabbed his crotch. Natalia bashfully looked away in a weak attempt to hide how horny she actually was.

"No more 'til you see me again. Aiight?" he sat next to her.

"Okay, fine, whatever." Natalia would have said absolutely anything at that moment.

He kissed her lips softly and slipped his tongue into her mouth.

Her body quaked. The kiss lasted a long time, and when he pulled away from her, she realized she was very wet. She watched him lick his lips as he pulled away from her and reached into his pocket.

She expected him to pull out a condom. But instead, he pulled out a pen. He took her hand and wrote his cell and beeper numbers on her right palm.

"If you want me, you can get me anytime. So call me when you need your next fix," he cooed as his hand made it's way to her thigh. "Nay-Nay, you have access to me at all times," he said as he left the room.

Natalia was on fire and couldn't believe he was leaving without putting it out. She desired him, needed him. She was hooked. If he were crack, she'd be scrounging for money for the next hit. But she would never beg.

The door slammed as she rushed to the hall balcony. From up high, she watched as he slid into his car and drove off. With a sigh, she dragged herself back to her room and flopped on the bed. Her mind drifted to her adventures, and she laughed to herself. *With a million other things to take care of, all I can think about is him!* Natalia knew that she would see Shawn again and understood just what that meant.

She raced downstairs to her office and transcribed his phone numbers onto a small piece of paper which she folded in half. Then she ran upstairs and tucked the scrap of paper under a pile of bras in her lingerie drawer. With a tinge of sentimentality, she scrubbed the ink from her palm and applied lotion to her hands. Then she went downstairs again to her entertainment room. With a click on a special remote control unit, the wall behind the bar parted to expose four surveillance screens. She pressed another button and rewound the VHS tape already in the recorder deck. She played it back and watched as Shawn and his crew crept up to her house and gained access. Rewinding to just before their appearance, she pressed another button to erase the tape and then turned off the entire system. There would be no evidence of her urban Fabio.

Chapter Five

❤

HELLO DECEIT

After Natalia closed up the entertainment room and emptied her overnight bag, she was sufficiently relaxed to fall across the bed and call André.

"Andy. Hi! Have I got something to tell you!"

"Uh-uh, missy. You most certainly do. Do you have any idea how worried you had us?"

"Would you just listen. I have something important to tell you."

"Like what? What could be more important than your fiancé calling all over New York looking for you? He sounded like he was gonna commit suicide or something."

"Really?"

"Yes, really. What in the hell is wrong with you? Pulling a Whodini and making me have a panic attack? Shit, I was about to put your face on a milk carton," he scolded. Natalia laughed but was interrupted by thoughts of Mark and of how worried and angry he might be.

"I'll call you right back, Andy. I better call Mark. I don't want him to worry anymore. Okay?"

"Yeah, but you better call me back. 'Cause ju got a lot of splaining to do, Lucy."

She pressed the flash button and waited for the dial tone. Her fingers nervously tapped out the numbers. What if Mark didn't buy her story? Would he be able to detect that she wasn't telling the truth from the tone of her voice? Would the story be too weak? Or would...

"Hello?"

"Markie. Hi."

"Nat! Oh my God! Where have you been? I've been worried sick about you. I called all over town looking for you. I called André practically every hour on the hour. Not even Renée knew where you were. In fact, she's looking for you too. What happened to you?"

"Oh...Mark. I,um, took a pill to help me sleep and it worked a little too well if you ask me. I slept for hours and hours and then had trouble waking up. And when I finally did wake enough, I called you but my phone wasn't working properly. You couldn't hear me."

"Oh, so that was you! I did get a call but all I heard was static."

"Yup, that was me."

"Nat, I'm just so happy to hear your voice. I have to see you."

"Markie, I have so much catching up to do. I missed an entire day's worth of meetings. Maybe tomorrow night we can get together."

"Can't I see you tonight?"

"No, please, I have a lot to do. First, I have to explain why I missed my last lecture and meeting, and then I have to re-schedule another lecture, that's if they'll have me now. There's the co-op board meeting and my itinerary and a bunch of other..."

Mark interrupted, "Blah, blah, blah. Look, Nat, I just want to stop by and drop something off. I've got a surprise for you."

"No, Markie."

"Oh, come on. I need to give you this surprise right away."

"It isn't a surprise if I've already sampled it," she giggled.

"Trust me, you haven't had this surprise sprung on you before," he chuckled.

"Tell you what, I'll call Sarah and see what my schedule will be like. I'll call you back, okay?"

Mark sighed then asked, "Why can't you just let me see you tonight?"

"I'll call you right back, okay?"

"Alright," he mumbled. "Just tell me you still love me."

"I still love you, Markie."

She called her assistant and listened to how she smoothed everything over with the angry board members and how she placated the principal of I.S. 219. Renée's expertise in damage control was one of the reasons Natalia had hired her in the first place. "Mr. Anderson agreed to have you lecture next Thursday morning. The co-op board insists that you be at their office tomorrow at 11:00am. And at 3pm, you are scheduled to meet the accountant at the 3rd Avenue McDonald's. Frank called to say that money was being shifted around, and he was unaware of where it was going to or coming from. He sounded pretty paranoid if you ask me. Almost as if he thought some laundering scam was going on."

"Really?"

"Well, I could be mistaken. But it was important enough for him to pester me all day yesterday about it. I called Lina, figuring you would want her to investigate immediately. But she told me that she'd prefer to meet you there and go over the books together."

"Oh, Renée, what would I do without you?"

"Hmmm...go insane perhaps?"

"Precisely," she chuckled. After the update from Renée, Natalia collapsed onto the bed and stared at the ceiling. Even though she couldn't get Shawn out of her head, she felt obligated to Mark. So she called him back as she promised and told him he could come over.

Shawn's pager went off. Then a second later, his phone rang. "Yeah," he grunted.

"Young blood, how you gon' disrespect me, like that?"

"What the fuck you talking about?"

"I asked you to do me a favor. So why you dis my lil' man. Then you go and tell him that you runnin' shit and fuck me? What's that all about?"

"Man, ain't nobody tell that niggah shit. I wasn't even up there. I told you I had my peoples up there already, so don't start this bull-shit. That niggah went up there like he was God, yo. That's not a smart move, nahmean? I don't have patience for that dumb shit, nahmean?"

"No need to get raw, young blood. He's young, ya know? He just hyped shit up to get me mad enough. But it's okay. I'll take care of him. So everything is everything on your end?"

"Yeah. I'm about to call up there now. So holla at me later."

"No hard feelings, young blood. I just had to clear shit up, ya understand?"

"Yeah, aiight," Shawn hung up and dialed Spank's cellular.

"Whut up son?"

"It's all love. It's movin', son!"

"Good, good. Call me after one, aiight?"

"Aiight," Spank replied. Shawn pulled up in front of Nut's house. He rang the doorbell and leaned up against the door. Nut peeked through the side window and after seeing that it was Shawn, flung it open. The doorstop bounced the hollow door from the wall right back at him.

"Yeah niggah!" Nut yelled and forced his chest into Shawn's as if they were at Madison Square Garden and the Knicks had finally won a championship.

"What the fuck is wrong wit you?" Shawn asked. He couldn't help but laugh. "I heard y'all upstairs."

"You heard what?"

"Oooh, ahhhh, ohhhh. Man you was killing that pussy. You had shorty screaming. I thought you was up there beatin' her ass," Nut laughed, wiping away specks of spit from his lip.

Shawn shot Nut a cocky smile then asked, "Why you ain't beep me?"

"Man, I beeped you twice, and you ain't call back. So I said fuck it. You always want somebody to beep you, but you don't know how to call a niggah back. I guess y'all was at it again, huh?" Nut elbowed Shawn. Shawn cracked another smug smile.

"I don't know what you be doin' to these bitches. You lucky muthafucka." Nut shook his head, "So was it worth all the shit we went through?"

"No doubt. She gon' be wifey," Shawn said with a serious face.

Nut stopped laughing. "What?"

"I said, she gon' be wifey."

"You feel aiight, man, 'cause I think she put it on your ass."

"I don't know what it is about her...I don't know," Shawn scratched the top of his head.

"Damn, it's like that?" Nut asked with a look of disbelief.

"Yeah, niggah," Shawn chuckled nervously.

Nut plopped down on his faded, dingy couch. Shawn sat next to him. Natalia filled his thoughts. He frowned. He couldn't even call her. He didn't have her phone number. He wanted to go to her house, but he couldn't chance it. He didn't know if she told the cops. He looked over at Nut and asked, "You got something to drink?"

"Just water," Nut said and scratched his knuckles. Shawn shook his head and sighed. "Let's go, man."

Natalia waited for Mark in the living room with a revised version of a speech in her hand. The original was on her lap. She had tried to read the edited copy aloud, but every time she did, Shawn crossed her mind. Was she crazy? It dawned on her that she didn't know why he had kidnapped her. But she pushed those thoughts aside. She wanted him, and as hard as she tried to clear her thoughts, it didn't work. She put down the speech and ran upstairs. She opened her lingerie draw and pulled out the piece of paper with his numbers. She called the first one, his cell.

Shawn's phone rang as he drove down Jamaica Avenue. He asked Nut to answer it. Nut grabbed the phone from the dashboard and ordered, "Speak," as if training a dog.

Natalia became nervous and hung up.

"Who is it?" Shawn asked eagerly. "I dunno, they hung up." Nut shrugged. Shawn drove to the Linden pool hall, hung out with his friends, drank and played pool. Slowly, thoughts of Natalia faded from his mind.

Natalia had returned to her speech and was reading aloud as Mark quietly came into the living room.

"Hi gorgeous," he said cheerily.

"Hi, handsome. Come here," she gestured and put the papers on the couch.

Mark grabbed her hands, pulled her into him and hugged her tightly in his arms. "I missed you."

"Me, too, Markie," she looked into his blue eyes and saw that they were peaceful. She did miss him and hugged him in return even more tightly, rubbing her hands up and down his back. "Now where is my surprise?" she asked in a little girl's voice.

"In my pocket," he grinned. She looked at him sternly and folded her arms. "Let me see."

"Get it yourself," he patted his jacket.

Natalia stuck her hands into his pants pockets instead. "Oh, not these pockets," she teased and then reached into his suit jacket. She felt bulky papers and cards and pulled them out. After examining all of the papers, she jumped up and down excitedly. "We're going to Hawaii!"

She waved the tickets in the air. "When?"

"As soon as you're calendar is clear."

"Really?"

"Yes, really," he pulled her close. "I love you."

"I know," she smiled.

He kissed her forehead. She remembered when Shawn kissed her forehead and how it made her feel. Guilt washed over her and she involuntarily took a step back from her fiancé.

"What's wrong, Nat?"

"Oh, nothing. I just can't believe you did this!" she lied. She turned to look at the tickets again, to hide her face from him. He hugged her from behind and whispered, "Can we celebrate?"

"How?"

"Let's see we can dance or..." he twirled her around. "Actually I have two surprises," he grinned. "I'd like to take you someplace special."

"I can't go anywhere. I told you—"

"It's right outside."
"What is?"
"Just come with me." Mark grabbed her hand, pulled her out the front door, and they stepped onto the veranda. Natalia looked around. "Well, where is surprise number two?"
"Come on," he took her hand. She followed him to his car. "Get in," he said and opened the door for her. Natalia looked down at her feet. "But I'm barefoot," she whined.
"Don't worry about it," he said as he helped her into the car.
Mark drove her to a big open field. Natalia's jaw dropped as a helicopter landed directly in front of them.
As he pulled her towards it, the propellers whooshed over their heads. They boarded the helicopter with windblown hair and rosy cheeks and sat on plump suede seats. A tinted plexiglass partition separated the back of the cabin from the pilots and the floor was covered with a velvety soft carpet. Mark lifted her up onto his lap.
"Excited yet?" he asked with a bright grin.
Natalia was astounded. Mark was really trying to win her heart again.
"Where are you taking me?"
"Nowhere. I just wanted to make love to you under the moon and this is as close as we can get."
The helicopter lifted off the ground. Natalia giggled as he slid his hand under her nightgown and tickled her. Marked probed and stroked until he found her panties. She helped him to pull them off. On the padded velvet floor of the helicopter, two thousand feet off the ground, she straddled him. Moonlight illuminated the cabin and the humming of the rotors covered her moans of pleasure. For the first time in a long time, she truly enjoyed their lovemaking. But making love to Mark did not dispel thoughts of Shawn, helicopter or no. As they descended to land, Mark wrapped his arms around her and rested his head on her breasts. Natalia looked at the moon and wondered where Shawn was.

As scheduled, at 11:00 a.m., Natalia met with the co-op board. Afterwards, she met her accountant at her McDonald's on Third Avenue.
Both meetings went well — the board's business concluded with no mention of her absence and the potential problems to which Renée alluded to turned out to be no problem at all.
Finished for the day, Natalia was about to pull out of the parking garage and head home when her cell phone rang. She put the car back in park and dug it out of her purse, "Hello?"

"Hi, sweetie. It's Thursday. You ready for Hawaii, yet?"

"Well, as a matter of fact, I am. I don't have anything on my calendar tomorrow or Monday."

"I can come and get you right now. You don't need to pack. I'll buy you some clothes when we get there. Besides, you won't be needing much clothing."

"Mark, what are you talking about?"

"Hawaii, silly! Or did you forget already?"

"You want to go today? Now? Really?!"

"Of course now."

Natalia was too excited for words.

"Nat, are you there? Listen, did you drive in today?"

"I'm here," Natalia finally replied. "Um, yes. I drove in today. Mark, where should I leave the Navigator?"

"I took a cab to work, so I'll take a cab to you. We can drive out to Newark together and leave the jeep in the garage."

"Great! OK, I'm on Third and fifty-ninth. I was on my way to Andy's."

"I'll meet you there. The Madison Avenue salon?"

"Yep."

"Great. I'll see you in an hour." And with that, Natalia was going to Hawaii!

She hurried to the salon, filled with excitement and dying to tell somebody about it. Two men were providing her with the time of her life, and she had to tell someone before she exploded. André was so happy to see her that he left a client's head in the sink and hugged her enthusiastically. He noticed her glow right away.

"You have been up to something, haven't you? I can see it all up in here," he shook his hand in her face.

"Let's go in your office," she pulled on his arm.

"Cybil, please finish Mrs. Tramindo's rinse," André said as they headed to his office.

"Start talking missy."

"I don't know where to begin."

"You better begin somewhere. Cause' I know something is up."

"Okay...well you know I was missing?"

"Yeah?"

"Wellll...I was really missing. I was kidnapped by this guy and..."

"Whaaat? Hold on, are you kidding me?" André was stunned.

"No, I was kidnapped. And, oh Andy, the guy who kidnapped me was sooo cute and sexy and sweet. He bought me flowers and clothes...he was just so sweet. Oh, and when he made love to me,

I thought I was in another world. I mean, it was so fabulous. Oooh, I can't believe I did that, but I did."

André's mouth hung open in shock. When he finally caught his breath, he pinched himself then asked, "Did you just say that you had sex with a strange man who kidnapped you?"

"Uh, yes," she replied, embarrassed.

"Nat, what were you thinking? Gurl, I hope y'all used condoms."

"You see, that's just it. He protected me. He was just so..."

"What do you mean, he protected you? What are you talking about? Make some sense, girl, please. What about Mark?"

"Oh, uh, now you're really going to be mad at me."

"What now? Don't tell me there's more to this story."

"Yes, there is. The same night that Shawn — oh that's his name by the way — brought me home, Mark hired a helicopter, and we did it thousands of feet in the air."

"Let me get this straight...you were kidnapped and had sex with a stranger and the same night you get back home, Mark takes you in a helicopter and y'all had sex, too?"

"That sounds about right."

"Gurlllll, you are so nasty. Sick, sick, sick," he said with a look of disgust. Then with a quick laugh, André said, "You know, I'm just kidding mama. Shit, I wish I could've been in your shoes! But I don't believe it. You of all people getting your freak on like that. You really are getting out of hand Ms. Thang," he laughed his husky laugh. Natalia giggled uncontrollably. She was relieved to be telling her secrets to her friend.

"What am I going to do? I love Mark...but Shawn...he's so exciting! He makes me tingle all over."

"Missy, you should know better. First of all this guy kidnapped you. He could be a wacko. What was that about anyway? Why did he kidnap you?"

"I don't know. He didn't mean to."

"What? You must be crazy. He's a criminal. Only God knows why he did that to you mama. If I were you, I'd just chalk that up to a one nightstand and forget about him. You better hope he forgot about you. That maniac just might try to kidnap your ass again."

"He won't."

"You don't know that. Besides, the man is a complete stranger. You know Mark. Mark is a good man. He is your fiancé. Remember that?" Natalia was confused. Her love life had never been complicated before because she never let anybody in — until Mark. He was the first man she allowed to touch her heart. He was good for her, and he was worthy of her. Now, she desired a total stranger, and did not know how to reconcile her newfound feelings. André was right, he made sense. But her feelings for Shawn were strong, and she wanted to continue to experience them.

"Andy, I think I love Mark, but I feel something for Shawn. I can't explain what I feel but...," she glowed.

"Nat, Nat, Nat. I know how bad you want excitement in your life. But you have got to see that this wouldn't be right. You can't base a relationship on a whim. A relationship takes time and a lot of patience. And Mark has definitely put in overtime, okay. You can't deal with this guy. He kidnapped you! That is not normal!"

"Andy, you don't understand."

"I know, I know. I can talk 'til I'm blue in the face and you're gonna do what you want to anyway. So, all I can say is please be careful," he sighed.

Natalia smiled her delightful smile and hugged him. There was a knock on the door and a voice said, "Can I have my woman back please." It was Mark.

"I've got to go," Natalia grinned.

"You leaving? You just drop this bomb in my lap and leave?"

Putting a finger to her lips out of view from Mark, Natalia said. "Mark and I are going to Hawaii!"

"Oh, really? Damn girl! You are way too much for me," André shook his head and laughed. "I'll let you off the hook this time. Just think about what I said, OK?"

"Yes mother," she laughed. André rolled his eyes.

Shawn and Nut left the pool hall mostly drunk. They fell all over each other and giggled all the way to the car. As they fell in, cracking jokes about each other's mothers, Shawn's pager went off. He called the number back. "Who dis?" He asked wearily.

"Ay, yo, it's one o'clock, you said to beep you."

" Yeah, whut up, Spank?" Shawn asked, trying to sound sober.

"Yo, we makin' mad cheddar, son."

"Aiight. You loaded down or what?"

"Nah. We aiight."

"Well, you know what to do."

"Yeah." Shawn put the phone back on top of the dashboard. He turned to Nut and said, "That park is a fuckin' gold mine."

"Yeah, yeah, whateva. Take me home."

"Come wit me to her house."

"Who?"

"Natalia."

"Who da fuck is a Natalia?"

"Wifey."
"Hell, Naw, niggah! I ain't fuckin' wit you."
"Come on man, just go wit me."
"What you goin' up there for?"
"I gotta see her."
"What if she got cops up there stakin' out and shit?"
"Just come on. Scary muthafucka," Shawn laughed.
"Damn, whatever she did to you, I hope that shit wears off soon," Nut shook his head.
Shawn chuckled and retorted, "Don't worry, your ass gon' get caught out there soon."
"Not the kid, yo. Not the kid," Nut waved his hand frantically.

Alo-ha, welcome to Wai-ki-ki," said a beautiful Hawaiian woman with a bright white smile.
"My name is Mai, and I am your hostess." She ushered Mark and Natalia into the jeep and acted as their tour guide while she whisked them to their private bungalow.

Here we are," Mai announced as she parked the jeep and gracefully stepped out. "You will have private maid service and maintenance. Please follow me."
She held the door open. Mark squeezed Natalia's hand. Inside, the airy bungalow was decorated with rattan furniture and marble tiles. Natalia pulled Mark to the window and took in the breathtaking scenery below.
"Look, no glass!" she exclaimed, "Mark, it is so beautiful here."
Mai chimed in, "Enjoy your stay. If you have any needs, please don't hesitate to call me. My number is programmed into the phone, see?" She pointed to the word "hostess" under the clear plastic on the phone.
"Thank you, very much, Mai," Mark said as he handed her a twenty dollar bill and ushered her out the door.
"Excited, yet?" he asked as he turned to Natalia. Mark had repeated that same question over and over for the past fifteen hours, beginning at the airport gate at Newark.
"Stop asking me that! Yes, yes, yes! I am! This is so lovely, Mark. Lets go see the island sights."
"I was hoping to see Natalia's sights."
"Be good," she simpered.
"I am being good. There is no natural beauty out there that can compare with the one I have right here."
"Oh, Mark," Natalia cooed.

"Come on, then. I'll take you wherever you want to go. Remember, this weekend, it's all about you."

I don't see nothing," Nut complained as he strained to look out the car window.

"Shit!" Shawn grumbled.

"Man, I told you this was a waste of time."

"Fuck! Just wait here. I'ma be right back."

Shawn hoped that Natalia's back door would still be open. And lucky for him, it was. He slipped into the kitchen and ran up to her bedroom. In her bathroom, he searched the cabinets and finally found what he was looking for — a tube of lipstick. With it, he wrote on the mirror: I need a fix.

He threw the lipstick in the sink and ran back out to his car.

"What happened?" Nut asked as he watched the house.

"Nothing. She ain't here."

"So we came down here for nothin'?" Nut complained.

Ignoring him, Shawn stepped on the gas.

Mark drove while Natalia read Newsday. They had just landed and Natalia wanted to catch up on the news. Five days wasn't very long, but she felt that she had missed out on a lot. Both were jet lagged and burdened with two heavy bags of unnecessary things they bought in Hawaii — clothing she would never wear again and gadgets that Mark just had to have.

Natalia rushed to the house as Mark struggled with the bags.

"Hurry up, slow poke!" she chided.

"Hey, you could help me ya, know."

"Oh, stop complaining and get in here."

Mark hurried past her and set the bags on the floor.

"I'm thirsty. You want anything?" he asked.

"No thanks. I'm going upstairs to change. But help yourself."

She went into her bedroom and saw clothes strewn on her bed. *This place is a mess,* she thought as she hurried to straighten up and throw things in the hamper. When she turned on the bathroom light, the writing on the mirror shocked her at first. She read it quickly then grabbed some toilet paper to wipe it away. *Thank goodness Mark hadn't come up here with me,* she thought. Shawn's persistence both frightened and excited her. And the fact that he could so easily get into her house unnerved her. But she smiled anyway at the thought of his being there.

Natalia had just finished wiping away Shawn's message when she heard Mark coming up the stairs. She hurried to clean the glass but the lipstick's waxy texture smeared, and made more of a mess. When Mark entered the bedroom sipping a glass of cranberry juice, he called out, "Honey, where are you?"

She slowly pushed closed the bathroom door and frantically finished the job. "Whew!" she whispered to herself.

Mark knocked on the door. "You okay?"

"Mm-hmmn," she muttered and flushed the toilet. When she came out of the bathroom, she found Mark sitting on her bed. She sat next to him.

"I've got a lecture tomorrow so I'd better go to sleep. Back to reality, I guess."

"Yeah, it's late. I'm gonna go. I have to be in the office early tomorrow morning."

"You've got clothes here. Just spend the night."

"I am so glad you said that. I thought you wanted me to go," he said as he stretched out next to her.

She unbuttoned her busy floral blouse and pulled down her shorts.

"Yesss," Mark grinned.

"Nooo. I'm going to sleep."

"You're lucky I love you."

"Why?"

"Never mind. I guess we both need to sleep. Goodnight, Mrs. Delucchio."

"Goodnight, Mr. Foles."

"Ha, ha," he laughed and rested his head on her stomach.

Shawn stood outside his house talking to D.L. Nut was inside tallying the profit from the night before. The phone rang, and he answered it. "Yeah?"

"Who dis?" Tymeek grilled.

"Who dis?" Nut asked.

"Where my fuckin' brother at?"

"Oh, Ty, whut up man? Dis Nut. You aiight?"

"Whut up? Where's Shawn?"

"Hold up." Nut ran to the front door with the cordless phone in his hand and his two-sizes-too-big jeans falling to his knees. He pulled them up quickly with his free hand and shouted, "Ay, yo Shawn."

"What?" Shawn turned around. "The phone. Here, catch."

"Who is it?" Shawn asked as the phone landed in his hands.

"It's Ty," Nut replied as he went back inside. Shawn put the phone to his ear and said, "Whut up niggah?"

"Why you ain't been up here to see me?"

"Man, I got the park now and shit just been hectic."

"What's the status on that?"

"It's doing well over the reg."

"I knew it would. So what Jigg say?"

"That nigga be on some shit but he got his sixty so far."

"Good. Good. How's moms?"

"She aiight. She still mad though. Every once in a while I stop by and drop her sumpin'. She act like she don't want it, but she be takin' it wit her frontin' ass," they laughed.

"That's how she do. But you gotta love her," Tymeek chuckled. "How is aunt Free?"

"She still cool as ever. You know she miss you right?"

"Tell her I love her and miss her too. That's my girl right there."

"Aiight."

"You taking care of her?"

"No doubt."

"So what you doing wit yourself?"

"I'm chillin'."

"Niggah, I know you out there slangin' dick like rock ain't you?"

"Nah. I got a girl."

"You got a girl, huh? Just one?" Tymeek laughed.

"Yeah."

"Don't get caught out there. I know you ain't tryna make no babies."

"Nah, not yet."

"When you gon' come see me?"

"Wednesday."

"Aiight, lil' bro. Keep taking care of my shit."

"No doubt."

"I'ma holla at you on Wednesday."

"One," Shawn replied. He missed his brother. He wanted to tell him all about Natalia, but he didn't know how Tymeek would react.

Nut came back outside and called to Shawn, "Ay yo, PB!"

"What?"

"We did three double," he grinned.

"I told you that park was a gold mine, didn't I?" Shawn asked. Nut nodded. Shawn could hardly smile. His mind was on other things.

"Ty want me to come up there on Wednesday," he sat on the top step and looked up at Nut. He needed to talk about her.

"She ain't call me."

"Who? Oh here we go again. You think she was gon' call you after what we did?"

"Yeah, 'cause she came to me. Me and her was cool."

"That don't mean shit. Women are funny like that." He scratched his head and continued, "Why don't you get Kamani to get you her phone number and call her. Just get it over with you, whipped muthafucker!" Nut laughed. Shawn laughed, too.

Natalia drove home early and beat the rush hour traffic. Her part-time maid was still cleaning when she walked in.

"Hi Lottie."

"Hello, Ms. Foles. I'll be done in another hour or so."

"That's fine, take your time," she said as she went through her mail.

Natalia picked up her briefcase and handbag along with the mail and went to the study. She sat in the swivel chair behind her desk and pulled from her briefcase a small stack of photos of her trip with Mark. A few of the photos showed the both of them sunburned and smiling, arms wrapped around each other in various gorgeous locations. Instead of feeling happy, guilt washed over her. She looked away from the pictures and thought of Shawn. More often than not, she found herself thinking about him and the time they had spent together. The memory of him sent shivers throughout her body. She wanted him — even after the impulsive trip to Hawaii. Mark had used his imagination but it involved a helicopter and a plane. He proved that he could change their environment, but his imagination in bed was still desperately limited. Shawn, on the other hand, was her very own action hero.

As she showered, Natalia fantasized that Shawn was lathering his hands with soap and rubbing it all over her body.

She stepped out of the shower and dried herself with a plush towel. After shaking out her wet hair, she pulled on a cotton tank and silk pajama bottoms and went downstairs. Lottie had apparently gone for the day.

Natalia made some microwave popcorn and carried the steaming pouch to the entertainment room. Zombie-like, she pressed the pay-per-view authorization button on the cable remote and started watching the movie, 'Life'. Just as the movie started, the phone rang. She turned the volume down.

"Hello?"

"Nay-nay?"

"Shawn?!" she exclaimed.

"You lied to me."

"Excuse me?" she asked confused.

"You promised me I'd see you again."
"I've been kind of busy."
"I don't care. I want to see you. I need to see you." His sexy voice made it impossible for her to say no.
"Where?"
"I'll come get you."
"But...," she weakly began to protest.
"I'm comin' to get you now," he insisted.
"Okay," she gave in.
"Wear a dress. Get sexy for me, okay?"
"Okay," she answered sweetly. Shawn hung up without saying goodbye.

Natalia was excited again. She threw the popcorn in the trash and ran to her room. She searched for the perfect sexy dress and found it — a tiny black mesh mini. She smoothed raspberry scented lotion all over her body and slipped on a black thong. Then she snapped on a strapless push-up bra. She slipped the dress over her head and tied the crisscross straps around her neck. To complete the outfit, she slipped into a pair of sandals with three inch heels that accented her pink polished toenails. As an afterthought, she added a pair of three-carat, teardrop-shaped, diamond earrings. She pinned her hair up in a roll and left a few strands loose on the right side then went into the bathroom to find the perfect shade of lipstick. She glided a sultry wine-colored stick over her lips and pressed her lips together to even out the color. After a final check in the mirror, she hurried down the steps to the living room and sat on the chaise. She wriggled into a comfortable position and waited for Shawn to arrive.

It was getting late and she felt silly. *He probably isn't coming after all,* she thought. She uncrossed her legs, went out on the veranda, leaned against a column and pouted. Moments later, a white vehicle pulled into the driveway. Excitedly, she ran inside and grabbed her purse. After hastily locking the door, she casually walked towards the car trying to disguise her nervousness. Shawn got out and met her halfway. He was incredibly handsome in a sky blue suit and brimmed hat that tilted on his head. Natalia could hardly see his sexy slanted eyes. As he got closer, she saw his broad smile.

"You are so beautiful," he said sensuously as his hands slid around her waist.
"My, aren't we all dressed up. Armani?" She pulled off his hat.
"Yeah. Now why you go do that?"
"I wanted to see your face," she smiled up at him. He was even

more handsome than she remembered.

"Can I get a kiss?" he said and puckered his lips.

"No kiss for you," she smiled seductively. He pressed his lips to hers anyway.

"I missed you," he breathed into her ear.

"Me, too." She reveled in his caress. "Where are we going?"

"A club."

"Oh. I thought we were going somewhere special," she said sarcastically.

"Anywhere you are is special," he grinned. She blushed.

"Let's go," he said and took her hand.

Shawn pulled up in front of a crowd waiting to get into the brightly lit Stardome. The women on line wore tight, skimpy dresses that made them look like high-priced hookers. Natalia wondered how they managed to get into them. The men leaned against fancy cars parked along the street. All of them looked as if they were posing for photos. Every last one wore a hat and gaudy diamond jewelry.

Shawn's gold trimmed Lexus sparkled in the night. He opened the door for Natalia, and she stepped out of the car like a princess. All the women stared. She felt like a superstar. A guy with a mouth filled with gold teeth ran over to them.

"Hey-eee man. Whut up?"

"Ain't nothin," Shawn handed him a few folded bills.

"Thanks, P.B.," he rested the side of his body on Shawn's car.

"P.B.?" Natalia asked. Shawn chuckled and explained, "They used to call me Pretty Boy. So now they just call me P.B."

"Oh." Natalia giggled. "Is it safe to leave the car here like that?"

"Yeah, he's my human car alarm," Shawn replied.

"You trust him?"

"Every time," he put her arm in his.

He led her directly to the door, bypassing the crowd. No one attempted to stop them. In fact, everyone greeted Shawn like he was the President. He didn't even pay the entrance fee.

They stepped down into a huge ballroom. Glitzy chandeliers hung from the high ceiling. Enormous speakers were bolted on the wall in every corner of the room and trembled with each bass line of the music blasting from them. Shawn guided her to stairs that were roped off with a thick burgundy velvet rope. A small gold plaque on the rope announced that they were entering the VIP section. A lovely honey brown woman greeted them with a smile and moved the rope so they could pass.

"Thanks, Kelly," Shawn smiled.

He led Natalia to a round table elegantly set with gold candles in the middle of the room. A plaque with his name was positioned in the center of the table. Natalia batted her eyelashes and asked, "Are you trying to impress me?"

Shawn smiled and asked, "Is it working?" He smiled with pride as he pulled out her chair.

A waitress in a tight metallic gold dress approached the table.

"Hi, I'm Tranay. If and when you need anything just let me know."

"Could you bring a bottle of Cristal right now? And please tell Michelle that Shawn is here."

"You got it," Tranay winked.

Natalia unexpectedly felt jealous. She folded her arms and crossed her legs. "So who's Michelle?"

"Why? You jealous?" Shawn grinned.

Natalia rolled her eyes and looked away.

"Don't worry, I'm here with you. Trust me, I got what I need." He reached over the table and caressed her hand. She pulled away.

"Don't start that shit. No games," he said sternly.

"What?"

"Why you pull away from me?"

"No reason..." she sighed then said, "So, you come here often?"

"Not really, once in a while."

"I see."

"You like it so far?"

"It's okay."

"Okay?"

"Yes, it's okay." She fluttered her eyelashes and looked away from his piercing stare.

Shawn shook his head and smiled. A short, dark skinned girl approached their table. Behind her back, she held something. "So you must be the infamous Natalia. Hi, I'm Michelle."

Natalia smiled a phony smile and Michelle understood immediately. "Don't worry, girlfriend. Shawn is my cousin. We family," Michelle smiled then and continued, "I have something special for you."

Natalia lit up. "Something for me? Really?"

"Surprise," Michelle pulled her hands from behind her back. She handed Natalia a small slender jeweled box and a long golden box.

"Th-thank you," Natalia stuttered while laying the boxes on the table.

"Come on open them up! I wanna see too," Michelle giggled.

"Yeah, open them," Shawn grinned.

Natalia glanced at him from the corner of her eye and opened the pretty jeweled box first. Inside was a uniquely designed diamond bracelet set in white gold.

"Oh, Shawn. It's lovely." She reached for his hand. "Thank you."

"Now, open the other one," he motioned.

She reached over and picked up the long gold box. From the length of it, she assumed it held roses, and she was right. Shawn had given her one dozen red roses and one white rose. She looked into his eyes appreciatively, "You are so sweet, Shawn."

Michelle leaned over and hugged her. "Girl, I don't know what you did to him. But you got him open." She laughed then patted Shawn on the back before walking away.

Shawn was extremely pleased with himself. He leaned back in his chair and watched Natalia. She smiled a bit self-consciously then asked, "Shawn, do you see other women?"

"Not anymore," he replied, sitting up straight and resting his elbows on the table.

"Oh." Natalia looked down at her bracelet and said, "Put it on my wrist, please."

Shawn got up and held her wrist gently. He secured the latch and then stopped to admire it. Spectrums of light danced and sparkled through each diamond.

"It's almost as beautiful as you," his voice was filled with adoration.

She stared up at him lovingly. He kissed her slowly and sensuously on the lips, but Natalia nervously pulled away. His slightest touch made her hot.

"Where is the ladies room?"

"I'll take you," Shawn said extending his hand. He waited for her to rise from the chair. She got up slowly and said in a child's voice, "I can go potty all by myself, daddy."

Shawn couldn't help but laugh. "I was just gon' show you where it is because you've never been here before."

"Just point me in the right direction, and I'll find it."

"Go down the steps the way we came in. It's near the coat check room."

"See? So simple." Natalia smiled and said, "I'll be right back."

"Don't overflow the toilets, aiight?" Shawn laughed.

"Oh, be quiet," she giggled and paraded toward the stairs, switching her ass hard on the way. Shawn watched until she disappeared. "Mmn," he sighed as leaned back in his chair and exhaled.

The club was packed and men grabbed at Natalia as she tried to squeeze past them. It took her a long time to reach the bathroom.

When she finally did get there, the bathroom was filled with hoochies. Most of them wore tacky weaves and too much makeup. Skin was everywhere. Natalia patiently waited on the long line for an available stall. The girl in front of her was wearing a micro mini dress. Her butt hung out from under the flimsy material. Natalia cringed at the sight of the lumpy, dimpled mounds. Three girls were whispering at the sink. One turned around to look at Natalia, snickered briefly, then turned back to her friends. All the girls turned and stared. At first, Natalia thought that maybe she had a rip in her dress or a strap was loose or something was out of place. So she checked herself in the mirror, found nothing wrong and ignored them.

A stall finally became free, and she hurried inside. Just as she finished wiping herself and began to pull up her panties, someone banged on the door.

"It's occupied," Natalia said in a melodic tone.

"What?" a raspy voice asked.

Natalia fixed her dress and opened the door. There stood a light skinned, curvaceous girl with big curls in her hair. She stood with her hands folded, chewing gum like a cow chews grass. Animated and with too much attitude, she asked "Who you here wit?"

"I'm sorry?" Natalia asked confused.

"I said, who you here wit?" she asked again, cracking her gum.

"Excuse me?"

"Don't play wit me, aiight. Who you here wit? 'Cause it looked like you was wit my man." The girl rolled her eyes and waved her hands around with each word.

"Your man? I don't know what you're talking about."

"You came wit Shawn?"

"Yes. And?" Natalia became agitated.

"And? Bitch, that's my man. Ya better leave before I fuck you up." She waved her finger around scoffing and occasionally glancing over her shoulder at her back up.

"What? I don't have time for this." Natalia dismissed her with a wave of her hand and turned to walk away. "Don't walk away from me bitch! You better leave my man alone, ya heard?" Natalia spun around and spat, "If Shawn is your man then why is he here with me?" Natalia was angry now. The fact that she was outnumbered didn't scare her. She knew tae kwon do and had recently taken boxing aerobics and self-defense classes. Natalia knew how to snap a neck. In fact, she had always wondered what it would be like to take a life with her bare hands. Maybe now she would find out.

The girl hadn't expected Natalia to be so courageous. She

assumed she would run. So sucking her teeth, she spat, "Bitch, I will fuck you up." She moved in closer to Natalia and put her hand in Natalia's face. "Kick that bitch's ass, Tina," one of the friends instigated. Natalia didn't waste any time. She took a step away from Tina and leaned backwards on one foot, readying to kick Tina in the face. Tina lunged, her outstretched hands loosely clenched into fists and ended up getting a face full of scuffed, hard leather sole of Natalia's Manolo Blahniks. Tina's friends were about to pounce when a tall, chunky woman with a circular pattern of cornrows in her hair and an orange and blue parka that read Security in bold blue letters pushed her way through the cheering crowd.

"Ain't no fightin' in here. Take that shit outside." The security guard stepped in front of Natalia and looked down at the woman on the floor holding her red cheek.

Tina struggled to get to her feet. "I'ma kill you bitch," she shouted, flailing her arms. Natalia bounced up and down like a boxer jabbing at Tina's face. The woman pushed them apart with her chunky elbows. "I said take that shit outside."

Tina leaned behind the security guard, rolled her eyes at Natalia and spat, "It ain't over bitch, I'ma catch you outside. I'ma kill you bitch."

"Whatever," Natalia said as she snatched her arm from the security guard and stormed out of the bathroom.

What took you so long?" Shawn asked as he met her at the top of the steps.

If looks could kill, he would've been in a body bag on his way to the morgue. She didn't say a word.

"What's wrong?" Shawn tried to hold her hand.

"I just want to go home." Natalia pulled away from him and turned her back. Shawn spun her around and grabbed both of her arms, pulling her to him.

"What the hell is wrong wit you?"

"Your girlfriend just attacked me in the bathroom."

"My girlfriend? What girlfriend?"

"Does Tina ring a bell? She said she's going to kill me outside."

"That crazy bitch is here? Where the fuck she at?" He let her go and ran down toward the bathroom.

"Shawn! Wait!" She ran after him as he pushed past the security guard and into the bathroom.

"What happened, P.B.?" the security guard asked.

"Tina!" Shawn shouted as he scanned the bathroom. Girls watched him, wondering who was this lucky Tina. "Anybody see a light skinned, nasty lookin' hoe named Tina?" he asked, knowing that upon hearing him, Tina would surely come out of her hiding place. But she didn't because she wasn't there. A short girl with blue contact lenses and a busy, poofed hairdo said, "No, but I'll be Tina or whoever you want me to be!" The women admiring their reflections in the mirror giggled. Shawn looked her up and down, shook his head in disgust and walked out. He pulled the security guard to the side. Natalia was already waiting by the coat check-room.

"Come here, Nay-nay," Shawn motioned.

"What?" she shouted.

"Come over here," he said motioning her to come closer. "Tell Casey what Tina was wearin'."

"I don't know. I didn't have time to critique her clothing. I was too busy defending myself," she said sarcastically.

The chunky woman tried to get a closer look at Natalia's face.

"I know what she looks like. I just stopped them two from fighting. She high yellow with a big ass right?"

"Yeah." Shawn glanced at Natalia before turning back to the woman.

"Aiight, P.B. Don't worry. I'll take care of her for ya."

"Good lookin', Casey," Shawn said and tugged gently on Natalia's arm. "You really wanna go?"

Natalia sighed and looked away. She wasn't just mad, she was jealous too. She folded her arms and shifted all her weight to her right hip.

"Aiight, let's go then." Shawn started to walk off but Natalia yanked his arm, and he abruptly stopped.

"Shawn, why did you bring me here? To make her jealous?"

He sighed and pulled her into a corner. He gently pushed her up against the wall and held her chin up with his forefinger.

"Baby girl, you know how I feel about you. I've broken every rule in the player's handbook just for you. Yeah, I used to fuck Tina. But that was it. Straight fuckin'! I don't give a shit about her. I don't even know why I kept fucking her cuz she's wack. Before you, yeah I fucked a lot of girls. But now all I need is my woman. That's you. Look at me. You got me acting like a punk. If I didn't want you so bad do you think I would be dealing wit you havin' the next man. I'm not gon' allow that to go on, but I'll accept it for now cuz I'm really feeling you." He caressed her cheek and continued, "Nay-nay, don't ever doubt me." He pulled her face closer to his. "I'ma marry you someday." He grinned then kissed her nose. Natalia rested her head on his chest, relinquishing all her doubts and jealousy and yielding to his dominance.

"So, you ready to go?"

"Not before I get to dance with you," she said, looking up at him.

"Come on." He took her hand and made his way over to the DJ booth. He whispered something to the DJ and seconds later the song 'All My Life' by K-Ci and Jo-Jo surrounded them. Shawn pulled Natalia to him and wrapped his arms around her waist. They rocked together in sync. He spun her around and hugged her from behind. Resting his chin on her shoulder, he whispered in her ear, "All my life I waited for someone like you and that's my word."

As they left the club, it was pouring rain, and the air was hazy and humid. As they waited under the awning over the club's entrance, Natalia cuddled up to Shawn. He looked down at her, "You wanna run for the car?" She shrugged, "Oh, I don't care."

"I'm sayin', I know how you women are about your hair," he chuckled. Natalia giggled and said, "It's okay if I get wet. I'm not a Gremlin."

Shawn smiled, pausing for a moment before saying, "Nay-Nay, do you get sea sick?"

"Not that I know of," she smiled.

"Good. Let's go." He pulled her by the hand into the downpour. The man with the gold teeth jumped out of the backseat of the car and gave Shawn a pound. Shawn held the car door open for her and after Natalia got in, she reached over to push the handle on the driver's side and opened the door for him. Shawn was smiling when he plopped down next to her.

"What's so amusing?" she asked.

"You ever see that movie, 'A Bronx Tale'?" Natalia shook her head. "Well, in the movie if a girl didn't open the car door for you after you let her in, it meant that she was selfish."

"Yeah, and?"

"And you got a fresh mouth. You better watch your tone," he pushed back the wet strands of hair sticking to her face.

"Yes, daddy," she said as she leaned back in the seat. *What was happening here?* Slowly but surely, Shawn was easing his way into her heart, and Natalia knew that sooner or later she'd have to make a choice.

Shawn drove cautiously to Pier 72 in Manhattan and parked the car near the boarding ramp. They walked hand in hand onto a huge yacht. Shawn knocked on the manager's door and a round-faced, pudgy man opened it. "Ay, paisano. How ya been?" the man asked with outstretched arms.

"I'm hangin' in there, ya know?" Shawn replied. They briefly embraced and patted each other's back.

"So, who's your gorgeous friend?" the man smiled.

"Tony, meet my future wife." Shawn put his arm around Natalia.

"Hi, pretty lady. He taking good care o' ya?" Tony asked, grinning.

Natalia shyly replied, "So far."

Shawn squeezed her shoulder. "So Tony, my man, can I get a hook up?"

"You're lucky I like you. How long ya talkin'?"

"A couple of hours."

"You got it, pal." Tony patted Shawn on the shoulder and went back into his office. Shawn took Natalia's hand and led her to the deck facing the city's skyline. A smooth voice came over the loud-speaker. "You're in for the time of your life."

Classical music played as the boat started to rumble out of the dock. Natalia leaned over the railing and watched the ripples in the water. "How is it that you have so much influence? I mean, it's seems like everyone loves you."

"Cuz, I'm the man, Nay-nay," he grinned and grabbed her from behind. Their clothes were soaked through from the heavy rain. Shawn rubbed his hands over her breasts and slowly made his way down her stomach to between her thighs. He massaged her and stimulated her center then removed his hat and jacket and lay them on the floor. "You ever made love in the rain?" he asked seductively, water dripping from his lips.

"Never," she whispered. He plucked the hairpins from her hair, dropped them to the floor and smoothed his fingers over her forehead, pushing the wet locks from her face. He then pulled her dress up very slowly, exposing her thighs to the rain, and gently squeezed her bare buttocks. "Yeah, you got sexy for me. I like that. You're a good girl." His voice was deep and sexy. "You want me?" he asked as he spun her around and looked intently into her eyes.

"Yesss," she hissed.

"Say it. Say I want you Shawn." He teased her covered nipples with his fingers.

"I want you Shawn."

He unbuttoned his shirt, yanked it off and threw it on top of his jacket. Then he pulled her dress up over her head and threw it into the puddle of soaked clothing. She watched in awe as he unbuttoned his pants. When he unzipped them, he ordered, "Get on your knees and take my pants off."

She knelt in front of him and slowly slid them down to his feet.

He stepped out of his shoes and let his pants fall to the floor. The rain soaked his black silk boxers so they clung to his buttocks and long, hard penis. Natalia's eyes were glued to the huge bulge.

"Take them off," he ordered.

Natalia pulled his boxers down slowly. She had to stretch the elastic wide for the fabric to pass over his enormous erection. She gazed in amazement at his jewels and glory as if they were alien beings.

When he was completely naked, he pulled her to her feet. Natalia stepped back to look at him. Shawn was beautiful and hard with broad shoulders and well-developed biceps. His muscles rippled like waves in the ocean across his torso. And his legs weren't skinny like Mark's. They were long and carved like those of a statue. He had many tattoos on his chest and arms. And his cock was at least nine inches long with a head as big as one of the roses he had given her and as thick as her wrist.

Natalia could hardly contain herself. She started to remove her bra, but Shawn stopped her. "Leave it on," he said and scooped her up in his arms and lay her on top of the pile of clothes. The rain pelted his back as he lowered himself on top of her. "What do you want?" he asked, placing juicy kisses on her lips.

"Wha-what?" she whispered incoherently.

"Tell me what you want."

"I-I want you."

"And what do you want me to do?" he asked as he stared deeply into her eyes, digging into her soul.

"Make love to me," she said passionately.

"No, you don't want that," he whispered.

"Yes I do," she replied, confused.

"Tell me what you really want me to do."

Nearly breathless, Natalia whispered, "Fuck me."

"That's my girl." Shawn pushed her thong to the side and oh so painfully slowly slid his cock into her just a little and pulled back. He slid into her again just a little bit more and pulled out again. Natalia was writhing on the floor in exquisite agony.

"Please, Shawn, fuck me," she begged.

He pretended not to hear her as he slid in just a bit deeper.

"Shawn, fuck me," Natalia pleaded.

"I can't hear you," he said as he thrust into her just a little bit deeper again.

By now, Natalia was frantic with passion. Raindrops splashed cold in her face, and his warm, slick body slid heavily across hers.

"What is it you want me to do to you?" his throaty whisper filled her ear.

"Fuck me!!" she screamed. And with that, he pulled her feet to his shoulders and rammed the length of his enormous cock into her.

Fireworks exploded in her head as he pounded into her over and over. Natalia was flying on the wind of pleasure. Rain pelted her, but she hardly felt it. She contracted her vaginal muscles, massaging his cock, adding to his pleasure. Slowly, he stood up while keeping her feet on his shoulders and held her upside down. She placed her hands on the wet deck for leverage as he pumped his full length into her over and over again. Her breasts bounced up and down and fell out of her bra. He held her like that and fucked her until he released his heavy load into her, moaning loader than the yacht's engines. The force of his orgasm buckled his knees, and he fell weakened to the deck.

He laid her down on the clothes and licked and kissed his way down between her legs. She drenched his face with warm nectar as he brought her to an explosive orgasm. Five minutes later they were at it again.

Their insatiable appetite for each other left them both still hungry and drained at the same time. But their "couple of hours" had run out — the yacht was headed back to the dock.

They were huddled in the bathroom, kissing like newlyweds, when Tony knocked on the door. "Shawn?" he shouted.

"I'll be right there," Shawn said as he grabbed his drenched pants. He fought his way into them and opened the door.

"You done pal? Cause I gotta go," Tony whispered.

"Yeah. Uh, Tony, I need another favor."

"What now?"

"Can you get us some dry clothes...something, anything."

The pudgy man laughed loudly. "You kids are something else." He scratched his head and smiled, "All we got are uniforms."

"That's cool," Shawn winked and gave him a thumbs up. "My man. Good lookin' out."

Shawn put the key in the ignition and popped the trunk. Natalia got in the car and tried to blot her face dry with a piece of paper towel. Shawn threw the plastic bag of wet clothes into the trunk. Natalia locked all the car doors with the automatic lock button and refused to unlock them so he was left out in the rain, tapping on the glass.

"Say please," she mouthed through the spotty window. Shawn pressed his lips against the window and mouthed the word please. She giggled and unlocked the door.

He jumped in, put her in a headlock and started tickling her until she threatened to pee all over his tan leather seats. He burst out laughing.

"You look so cute." He pinched her cheek.

"And you look adorable, Chef Boyardee."

"Look at you, Julia Childs." He grabbed at the chef's jacket she was wearing.

"At least mine is clean. And what do you know about Julia Childs?" she smirked and tugged on the yellow stained collar of his chef's jacket.

"Damn, you must think I'm real ignorant, huh?"

"It's not that. It's just that I can't picture you watching the cooking channel," she laughed.

"Yeah, yeah. Let's get outta here, before someone sees me."

She stared at him while he drove, completely smitten yet confused. Why had they met the way they met? It bothered her that he never mentioned and never explained. He felt her stare and took one hand off the wheel and rested it on her lap. She looked down at his hand. "Shawn, why did you kidnap me?"

Shawn sighed. He switched into the right lane, and as soon as it was clear, he pulled the car over on a side street.

"Do we have to do this? Can't we forget that?" He looked out the window, avoiding her eyes.

"I need to know. I keep wondering why you did what you did?"

"I didn't mean to do it. In fact I...let's just forget it."

"I'm entitled to know, Shawn," she frowned.

"Just forget it," he yelled, annoyed at her persistence.

She was quiet for the remainder of the trip.

Shawn pulled into his driveway and put the car in park. He turned to Natalia and rubbed her thigh. "Don't be mad at me. I need you to know that I will never hurt you. You mean a lot to me. You just don't know, baby girl. Trust me...you just don't know."

"Are you a crazed psychopath?" she asked sarcastically.

"If I was, would I admit to it? Silly girl," he chuckled.

"I got your silly girl..." She hit his arm repeatedly. He just laughed it off and got out the car. He opened the door, grabbed her and threw her over his shoulder and began spanking her exposed bottom.

"Stop it!" she laughed.

Two weeks passed and Natalia saw Shawn every day. She completely neglected Mark. Every time he called, she was out. When he called her cell phone, she'd give him excuses as to why he couldn't see her. He became suspicious one Saturday night and invited himself over. He pulled up in her driveway and didn't see anything out of the ordinary.

But that night, Nut had driven Shawn to Natalia's house and left with the car. So there wasn't a strange car in the driveway to help Mark's investigation. Mark saw lights in the windows and knew that she was home.

Natalia and Shawn were playing hide and seek — naked. Natalia was it. Shawn hid in one of the guest bathrooms. Natalia was searching the television room when she heard Mark calling to her. Her heart nearly stopped. She ran into her bedroom, grabbed a silk robe and quickly put it on. "Mark?" she tried to act casual.

"So you are here. Why didn't you answer your phone?" He hugged her tightly.

"Oh, I was probably in the shower," she smiled trying to mask her guilt.

"Jeez, I finally get to see you. What a privilege!" he said sarcastically. He looked her up and down and glanced around the room.

"Mark, what are you doing here? I told you I didn't like it when you popped in unannounced."

"I'm going to be your husband soon, so what's the big deal?"

"I just want my space. Don't you understand that?"

"What I don't understand, Nat, is why you're avoiding me. I'm starting to think something is going on."

"Oh Markie...I just haven't been feeling well lately. I just wanted to be alone," she lied. She sat on the bed and crossed her legs, shaking them nervously.

"I've missed you." He knelt in front of her and laid his head on her lap like a puppy in need of comfort. It made her feel even guiltier. She ran her fingers through his curls. "I missed you too. I just wanted to be alone tonight. I've got a lot on my mind. It's just that..." she noticed a shadow in the hallway. She gulped and put her hands over Mark's face.

"It's just what, sweetie?" Mark tried to maneuver his face so that he could see past her hands. Natalia lovingly caressed his face, stroking his cheeks with her fingers. All the while she kept her eyes glued to the hallway. The silhouette of a masculine frame appeared in the doorway. Mark lifted his head to look at her. She nervously trickled her fingers over his forehead blocking his left peripheral view with her hand. He stared into her face and asked, "What's the matter?"

She looked at the hallway again. It was empty.

"N-nothing, I just..."

"What is it? A fever? A tummy ache?" he rubbed his hands over hers.

Shawn reappeared in the hallway. This time he gestured for her to come then disappeared. She nodded and turned her attention back to Mark. "Markie, I just want to be alone. I promise you I'll see you tomorrow. But right now I need to be alone. I'm just not in the mood for company."

Mark got up and said, "I love you. No one else can love you like I do. I hope you know that." His eyes saddened. She couldn't look him in the face so she stared down at his shoes. He turned to walk out and from the corner of his eye he noticed an empty condom packet on the floor near the foot of the bed. He turned back to her and calmly asked, "Where is he?"

She jumped to her feet and tried to hold him. He pulled away with so much force that she fell to the floor. He grabbed her by the shoulders and forced her onto her feet. "Where is he?" he spat through gritted teeth. She could see anger and pain in his eyes. She was at a loss for words. Her guilt escaped through her tear ducts, and she cried and cried. Mark held her face in his hands and wiped away the tears with his thumb. "Talk to me."

"I-I can't deal with this right now. Please go, Mark. Please...just go." She tried to push him towards the door.

"Why, Nat? Why?" his voice trembled with anger.

"I can't do this now. Go," she pleaded. She was worried that Shawn would come into the room. "Is this it? So you've been fucking somebody else, and you want me to leave. I'm the one you should be worried about. You're just going to throw everything we've built away? I don't understand you. What the hell is wrong with you?" Natalia looked away.

"She asked you to leave didn't she?" Shawn stood in the doorway fully dressed. Mark charged at him. Shawn jumped out of the way and grabbed Mark, putting him in a headlock.

"Stop it!" Natalia shrieked. Shawn loosened his grip. Mark wriggled out from Shawn's hold then swung at him. Shawn effortlessly moved out of the way. He laughed at Mark and said, "Man, she don't want us to fight, so just go."

Mark turned to Natalia. His face was flushed and his shirt rumpled. *How could I have done this to him?* she thought.

"So I guess he wins," Mark huffed.

"It's not like that. I-I'm sorry..." she sobbed and moved closer to him. He turned away from her and bolted from the room. *What have I done?* she thought and ran after him. "Mark wait! Please...waaaiiit," she shouted. He stopped and slowly turned.

"Why did you waste my time if you didn't love me? Why?"

She didn't have an answer. He shook his head and stormed out the front door.

"You love him?" Shawn asked, standing behind her.

"I think I do...Y-yes," she sobbed.

"I know you need to think. So I'ma leave." He kissed the top of her head, then her lips.

She was too confused to protest so she watched him leave, too.

Chapter Six

❤

BREAK UP TO MAKE UP

Mark drove like a madman back to Manhattan. His pride, his heart and his head were all hurting. In his mind, he kept envisioning Shawn on top of Natalia. The angrier he got, the more the car crazily swerved. He drove directly to an exclusive cocktail lounge he brought clients to and took a seat at the bar.

He was agitatedly running his fingers through his hair when the bartender approached and asked, "What'll it be?"

Mark wasn't a hard drinker, but, tonight, he wanted to forget everything. "Hennessy straight," he replied as he rubbed his temples. The bartender put a short crystal glass in front of him, and Mark slid three twenty-dollar bills on the counter. "Keep them coming until you run out."

The first sip felt like fire in his throat, but he emptied the glass anyway. He wiped his mouth with the back of his hand and tapped his fingers to the beat of the music. He downed two more glasses of Hennessy and started to unwind. "Give me a rum and Coke. I need a change," he said to the bartender and within seconds, it appeared. Mark rubbed his hands across his face and when he opened his eyes, a slim blonde with silicone breasts bumped into him as she slid onto the empty stool next to him. "Oops! So sorry. I think I'm a little bit drunk," she giggled.

"It's, okay. I'm a lot a bit drunk," he said and returned his attention back to his glass.

"You're new here, aren't you?"

"No," he said as he sipped his rum and coke.

"I usually come here after work, every Saturday. I would have remembered seeing you," she said as she crossed her legs, exposing some thigh.

"Well, I have been here before." Mark ignored her legs and finished his drink.

"Have you ever seen me?" she leaned closer.

"No."

"Dance with me." She held out her hand.

"I don't feel like dancing," he grunted as he gazed at her perfect, manufactured cleavage.

"Oh. Well then, what do you feel like doing?" She slid off the stool and pressed up against him.

"I feel like going home," he said with his eyes still glued to her chest.

"With me, I hope." She put her hand on his lap.

"Sure. Why not?" he replied matter-of-factly.

"Well, I'm not ready to go just yet."

"I'll be right here when you are." His glass was empty. "Hey, bartender," he drooled, "'nother one of these."

Mark didn't bother with the lights and led the blonde directly to his bed. She clung drunkenly to him, her fingers trickling erratically up and down his arm. She smiled at him, backed away and undressed.

"I see you're either a real blonde, or you're not afraid of chemicals," he chuckled.

"Take your pick," she said as she spread her legs wide.

Mark reached into his night table drawer for condoms and then realized that Natalia had thrown them away after their second negative HIV screenings.

"Shit," he swore. "Do you have any condoms?"

"In my purse." The blonde almost rolled off the bed reaching for her purse. She gave it to Mark. "In my make-up bag," she said. Mark found the rumpled packet and ripped it open with his teeth.

"Come here," she said as seductively as she could manage, and he stumbled over to the bed. She pulled his zipper down and pulled out his penis. She opened her mouth and latched on. "Mmm," she muttered between slurps.

Mark had felt Natalia's mouth on his cock only a few times. Either her teeth got in the way or she gagged. But ultimately, she didn't perform oral sex on him. So this moment with the blonde was definitely a treat. He enjoyed it so much that he came almost immediately. But sensing his excitement, the blonde took the condom from his hand, placed it in her mouth and slid it on him. She then reclined on the bed and spread her legs. Mark flopped onto her and into her. With the liquor as fuel, he went wild on her for twenty minutes and then collapsed. She rubbed her hands up and down his back.

"By the way, I'm Karen," she said.

Mark raised up on an elbow and said, "Nice to meet you." He let out a breathy sigh, rolled off of her and fell into the softness of the bed.

The phone rang at least 5 times before Natalia heard it. She had cried herself to sleep. As she scrambled for the phone, she glanced at the alarm clock on the nightstand. 5:42 am.

"Hello?" she whispered.

"Good morning, baby girl." Natalia recognized Shawn's deep voice right away.

"Mornin'," she replied weakly.

"Are you okay?"

"Uh-huh. What are you doing up?"

"I couldn't sleep. I can't stop thinking about you. So what the deal wit that white boy?"

"Shawn, I've known him for years. We're engaged," she sighed into the phone. "I've only known you a month, Shawn. It's a difficult situation for me."

"I'm not trying to force you into anything, Nay-nay. But I can't let you go." There was a brief silence before he asked, "Do you still want me?"

Without hesitation, she answered, "Yes."

Shawn's worries diminished. He was still in the game.

"But I can't end it with him just like that, Shawn. I don't even know if I want to. I-I don't expect you to wait for me. And really, what do we have? All we have is sex. We don't really know each other." Natalia put her hand to her forehead and fell back onto the pillows.

Shawn was quiet. He knew that he was in love with her, but he couldn't tell her. "That's not all we have. Don't I make you happy?"

"Yes...sexually, you do," she smiled.

"So, what you sayin?"

"I'm saying that I want you to understand why I can't just say to hell with Mark and be with you. There are other things to consider. I hardly know you. I don't know what you do for a living or where you're from. I really don't know anything about you."

"You will know...in due time," he replied matter-of-factly.

"Why can't you tell me something, anything, now?"

"When can I see you?" he asked, avoiding her question.

"I've got things to do today. Besides, I need time to...think."

"Think about this. I don't take good-byes very well." His deep tone both turned her on and frightened her.

"Was that a threat, Shawn?"

"Like I said before, I can't let you go."

Natalia didn't believe it could be possible, but she loved both men. Shawn's dominance provided her with the excitement she lacked. And Mark's loyalty and passivity provided her with the security she needed. She didn't want to lose either of them.

"Shawn, we shouldn't see each other for a while."

"I'll try to stay away," he chuckled then asked, "Can you?"

She giggled and replied, "I don't know, Shawn, I might need a fix. Yaknowwhuti'msayin?"

"Listen to you. You mad funny, Buffy."

"Whatever!" she said, emphasizing each syllable.

"Okay, get your beauty sleep. I won't call you...unless you want me to."

"Let's see how things go without seeing or talking to one another."

"It's gon' be tough. But for you, I'll do it. Get at me when you ready, baby girl."

"Bye, Sha," she sang as she hung up.

The truth was that Natalia wanted them both. She realized that Shawn wouldn't leave her and that Mark probably hated her. And she felt that Mark had every right to. Still, she had to talk to him.

Swallowing hard and not knowing what she would say, she dialed his number. Mark's voice was barely recognizable when he finally answered. "Mark?" she asked, unsure.

"Natalia?"

"P-please don't hang up on me."

"I wasn't going to," he assured her.

"I am so sorry for..."

"Wait. Do you still love me?" Mark interjected.

"Yes," she said weakly.

"Then why, Nat? Why did you betray me?"

"It's a long story, Mark. And I'm quite sure that none of it would make sense to you. I guess I was confused. Markie, I don't want to lose you."

Mark had forgotten about the blonde sleeping next to him. She stirred, reached over and ran her fingers through his hair. Then she nuzzled his neck and made humming noises as she kissed it. He pulled away and covered the receiver with his hand. "Shhh," he whispered.

"Why?" she asked, puzzled.

"Just be quiet...please."

She frowned and asked, "Are you married?"

He bluntly answered, "Not yet," and put the phone back to his ear. He heard Natalia repeating, "Hello? Hello?"

"Sorry, I dropped the phone," Mark lied.

"Mark, do you still love me?" she asked nervously, afraid of his answer.

"Of course I do. I love you too much," he answered sweetly.

The blonde cocked her head in disbelief. "I'm leaving!" she snapped then hopped out of bed. She snatched her cheap dress off the dresser and quickly put it on. Mark put his finger to his lips and searched the floor for the television remote.

"Mark, is somebody there with you?" Natalia quizzed.

He couldn't find the remote. "No, no. I turned on the TV by accident."

"By accident?" she asked suspiciously.

Mark didn't want to lie. And why should he? "Nat, hold on, please. Don't hang up." He put down the phone and jumped out of bed. Searching his pants pockets, he found his wallet and pulled out a twenty dollar bill. "Here, take a cab."

The blonde glared at him. "I hope she dumps you, you dog!" She snatched the money from his hand.

Mark snapped back, "Hey! I was drunk as hell. Besides, you seduced me! Look, I don't want any hard feelings here. Friends?" He held out his hand to shake hers.

She managed a slight smile. "Well if you don't get married, and you want to see me again, here's my card." She reached into her purse and pulled out a pink business card.

Natalia was fuming at the other end of the phone. She was able to hear voices and determined that one of them belonged to a woman. She didn't like it one bit.

Mark hurried back to the phone. "Nat?"

"What?" she answered coldly. Mark could tell she was upset so he took a breath and said, "Okay, let me explain. Last night I felt like my heart was ripped out of me. So I went to a bar..."

"You slept with someone, didn't you?" She felt as though her insides had been ripped out and the wind had been knocked out of her.

"Yes. I got drunk after seeing you with th-that boy...I thought it was over between us." They both fell silent.

Natalia exhaled. "I have no right to be angry. This is probably none of my business... but did you use a condom?" She tried to hold back tears.

"Of course. Did you?"

Natalia's thoughts flashed back to the night on the yacht. *Oh my God!* her brain screamed. She and Shawn did not use a condom that night. But before she could answer, Mark blurted, "Oh, you did. I remember seeing the wrapper. Well," he paused, "at least we both had enough sense to use them."

"Th-thank God for that," she stammered.

"What now?" Mark asked.

"I don't know. I guess we should talk in person. What do you think?"

"How about now?"

"Um...Okay."

"Okay then. I'll take a shower and be on my way."

"Okay," she said as her mind raced a mile a minute. *What if Shawn has AIDS or a sexually transmitted disease? What if...?*

Mark rang the bell. Natalia took a long time to open the door.

"Hi," she smiled nervously.

"Hi," Mark smiled back and walked past her into the living room.

"Do you want something to drink?"

"No, thanks," he said as he scanned her from head to toe. God, he loved her body. But the thought of her with another man dirtied the perfect picture he used to have of her.

Natalia grew restless and ended the silence. "So what happens now?"

Mark spoke in strained sentences. "I don't know. I still love you, Nat, but you lied to me. You had him here, Nat, in the same bed that I've made love to you in. I have keys to this house, but you didn't care. It didn't matter to you if I walked in. *I* didn't matter. That's scary. How can I ever trust you? We're supposed to be getting married!" He paused and patted the space next to him. "Sit down."

Natalia went to him with her head hung low. Mark was right. Everything he said was understandable. Salvaging their relationship would be difficult for him, and she knew he wouldn't marry her now. She sat next to him without looking in his direction. She was too ashamed. He turned to face her.

"Nat, I can't help loving you. But, I can't stop thinking of how you betrayed that love. How do I know you won't do it again?"

"Mark, I love you. And I can't really say what I'm going to do. I still want you to be a part of my life. But I'm confused right now."

"Do you really expect me to accept the fact that you are sleeping around?"

"Excuse me! I don't sleep around. You do! You're not innocent.

What was it? An hour before you found someone else to fuck?"
"Calm down. I didn't mean it like that. It's just...it's just that I am angry knowing that he was with you, that he was inside you. And now you're telling me that you're confused! Nat, do you love him?"
"Even if I do, it doesn't change the fact that I love you. What I did was a mistake."
"Nat, you just told me that you might do it again. So, how was it a mistake?"
"When did I say that?"
"You said you don't know what you'll do." Natalia became very still. Mark continued. "It seems to me that you want things both ways."
"No, I don't," she lied. "Oh, I don't know Mark. I've never had to deal with something like this before. You know how hard it was for me to let you in the door just now. I don't know how to handle this!" she moaned.
Mark put his arms around her. "I can't take it, knowing you'll be with another man. I can't."
"So that's it? It's over?" she sobbed.
"Do you think you could be with me and only me?"
"Y-yes." She didn't sound convincing.
"Nat, I don't know. I just don't know." He withdrew his arms from around her and watched her cry. She had buried her face in her hands and sobbed. Natalia realized that, in no uncertain terms, Mark was letting go.
Mark held in his pain. His anger kept him from consoling her and prevented him from shedding his own tears. He stood up and headed for the door. Without turning, he said, "I still love you, but I just...I won't share you." The door creaked as he slowly pulled it closed behind him.
Natalia was inconsolable. He was gone, really gone and she couldn't remain in her house a second longer. She dashed out to her jeep, and as soon as she reached the highway, she called André.
"Salondre," a cheerful voice answered.
"Lauren?" she asked.
"Yes?"
"Hi, it's Natalia. Is he there?"
"Hi, Natalia. Yes, he's in his office. Hold on and I'll transfer you."
André picked up a second later. "Hey, you. Why haven't I heard from you?"
"I'm, so...so messed up right now. Oh Andy, I fucked up."
"Oh, boy. What happened?"

"I'll tell you the details when I get there, but to make a long story short, Mark just dumped me."

Shawn sat quietly in his bedroom waiting for his 3pm appointment with Tymeek's lawyer who claimed that he had found a loophole that would overturn Tymeek's conviction. Tymeek was elated, but Shawn wasn't. He was worried about Tymeek's return home. Things would change drastically.

As he waited, Shawn thought about what Natalia had said about not knowing him. He knew she'd have nothing to do with him if she discovered the truth. He couldn't get her out of his system and he couldn't lose her. Being in love, as it turned out, was one big pain in the ass. He picked up the phone and called her, but the answering machine picked up. "Baby girl, I need to see you. Get in touch with me." He hung up and wondered aloud, "Is she playin' me like she did that white boy?"

Shawn left for Nut's house with a lot on his mind. Nut was standing on the steps waiting when Shawn pulled up.

He strolled over to the car and stuck his head in the window. "Whut up, dog?" he grinned.

"Get in," Shawn ordered.

"What's wrong now?" Nut sighed.

"Ty might be coming home soon," Shawn answered.

"Say word. That's good. So how they gon' get him out?"

"I don't know. But I gotta go see his lawyer at three today."

"You don't sound happy."

"You know how shit gon' be when he get home."

"You still gon' be paid. What you worried about?"

"Shit gon' be different when he find out about me and Nay-nay. He gon' go ballistic."

"True dat. You sleeping wit da enemy." Nut chuckled and continued, "But you ain't gotta tell him all that."

"But you know how them playa hatin' muthafuckas are. They broadcastin' my shit now."

"So just stop seeing the bitch."

Shawn's expression changed, although his voice remained calm, "Son, watch your mouth. She ain't a bitch. She gon' be my wife."

"Oh man. You still on that shit?" Nut looked at Shawn and saw it. He was in love.

Nut never imagined it could happen to his 'Pretty Boy' but it did. He blew hard, then lowered his voice. "You done fucked up, didn't you? You went and fell in love wit her?"

"Man, I been trying to fight it. But I get KO'd every time, dog." He laughed to himself. "I'm all fucked up in the head over her." He laid his head on the steering wheel.

Nut patted his back. "It happens to the best of us man. So, why don't you just tell Ty before he gets out? Try to explain it to him. He ain't gon' kill..." Nut leaned back in the seat as it dawned on him that Tymeek was feared for many reasons. Murdering someone who fucked up his money or got in his way was one of them. He knew killing Natalia in retribution was not a farfetched idea.

Shawn lifted his head and said, "You know how Ty do."

"I know. I was just thinking about that. Damn, that's fucked up." Nut shook his head and said, "I'm sayin', though, you're his brother. Just talk to him."

Shawn stared out the window. "So you think I should tell him before he get out?"

"Yeah. Just tell him you in love wit her. But yo, I hope she love you too."

"She do, man. I know she do, cuz I take care of my BI nahmean?" he grinned and Nut laughed. "I hope she's worth all this and it ain't just the pussy talkin' to your whipped ass."

"It ain't just that. She just got a way about her, nahmean? She got class. I'm tired of these low class bitches out here." They both laughed.

Nut gave him a pound. "I feel you."

The lawyer's office was damned cold. The AC was turned on full blast.

Shawn paced in front of the receptionist's desk. "Excuse me miss, how much longer do I have to wait?" he asked.

"I'm sure he'll be out soon." She looked up briefly then returned to her work.

Shawn pulled out his cell phone and called Natalia's house. No answer. Just then the door to the lawyer's office opened. An elderly couple and a young preppy kid came out. The lawyer followed and reached out his hand to Shawn. "You must be Shawn. I'm Joseph Kahn. How are you?"

"Fine." Shawn smiled a phony smile.

"Come in," Mr. Kahn said as he resumed his seat behind his steel desk. With an outstretched his hand, he motioned for Shawn to have a seat.

"I finally got a judge to order the DA's office to release tapes to me that weren't submitted in court during trial. And I've reviewed them. In all the transactions captured, Tymeek was simply there, a bystander. His hands never touched anything illegal. In fact, I believe he was convicted solely because of his association with Lou."

"So can you get him out?"

"I've started the proceedings, and it looks promising. In about a week, I should have some news for you."

"So, that's it?" Shawn asked, both surprised and annoyed.

"So far. Give me a call at the end of next week."

"I will, thanks." They shook hands.

"What a fuckin' waste of time. He could've told me that shit over the phone!" Shawn complained to Nut once back in the car.

Natalia spun around in André's leather chair.

"I can't believe you! I hope gettin' your freak on with that little boy was worth losing Mark." André reprimanded from the edge of his desk.

"Andy, really, I don't need to be scolded right now. I feel awful as it is."

"I'm not going to sugar coat anything. You went out, got some young dick and let it go to your head. Now you lost the one man who would die for you. I am furious with you right now."

"Andy, pleeeease."

"Nat, what were you thinking?"

"I don't know. I don't know!"

"And Mark's fuckin' some other woman already. Oh well, now she's got your man." He snapped his fingers in a zig zag motion in front of her face.

"Stop it," she whined.

"Hey, I just call em' like I see em'!"

"I'm glad to see you're happy...as usual." She spun around in his chair.

"Don't go breaking my chair, missy. You made your bed, now lay in it."

"Andy, if you met Shawn, you would see just how captivating he is. He is sooo incredibly hot. When we do it, I explode every time!"

"That's you're damn problem. All you're thinking about is the sex. You don't know anything about him."

"He makes me happy. That's all that matters."

"Get a grip, Snow White, and come out of the woods. When you bore him, he'll move on to the next. In fact he's probably out fucking some little tramp younger than you right now."

"Whatever," Natalia grumbled. She rifled through her bag looking for Shawn's cell phone number. When she found it, she dialed it and pressed the speaker phone button.

After the first ring, she whispered to André, "Listen to his voice."

André shook his head and whispered back, "Tsk, tsk. You're strung out." She ignored André's sarcasm and continued to nervously wait for Shawn to answer.

Shawn picked up on the third ring. "Speak."

"Hi, Sha," she cooed like a little girl.

"Hey baby girl. Where you at?"

"I'm in Manhattan. Where are you?"

"In Manhattan. Can I come get you?"

"I have my car."

"I'm glad you called me. I left a message on your answering machine. Did you get it?"

"No. I don't check my machine until I get home."

"You need a beeper. I wanna get you when I want you."

Natalia batted her eyelashes and grinned at André. André rolled his eyes, and shook his head.

"I have a cell phone. Do you want the number?"

"Yeah, hold on." Shawn pulled out his Palm II organizer. "Go ahead."

"Nine...one...seven,"

"I know that. What's the number, sexy?"

Natalia giggled and told him the number.

"I wanna see you."

"Uh, hold on." She pressed the hold button. "Andy, please keep the Navigator for me," she pleaded with a pitiful face.

"He acts like he's your daddy. And you are just feeding his ego."

"Come on, pleeease. I'll have him pick me up here so you can meet him, okay?"

"Yeah, you do that, because I've got to shake the hand of the one and only man that has princess Natalia strung out like a freakin' crackhead." She took Shawn off hold and said, "Where in Manhattan are you?"

"Just tell me where you are."

"I'm at Madison and 72nd at a beauty salon called Salondre. Got that?"

"Yeah. Blow me a kiss."

She pressed her lips against the mouthpiece on the receiver and blew him a loud kiss.

"That was sweet. You need a fix?"

"Nooo," she simpered.

"Yes you do." He paused. "I'm on my way." He hung up, with no goodbye as usual.

Natalia was so giddy she couldn't stop grinning.

"Girl, that boy got you in deep check. And what is he talking about, a fix? He got you on drugs or something?" Natalia burst out laughing.

"No, silly! He means sex."

"Oh, puhlease. Did he put some voodoo curse on you or something?"

"So, what do you think?"

"He has a sexy voice and all that, but he talks like a thug."

"Even if he is one, he's got the perfect balance. He's sweet and domineering."

"Does he work?"

"I don't know."

"I bet you don't even know his last name."

"I don't. But I'll find out when he gets here," she sneered.

Shawn arrived at the salon in no time at all. André was flabbergasted when he walked in. Shawn was a Gucci model from his tan nubuck shoes to his tortoise shell shades. The goldtone Gucci logos twinkled as if they were winking. And his baggy slacks had not one wrinkle. André knew designer clothes when he saw them, and Shawn's taste impressed him. A diamond stud and diamond pinkie ring glittered under the track lighting. Everyone in the shop gave him their undivided attention. Jean Paul positively drooled at the sight of Shawn.

Natalia smugly walked over to him. Shawn pulled her close and kissed her sensually, not giving a damn about their audience. André walked over to them as the kiss ended. "Hi," he beamed. Natalia smiled and tugged on his arm. "Shawn this is André, my best friend in the whole world."

"Nice to meet you," Shawn said as he firmly shook André's hand. He looked him up and down and instantly knew what kind of man André was. He turned his attention back to Natalia, looked at her dreamily, and said, "I missed you."

"Me too," she simpered.

"I'm hungry. Are you?"

"Yes."

"What do you want to eat?"

"How about Greek?"

"Hmmm, I never had Greek food before," he said with a far off look in his eyes.

"Well?"

"Yeah, okay. I'll try it. Let's go." He turned to André and all the staring faces. "Nice meeting y'all."

André waved goodbye then grabbed hold of Natalia's shirt as she started to walk off. When she turned around, André fanned himself and mouthed the word 'sizzling'.

She pulled him to her and whispered in his ear, "Told ya."

André grinned and whispered back, "Damn! You go gurl!" He hugged her and walked her to the door. Natalia was glad for his blessing. She took Shawn's hand, and they walked down the block to his car.

They ate at a trendy Greek restaurant then went to a comedy club. After the last comic did his bit, they left.

"So, what do you want to do now?" she asked him with a mischievous look in her eyes.

"Go home," he answered wearily.

"You look sleepy."

"I am," he yawned. "Oh, but don't worry, I'm not too sleepy to give you what you need."

"And what do you think I need?"

He grinned. "You know."

Shawn turned on the TV and lay next to Natalia on the bed. He rested his head on her stomach, and she stroked his head thinking about what André had said. *Did Shawn have a job? And worst of all, did he have any diseases. And his last name. What was his last name?* She blew hard and sat up straight, propping herself against the pillows.

"Shawn, I want to know more about you."

He knew this was coming and sat up next to her. "What do you want to know?" He prepared himself for her questions.

"Well...let's start with your last name." He gave her his mother's maiden name. He didn't want her to figure out the connection he had to Tymeek. "Reynolds," he replied.

"Okay. How old are you? Do you work and where?"

"Damn!" he exclaimed. "Do you work for the FBI?" he chuckled.

"No, I just have a lot of questions and I want — no, I deserve answers."

"Okay, okay. I'm twenty-two, and I, um, run the family business."

"Really? What is it?"

"Uh, it's a store...retail."

"Oh...okay. I have one last question. This one is a biggie." She watched as his eyebrow arched, and he leaned back against the pillows.

"Have you ever had or still have any venereal diseases? I mean like...HIV?" She seemed uneasy asking the question.

He looked her calmly in the eyes and answered, "I've had gonorrhea. That was when I was thirteen years old. I was treated for it. Ever since, I've been using condoms. A couple of times the condom broke, but I went straight to my doctor. I never took an AIDS test though."

"Oh, Shawn," she shook her head in disapproval. "I take one every six months. I think you should take the test. I'd like to go with you if that's okay with...wait a minute. Did I hear you right? Did you say you had gonorrhea at thirteen?"

"Yup," he answered without blinking.

"You were a busy little boy, weren't you? When did you study?" She giggled.

He just smiled at her and caressed her face. He dropped his hand on her leg and slunk further into the pillows. He was willing to do anything for her. "Yeah, that's cool," he said without looking at her.

"What is?" she asked.

"I'll take the test. And you can come with me."

They smiled at each other, but Natalia couldn't help but wonder, "How many times did the condom break again?"

He looked down at his hand on her leg. "Twice." He slowly turned toward her and saw that she was worried. He also knew there would be no nookie tonight. She moved down and lay her head on his chest, tracing his stomach muscles with her fingers. He twirled strands of her hair. Until now, he never thought about AIDS. He always believed it couldn't happen to him since he used condoms faithfully. He'd take the test to please her and to appease his own curiosity. Deep down, though, he truly believed that he had been careful enough. "We'll go tomorrow morning." He said matter-of-factly.

She raised her head to look into his face. "Go where?"

"To see the doctor," he continued twirling her hair around his finger.

"Okay," she said and sunk back onto his chest. She was relieved to not have to debate the matter with Shawn as she had to with Mark. In the race for her heart, Shawn was definitely in the lead.

When will we get the results?" Shawn asked, tapping his fingers on the armrest of his chair.

Natalia leaned across the armrest and wrapped her arm around his. "Three days," she whispered.

Just then, a tall, pale, platinum haired woman with a white lab coat stepped into the room. In her right hand, she held a clipboard and in her left, a pair of rubber gloves. She looked down at the clipboard and called out, "Foles?" She looked around the room. Natalia stood up and followed the woman into a lavender room.

Minutes later, she returned to the waiting area pressing a piece of cotton onto her arm. She sat next to him and smiled. "Dracula bit me," she joked. After a fifteen-minute wait, Shawn went to have his blood drawn. He, too, came out with his cotton pad in his hand. "Dracula bit me, too," he chuckled.

Shawn noticed right away that Natalia was worried. He took her hand in his and asked, "I bet you're thinking, what if he has it and gave it to me? Aren't you?"

"No, I'm not. I'm thinking positively." Her mouth curved into a smile.

"All I know is that the condom broke on me only 2 times. That was when I was like fifteen years old. I really didn't know what I was doing then. And the way I understand it, AIDS starts fucking you up in like five or ten years right?" he tried to justify himself.

"Something like that." She let go of his hand and moved closer to the elevator.

"What's the attitude about?" He looked down at her.

"Why are you asking me that?" she asked, annoyed.

"Never mind." He banged on the elevator button. "Where you want to go now?"

Her eyes lit up. "I know what we can do. Let's go to V-World."

"What the hell is that?"

"It's a virtual reality game room," she beamed.

"Computer games?"

"Yeah, but you're in the game. We'll wear these special suits that allow us to move in the game."

"How do you know all this?"

"I gave a lecture at an elementary school once. Because their attendance was the best in the entire borough, the principal and I rewarded them with a field trip. I went with them and it was great."

"You know how to get there from here?"

"Yeah. Do you want me to drive?"

"I...don't...know," he said, feigning fear.

She patted his pockets. "Just give me the keys."

He pulled them out and put them in her hand. "My life is in your hands," he whispered passionately into her ear.

POW! Take that!" Natalia squeezed the laser gun trigger hard.

"Arrrgggh!" Shawn shouted.

"I got you!" she squealed.

"Yeah, yeah. Let's bounce. I'm bored."

"Awww, you party pooper," she pouted as she wriggled out of the oversized suit.

"I'm gonna drop you off, okay?"

"Drop me off where?"

"My house. I've got to take care of some business right quick."

"Why can't I come see the store?"

"Because...it's not up to par, nahmean? But after we finish renovating it, I'll give you the VIP tour."

Natalia patiently waited for Shawn in his room. She laid across his smooth silk sheets and flipped through a hip-hop magazine she found on his dresser.

After a while, she became bored and decided to take a look around the house. She ventured into the attic where she found a twin bed, a couple of chairs and several boxes. The gray carpeting was surprisingly spotless.

Then she investigated the living room. She ran her hands over the soft gray leather couch and recalled the first time she saw Shawn's handsome face. The shiny black entertainment center beckoned her. Picture frames curiously lay face down on glass shelves. She picked one up. It was a slightly stained photo of a light skinned woman wearing a pair of dark sunglasses. Her arms rested on the shoulders of two young boys. She couldn't make out the other boy, but she recognized Shawn's bright smile and slanted eyes right away. She giggled at his plaid shirt and tight polyester pants. Although the other face seemed familiar, she kept her eyes on Shawn. She said aloud, "He must have driven the girls crazy in high school." She replaced the frame face down on the shelf again and was about to pick up another when she heard a noise at the front door. Keys. She quickly crept back upstairs into the bedroom, grabbed the magazine and pretended to read. She didn't want Shawn to think she had been nosing around.

Shawn entered the house quietly and slipped into the bedroom. He crept over to the bed. "Ah-ha!" he yelled, startling her.

"Oh, my goodness! You scared me!"

He sat next to her and rubbed her thigh. "You missed me?"

"Uh-huh." She smiled. He stared at her face. "You are so adorable, you know that?" He pinched her cheek.

"I know," she said smugly.

"Guess what?" he grinned.

"What?"

"I'm gonna take you somewhere special. Right after we get our results back."

"But what if…we get bad results?" Natalia asked with a long sigh.

"I thought you were thinking positive. I am," he said with a knowing smile. He looked so confident that it convinced her.

"You're right…so where are you taking me, Sugar Daddy?" she cooed.

"Jamaica, baby. Me gwan mek you sweat, gal," he answered in a sexy voice.

"Oh. How nice." *Did Shawn know somehow that her parents were from Jamaica? Of course not.* And he also couldn't know that she had been there many times in her life. She decided to enlighten him. "Shawn, this is why we should really take the time to get to know each another."

Shawn looked confused. "What are you talkin' about?"

She paused and exhaled as memories flooded her head. The words didn't flow smoothly as she began to explain.

"I'm Jamaican. My mother was half Polish and half Jamaican, and my father was Jamaican. I've been to Jamaica so many times, I can't even count."

"Shit, I've never seen no Jamaican girl that looked like you before," he laughed

"What's that supposed to mean?"

"I'm sayin' I know these Jamaican girls from around my old way. They all got fake hair with rainbow streaks, and they're real crusty black and all scarred up. They fuckin' look like monsters. On the real!" He laughed hard, then continued. "But I did have a feeling that you were mixed…I guess you can't always judge people by shit like that."

"Your mouth is such a gutter." She shook her head and spoke softly as she continued, "There are many different types of people in Jamaica just like here in America. Has the thought ever crossed your mind that you're probably mixed too? You have slanted eyes. Who's your father, Jackie Chan?" she giggled.

"Ha ha, very funny. No, he was a black man. He's also dead."

Natalia stopped giggling and her expression turned solemn. "I'm so sorry," she said in a voice close to a whisper. "My mother and father are dead, too," she struggled to keep the tears from falling.

"I didn't mean to bring up bad memories, baby girl. I'm sorry." He took her in his arms and gently rocked her.

"I'm fine. It's been a long time. I finished my grieving years ago." Natalia wanted to change the subject. "Um, can we go somewhere else?"

"Anywhere you want. Just tell me." He caressed her cheek. She closed her eyes and savored his touch. The warmth radiating from his palm soothed her. "Anywhere?" She asked with a mischievous grin. "Yeah...anywhere." Shawn answered with a curious look.

Natalia perked up again. "How about the Virgin Islands?"

"I heard about that place."

"Well, I own land on one of the islands. It's called St. Croix. I have a bed and breakfast right on the beach. Do you want to go there?"

"It sounds good, but Sugar Daddy wanted to take care of everything, nahmean? I wanted to be the big spender and splurge on you."

"You've already done that. You don't have to impress me anymore. It's time I take care of you," she said as she seductively rubbed up against him.

"Don't start nothing you can't finish," he grinned. She kissed his lips gently.

Their test results came back negative, and the three days they spent on St. Croix were incredibly hot and sexy. They made love on the beach as the sun set and under a waterfall as the sun rose. They did it on the roof of an abandoned bungalow in broad daylight with an audience of couples watching from hotel room terraces. Natalia and Shawn were carefree and relaxed...and in love.

When Shawn dropped her off at home, he squeezed her tightly in his arms. "I'll call you later, okay?" he said before kissing her lips goodbye.

Natalia unpacked and ran a bath. As she soaked in the tub, she thought of Mark. He had been on her mind a lot. Mark was a good man, and she had ruined him with her affair. Her guilt compelled to call him, "Just to see how he's doing," she tried to convince herself.

She dried off, put on a robe and padded down to the TV room. Leaning back in the couch, she sighed. "I'll just ask how he's doing and hang up," she thought. She picked up the cordless phone and called him.

"Yeah?" Mark answered glumly.

"Hi Mark," she said nervously.

Mark paused before responding. "Hello, Natalia."

"How have you been?" she asked, her rattled nerves beginning to calm down.

"I'm okay. How are you?"

"I'm fine."

"I know you are, but how are you, really?" he joked, hoping to break the ice.

"Mark, I miss you," she confessed.

"I miss you, too," he sighed with relief. He was happy to hear her voice. Even happier to know she was thinking about him.

"So, are you still the best stockbroker on Wall Street?" she probed.

"I certainly am. And are you still the best darn entrepreneur slash motivational speaker in the universe?" They giggled simultaneously.

"Yes, of course I am, thank you very much," she answered proudly.

He hadn't forgotten her. He wanted her. But his pride kept him from contacting her. Now, upon hearing her voice for the first time in what felt like an eternity, he couldn't hold back.

"I love you so much, Nat. I've been going crazy without you. I don't know how we can do this...b-but I've got to be with you again. I can't stop loving you. I tried, but I can't." He paused to gather his thoughts and continued, "We had so much going for us. I think about you all the time. I couldn't call, because I was so mad at you. I couldn't bring myself to talk to you. I kept seeing you and him together." He paused again. "But I knew that sooner or later, I would've caved in and called you. You do know that, don't you?"

"I guess...actually, I didn't think I'd ever hear from you. You were really angry." She exhaled and continued, "I'm so sorry that I hurt you. I know you deserve better. I know that. But I do still care about you, Mark. I want us to be close again. We were friends before we were lovers. Can we be that way again?"

Mark answered quickly, "Of course we can. Well friend, are you too busy to hangout with me?"

"No, friend, I am not."

Shawn drove to Riker's Island and suffered through a grueling search and wait before getting on a cramped van to yet another waiting area.

A corrections officer approached Shawn as he was signing his name in the visitor's log book. "Whut up Pretty Boy?"

Shawn looked up to see the burly officer grinning.

"Oh shit. Whut up niggah?"

"How you been man?" The corrections officer smiled, and they gave each other a pound and a brotherly hug.

"I've been good, man. You look like you doing real good too." Shawn chuckled.

"No doubt. Ty told me you were coming so I switched posts. You know I gotta look out for my peeps," he said under his breath so no one would hear him.

"True." Shawn nodded with approval. Mike led Shawn past the metal detectors and into another visiting room. An officer read names off of a list and visitors lined up in front of him. Mike whispered to the officer who nodded and shuffled through papers and called another name.

Mike told Shawn, "You all set. I had already pulled some strings so that Ty could be on standby, nahmean? So he'll be in the next bunch when you get over there, aiight?"

"Aiight," Shawn discreetly gave him another pound.

Once again, he rode in a packed van to another security checkpoint. He presented his paperwork and was ushered into what appeared to be a gymnasium. An unfamiliar officer approached and said, "You come with me." Shawn followed him over to a couple of bright red chairs that looked as if they belonged in a kindergarten class. Two doors near the bleachers opened. Shawn saw nothing but orange jumpers. The officer made a signal with his fingers then turned to Shawn, "Ty is coming out now. One."

Damn, Shawn thought. *Tymeek sure got a lot of niggaz in his pocket.*

A sea of orange moved through the doors. Tymeek spotted his brother first and walked over to him. They hugged each other. "Look at you, man. Damn, I feel like I been in here for decades."

"What up niggah? They treatin' you right?" Shawn asked.

"I'm aiight. What about you?"

"I'm holdin' it down. Just tryna hang in there until you come home. I spoke to your lawyer, and he said he didn't hear from the judge yet. Yo, does this guy know what he's doing?" Shawn asked.

"Don't worry. He's doin' what he gotta do. They just tryna drag this shit out a while longer before they hafta set a niggah free."

"When you come home, shit gon' be right," Shawn smacked his hands together.

"It better be," Tymeek chuckled. "So what's good?" He could see Shawn's pensiveness.

"I wanna tell you something...but I don't know how you gon' take it," Shawn spoke hesitantly.

"You can talk to me about anything. I love you bro, no matter what." He patted Shawn on the shoulder. It was true. Shawn, Aunt Freda and his mother were Tymeek's only weaknesses.

"Ty...this...this shit caught me off guard."

"What shit?" Tymeek asked, interested. Shawn exhaled then

whispered, "Aiight, I'ma come out and tell you. It's about that lady that helped get you locked up. You know the one that, um, testified at your trial."

"Yeah?" Tymeek looked confused now.

"I went to her house to...take care of that snitchin' situation. But when I saw her, she put me in a trance, son. You ain't warn a niggah about her looking so damn good. But, um, me and her...we together now. She's my girl." Tymeek hunched over with his hands folded, expressionless.

Shawn waved his hand in front of his brother's face. "Did you hear me?"

Tymeek shook his head and buried his face in his hands. Shawn's confession had left him speechless. Shawn sat quietly waiting for his brother's outraged response. But there wasn't one. After a few minutes of no movement at all, Tymeek finally raised both his head and a thick brow. "I don't get you. I told you not to fuck wit that bitch. Now, you tellin' me that you in love with this broad? How the fuck...What the fuck...?" Tymeek shook his head to gather his thoughts and let the shock marinate.

After a minute, he said, "You think she don't know who you are?"

"Nah," Shawn answered, putting his hands to his temples. "I can't help how I feel, Ty. I know it's crazy, but I can't help myself. When we took her to the house, I..."

"You what? You did what? You crazy? You took her to my house?" Tymeek tried hard not to raise his voice. "You fucked up." He scolded, pounding his left fist into his right hand.

"It's a long story, yo. But she don't know nothin' about you being my brother or what I do. She don't know none of that. I know this is crazy, Ty, but she got me...I love her. I didn't wanna tell you cause' I know how you get. But, I don't want you to hurt her when you come home. Now you know this is some real love shit cuz you know I don't ever act like this over no woman."

Tymeek rubbed his hand across his chin and said, "Shawn, she's probably using you to get my appeal shot down." He seemed calm and composed now. "You don't know what she's up to. You better cut her loose, before you end up in here too."

"Ty, I'm telling you, she don't know nothing." Shawn didn't doubt his words. He felt that what he and Natalia had was real. "I'm asking you as a favor to me bro, don't hurt her. I'll make sure she don't get in your way. Just try to understand where I'm coming from."

Tymeek thought Shawn was an idiot for falling in love. But he had been in that same predicament once and understood how love could make you do stupid things from time to time. He was sure that the relationship would end in heartbreak for his little brother, and he felt sorry for him. Tymeek leaned close and whispered, "I love you, P.B., like a father loves his son. You know I'd do anything for you. So, I'm gon' leave it in your hands. You take care of shit while I'm in here. But when I come home, if shit ain't right, I'm gonna clean house. You understand?"

"Yeah...I feel you. Thanks."

"Don't thank me yet. I'm tryna tell you Shawn some of these women out there are snakes. You gotta be on your guard at all times. I hope she ain't playing you. I don't wanna see you get fucked over. And don't fuck up and get loose wit your tongue over no pussy." He sighed, then continued, "Tell me this, little brother. If you love her so much, why don't you tell her the truth? I bet if you do, she'll run to the police," he scoffed.

"Right now, I can't tell her. But trust me, I got that ass locked."

"I wish you luck." And with that said, they switched subjects. Before they knew it, visiting hours were over. "Be good. One." Tymeek hit his fist against his chest, and they embraced once again.

Natalia walked into the café wearing tight bootcut pants and an ecru merino wool cardigan over a red tube top. She spotted Mark sitting at a corner table and walked over to him. "Hi Markie."

"Well, you certainly know how to enter a room, don't you?" he grinned. "Sit, please, before all the men in here have heart attacks."

"Oh, stop. They're not paying me any mind."

He chuckled, knowing better. "I really, really missed you."

"Ditto," she replied.

"Are you ready to order?"

"I'm in the mood for ice-cream."

"Ice-cream?" he asked, puzzled.

"Yes, that's what I'm in the mood for."

"Nat, eat some dinner first."

"I don't want to," she said in her bratty voice. They both laughed.

Natalia was excited to be with Mark again. They saw a movie in the East Village, a supernatural thriller, and huddled close through the scary parts. When it ended, it was late so Mark decided to end the date. "How did you get here?" he asked.

"I took a taxi." She wanted to spend the night with him, but he didn't offer. Instead, he hailed another taxi, gave the driver eighty dollars and said, "Please take this lovely woman straight to her door and make sure she gets in safely, okay?" The driver nodded.

Mark took her hand and gently kissed it. "Until we meet again, my lady," he said with English accent.

As he closed the cab door, she sweetly said, "I still love you."

"And I love you more."

Chapter Seven

❤

IN THE MIDST OF MADNESS

Shawn and his crew waited outside the billiards room on Linden Boulevard. The streetlight was out, and the corner was darker than usual. A black Range Rover screeched to a halt in front of the crew, and a group of men with hoods over their heads hopped out toting guns. Everyone scattered. Shawn ran around the corner and hid behind a rusty green dumpster. He pulled out his Glock and cocked it. Peering out from behind the green metal, he saw D.L.'s jerking body sprawled out on the ground across the street. Cautiously, he emerged from his hiding spot and ran to safety behind a parked car. He crept down low behind a line of double-parked cars, peeking over the trunk of a red Hyundai to check the corner. He pulled another gun out from his belt, jumped up and ran around the corner, blasting. One of the hooded thugs was hit as he climbed into the Rover and fell backwards. His head cracked loudly as it hit the concrete.

Slowly, the car backed up towards Shawn, and the driver let off a round of shots out the passenger window. Shawn dropped to the ground and rolled. The driver continued to shoot in spite of the lack of a target. As soon as he reached the side door, Shawn sprang to his feet, stuck his gun into the passenger's window and pumped the driver with bullets. The Rover lurched and rolled down the street.

Shawn ran across the street towards D.L. When he reached him, he felt a bullet tear into his forearm. "Shit!" he shouted as he spun around with gun pointed straight ahead. He pulled the trigger. The Rover was in motion, and as it sped off, the body of the dead driver was tossed out.

Before Shawn knew it, sirens were blaring. He ran as fast as he could to his car holding his arm. The Lexus was parked a block and a half away. A cop car drove past without noticing him. Hopping into his car, he peeled off his shirt, tied it around his arm tightly and floored the gas pedal. He kept his arm in his lap so that his blood wouldn't leak all over the tan leather. The pain was excruciating, but he couldn't go to a hospital in Queens. The police would most likely be looking for him at all the hospitals. Instead, he drove to Kings County hospital in Brooklyn, and although he felt faint, he managed not to pass out. He parked his car behind a disabled ambulance near the emergency entrance and ran in holding his arm. The nurse at the triage desk filling out a form didn't notice him. He slapped his uninjured blood soaked hand on the desk and yelled, "Can I get some fuckin' help here?"

A doctor in a blue mask said, "Count backwards from one hundred for me." Shawn felt pressure on his wrist and after a few moments, could no longer feel his arm at all. The bright ceiling light bothered him so he turned his head to the side and closed his eyes. The evening's scenario played out in his head; he could see D.L.'s body clear as day. The more he dwelled on it, the more aggravated he became. Time passed quickly as he lay there trying to figure out who had set him up. He didn't even notice the doctor operating on him.

When the doctor was finished, a nurse appeared. She advised him on the healing process of his injury. She also informed him that the hospital had notified the police and that Shawn would have to file a report.

"I'll be back with your prescriptions and instructions for after-care," she said.

Shawn looked down at his arm in the sling and shook his head. "Damn!" he muttered. He tried to ease off the gurney and almost fell.

The nurse returned, saw him struggling and helped him down. She patted his back and said, "You really need to change your occupation."

Shawn ignored her. He wanted out of the hospital as quickly as possible. She frowned and handed him his prescription. He dashed for the door. Outside, the sun was rising through swirls of red orange in the sky. Once in his car, he checked his pager. He called the last number that appeared on the screen.

"Yo, niggah! I thought they got you!" Spank shouted frantically.

"Nah, son. Where's Nut and em'?" Shawn asked.

"They here," he answered. Nut grabbed the phone from Spank's ear and asked, "You aiight?"

"Yeah. I just got shot in my arm. The shit don't hurt. But it's a pain in the ass not being able to use both my hands. Now I gotta squeeze one tit at a time," he chuckled and asked, "Is D.L. aiight?"

Nut's silence spoke volumes. "He's dead, right?"

Nut filled him in. "He died in the ambulance. We watched the shit on TV. The cops was all over like roaches. But two of em' punks is dead too. One of em' is in intensive care. I only shot one, so I know you must've taken them other two out. You wannabe Clint Eastwood muhfucka!" They both laughed. Then the silence returned.

Shawn couldn't believe it. D.L. was dead. "Y'all heard anything yet?" he asked.

"Nah. But, yo, niggaz around here know better. Them muhfuckas couldn't be from around here. We ain't got beef wit nobody."

"We gon' find out."

"Come get me."

"Why did you go over there in the first place?"

"His house was closer. Man, just come get me."

"Why? You scared that ass gon' catch a bullet?" Shawn laughed heartily.

"Nah, punk. But somebody gotta watch out for your ass. You da one who caught a bullet in ya ass." Nut laughed.

"I'm on my way niggah," he said, trying not to laugh. Somebody wanted him dead. But who?

Andy, please come over," Natalia pleaded over the phone.

"For what?" André asked sarcastically.

"I need counseling," she replied.

"That's the only time you want to see me? Where's you're little boy toy? Did he leave your ass, too?" André chuckled.

"No, and I can do without your sarcasm. Just get your sexy butt over here, ASAP!"

"Why? What happened now?" André sighed.

"I saw Mark last night. Oh, by the way we're friends, now."

"Yeah, right. You're both getting on my last nerve. Well, I'll probably come by later tonight."

"Tonight?"

"Yes, tonight. I've got things to do. So just hold your horses."

"Okay, I guess I can wait. Bye." She let out an exasperated sigh. The house was too quiet for her. She decided to go outside and pick peaches. When the fruit on her trees ripened, she would pick all of it and give it to shelters and churches. She grabbed a bushel, a ladder and a brand new pair of garden gloves from the garage and went peach picking. The fruit was so ripe, she had to be careful not to squash them in her hands.

When her hard work was complete, she relaxed on the grass and called Shawn. She recalled that evening when he pinned her down in the grass — the night of her kidnapping. "That crazy boy," she giggled.

On the second ring, an unfamiliar voice answered. "Uh, can I speak to Shawn please?" she asked sweetly.

"Hold on," Nut replied and threw the phone at Shawn. It landed on top of his chest. "Ouch, muhfucka. Who is it?"

"Your wife," Nut grinned.

Shawn's face lit up and he put the phone to his ear and said, "What up ma?"

"Hi, big daddy," she giggled.

"You miss me?" he asked.

"Mmn-hmn. Whatchu doin', boo?" she attempted to talk like him.

"Nothing." He thought about whether or not he should tell her about his arm but realized that he would have to explain sooner or later. Better sooner. "Baby girl, you've gotta come over here and take care of me. I'm hurt."

"What happened?" she asked anxiously

"It's my arm. It's all fuc...I mean messed up. Come take care of me."

"Oh, I get it. You want to play doctor."

"No, Nay-nay. It sounds good, though. But seriously, I'm really hurt. My arm is outta commission, nahmean? So you coming?"

"Of course I am. I've got to take care of my baby."

"How long it's gon' take you?"

"I don't know. So just kick her out now, and I won't have to hurt somebody when I get there," she joked.

Shawn laughed heartily. "I want you here, pronto. You got that?"

"Yes, daddy," she answered in a baby voice. There was something about him that made her obedient. She rushed in the house and got ready. Before she left, she called André's salon and left a message for him. "Sorry, Andy, but my daddy wants to see me, and I know you wouldn't want me to get a spanking."

She hopped in her Navigator and headed for Shawn's house.

So, I guess you want me to leave now?" Nut asked.

"You ain't gotta leave...right now," Shawn joked. He attempted to sit up and a sharp pain shot up his arm. "Fuck!" he shouted.

"What happened?" Nut rushed to his aid.

"That shit is startin' to hurt now. Help me sit up." Nut took

Shawn's good arm and helped him lean against the pillows. He handed Shawn the remote and said, "I'm gonna go talk to this kid from Baisley. He said he knows one of them niggaz from last night."

"Aiight, son. As soon as you hear something call me."

"No doubt," Nut said, gave Shawn a pound and left.

Shawn's car was in the driveway when she pulled up. She wondered why it wasn't parked inside the garage. She got out of her car and smiled at the sight of the quaint house. She rang the doorbell and turned her back to it. Her plan was to flash him when he answered the door.

A couple of teenaged girls passed by and stopped in front of the house. One girl pulled out a cigarette and lit it. Another girl boldly asked, "You here to see Pretty Boy?"

"If you mean Shawn, then yes I am." She hoped these teenyboppers weren't here to see him too.

"Oh," the girl said and looked Natalia up and down. "It's gon' rain?"

Natalia laughed. It was apparent that the weather didn't call for a long trench coat. But, then, she couldn't have come out of the car without it. She smiled and replied, "No, not that I know."

Natalia turned around to ring the bell again. Shawn was standing in the doorway, shirtless.

The teenage girls seemed to be in heat. They moved in closer trying to get a better look at him. "Hi-eee, Shawwwn," they sang like a choir.

"Whut up?" he replied with a nod of his head before turning his attention back to Natalia. He examined her from head to toe, his mouth forming a knowing smile.

"You have a fan club, I see." He ignored her remark and closed the door behind her.

"Well, don't you feel sorry for me?" he asked as he motioned for her to look at his bandaged arm.

"Of course I do, you poor baby. What happened?"

"I got shot...with a nail gun," he lied and embellished even further, "Remember I told you that we were renovating the store?"

"Yes. But, honey, you should've left that work for the construction crew."

"I know that...now." He slipped his good arm around her waist. and kissed her forehead. "Where's my sugar?"

She lifted her head and planted a juicy kiss on his lips. His tongue wormed its way into her mouth, and he lowered his hand to rest on her butt. "Mmn!"

She smiled and stroked his bandaged arm. "You poor, poor baby. Now you can't do anything for yourself."

"Nope. But now my girl will take care of me." He smiled at her.

"So what do you need me to do?"

"Cook me something to eat. I'm starving," he rubbed his washboard stomach.

Natalia grimaced and replied, "I don't even cook for myself."

"You're gonna cook today."

She gave him an evil look. He kissed her cheek and said, "I'm just playin' wit you. I'm gonna take you out to dinner. Is that alright wit you, brat?" he laughed.

"You better be playing," she pouted.

"I love that face," he said and pinched her cheek.

He led her into the living room and fell back on the couch. He put his good arm around her neck and pulled her to him. "So, did that guy call you?" he asked nonchalantly.

"What guy?"

"Your man," he answered sarcastically. She couldn't tell him about her rendezvous with Mark, so she simply said, "No."

He raised his eyebrow and said, "Then he don't really love you. I know I couldn't just give you up like that." He wiggled into a more comfortable position, moving his injured arm further away from her.

Natalia knew the truth. She knew that Mark still loved her. She glanced at the entertainment center. The pictures were no longer face down. She giggled as she remembered his polyester pants. Shawn looked at her as if she were crazy. "What's so funny?"

"Nothing," she smiled and lay her head on his shoulder.

"You know, you're hot as hell in that coat. Take it off and show me my surprise."

Natalia stood up and untied the belt. She opened the coat slowly. Shawn's eyes bulged at the sight of her shining naked body. "Damn!" He licked his lips. "Come here."

She dropped the coat to the ground and sat on his knee. "You trying to give me a heart attack?" he asked with a smile. She smiled back and kissed his lips. The phone rang as their tongues intertwined. They continued to kiss and ignored the phone. It was about the 5th ring when he realized that the answering machine was off. He pulled his tongue from her mouth and asked her to pass him the phone.

"Yeah," he said annoyed.

"Yo, it was Jigg and that kid that came to the park askin' for work that set us up. We need to pay that muthafucka Jigg a visit." Nut said in one breath.

"Where you at?" Shawn asked.

"The G-Spot."

"I'm on my way," Shawn slammed the cordless phone down on the end table. He gently nudged Natalia off his lap and got up.

"Where are you going?" she asked, confused.

"I gotta go take care of something. Go home. I'll meet you there later."

"But why? I just got here."

"I've got to take care of something now. It's real important. Go home, and I'll be there later on tonight, aiight?"

Natalia picked her coat up off the floor and put it on. But instead of heading for the front door, she ran upstairs.

Shawn had pulled out two guns and a small rectangular box from a hole in his closet floor. He turned to see her standing there with her mouth wide open. "Nay-Nay, please go home. I'll explain later," he told her while putting the cover back over the hole.

Natalia couldn't move. "What's going on?" she asked.

"Just go!" he yelled. "Wait. I'm sorry. I didn't mean to yell at you. But I've got to go. I promise you, I'll explain everything later." He took a deep breath and said, "I love you."

He kissed her forehead and hugged her tightly. There, he said it, and it wasn't as hard as he thought it would be.

Natalia was more shocked than he was. He looked down at her and asked, "Do you love me?" She couldn't answer him. He shook her gently and repeated the question. "Do you love me, Natalia?"

For the first time, she looked into his brown eyes, really looked into them. She wanted to melt. Wasn't it obvious that she loved him? Perhaps he just needed her to validate it by saying it out loud. So she did. "Yes, I love you."

He squeezed her again. "Please go home and wait for me." He touched the side of her face lovingly. She kissed his bare chest and looked up at him with a hint of sadness. "See you later?" she asked, worried.

"Most definitely," he answered with a slight smile. She went down the steps slowly and kept turning to look at him until she couldn't see him anymore.

Jigg lived on a busy street in Harlem. Even with all the hustle and bustle, Shawn knew that anyone or anything out of the ordinary would fall under suspicion and be reported back to Jigg by one of his lookouts. So he parked the car three blocks away.

Shawn entered Jigg's building alone, took the elevator up to the

3rd floor and then took the stairs the rest of the way to the fifth. Nut and the four others he brought with him discreetly followed.

Shawn peeked out from behind the stairwell door and kept his eye on Jigg's apartment door. In his peripheral vision, he saw Spank followed by Nut slowly creeping up the stairs.

"How we gon' get him to open the door?" Nut whispered while pulling his gun from his pants.

"We just gonna hafta bust in. He probably think I don't know it was him anyway." Shawn peeked out again at the door then whispered, "Y'all ready?" Nut and Spank both nodded.

They crept to Jigg's door with guns drawn. But just then the elevator doors opened and two young girls got off. Shawn watched as they went to the apartment adjacent to Jigg's, and he had an idea. He went over to them. "Hey, can y'all do me a favor?" he asked in a friendly tone. The girls looked at each other and bashfully giggled.

"I'm serious. I need y'all to do me a little favor," he persisted.

"What's that?" the braver of the two girls asked.

"I need you to knock on that door for me, okay?" he smiled widely.

"But why?" the girl asked, confused.

"Cause I'll pay you to," Shawn promised, patting his pocket.

She looked at the other men anxiously waiting near Jigg's door and understood. She was streetwise and knew all about the drug game. "How much?" she asked.

Shawn pulled out a wad of bills, separated out a fraction of it and held her share in front of her.

"Y'all gonna kill him?" she whispered. Shawn smiled but didn't answer.

She threw her keys at her friend and whispered, "Open the door and hold it." Then she turned to Shawn and said, "Aiight, I'ma do it." Shawn handed her the money.

She walked over to Jigg's door and rang the bell. Shawn could hear Jigg's heavy footsteps as he neared the door.

The girl's face smiled at Jigg through the peephole, and he unlocked the door. When he pulled the it open, however, Shawn was on the other side — not the girl. He tried to slam the door closed, but Shawn forced his way in and hit Jigg in the head with the handle of the nine millimeter. The rest of his crew ran into the apartment and attacked Jigg, beating him unrecognizable.

Shawn put the gun to Jigg's temple. "I want all them niggaz. Start talking, bitch."

Jigg's swollen lips were covered with blood and he could barely speak. "M-man, whatchu talkin' bout?"

Shawn cracked Jigg in the head with his gun again. "Stop playin' wit me. You know what the fuck I'm talkin' bout. Give them niggaz up."

Jigg groaned, "Man it wasn't me. That lil' boy set y'all up."

Shawn grabbed Jigg's neck and tightened his grip. "What little boy?"

"Q-quest...he live on a hundred and tenth corner of Frederick Douglas. It's um...tw-twelve ninety-three."

"What's them other niggaz names?" Shawn applied more pressure to Jigg's thin neck.

Jigg gasped for air. "I-I c-c-can't b-breeve..." he pleaded. Shawn let up just enough for Jigg to speak clearly, and he spilled his guts. He even wrote down cell numbers and addresses.

Jigg begged again for mercy. "Come on, young blood...that cat set y'all up, not me. I told him not to fuck wit you." The blood on his battered face was beginning to dry and cake.

"You slippin', you know that? You fell off. Nobody got your back. Look at you. I thought you was big time niggah. I'm not supposed to be able to get at you. You fucked up, though, trusting some punk ass kid. You fucked up." Shawn could barely stand to look at him. He spit on Jigg's face and said, "Put that bitch out his misery."

Nut grabbed a corduroy pillow from the couch and put it in front of his gun. Jigg's eyes grew wide. "Nooooo! Come on young blood don't do a niggah like that!" he screamed. Shawn turned his back to him.

"Roll over bitch," Spank yelled. Jigg started blubbering like a baby with snot bubbling from his nose like boiling soup. "Pleassse, man. Pleassse!"

Spank flipped him over onto his stomach and Nut pressed the pillow to the back of his head and pulled the trigger. A puddle of urine spread on the bare wood floor. Jigg's body trembled for a few seconds then went rigid. "Look at that fuckin hole," Nut said proudly, pointing to the gaping hole in Jigg's skull. Shawn shook his head in disgust and headed for the door. "Let's bounce."

Shawn pulled into Natalia's driveway and called her from his cell phone.

"Hello?" she answered anxiously.

"Baby girl, I'm on my way," he lied.

"Okay," she simpered. She rushed to change from her flannel shirt into a silky pink chemise. She brushed her hair, applied a pale pink lipstick and slipped her feet into a pair of fuzzy white slippers with frilly pink ribbons.

As she sat on the bed going over all the questions she needed to ask Shawn, the doorbell rang. Damn! Mark was dropping by unannounced once again. *Will that man ever learn?* She stomped down the stairs and yanked the door open.

"Surprise!" Shawn grinned at her.

"Shawn!" Natalia jumped into his arms and wrapped her legs around him. They looked at each other as if they had been apart for ages. Shawn pressed his lips against hers and kissed her passionately.

Without saying anything more, they went upstairs hand in hand. They went to the bedroom and lay next to each other. She rolled onto her side, rested her head on his chest and gently ran her hands over his bandaged arm.

"Are you okay?" she asked.

He raked his fingers through her hair and answered, "I'm aiight." It was nice being with her. He was happy.

"Nay-Nay..." he said, hardly loud enough for her to hear. "I love you. Don't ever forget that...I didn't know what I wanted before I met you. I was out there, fuckin' every pretty broad that came my way. But now I don't even notice 'em." He swallowed hard, cleared his throat and continued, "I want a life with you. Marriage, kids, everything." He swirled his finger on her back and butterflies fluttered in her stomach.

"I love you, too," was all she could think to say.

It was an awkward moment for Shawn; he had never felt this way about a woman before. Maybe he had said too much. She probably took him for a sucker now. Maybe she really didn't feel the same. Maybe she would go back to her fiancé. Maybe, maybe, maybe.

Natalia couldn't remember any of her questions. Shawn was vulnerable right now because of his injury and his emotions, and all she could think about was sex. She wanted him and decided to take control and have him.

It had been a long time since she went down on a man. She knew that she wasn't very good at it. But, tonight, she was going to give it her all.

Slowly, she slithered down the bed until her face was directly above his crotch. Shawn understood what she was up to and watched in excited anticipation. The bulge growing in his pants made it difficult for Natalia to pull his zipper down so he helped her by guiding her hand with his own. She pushed his pants down his hips as he lifted his butt off the bed and then pulled them down to his ankles. She crawled back to his crotch and took his cock into her mouth, trying to take it all in but gagged instead.

Shawn realized that she was an amateur so he instructed her. "Relax your throat. Don't tense up and open as wide as you can. Get it nice and wet," he whispered seductively. She followed his instructions and took him deep into her mouth. She didn't gag — his instructions actually worked.

"Sss-ah, yeah. Now move faster," he whispered passionately. He closed his eyes, leaned back into the pillows and grabbed two handfuls of her hair, groaning with pleasure.

Natalia was proud of herself to have brought him to the point of no return (or so she thought). She was in charge as she licked the length of him all the way up to the tip, watching his face the entire time.

When he opened his eyes, she raised her head, lifted her chemise and slowly climbed on top of him, gazing into his eyes mischievously.

"Rip my panties off!" she commanded.

Shawn did not hesitate. He ripped them to shreds. She grabbed his cock, positioned it straight up into the air and slowly sat on it.

"Take it all," he coaxed. And she did, riding him like a bull in the rodeo until his face contorted, and he completely let go.

So what did Ty say?" Nut asked, reaching over to push in the lighter. They were stuck in traffiic on the 59th Street bridge.

"What?" Shawn asked, annoyed at the delay.

"What did Ty say about your wife?" Nut chuckled.

"This shit is funny to you?" Shawn asked.

"I'm just fuckin' wit you. So what did he say?"

"He's aiight with it — for now." Shawn blew his horn and shouted, "Move bitch! Damn, she act like she scared to drive." He pressed down on the horn again. "These muthafuckas can't drive for shit," he grumbled. He finished answering Nut's question. "When he come home, he gon' take over. I ain't gon hafta do nothing."

"True. You's a lucky niggah. So whatchu gon' do wit all that free time? Honeymoon wit wifey?" Nut asked with a sly grin. Shawn smiled wide. The thought made him feel good. "Hell yeah! We gon' make some rugrats."

Nut looked at him surprised. "You for real?"

"No doubt," he replied dreamily.

"Man, she got your ass on lockdown. She got a niggah trippin'. You mad open, yo. She got platinum pussy!" Nut laughed hard and said, "But I'm not gon' front...I kinda envy what you feel, nahmean. I wonder what that love shit is like." Nut caught himself and ended the conversation. "But ay, whateva makes you happy."

"She does man. She does."

After Natalia's lecture, she stopped by the salon to make up with André. She had been neglecting him for Shawn and knew he wasn't too happy with her right now.

"Hi, Andy," she chirped.

André turned his back to her and continued his conversation with Lauren. "You know, I think friends who desert their other friends for hot sex with a teenager should be on the next Jerry Springer show, don't you?" he said sarcastically.

Lauren giggled and slapped his arm. "Be nice," she said and greeted Natalia. "Don't pay him no mind, Nat. He wishes he could get him some young stuff. That's all it is, just plain ol' jealousy."

André snapped his fingers and said, "I don't think so, missy. And oh, by the way you're fired!" Everyone laughed. "Poof, be gone," he snapped his fingers then waved his hand at Lauren. Then he folded his arms and turned his attention to Natalia. "What do you want?"

Natalia batted her eyelashes and tried to look pitiful. "That's not gonna work," André said and sucked his teeth.

"I'm sorry, Andy," she said innocently.

André hugged her. "I just don't know why you couldn't call me. It's not hard to pick up a phone." He kissed her cheek.

"I know, I know. I've been a horrible friend. Do you forgive me?" she asked.

"I don't know...um, hmmm...I guess so." He laughed as they went into his office. He was dying to hear the latest news.

"So what's been going on in Natalia's world?" he asked, excited.

"Well, I'm still seeing Shawn...and, of course, Mark. But it's strictly platonic."

"Strictly platonic, my ass. Please honey. I wish my life was action packed like that." André sighed then said, "You are just living it up, gurl."

Natalia felt like she was losing control over her life not living it up. "Andy, I don't know if I'm coming or going anymore," she confessed.

"Well, it certainly seems like you're coming, honey! Multiple times," André laughed.

Natalia didn't laugh.

"Honey bunny, what's the matter? You look like you're a million miles away."

Natalia perked up. "You know, everything's your fault."

André's jaw dropped. "I beg your pardon?"

She moved closer to him, touched his hard chest affectionately and replied, "If you would have just given into your true feelings and admitted that you wanted me, I would be with you instead."

André broke out laughing. "Nat, you are too funny," he said with tears in his eyes.

She pretended to be offended, "What the hell is so funny?" she tried to contain her laughter.

André hugged her tight. "I love you, gurl." He pressed his lips on her forehead, leaving a wet smudge.

"Ewww!" she playfully shrieked as she wiped away his saliva. "Do my hair, Andy. I need a different look. Sexy but not slutty. You know what I mean?"

"I am an artiste, honey bunny. I'm going to turn all of this into a masterpiece," he said as he ran his hands through her hair.

At the same moment, her cell phone rang. She hoped it was Shawn and was quickly disappointed. It was Mark calling to invite her to a play that evening. Natalia wasn't in the mood for a play — she wanted to play. André spoke the truth. She wasn't ever going to go back to being platonic with Mark. And tonight she would reclaim him by being irresistible.

André really outdid himself. Natalia's hair looked as if it had slid off the page of a fashion magazine, bouncy and shiny. He even made her up. She left the salon looking like she was ready for a photo shoot for Vogue. Mark would be putty in her hands.

Natalia didn't have time to drive all the way to Long Island to get ready for her date with Mark, so she decided instead to go to her condo in Brooklyn. It was just after five o'clock and rush hour traffic conspired to keep her in the car for as long as possible. She was anxious to see her father's building again — *it has been so long,* she thought. Instead, she was stuck in the car alone with her thoughts.

Mark. Shawn. Her relationship with each of them developed in such completely different ways, she couldn't really compare them.

Mark. She had toyed with him, not allowing him to get close because she wanted to have the upper hand with him as she had in all of her previous relationships. He wasn't weak, but he wasn't strong either, and he fell for her mainly because she made him fall for her. Natalia realized she loved Mark but not passionately. Her love was tame and comfortable. The exact opposite of what she felt for Shawn.

Her love for Shawn was explosive. Dynamic. Crazy. He was primal, sexy, hot. He dominated and made her feel weak and out of control. And she surrendered to him. But what was she really surrendering to? She didn't know him like she knew Mark. But that element of danger both thrilled and excited her.

Lately, however, Mark was showing strengths that she hadn't seen before. She had come to think of him as a sniveling yes-man. Yet his I'm-not-having-it attitude impressed her. He wasn't calling her every day, five times a day. And he hadn't put the moves on her at all. Natalia was intrigued and determined to dominate him again. *Tonight*, she thought.

She hadn't been to her condo in Brooklyn Heights in almost two years. Yet the short, elderly doorman recognized her immediately.

"Natalia!" he happily shouted as he hugged her. "Where have you been? It's so nice to see you!"

Natalia smiled and hugged him back. "It's so nice to see you again, Mr. Drelpher."

"Will you be staying a while this time?" he asked.

"I'm thinking about it."

"Well, it sure would be nice to see a little more of you," he said enthusiastically as she headed up the stairs.

"Oh, don't worry. You will!"

The condo was dark and smelled of stale air. Natalia walked across the living room and opened the heavy silk drapes and slid open the patio doors. Then she went up the spiral staircase to the second level and opened the windows up there as well.

In her bedroom closets, she searched for the perfect outfit. Mark loved to see her in black, but the only suitable dress she had was beige. It would have to do.

She inspected all the rooms and everything was as sparkling clean as she had left it. Then she glanced at the clock and realized that if she was going to meet Mark on time, she was going to have to hurry.

You look great." Mark said as he briefly hugged her.

"Thank you," she said as she hugged him again with her whole body. He nervously chuckled and pulled away. She stared at him incredulously. "Are you afraid of me or something?"

"No." He laughed it off. "It's just that we've got to get inside and take our seats." He took her hand and led her into the theater.

The play was long and monotonous. Natalia was careful to keep her yawns to a minimum though Mark wouldn't have noticed anyway. He was lost in his own thoughts. He felt uncomfortable around Natalia now. As hard as he tried, he couldn't push from his mind images of Shawn and Natalia together. And he wondered just who Shawn was and what trait or attribute he might have that would steal Natalia's heart. Mark was determined to marry Natalia and turn her against Shawn. So he had taken steps towards finding out all he could about Shawn and hired a private detective.

The play was apparently over. The applause was deafening, not that Natalia could understand.

She stood up, stretched and announced, "I'm starving."

"Really?" he asked surprised. She wasn't one to eat much, and when she did eat, it was mostly fruits, salads and other healthy stuff. Once in a while, she'd splurge on a real meal or go overboard on junk food.

"Yes, really. So what we gon' eat, boo?" she giggled.

This shit is hot!" Nut exclaimed.

He pulled the trigger of the empty gun in his hand. "Ay, dog, how much you want for this?"

The dealer sat across from Shawn at a long metal table. Long dreadlocks were wrapped around his head like a turban. "Gimme four bills, seen."

Nut happily slapped four one hundred dollar bills on the table. The Jamaican checked each one under a small lamp. Nut laughed and said, "All that shit is real, dread." Then he turned to Shawn. "This shit is hot!"

Shawn paid no attention to him. He was busy sampling the contents of a plump white bag. He flicked his tongue against his pinkie, tasting the white powder. "I want my usual," he said, nodding his head in approval.

"Awright, yoot. You have a way fi transport dem tings deh?"

"Yeah," Shawn answered as he began stacking the packages on the table. In the corner of the room, a scrawny boy with a beat up baseball cap was smoking a blunt. The Jamaican ordered, "Ay, Tekk, gwan go get me one of dem big box from off de counter deh." Tekk nodded, drew deeply from his blunt and left the room. He returned carrying a long cardboard box with handles which he dropped on the table.

From the box, the Jamaican pulled a new bubble goose down coat, and into several Velcro lined slits on the inside of the coat, he inserted the packages one by one. When he was finished, he folded the coat neatly, slid it into a Macy's shopping bag and handed it to Shawn. From a paper bag, Shawn pulled out a stack of badly crumpled bills. These bills were checked under the lamp as well.

Shawn waited until the Jamaican was satisfied. "Awright, unah tek care." They gave each other brotherly pats on the backs.

Shawn idled in the beat-up Toyota Celica. "When you finish, call me. I'ma go home right quick," Shawn whispered in Nut's ear. Nut nodded.

Shawn was always paranoid when he did the actual buying. He never used his own car, and wouldn't speak out loud in whichever vehicle he did use for the pick-up. He believed that Federal agents could easily bug his car. They were careful not to bust drug dealers at the time of the purchases. Instead, they patiently collected evidence, staked out possible business hang outs and waited until they could actually round up everyone in the operation. The Fed's mission was to catch drug dealers and get a guilty verdict in court. They took all precautions possible so that perpetrators would not slip through the cracks and go free due to technicalities, clever lawyers, botched evidence or lack thereof.

Once in a while, the Feds followed Shawn. He would take them on wild goose chases to insignificant locations like the Department of Motor Vehicles, a McDonald's drive-thru or a mall parking lot. Then he'd lose them on the parkway. When he confirmed that he was no longer being followed, he'd take the vehicle to his mechanic and have him search for taps. Finally, all traces of the car would be destroyed at a chop shop.

After dropping Nut off, Shawn headed home to clean up for his date with Natalia.

A half hour later, he picked up Nut, and they drove out to Long Island.

He pulled up to the house again behind the trees and dialed her number. He looked confused when she didn't pick up. "I don't know what's up wit her. She know I'm comin' over here." He seemed to be talking to the air freshener dangling from the rearview mirror.

"She wit her next man," Nut snickered.

"Fuck you." Shawn laughed and dialed her number again. No answer — just her voicemail, again. "Fuck it. I'll catch her tomorrow," he said wearily.

Shawn wanted to see her beautiful face, and now that his arm was almost healed, he could explore her body again with both of his hands. He felt in his heart that she wasn't alone, and it made him jealous. But he couldn't sweat Natalia in front of Nut.

Thank you for a lovely evening, Mark."

Natalia looked up at him lovingly. His eyes glimmered with the city lights, and he smiled as he held her in his arms. It felt good, like old times.

Natalia reminded herself of her agenda for the evening. She wanted Mark to beg for her company. She wanted to hear him say, "I don't care about what you've done. I'll take what I can I get. I'm willing to share you." She wanted her cake and eat it, too. If only they could both accept that.

She gently pulled away and sighed. "I guess I'd better catch a cab."

"You took a cab all the way here?" he asked.

"No, not from Long Island. I'm going to stay in Brooklyn for a couple of weeks."

Mark looked surprised. "Really?"

"Yes, it's a bit more convenient. I've got a few meetings lined up this month, and I'm tired of driving back and forth...back and forth..."

"Well, that's a good idea. I was wondering when you were going to get fed up with the long drive into the city." He let go of her hand, stepped off the curb into the street and gestured for the available cab at the corner to come for them.

"Gotcha!" Natalia said to herself.

They made out in the back of the taxi like two lovebirds.

Mark missed her soft lips. She missed his thin ones. The taxi had reached their destination, and they didn't even realize that the car had stopped.

Politely, the driver tapped on the Plexiglas partition to get their attention. "Iz heah stop," he said in a heavy African accent.

"Huh?" they both asked. The driver pointed out the window.

"Oh, yeah. Thank you," Mark laughed and pulled out a twenty dollar bill from his monogrammed money clip.

Natalia waited for Mark to open her door. "The Promenade?" she asked, puzzled.

"I wanted to talk to you in our spot," he smiled. The place brought back good memories.

They reminisced about when they met, their first official date, the first time they made love, the day he asked her to marry him. He wanted to marry her — still — and was convinced that she would come to her senses and realize that she should be with him and only him. The night was special to him, and he didn't want to cheapen it with sex. It was in his best interest to wait until they fully repaired their relationship.

But Natalia had other plans. She assumed that they would spend the night together, and she would hold out on him. She would be in control again.

He put his arm around her shoulder and said, "Come on, I'll walk you home."

Walk me home? she asked herself. *Maybe he wants to seduce me at my place.*

Natalia expected Mark to follow her inside, but, instead, he lingered in the opulent doorway. She stopped short when she realized that he wasn't right behind her and went back outside.

"Aren't you coming in?" she tried not to seem eager.

"No, I've got to get up early tomorrow...ya know, run that rat race," he chuckled. Natalia was not amused. Her plan was torn to shreds and Mark still had the upper hand.

His incessant aloofness was starting to take a toll on her otherwise high self-esteem. Could it be that he had another woman in his life? A female equivalent to Shawn rocking his world the way Shawn rocked hers? She shuddered at the thought. It would kill her to know that her loyal puppy dog was really a pit bull waiting to be unleashed.

It didn't add up. But then, Mark did have a one-night stand with a stranger. Damn!

Afraid of exposing herself, Natalia gingerly kissed him on his cheek and said, "Well, get a good night's rest...it was nice hanging out with you again, friend."

He watched as she went into the building, wanting to run after her but knowing it would only be counterproductive. He sighed. He wanted her to be sure of what she wanted before he would commit to any course of action.

Once inside her apartment, finding her cell phone was her primary objective. She had left it home on purpose.

"You have two messages," the digital voice informed her.

"Nat, you have a ten o'clock with Dianne Shelby on Thursday. I forgot to add that to this week's itinerary. Sorry. Oh, and I hope you didn't forget about Lifetime's breast cancer charity function Thursday night. Okay, see ya Thursday evening. Buh-bye!" Her assistant Renée sounded so jovial.

Damn I forgot all about that, she thought. *Who should be my date?* she asked herself. Maybe she should go without a man for once. "Decisions, decisions," she sighed, pushing the pound key to hear the second one.

"Where you at, huh?" Shawn's voice seemed to echo. Then silence. *Is that all he had to say?* she asked herself.

Mark hunted her down and was concerned about her. Shawn

didn't sweat her like other men did, and it drove her crazy. Out of pure stubbornness, she did not call him back. "He's just a man," she kept repeating to herself.

Chapter Eight

❤

BIG WHITE LIES

Mark's office was dead quiet for a change. He rested his head in his hands and watched the screensaver on his computer. Different photos of him and Natalia floated across the screen every ten seconds. He checked his watch. He looked out his office door and down the hall. He grew restless waiting for the private detective to get back to him.

Even though he was sure that Natalia's fling with Shawn wouldn't last, he had to ensure it. So he hired the detective to tail Shawn. Mark knew that there had to be some dirt on him.

He instructed the detective not to photograph or videotape Natalia and Shawn together. Mark would not be able to handle actually seeing them together.

As Mark watched one of their Hawaii photos float across the monitor, a slim man in a pair of Levi's and a pale blue, short sleeved dress shirt knocked on the door.

"Come on in," Mark said and sat up straight in his chair. The detective entered carrying a thick folder under his arm. He seemed pleased with himself.

"Well?" Mark asked eagerly.

"Mission accomplished, Mr. Delucchio."

Mark reached for the folder, but the detective slapped his hand away. "Let me just say that this was a very dangerous job. I could have been killed. So the price has gone up."

"OK, whatever. Just show me what you've got," Mark scowled.

The detective opened the folder and pulled out a large photograph. "This guy was real busy. You're gonna love this," he said as he laid it on the desk.

Mark stared at the photo. "Are you kidding me?" he asked, bewildered.

"He's just one of the dangers I faced during this assignment," he said pulling out a cigarette from his shirt pocket. "Do you mind?" he asked, holding up the cigarette. Mark shook his head as he stared at the photo.

After the cigarette tip was glowing, the detective continued, "You know, I was a narcotics officer before I retired. So I asked my old precinct for a little help, and voila! His name is Shawn Wilson, and he's a drug dealer." The detective jabbed a finger at the photo. "Dumb bastard is about to get pinched soon, real soon. My buddy tells me he's the kid brother of that big shot drug dealer, Tie-mickey, or something like that, Wilson."

He took another puff of his cigarette and continued, "I was able to get copies of his rap sheet and mug shots. Everything is in the folder."

Mark recalled Tymeek Wilson's trial. He proudly sat in the second row behind the prosecutor's table when Natalia testified.

"The brother's name is Tymeek," Mark corrected.

Natalia couldn't possibly have known what she was getting into. The first thought that came to his mind was that Shawn was out to avenge his brother. "Is this the only picture you have?"

"No, there are others in the folder." He flicked his ashes into a black ceramic mug next to a framed photo of Mark and Natalia. Mark pulled out more photos of Shawn. He had to save her.

"How much?" he asked. The detective removed an invoice from his pocket and handed it to Mark.

"You don't come cheap, do you? But you've done a remarkable job." He dug into his pocket and pulled out his wallet. He placed a pile of one hundred dollar bills on the desk in front of the detective. "There ya go. Cash, as you requested."

The detective scooped them up and grinned. "It was nice doin' business wit ya, Delucchio. You know how to reach me if you ever need me." He took a rubber stamp and ink blotter out of his back pocket. He pounded the ink blotter with the rubber stamp and pressed it onto Mark's receipt.

Mark read aloud, "Paid in full."

"Yep." The detective dropped the cigarette butt in the mug, got up and shook Mark's hand. "Oh, and uh, tell your friends about me. It's good for business, if ya know what I mean."

Mark escorted him to the elevator, then ran back to his office. He grabbed the folder and looked at the photos again. His fingers trembled as he called Natalia.

"Hello," she answered groggily.

"Nat, I really need to see you. Can I come over?" Mark sounded troubled, but she wasn't concerned enough to oblige him. She was too tired.

"Mark, I've got an important meeting in the morning. I need to get some sleep. What's wrong?" she asked wearily.

"I don't want to tell you over the phone. But it's really important. It's about your..." Mark stopped himself. An accusation would make her defensive and kill his chances of seeing her. "Nat, it's really, really important. I've got to show you something."

"Mark, please, not tonight. I promise I'll come to your office tomorrow. What time is good for you?" It wasn't what Mark had in mind, but he'd take what he could get. He wanted to be the white knight in shining armor who saves her from the dark knight.

"How about one o'clock?" he asked.

"Okay, I'll see you tomorrow...friend," she giggled. Her sweet voice rang in his ears. He could see how easily a man could fall for her. Maybe that was Shawn's dilemma, Mark thought. Maybe Shawn couldn't avenge his brother until he sampled Natalia's sweetness and broke her spirit. And just maybe, he was hooked. *Well, that's too damn bad,* Mark thought. He wanted her all to himself, and he would have her.

"Nat, wait. Before you hang up I must say this. I love you. And the love I have for you transcends the limits of space and time. And even in adversity, it will not falter. Sleep on that...friend."

The music was so loud, Nut had to shout, "Yo, that one look like a pit bull." Colorful lights danced over his head as he sank into the vinyl seat of the booth. Big ass women with long weaved hair gyrated on the stage in front of them. "But yo, I'm mad happy for Ty." Nut leaned forward to check his glass in the light. Shawn nodded in agreement. "I know he can't wait to get home."

"When he gettin' out?"

"Next week. So we gotta get everything situated, 'cause I want shit to be right when he come through. Nahmean?"

"So what da deal wit your girl?" Nut asked as he emptied his glass.

"I don't know. I'm just not gon' bring that shit up though." Shawn glanced at a thick girl bouncing up and down at the edge of the stage. She flashed a broad smile at him then stretched out her arms, motioning for him to come to her. He smiled back then turned away. He needed Natalia tonight.

Nut rested his elbows on the table and shook his head, "Damn! Bitches just love your ass. Look at that shit."

Shawn just smiled in his usual cocky way and took his cell phone from its clip. "Yo, I'ma be right back," he said as he slid out of the booth.

A mocha colored beauty with shimmering silver eye shadow delivered drinks to the table.

"Damn! Sharaina when you gon' stop frontin' and get wit me?" Spank asked, grinning mischievously.

"I'm not tryna hear you right now 'cause you are drunk as hell! Just gimme my tip." She held out her hand in front of his face.

"Beat it bitch, ya bother me."

She sucked her teeth and began to walk away. Spank grabbed the string on her bikini bottom. "Stop, Spank," she smacked his hand. "I'm just playin' wit you, shorty. I'm sayin' though I'm tryna holla at you." He looked serious.

"If you really serious, you would wait to talk to me after I get off work."

Spank looked over at Nut who didn't seem to be paying them any attention.

"What time?" he asked as he caressed her hand.

"Four," she answered.

"I'ma be waiting for you, aiight?" he said as he looked her up and down.

He caught Nut snickering when he turned back around. "Fuck you laughing at?" he asked, grimacing.

"I'ma wait for you," Nut mimicked.

"Yeah niggah, I don't mind waitin' for that big ass. Nahmean." Spank chuckled. Shawn returned and sat down beside him.

"You finally gon' get some ass huh?"

Spank faked a laugh. "Niggah I been gettin' ass. You ain't the only Mack up in here, pretty muthafucka."

One of the voluptuous strippers wearing a patent leather bodysuit came over to the table. Her nipples poked through two peep holes.

"Lap dance, baby?" she asked Shawn as she stuck her tongue out. A steel ball protruded from it.

Shawn smiled a phony smile and said, "No thanks. But you can have this anyway." He stuck a twenty-dollar bill in her hand.

"You sure, baby?" she persisted.

He just looked past her.

"Alright then. Thanks, baby." She inched closer and kissed his cheek. Shawn wiped her kiss away.

"Y'all still going to Stardome?" he asked as he turned his attention to Nut and Spank. Nut put his glass down and answered, "Yeah. We leavin' around twelve." Shawn patted his pants pocket. He reached in and took out his car keys. "Aiight then. I'ma bounce."

"Where you goin'?" Nut asked, already knowing the answer.

"I'm out," Shawn snapped and left.

Markie, I'm so sorry. This meeting is running longer than I expected." Natalia spoke softly into her cell phone as she left the noisy boardroom.

"Well, then, can I see you later? I can meet you at the condo."

She didn't have any plans, so she agreed. "I'll be home around three."

"Okay, I'll be there at three-thirty." *Finally,* Mark thought.

"Okay. See you later then."

The meeting ended, and Natalia had a few hours to kill. As she sat in midtown traffic, she called André.

It took her only a few minutes to get to the salon. André rushed out and hopped in as she signaled her arrival with the horn. "That was so ghetto. Don't you know that honking is considered noise pollution around here?" he hissed.

"Oh, whatever!" she shouted and pulled away. André stared at her as she drove, a mischievous grin on his face.

Natalia noticed. "What is it?" she asked.

"Oh, nothing," he giggled to himself.

"What, Andy? Tell me!" she insisted.

"I still can't get over this thing you got going with this Shawn character. Girl, you are buggin', trippin'...all of the above."

"Andy, I thought you said you liked him. I mean you did say that he was sizzling. You can't possibly tell me now that he isn't worth buggin' over."

"Damn, look at that. All somebody has to do is mention his name and you lose your damn mind," André cackled. "You make me sick!"

She giggled.

"Just drive," he ordered as he pulled out his phone and made a call. "Yeah, baby. I'm not at the salon so just call me on the celly, okay?"

Natalia stared at him, surprised. "Who's that?" she asked excitedly.

"Well, if you were a real best friend, you'd know already. But you've been just too busy with that little boy," he replied sarcastically.

André said nothing until they reached Surli's restaurant. Then, in the middle of his juicy confession, Shawn called.

He told her he wanted to see her right away. Natalia knew it would be wrong to just pick up and leave André so she excused herself from the table to talk to Shawn in private.

"I can't just leave him. Can't we compromise, Daddy?" she asked in the sweetest voice he had ever heard. He wanted to reach through the phone and squeeze her.

"Yeah, I can do that. So, what time?" he asked.

Natalia was in a bind. She had made a promise to Mark, and he would be angry if she called and cancelled. It would seem to Mark that she was playing games. Then there was Shawn. She was simply unable to say no to him.

"You ain't hear me? I said what time you coming?" his voice cut through her thoughts.

"How about I just surprise you? Or maybe you need to reschedule your date with me so your mistress won't get mad," she joked.

"You are my mistress," he laughed. "But look. I'm not gon' stay in the house all day waiting for you, understand?"

"Yes, sir," she giggled.

"Who loves you?" he asked in such a silky smooth voice she felt herself get wet.

"You?"

"You don't sound like you believe that. Let's try this again. Who loves you?"

"Shawn loves me," she answered like a child.

"That's my baby. Aiight. I'ma run take care of some things right quick. But I'll be right back. I'll be waiting for my surprise." He hung up without saying goodbye, as he always did.

A musky fragrance floated on the air and relaxing R&B music filled the room. Natalia laid on the sheepskin rug in front of the lit gas fireplace and thought about how crazy her life had become.

She was in love with two men, and she couldn't view them as separate entities. They served one single purpose...to make her happy.

She got up and went into the kitchen and prepared a big bowl of shrimp salad — one thing she didn't mind making. Then she changed into a pair of washed out jeans and a white tank top. Afterwards, she lay on the soft rug, soothed by the earthy smell and calming music. Eventually she fell asleep.

A loud thump jolted her awake. She jumped up and hurried to the door. Through the peephole, she saw Mark in all his Italian splendor carrying a large manila envelope.

She straightened herself out and opened the door. "Hello," she said sweetly. "Come on in."

He walked in without hugging her and removed his suit jacket. "Wow, it smells nice in here," he said as he sat down on the sectional. Fluffy leather covered pillows engulfed him.

"I forgot how comfortable this place was. Sit down with me." He tugged at the front of her jeans.

"I don't feel like sitting. What's in the envelope?" she asked.

He didn't know how to break the news, yet he couldn't wait to expose Shawn.

"Well? What is it?" Natalia asked impatiently, assuming that in the envelope, Mark had tickets and travel brochures to exotic places. A make up excursion.

"Sit with me, and I'll show you. But, Natalia, I just want you to know that I did this to save our relationship. You deserve the best."

He was so serious that Natalia began to worry. "What are you talking about?" she asked apprehensively.

"Take a look in here," he said as he passed her the envelope.

"You're scaring me, Mark. What's in here?" Mark looked down. He couldn't put words together. Instead, he rubbed his hand up to her shoulders.

"Mark..." she started but he pressed his fingers to her lips. "Here," he said as he pulled the folder out of the envelope and lifted its lid. She took it from him and began to pull out 8x10 black and white photographs and copies of official-looking documents.

The oxygen left her body as she stared at the first photo. Shawn with a gun, sparks coming from it. The next photo was apparently his victim laying in a puddle of blood. Every photo was incriminating. She scanned a copy of Shawn's rap sheet which listed many misdemeanors and stared at his enlarged mug shots. She learned his real last name. Another report declared him heir to a drug dynasty. He was conspicuously linked to Tymeek Wilson, the renowned New York City drug kingpin. Natalia looked at the photos again and saw the similarities. Shawn was Tymeek's brother.

Mark didn't know what to do. Resuscitate her or console her? She didn't blink, she didn't move. He saw a range of mixed emotions flash across her face. He wanted to reach out and hold her.

Natalia was stunned. *How could she have been so gullible?* And then the truth — she was in love with a murderer. Mark tried to hold her in his arms, but she pulled away. The folder and its contents spilled to the floor as her arms went limp. Mark bent down and began to pick them up. She watched him. *How did he come by all of this information? Where did he get it? It doesn't matter,* she told herself.

She went into the bedroom, slipped into a pair of mules and a cardigan. She felt cold, very cold. Mark followed her, attempting to console her, but she didn't want him near her. Instead, she grabbed her keys and left. Mark didn't try to stop her. He understood.

When the tears finally came, Natalia couldn't stop them. She walked alone to the promenade and sat on a bench facing the Manhattan skyline. "That bastard!" she mumbled under her breath. She stepped up to the railing and looked down. Cars whizzed by beneath her as the sun set in front of her. Behind the clouds, the sky turned orange and violet as the sun slowly descended behind tall stacks of concrete and brick. The lights brightened on the isle of Manhattan.

With her arm hanging over the railing and her head lowered onto her forearm, she rested and thought for a long time. No matter how many times she resisted believing, the truth could not be undone. Shawn was supposed to kill her. Maybe he toyed with her to experience some sort of perverted thrill. Maybe it was part of his grand plan to gain her trust before lowering the boom.

As Natalia struggled with her feelings, a glimmer of hope shone in her mind — maybe, just maybe, it was possible that in the midst of his ghastly assignment, he actually fell in love with her. But whatever he might have intended or felt didn't really matter. The truth was that she was meant to die. Period.

As she sat very still on the bench, her body went numb. As if it had a mind of its own, her body rejected the idea that it would never again be touched by Shawn. Her every cell craved him.

She recalled Tymeek at the trial, his threatening gestures, his sneer, his complete lack of remorse for his brutal crime. *How could Shawn be related to such a monster? How could Shawn be a murderer?* She thought of all their intimate moments together, his gentleness and his love. No, her brain just couldn't accept that he was bad. But, then, her heart was influencing her mind.

She sat on the bench until the sky was completely dark and had come to a decision. She had to confront him; she wanted — no needed — answers. She needed to look him in the eyes and determine if he was answering her questions truthfully. *But how do you face your executioner?* It would take all the courage she could muster, but she was determined to hear the truth from the horse's mouth — even if the horse might hoof her to death.

Shawn had decorated Natalia's bedroom with lit candles and waited for her to arrive. As he lounged on her bed, his cell phone rang. It was Tymeek.

"I need you to go to Aunt Freda's house and get my ride and then go by Kendell's and do that thing for me.You understand?"

Shawn thought about all the new arrangements he'd have to make for himself. He wouldn't be able to live in Tymeek's house any longer now that Tymeek knew about his relationship with Natalia. Shawn had his eye on a condo in Flushing anyway. The condo reminded him of her. She was refined and appreciated classy living.

"You listening, bro?" Tymeek's gruff voice snapped Shawn back to attention.

"What?"

"I said get that shit I left over by Kendell's crib. I already told him you comin' for it, aiight?"

"Yeah. I'll see you next week."

"No doubt, baby. The eagle is landing," Tymeek laughed. Then in a much more serious tone he said, "On the real, yo. I ain't get the chance to tell you. I'm proud of you. I'll see you on the outside. One." And with that, Tymeek hung up.

Hey, Miss Cee, can I speak to Aunt Freda?" Shawn asked as he lay back.

"Stretch! Why y'all don't call no more?"

"Been busy, ya know. But I still love y'all. Is Aunt Freda there? It's real important."

"Hold on, honey. Freda! Freda, come get the phone."

"Hello?"

"Hey, Aunt Free!" Shawn smiled when he heard her voice. He was truly fond of Aunt Freda, the coolest adult he had ever known. When he and Tymeek were little, she never scolded them or deprived them of just being children. She was always there when they needed her and would even stand up for them to their mother. After they stayed out too late, and their mother locked them out, she would take them in. She even bailed Tymeek out of jail the first time he got knocked by putting her house up. She was hip, always down to do whatever, and Shawn knew that, no matter what, Aunt Freda had his back. Sometimes, he wished she was his mother.

"Hi, baby. What happened to you? Why did you miss our Fourth of July picnic?"

"I forgot. I must've been taking care of some business. I'm sorry. You know I would've been there if I could have," he said humbly.

"You missed my macaroni and cheese, and please! All that chicken I made...child it disappeared quicker than a purse around your Uncle Derrick." They both laughed hard.

"You crazy aunt Free. How's Tasha?" he asked.

"You missed her, too. She came up for the holidays. She left last weekend. She asked about you. You know she moved to Rochester so she can start college this year?"

"Say word?"

"Word. You know what I mean, son?" she said in a manly voice. Shawn cracked up on his end, holding his sides.

"Aunt Free, I love you to death. I can't believe lil' boogabear is in college already."

"That's right. My baby studying to be a teacher. So when am I gonna see you?"

"Soon. Guess who's coming home next week?"

"Ty-Ty?" she asked excitedly.

"Yeah. I'm gonna come get his car. I'm gonna pick him up in it."

"Oh, I'm so glad he's getting out of there. I'm gonna have to talk to that boy when he get home. You know what I'll do? I'll throw him a welcome home party."

"Oh, yeah, that'll work. If you..." The door slammed. "Hold on a sec, Aunt Free," he laid the phone down and went to the foyer.

Natalia was leaning up against a wall with her arms crossed against her chest. Her eyes were red and puffy. Shawn knew right away that she had been crying. He approached her and was going to hug her but she pushed one arm out to stop him. Confused, he retrieved the phone and finished his conversation with Aunt Freda.

"Sorry about that...a party sounds good. Listen, if you need any money or anything let me know. I'll come tomorrow for the car, okay?"

"Okay, sweetie. See you tomorrow. Bring your appetite," she giggled.

"No doubt. See you tomorrow."

He threw the phone down and turned back to the foyer. Natalia was in the same place against the wall, staring at him, her body shaking with anger. He stared back.

"What's the problem?"

As she stood there looking at his handsome face, she nearly forgot about the problem. But then she came to her senses. "How long do I have left, Shawn?" she asked bitterly.

"What?" he asked.

She rolled her eyes. "Was I just a piece of ass to you? Tell me. How do you fuck someone knowing you're going to kill her? You'd have to be a sick, evil, insane!" she spat.

Shawn grew tired of her rambling and took a hold of her shoulders. "What...the...fuck...are you talking about?" he asked emphatically.

"I know everything...Shawn Wilson," Natalia cried out as she broke down. "You should've just killed me. It would've been better than this. I actually fell in love with you!" she sobbed.

Her face was wet with tears and her nose was running. She looked more innocent than Bambi.

Shawn let her go and sighed. The jig was up. He put one hand on the wall and rubbed the other over his face. "Nay..." he started but she cut him off.

"Don't. Don't call me that!"

He stared at the floor. It was impossible to look at her beautiful face now filled with disdain and hatred.

"Who told you?" he asked.

"What? Is that all you care about?" she shouted. "What about an explanation, Shawn? You owe me that much!"

"I know this shit looks real fucked up to you right now. But I wasn't gonna hurt you. I would never...listen, I'm gonna give up the life. I want us to be together, nahmean? I'm in love wit you. You know that." He had inched closer to her and tried to kiss her. She pushed his face away.

"I don't know any such thing. I don't even know you! But if you really love me, then you better stay the hell away from me."

He saw the anger flare in her eyes again as she turned to walk away.

He grabbed her arm. "Listen to me. You better believe that I love you. I wouldn't play myself if I didn't." He started to get loud. She tried to pry her arm free, but he tightened his grip. "Stop," he warned.

"Why? What are you gonna do? Huh? Kill me?" she said sarcastically. "I'm not afraid of you. I hate you. You're a liar and a murderer just like you're brother. You make me sick," she spat.

In response, he pushed her up against the wall and pressed his body up to hers. "I love you with all my heart. I never said that to no other woman. You know me. I'm the same guy you said you loved. Unless you were lying to me. Maybe it was all a game for you. But not for me."

Natalia looked away, but Shawn continued, "I'm about to make a major change. All that shit with my brother don't matter to me. I know you still love me. We could do this. Just gimme the chance to get shit situated." He kissed her forehead delicately. His lips were irresistibly soft. Natalia melted at his touch. He kissed her neck then her ear, flicking his tongue across her skin. Her heart was taking over...but then plain old good sense resumed control. She pushed him away and pounded his chest with her fists. Her anger didn't faze him in the least.

"I'm sorry," he whispered, nuzzling her ear. He pressed his lips against hers and said, "I do love you. Don't go." She could feel the vibration of his lips as he spoke. She wanted to collapse into his warmth. But she couldn't convince herself that what she now knew about him didn't matter. It did.

He caressed the side of her face and began to kiss her neck again. She fought the pleasurable sensations and smacked him. Again, he ignored her. She squirmed. "Do you really want me to stop?" he asked sensuously.

"Please," she answered flatly. He took a step backwards, looked into her eyes and saw that she was serious. He slowly backed away from her. She wiped her mouth with the back of her hand in disgust then turned on her heels and stormed out the front door.

"Fuck!" he yelled as he balled up his fist and punched a whole in the wall. He heard her start the car and ran outside barefoot. Natalia had already started to back out of the driveway. "Wait!" he shouted after her.

He ran back into the house to get his shoes and car keys. But by the time he returned to his car, Natalia was gone. He drove in search of her. He dialed her cell phone number, hoping that she would answer, but the phone just rang and rang.

André rubbed his thick fingers over Natalia's glistening back. "This is really starting to bother me now," he said as he poured more massage oil into the palm of his hand to rub onto her back.

"What is?" she asked with eyes closed.

"Shawn called the salon again yesterday looking for you." He kneaded his hands down to the small of her back.

"Aaaah," she moaned in delight. "Oh Andy, your hands feel so good." She pulled her hands from under her breasts and rested her chin on them. André pressed his thumbs more firmly into her back muscles.

"Did you hear what I said?" She turned over onto her back, displaying her erect nipples. "What are you doing, Nat?" he asked suspiciously.

"Oh, nothing," she said as she sat up and slid off the table. The towel fell to the floor.

"You just love parading your naked body around me, don't you?"

he shook his head.

"What's wrong? Getting horny?" she giggled.

"Stop trying to change the subject. What are you gonna do when he does find out where you're hiding?" André was afraid that Shawn would kill her now.

Natalia stepped into her purple panties and grabbed her bra from a wooden chair. "Can you hook this for me?" she handed the bra to him.

"Girl, I asked you a question." He snatched the bra and placed her breasts in the cups, holding them in place with his hands. "Put your arm in," he instructed. "Now the other."

"Andy, I don't want to think about him. But honestly, sometimes I find myself wanting to go to him. Deep down I miss him...oh how I miss him," she sighed as she adjusted the bra straps around her shoulders. Andre cinched the hooks and turned her around to look at him.

"Nat, I think you should see Mark again," he said as he buttoned her white cotton shirt. "He practically saved your life, and all you do is treat him like shit. That man truly loves you. He deserves more." He watched as she struggled to button the tiny button at the top of her leather jacket. He grew tired of watching her and helped her with it."

"Thanks, Andy." She removed her hair comb and let her hair fall past her shoulders. "I can't face him after all of this. I'm not ready to hear him say I told you so."

She grabbed her leather boots, slipped her feet into them and picked up her purse. André followed her into the stylists' area. "I'm going to Brooklyn to get some more of my things."

André pulled her to the side and spoke in a low whisper. "Nat, don't take this the wrong way...but I think you should go home now. You've worn out your welcome. I would like to have my place back to myself. It's been two weeks. I love you and the whole nine, but Adonis and I need to spend some time together."

"I'm sorry, André," Natalia smiled to hide her embarrassment. "I guess I've only been thinking about me, me, me. I didn't realize how selfish I've been. I'll take my things from your house tomorrow. Do you hate me?" she asked.

"Not yet," he answered with a chuckle.

"Well...I should go home and stay there."

André hugged her. "I love you, mammita. I really do. Keep movin' forward, baby. Don't let this stop you."

"Call me," she told him as she waved goodbye.

Thick smoke filled the room — as did hacking coughs.

"It's an honor and a privilege to have you wit us tonight, Pretty Ricky." Spank's eyes closed involuntarily as he spoke. He raised a blunt in the air in salute then brought it to his lips.

"You's a stupid muhfucka," Shawn laughed as he put the bottle to his lips and gulped the last bit of Moet. He tossed the empty bottle on the floor and grabbed another one. As he looked at the full bottle, he began to laugh.

"What's so funny?" Nut asked, blowing smoke out of his nose.

"I can't believe this shit. I'm high. I drank a whole bottle of Mo for dolo...I stopped doing this shit a long time ago and now look at me," he shook his head.

Nut patted his shoulder. "Pussy will do that to you," he said and burst out laughing. "Seriously, though, you can't let that shit get to you. I don't know why you stressin' her for. You know you can get mad bitches." Nut threw out an eight of spades.

Spank slapped his hand on the cards in the middle of the table and shouted, "Another book! Ha, ha!"

Shawn put the bottle down and leaned back into Nut's worn couch. Nut didn't understand. How could he? He never tasted Natalia's nectar. *I miss her,* Shawn thought. *I really miss her.* No other woman would do.

Tymeek burst into the room. "Freeze muthafuckas!" he shouted holding an imaginary gun in his hand. Everyone laughed. "I knew y'all would be in here loafing. Lazy slackers. Break it up and pack it up — now. Let's move." He took a swig from the Moet bottle. "I missed this stuff, sheeit!"

Nut and Spank giggled like children. Tymeek slapped Nut in the back of his head. "Come on, you fuckin' clowns, let's go!" He laughed at the sight of Nut rubbing his head. Spank laughed so hard tears came from his eyes. Tymeek turned his attention to Shawn. "You was smoking?" he asked.

"Yeah," Shawn answered with closed eyes and a goofy smile. Tymeek sat next to him.

"I thought you knew better," he said low so the others wouldn't hear.

"I do," Shawn replied, opening his eyes. "I'm just in a messed up mood...I needed something to mellow me out." His smile faded.

"Me and you gon' have a long talk later, aiight?"

"About what?" Shawn sat upright.

"About that fuckin' bitch that's got you whipped."

"Man, don't start that shit. I don't wanna hear that."

"What you don't wanna hear? I told you so or I told you so." Tymeek laughed.

Shawn sighed and rubbed his eyes. "On the real, yo, this shit is makin' me crazy. All I do is think about her."

"Don't let pussy rule you. I thought I taught you better than that." Tymeek shook his head in disapproval.

Shawn's eyelids felt heavy. He fought to keep them open. He didn't feel up to arguing. Tymeek palmed Shawn's head with his big dark hands and playfully shook it. "I told you this would happen, didn't I?" He got up from the couch offering Shawn his hand to help him up. "Hey, you too high to talk?" Tymeek asked.

"Dog, I'm tired," Shawn answered.

"You ain't tryna hear what I'm sayin' anyway," Tymeek chuckled.

"We'll talk when I get home." Shawn languidly followed him outside. The cold brisk air whipped around his face and woke him up a bit. "Damn! It's brick out here!" he exclaimed, shivering and trying to close his leather jacket. "Ay, yo, my ride is parked down the block. I'll meet you back at the house," he searched for his keys.

Tymeek stopped and turned. "You sure you aiight, man?"

"Yeah," he answered. He found his keys and headed down the block.

As he sat in the car waiting for it to warm up, his lids started feeling heavy again. He opened the driver side window all the way, but this time, the cold air didn't help much. He drove at a slow pace to be on the safe side, but then it took so long to get down the block, he changed his mind and started doing sixty.

Shawn was so glad to be home. He hurried inside and threw himself on his bed. Now that he was home, however, his fatigue started to fade — just when he needed it to stay. He didn't want to think of her, but Natalia crept into his mind anyway as he lay looking up at the ceiling. He had been celibate ever since she dumped him and was surprised to find that he wasn't the least bit interested any longer in sex with other women. Only when he thought of Natalia, did he become truly aroused. He came close to having sex with other women a few times, but they were all lacking once they got naked. Either they were too big in the wrong places, too small in others or had too many dents or stretch marks. Once he actually sprayed air freshener on a woman's pussy because of the odor. Of course, he did it to embarrass her, and after he put her out, he threw away his bed sheets. Natalia had a hold over him that no other could ever have. She was everything he had ever dreamed of and even though he swore that he would never become one, he had become a fool in love.

He looked over at the phone then at the bright neon green numbers on his alarm clock. It was two o'clock in the morning. "She has to be home," he said aloud. He realized that she would probably hang up on him, but as long as he could hear her voice, he didn't care.

He dialed Natalia's number and listened to the phone ring...and ring. He pressed the receiver to his ear, his breath suspended as he waited to hear the voice of his angel. He let the phone ring until the answering machine picked up. He waited for the beep. Then he waited until the machine disconnected.

He dialed again. Again, the phone rang and rang. But as he started to hang up, he heard her fumble to answer.

"Who is this?" Natalia asked sleepily.

Shawn's heart skipped a beat, and he knew it was real — he was in love with her. "I miss you, baby girl," he said weakly.

His deep voice was filled with a yearning that even she hadn't expected. She hadn't heard from him in weeks and assumed he had moved on. She had. Mark had given her a second chance and they resumed their relationship, back on the road to marriage. Shawn had become a memory but she hadn't forgotten him — she simply forced herself to pretend that he no longer mattered. The fact that he was a murderer who might have killed her helped stop her urges to see him. Some days were more difficult than others. She fabricated reasons to hate him yet kept certain memories etched in her mind to help spice up Mark's otherwise boring love-making. She fantacized that Mark was Shawn doing what only Shawn could do. But she constantly worried that one day she might slip and call out Shawn's name. How ironic that her fantasies of Shawn were the very thing that kept her renewed relationship with Mark stable.

"Shawn?" she asked, simultaneously surprised and thrilled.

"You're killing me, you know that?" he whispered.

She felt the flutter of butterflies in her stomach. She still wanted him so badly.

"Why are you calling me?" she tried to sound mean.

"Don't hang up. I can't say nothin' to change what I've done. But, I'm changing myself now, and you can help me. I can't give you up. I told you that."

"Are you threatening me?" she asked, raising her voice.

"Nah, baby girl, never that. I love you too much." The words echoed in her head. He must love me, she thought. If he didn't, she would have been dead by now. And if he didn't, he wouldn't keep after her. *But how can I love him in return knowing what I know?*

"Shawn you can't do this to me. Don't call me. Just forget about me." Her eyes filled with tears. It was difficult telling him to forget her when she didn't want to forget him. But it was the only reasonable thing to do.

"You know I can't do that. Now I know what I did to all those girls that I didn't care about. They would tell me they love me and how they wanna have my baby and shit like that. But I didn't care. I wasn't feelin' em' like that. Now the shoe is on the other foot. I'm the one gettin' clowned," he sighed and continued, "Please let me show you how serious I am. We can start over. I'll give up all this shit. I've been thinking about doing the legit thing, nahmean? I'll do it to get what we had again." He pleaded with such sincerity, she cried even harder. She covered the phone with her hand to stifle the sound.

"Baby girl? You heard me?"

She wiped the tears from her face and sniffled one last time. "I heard you," she answered in a shaky voice.

"Whatever I gotta do, just tell me."

He almost had her. But she realized that without trust, their relationship couldn't work. And she couldn't trust him anymore. She had to find a way to get rid of him, because the next time he tried, he probably would win her over. She couldn't be weak. She took a deep breath, and in a stern voice said, "I can't be with you, so please don't bother me anymore. If you love me like you say you do, don't ever call me again." She slammed the phone down.

Chapter Nine

❤

New Beginnings?

It was a cold, yet surprisingly sunny Autumn day. Hundreds of teenagers noisily filed into the auditorium. Natalia sat behind a desk covered with a cheap white vinyl tablecloth and a plastic vase with a bouquet of fake flowers. She checked her watch, remembering that she had one more school to visit after this one. The crowded auditorium became silent as the principal took the microphone from its stand. "Good morning students and faculty. We are privileged to have an illustrious motivational speaker with us this morning. I'm very pleased that she was able to meet with us so early. Let me introduce Ms. Natalia Foles."

The applause that followed her introduction signaled her cue. She took the microphone and walked to the center of the stage.

"Good morning, everyone. I hope that we're all wide awake," she smiled. A few snickers followed, but she ignored them and began her lecture.

"When I give lectures, I usually talk about the perpetual violence in urban communities. I do most of the talking then I take a few questions. But today, I want to ask you questions, and I want you to answer as honestly as possible. I don't have much time this morning, so I will select three students to come up on the stage." She walked to the edge of the stage and looked over the sea of faces. She randomly selected three students sitting in the first few rows. "Please join me on stage." As the teenagers strolled down the aisle and up the short flight of steps to the stage, Natalia put the microphone to her mouth again and said, "Okay, please quiet down. It's important that we hear what your peers have to say." The murmuring slowly subsided. The students stood in a line facing the audience. The first was a brown skinned boy with short dread locks piled on top of his head in four sections secured with rubber bands.

"What's your name?" she asked with a warm smile. She held the microphone near his mouth waiting for his response.

"Devin," he replied.

"My question to you is, What is it like in your neighborhood?" She passed him the microphone. He took it and began to fidget with it as he tried to come up with an answer. "It's kind of messed up. There's a lot of shootin' and cops come through a lot." He gave her back the microphone. The auditorium filled with laughter and snide remarks. Natalia hushed them.

"What do you think would make your neighborhood better? Maybe even make the people in your neighborhood act differently?" She put the microphone near his mouth again.

"Money," he chuckled, nervously shifting his weight back and forth.

"Exactly. Which brings me to my next question. What will you do to make money?" she asked with sincere interest. With his eyes fixed on the microphone he answered, "Well, I really wanna own a company. Like a production company...I like doing music. But first I'm gonna take up computers."

"I'm impressed, Devin. I wish you the best of luck and thank you."

She shook his hand, and he quickly left the stage. Then she turned to the audience and began part one of her lecture. "You see, the social economics of an area are always a factor when it comes to violence. People get depressed and desperate when they have no money, no means to support themselves and their families. It's a fact. If a gun can get you what you think is worth going to jail for, then you'll use it. But in the process, lives are wasted in the chase for the almighty dollar. Some would say that our capitalist system is the real culprit for the escalation of violence in this country. In truth, we all gain from capitalism in some form or fashion. Money is power all over the world — not just in America."

Natalia continued with more questions for the remaining two students on the stage and ended the next two parts of her lecture with a five minute educational film that she usually showed. She summarized her major points in closing and thanked the audience for its participation and undivided attention. And as always, she hoped that some of what she said would remain in the memories of the impressionable teenagers.

As she began to collect her papers and briefcase, the applause started. A mysterious man wearing dark sunglasses was standing and clapping in the back of the auditorium. Before long, all the students were standing and applauding. The man had started a chain reaction. Natalia squinted as she strained to look through the crowd. When her eyes found the man, she saw that it was Shawn. She grabbed her briefcase and her mauve Chinchilla coat from the chair, thanked the principal as he helped her with her coat and handed him a stack of pamphlets as she quickly left the stage. She wasn't quick enough. Shawn caught up with her and grabbed her arm.

"Don't treat me like that. You act like I'm gonna do something to you." His sexy lips moved slowly like in a dream. She searched for his eyes in his dark glasses. He removed them to help her.

"How did you know I would be here?" she asked, amazed at his persistence.

"I just wanted to talk to you." His hand was still on her arm. She looked down at it.

"Pardon me," he mumbled, quickly releasing her. She sighed and looked into his chiseled face.

"I told you to leave me alone, and I meant it," she said and began walking away. He only had to take a few steps to catch up with her. He jumped in front of her, blocking her path.

"Why?" he asked.

"Why? What the hell do you mean why?" she yelled.

"You trying to tell me you don't love me?" he asked raising his voice.

"Just leave me alone." She tried to get past him but he wouldn't budge.

"Tell me you don't love me, and maybe I will." It was a bluff. He hoped she wouldn't be able to say it. She couldn't. He tripped her up with his dare and it pissed her off. "I'm with someone, okay?" she shouted.

"So? That didn't stop you before," he quipped.

"You know what, Shawn Wilson? I've been as nice as I can possibly be considering all the shit you've done. But you don't deserve niceness. You kidnapped me! You're a drug dealer! You were supposed to kill me, and now you stand here and expect me to act as if everything is okay? Niggah, please! And for your information, I'm getting married so I don't need you stalking me. I've told you more than once but I'm going to tell you again since you act like you're deaf. I don't want to see you ever again!" Her hair whipped around as she stomped off. He followed her to her car, spun her around and wrapped his arms around her tightly.

"You don't want nobody else. I told you I'm willing to do what I gotta do to make this right and I'm gonna do it. You'll see..." He lovingly kissed her forehead. "I'm not giving up," he promised, looking deeply into her eyes as he caressed the side of her face. "I can't." He sensuously traced her lips with his thumb and gave her a peck on the cheek. Then he simply walked away. She watched him in silence. Her knees began to wobble, her face flushed. He left her intoxicated. The way he spoke, his mere essence, turned her to jelly. She fell into her car and sat there, stunned. She was unable to drive, let alone give another lecture.

Florida didn't look or feel like Florida this particular Saturday afternoon. It was pouring rain and there was a slight chill in the air. Shawn, Tymeek and his friend, Kam, waited outside the entrance of Budget Rent-a-car. Tymeek occasionally looked through the glass doors to see what was keeping his female friend. Inside, the Budget clerk placed the car keys on the counter and said, "Thank you for choosing Budget, Ms. Peterson."

"Thank you," she replied, and scooped up the keys. Her long, brightly colored nails hit the counter, and she checked to make sure they weren't damaged. Her very tight pants hugged her bubble butt and made it stick out even more. The clerk's eyes bugged out as he watched her leave. "Damn!" he exclaimed.

"Here you go," she said as she handed Tymeek the keys.

He slid his hand around her waist then downward and patted her ass. "Good lookin' out," he commended her.

She smiled to herself knowing that Tymeek was forever in business mode. This trip was no different. His main agenda was to hook up with his cousin who owned a successful real estate agency. The cousin was going to help him purchase land in Orlando. Tymeek planned to build houses and condominiums using his own construction company. In another year or two, he'd be able to retire.

They all piled into the car with their luggage and drove to a posh hotel. Tymeek and his companion reserved the presidential suite. And although Shawn and Kam's rooms were smaller, they were just as luxurious.

After settling in, Shawn left his room and knocked on Tymeek's door. His brother opened the door wide, and Shawn entered.

"Sit down and relax," Tymmek offered. Shawn looked like a small child on the huge sofa in front of the windows. Tymeek sat across from him in a cherrywood chair covered in elegant tufted velvet. Shawn was impressed. "This shit is real cool. This is what I want...all day, every day," he smiled.

Tymeek looked at his brother suspiciously.

"What you hinting at wit' your sneaky ass?" He knew that smile.

Shawn was going to ask for money.

"I want to open up a business for myself, buy a condo, ya know...go legit." Tymeek sat in deep concentration. His little brother was asking to get out and Tymeek understood. He never really wanted him in it in the first place. He couldn't say no to Shawn

"Don't do what I do even though I live and dress like a rich man." Truth be told, Tymeek wanted out, too, but Shawn said it first. His little brother wasn't in as deeply as he was so it would be easier for him. He had taught him the dos and don'ts of running the business. Shawn was older and wiser now — at least Tymeek hoped he was. And he was his only sibling, his baby brother, whom he had practically been a father to. If having a legitimate business was all he wanted, then financing his wishes would be the least he could do. He leaned forward and rested his elbows on his knees.

"Is fifty enough?" He folded his hands.

Shawn cracked half a smile. "Well, actually, Aunt Freda got the foreclosure list from her job and they gon' auction off this condo that I want. It's only gon' run about sixty. Plus I'm still negotiating with this car dealer on Merrick Blvd. who wanna sell me his dealership. But, it's gon' cost over a hundred."

"Come on, Shawn. I'm runnin' a business, nahmean? I can't give you all that. I got other shit I'm tryna do, damn." Tymeek rubbed his chin and shook his head. Shawn went into the kitchen and opened the small fridge. He took out one of the complimentary bottles of juice and opened it. Tymeek didn't pay him any attention. He was too preoccupied thinking about how to come up with the money. Shawn gulped down the juice and leaned on the counter.

"Don't pout like a little bitch, aiight? That's your damn problem. You too fuckin' spoiled. And it's all my fault," he sighed, sounding like a true parent. "What happened to the money Aunt Free got in those accounts?" Tymeek asked as walked over to the kitchen.

Shawn perked up. "Oh, yeah, I forgot all about those."

In the early days, when Tymeek first got into the drug game, he opened CD and IRA accounts at his aunt's bank using an expensive false identity. The money in them had grown over the past few years. Then with his business's expansion out of state into South Carolina, Virginia and Georgia, Tymeek decided to open another account. But for the large amount of money he had for the account, he needed a hook up — a friend whom he helped start an automobile insurance company (through which he laundered some of his cash). His friend made out a check in Aunt Freda's name as an award for a tragic non-existent car accident claim. For her assistance, Tymeek bought his aunt a car and gave her a substantially large down payment for her house. Luckily, he trusted her completely. Otherwise, his two hundred and thirty thousand dollars would have been long gone.

"I tell you what. I'm gonna find out how much is in that account now," he sighed and continued, "I'll see what I can do." Shawn couldn't hide his glee — it seeped right through his pores.

"I love you, man," he gushed and hugged Tymeek.

"Yeah, yeah," Tymeek chuckled and shook his head.

"But, you gon' pay me back little by little. Even if it's a free car. Understand?"

Shawn frowned. "Pay you back? Come on man, you know legit shit don't pay. Crime pays, niggah!" They busted out laughing.

Are you ready?" Mark asked enthusiastically.

Natalia grabbed hold of his hand. "OK! One, two...threeeeeeeee!" they shouted in unison and jumped from the platform. They dove through the air toward the water below, and, at the last second before they plunged into the swirling blue rapids, they were jerked upwards. They bounced back up into the air then fell down again before coming to a swaying stop. They dangled upside down inches from the frothy water, their fingertips grazing its surface.

Natalia's voice strained after screaming all the way down, "We did it!"

"That was incredible! Do you feel the adrenaline rushing through your body?" Mark asked.

"Yes! But how do we get out of this contraption?"

All of a sudden, a thick black cable attached to wide, heavy-duty metal struts was lowered between them. Mark grabbed Natalia, spun her around to vertical and secured her feet to the strut. He did the same for himself and then wrapped one hand around her waist as the other gripped the cable. She held onto him tightly. Once they were certain that they were safe, they began to kiss. Back on solid ground, they excitedly jumped up and down.

"That was soooo great!" Mark exclaimed as he shook the rig operator's hand.

"What now?" Natalia asked, exasperated.

"You tell me," he replied.

"I don't know, Mark. You're the director of this particular movie." The hot sun beat down on them, and Natalia realized that she couldn't take the heat anymore. "I need air conditioning!" she yelled.

Mark chuckled, "Of course, my princess. You wanna go back to the room?"

She shook her head up and down, "Yes, please!"

"OK." He crouched down. "Jump on my back, and I'll carry you back to the boat, my lady."

He tried to carry her all the way to the dock, but with the sun melting him and his hunger stealing his strength, he accepted defeat and put her down. By the time they reached the dock, they were pooped.

A string of white lights lit their path. The scene resembled a postcard.

The yacht rocked gently on crystal blue waters. Inside, they had everything they needed — a fully operational galley, two commodes, three televisions and four CD players — one in every room. Rave Chaunessy, one of Mark's most elite clients, designed the boat himself. He loaned it and use of his mansion to Mark as part of a generous reward for a job well done.

Mark helped Natalia aboard and turned on the light in the wooden and brass galley. Spending two days on a boat wasn't as bad as Natalia thought it would be, but she did feel like she was developing a case of claustrophobia.

As she sat at the table and caught her breath, Mark opened the refrigerator and found a can of guava nectar. "Here. Drink this. You look beat."

"I am. We've been up since the crack of dawn. We walked all the way to the beach, drove those stupid sand buggies, went jet-skiing, then bungee jumping, and we had to hike it all the way back here. Of course I'm beat!"

"Do I detect an attitude? Because I have the perfect remedy for that ailment." Natalia looked up from the Vogue magazine she'd been thumbing through. "Oh really? And what is that?" Her mouth twisted into a snide grin.

"I have to show you," he answered.

"You are such a bad boy. A very bad boy," she giggled.

Mark slid next to her and lay his head on her shoulder. "You know, in Italy when a man is hungry, the woman automatically starts cooking a huge meal for him," he smiled and put his arm around her. She went back to looking at the magazine, pretending not hear him.

"U hearah whut Iyah sayah toah U?" he asked with an Italian accent.

"I heard you...but I wasn't listening," she rolled her eyes. Mark laughed and tried to kiss her. She turned her head away. "Uh, uh, uh," she waved her finger at him.

"Well, I'm hungry. I'm going to make something to eat." He got up and began searching the cupboards for something edible. Natalia closed the magazine. She thought about how badly she wanted to sleep on dry land. They roughed it long enough. It was time to go back to civilization.

"Markie, can we please go to the house. I really don't want to spend another night on this boat." Mark slammed the cabinet door shut and put his hands on the sink in front of him.

"You are so damned spoiled!" He turned to look at her. "Would it kill you to sleep here one more night?" he shouted, startling her.

Natalia wasn't used to outbursts from Mark, but then, she had noticed that he hadn't been his usual agreeable self since they had gotten back together. In truth, she knew she didn't deserve the old, easy-going Mark and understood that he had every right not to kiss her ass anymore. She knew that she had to earn his trust again, and if that meant she'd have to walk on eggshells for a while, then she'd just have to put on a pair of galoshes.

"Mark, I'm feeling cramped in here. But it's okay, never mind." She picked up the magazine, left the room and went into the largest compartment with the biggest waterbed she had ever seen. She turned on the television and lay on her stomach. Mark came into the room.

"Nat, I didn't mean to yell at you like that," he apologized. "It's just that I thought this would be romantic. Just the two of us floating on the water in a gorgeous yacht. The mansion is great, but it's like being in a fancy hotel. At least we're alone on the boat. We can set sail and wake up to the horizon in the morning; make love as the boat sways on the ocean. I thought you'd be happy here. But if you're really unhappy, then we can go up to the house..." He sat next to her on the bed and stroked her hair. She rolled over onto her back and looked up into his clear blues. "I'm fine. I'm very happy." She ran her fingers across his chest. She slid her hand up his shirt, and whispered, "What was that you said about making love on the ocean?"

The boat rocked violently, waking Natalia. She jumped up and looked beside her. Mark wasn't there. She hopped out of bed and went up on deck. Mark sat behind the wheel smiling from ear to ear. He turned to look behind him as the early morning sun cast her shadow on the shiny wood deck. "Wow! I didn't know you were such an exhibitionist. Woohooo, mama!" He clapped and whistled. At first Natalia was confused but then it dawned on her that she was naked. She ran back down the steps into the main cabin's lavatory. She brushed her teeth and washed her face and put on a robe before going back on deck. "Okay, smart ass, where are you taking us? Better yet, do you really know how to sail this thing?" she asked, watching as the shoreline shrank. Mark took her hand and planted a precious kiss in her palm. "Don't be afraid. We're just going around the block, so to speak."

"Oh, that makes me feel so much better," she giggled. "I'm going to shower, okay?" she asked and gently pulled her hand from his. "Okay, honey," he said as he resumed his captain's stance behind the wheel.

After her shower, she flopped onto the wobbly waterbed and thought about his name, Delucchio. They discussed marriage on the plane. Mark was ready to jump the broom, step on the glass, whatever necessary to stake his claim and brand her a Delucchio. His mother was probably rolling over in her grave, wrestling with the fact that her handsome, blue eyed Italian son was marrying a black girl.

She rubbed her hands over her stomach. Mark was ready to be married, but she wasn't. Part of her still desired Shawn. But she also was not ready for the changes in her life. She'd have to compromise so much. And children. Mark would want to start a family right away. He had even mentioned it on the plane. To him, it was a prerequisite to marriage. *What am I waiting for?* she thought. *If I don't marry him. Some other lucky woman will come along and snatch him up!*

That one thought alone was all it took to convince her that first comes love then comes marriage then comes Natalia pushing a baby carriage.

The sky blue car glided down the smooth asphalt surface in Apopka. The trees lining the highways did nothing to block out the sun's persistent rays.

Shawn grew weary from the ride and rested his head on Denise's shoulder. "Get off me," she calmly muttered. He moved his head without hesitation, laughing as he slid a few inches away from her. "I guess only my brother got that privilege, huh?" he chuckled. A dreamy smile played on her lips, confirming his accusation. Tymeek peered into the rearview mirror and looked directly at her. She licked her lips sensuously and winked at him. Tymeek didn't give a damn about her — she was there only to help him remain anonymous and she knew it. The airplane tickets, hotel reservations and car rental were all in her name. There wasn't a trace of him in any computer in Florida. He wasn't one to play games and waste time pretending for any woman. He was always up-front and to the point about his intentions. Even still, women sought him out. If Shawn told him that he wanted to have sex with Denise, Tymeek would've given him permission and a few condoms. He was cold like that. She gave him a come hither stare as she watched his eyes dart from what she thought was her to the road in front of him. In actuality, he was only switching lanes and needed to see if any cars were coming from behind him.

Denise continued to adore the back of his hairless head. She looked like a twenty-year-old but was really thirty-three. Her skin was wrinkle free and her body was tight. She worked out fanatically to keep it that way. She enhanced her short hair by gluing in a couple of European weave tracks onto the back of her head. The front of her hair was parted into small sections of flat twists that made her look even younger. In the beginning, even though she was with Tymeek, she had a thing for Shawn. But over time, she realized that Shawn would never go for her. She looked over at him. He looked so good in his short-sleeved Moschino shirt. His low haircut accented the tiny natural curls on top of his head. The sun highlighted his curls and ricocheted off his three carat diamond earring. She shielded her eyes and gave him one last glance before she decided he wasn't her kind of man. She liked her men rough, rugged and raw — like Tymeek.

Tymeek didn't look anything like his brother. When they were children, they would accuse their mother of lying to them about having the same father. It wasn't until they were older that they realized she wasn't. Tymeek grew up to resemble his father, and Shawn looked exactly like his mother.

Tymeek had his father's ember complexion, light brown eyes and fuzzy brows. His looks weren't as refined as Shawn's. He had a keloid scar beneath his ear that reached down to his jaw — courtesy of a gangster-in-training he had beef with during his brief stay at Spofford. Tymeek wasn't as tall as Shawn, but his thick, bulging muscles made him look much bigger than he was. He wasn't reasonable like his little brother either. His temper, once ignited, made him a force to be reckoned with. Women were initially drawn to Tymeek because of his angelic eyes. But it was really his impudence and high street credibility that attracted them.

He pulled onto a wide strip of paved gravel surrounded by a freshly mowed lawn. Bright red tulip beds lined the driveway all the way to the yellow and white house. Tymeek blew his horn. Patience was definitely not high on his list of virtues.

"Lemme go ring the bell." Shawn opened the car door to step out.

"Nah, he knew I wanted to get there before noon," Tymeek assured him.

Shawn slammed the car door shut, and Tymeek blew his horn again. The curtains in the window parted and a small face peeked out from behind them. A pale palm swayed in the window, indicating that they should wait.

"Dis niggah, man. He know I got shit to do," Tymeek complained. He rested his hand on the steering wheel, nodding his head to the radio. The large white door opened and a lanky, beige man emerged holding a brown striped attaché case.

"Yo, Kam get in the back," Tymeek ordered. Kam got out, walked around to the driver's side and tried to squeeze his wide body into the backseat behind Tymeek.

Denise refused to give up her spot behind Tymeek. "Uh-uh, Kam. Go sit on the other side with Shawn." She waved her hand and rolled her eyes.

Shawn looked at her like she was crazy. "Who the fuck you think you are? I'm not gon' be squashed up next to that niggah. It's bad enough I gotta sit back here wit y'all in this fuckin Matchbox Pinto. Ay, yo Kam sit over there, man. Fuck what she say." Kam's jelly belly jiggled as he laughed. His stomach hung over jeans that were so low it looked like they were about to fall off of him. When he plopped down next to Denise the car jerked.

"Damn! You fat muthafucka!" Denise hollered. Kam just sucked his teeth and opened the window. Gerald opened the car door and sat in front, smiling when he noticed that Tymeek was laughing at all the commotion. "What up, cat daddy?" he asked, grinning, and he held out his fist. Tymeek pounded his fist down on it. "What up pimp?" Shawn patted Gerald's head as if he were a puppy.

"Hey, watch out there now, boy." Gerald chuckled then playfully punched Shawn in the shoulder. "Mr. Big, what's going on?" Gerald asked Tymeek.

"Ain't nuttin'," Tymeek replied with a weak smile. As a cousin to their father, Gerald was used to Tymeek's cavalier demeanor. He owned a prosperous real estate firm, and his wife owned and managed a daycare center. Gerald used to send money to them after their father died but stopped when they both passed the age of eighteen. Gerald's wife never forgot their birthdays and sent them cards every year. They always served as inspiration to Tymeek .

"You got the directions to the construction site?" Tymeek asked.

"Yeah. I went yesterday and checked it out." Gerald opened his attaché case and pulled out blueprints for Tymeek to review.

Tymeek glanced over at the blueprints. "I's rather see it in person, ya know?"

"I hear you, man."

When they arrived at the development site, they saw that two homes had been framed out, and the ground had been cleared for many more. As they drove down a pitted dirt road, they saw a dozen construction workers in sweat stained wife beaters and hard hats.

"So this is it?" Shawn asked Gerald.

Gerald looked out the window and nodded. "Yup. I know it doesn't look like much now, but believe me, it will be a magnificent development in a year or so. Trust me."

Tymeek and Gerald got out the car and walked toward one of the houses. Tymeek admired it. Kam, happy to stretch his chubby legs, got out of the car as well and stood next to Gerald. Denise slid over to the open car door, her cell phone antenna sticking out from the top of her Fendi bag. Shawn noticed it and snatched it from the bag without her knowing. She went to Tymeek, desperately trying to get his attention.

Gerald loaded them onto an oversized golf cart that the construction crew used to transport supplies from one end of the property to the other. Shawn remained with the car and made long distance phone calls on Denise's phone.

"You see, over there is the perfect spot to build the apartment complex. Im thinking condominiums. You could rent half with the option to buy and sell the other units," Gerald suggested.

"Yeah, I was thinking that the people out here ain't wit renting. Not when they can buy houses so cheap," Tymeek replied thoughtfully.

With Tymeek deep in thought, Denise grabbed the opportunity to get closer to him. She stepped to his side and threaded her manicured fingers between his strong thick ones. He didn't return her grip.

He marveled at the size of the property and of the income he could generate from it. He would finally be able to sit back and relax, have some real success and enjoy his money. Now, he had to work so hard just to protect it.

He was smiling to himself when he realized where his hand was. He snatched it from Denise's grip and gave her a stern look as if to say, you know better.

Tymeek decided that he wanted to own the development. All he had to do was come up with $750,000 and sign on the dotted line to seal the deal. Of course Gerald would hold the property for him — he wasn't stupid. He knew that Tymeek had the ability to make that kind of money in a matter of months.

"Well, what's the verdict?" Gerald asked, pulling out a cigarette from a gold-tone case.

Tymeek was pleased with what he saw. He could already see the sign that read: Welcome To Wilsonridge (the name he came up with a week before they flew into Florida). He could feel, smell and taste its success.

"Yeah, I want it, Gee. I just need a few months."

Gerald smiled as the word sold flashed across his mind.

"As a matter of fact, give me 'til February," Tymeek said with a far off look on his face. He rubbed his hand over his bald head and smiled. Shawn met him by the cart with Denise's cellular phone in his hand, "Y'all ready?" he asked.

"This is gon' be mine come February," Tymeek said with arms spread wide and a huge grin on his face. It was a smile Shawn hadn't seen in a long time.

"No doubt," he smiled back at his big brother. He wanted him to find peace...and it looked like this would be it.

They dropped Gerald off at his realty office then went to Universal Studios for the rest of the day. Shawn drove back to the hotel after dinner at a seafood restaurant in Miami. He and Kam got cleaned up and went out to a club. Denise and Tymeek retreated to their suite.

Tymeek undressed as soon as they closed the door and headed for the shower. Denise damn near tore her clothes off rushing to meet him in the shower. She dug into her bag and pulled out a condom. She knew that if she wanted him inside her she'd have to bring a raincoat for him. It was one of his rules. He had seen people die from AIDS and he vowed that he wouldn't.

She rushed into the bathroom, stepped into the shower and rubbed her body up against him. Her flat twists got wet but didn't unravel from the spray of water. The drop curls in the back of her hair went limp from the steam. Her pretty brown face looked into his adoringly. His eyes roamed her body before settling at her still perky mounds of flesh. Her tiny nipples stood erect, begging for his mouth's attention. He pushed her head back and licked her neck down to her eager nipples. He alternated nipples sucking them hard then nibbling gently. She moaned a high pitch moan and clasped her hands behind his head. He moved his fingers between her legs. Denise slid her hand down his neck then to his shoulders, grazing one of them with the plastic packet in her hand. He reached up and took the condom from her hand, turned her around and pressed on her back, pushing downward. She grabbed her ankles and anxiously waited her reward. He entered her slowly, then pumped with powerful, deep strokes. She arched her back with every stroke, moving her buttocks to match his rhythm. He moved his pelvis in circular motions exploring every inch of her inner walls with the length of his penis. After a while his pace quickened and his body went rigid. He pulled out from her, pulled off the condom and set it in the soap caddy. He began soaping up his body. She helped spread the lather over his bulging arms. When he was done soaping up he rinsed off and left her in the shower. She quickly rubbed soap on a rag and scrubbed herself clean and got out of the shower. She walked into the bedroom with a white towel bearing the silver hotel logo.

Tymeek was on his cell phone checking on his money, of course. She went through her bag and looked for one of the sexy lingerie sets she had packed. She found a black teddy with matching stockings. She took out her make-up bag and went into the bathroom. Using a cheap kohl eyeliner pencil she outlined her eyes then her lips. Later she filled them in with a matte shade of cappuccino. She put baby oil all over her body and put on the teddy and stockings. She turned out the bathroom light and went into the room. Tymeek was still on the phone. She was ready for round two, but it didn't look promising. She strutted in front of him anyway. He remained on the phone without acknowledging her presence. Frustrated, she left the room with an attitude. She plopped down on a dainty couch and propped her feet up on the throw pillows. Tymeek finished his call and went looking for her. He decided to give her what she wanted. "Come here," he said without emotion.

"No," she sulked. He took her hand and pulled. "Come on." That's all it took.

The line to get into the club was too orderly. Shawn and Kam were amazed.

"Damn, niggaz look like they waitin' at the DMV." Kam chuckled. Shawn searched for attractive women. Natalia still permeated his every thought, but he had gone too long without sex. It was driving him insane.

"Yo, I ain't waitin'. Let's go check out another club," Kam said as he checked his watch.

Shawn spotted a few pretty young things on line. He knew he would be able to get one of them without much effort. "Lemme holla at shorty first," Shawn said as he patted Kam's shoulder.

Kam shook his head and chuckled, "Aiight, Machiavelli."

They approached three young ladies who were already bashfully giggling. One was Hispanic, her long brown hair streaked with blonde, parted deeply on the left side and tucked behind her right ear. The tall one's skin was a darker shade of brown, but she looked like a transvestite with micro braids intertwined with blue yarn. Light blue eye shadow and glittery blue lips did nothing for her. The light skinned girl wore her hair just like Natalia's except it wasn't as long. She wore it parted in the middle with feathered layers framing her face. A few red scars dotted her cheeks. Shawn dismissed her and turned his attention to the bronzed Hispanic girl.

"This is a long line...why don't y'all go partyin' with us instead," he suggested in a sultry tone. The Hispanic girl smiled nervously. She couldn't look him in the eyes. He took her hand and held it with both of his. Sounding like Al Pacino in "Scarface" he said, "Come go wit me and my friend, mami."

His charismatic voice, model face and Versace suit was too much for her to handle. She surrendered. "Where to?" she asked without regard to her friends.

The tall one said, "I don't know about you, Brenda, but I'm not leaving." She folded her arms and leaned back against the brick wall. The light skinned girl looked at Shawn and asked, "Y'all are from New York?"

"Yeah," Shawn answered smiling his winning smile.

"Who else is wit you?" the light skinned girl asked as she glanced at Kam. "It's just me and my man right there." She sucked her teeth and sighed a long drawn out sigh.

"It ain't gotta be all that, ma. I'ma make sure you have fun." Shawn's eyes sensuously hinted at something more. She giggled at his New York accent.

"So whut up, mami? You gon' hang wit papi chulo or what?" he asked. She smiled bashfully and looked up at the tall girl as if to get permission. But the tall one just turned away, upset that none of Shawn's attention was on her.

"So where you gonna take us?" Brenda asked.

"Where y'all wanna go?"

The tall one blurted, "I wanna get my groove on."

Shawn turned to look at Kam who was busy smoking a cigarette and watching the fancy cars pull into the parking lot. "Ay, yo, Kam. You wanna go to another club?"

"It beats standin' out this bitch," Kam replied flicking his cigarette to the ground.

"Aiight," Shawn shrugged. "Let's go."

"We came in Darnisha's car," Brenda said with a worried look.

"Oh, aiight. You ride wit me ma. Your girls can follow," Shawn said. They all piled into their cars and were off to Island Z, a club that played mostly reggae music.

My name is Shawn, by the way," he whispered into Brenda's ear as their bodies swayed together on the dance floor to the rhythmic pounding of the bass.

"I'm Brenda," she giggled in response.

"You look mad young...so am I fuckin' wit jail bait or what?"

"No, I'm not jail bait. I'm twenty-one going on twenty-two the end of this month."

"Oh aiight, cuz I'm not tryna get locked up tonight," he laughed and pressed her closer to him. "You Puerto Rican?"

"Cuban," she answered. She loved the way he smelled, an exotic combination of coconut and Gió cologne. And she loved the way his warm hands caressed her waist. He made her feel like she was the only woman in the club. Even when he went to the bar and ordered her a drink, he ignored a curvaceous woman wearing a fish net gown over a thong.

Shawn knew that he had Brenda right where he wanted her, and the beauty of it was that she had no idea.

It was well past two a.m. and Shawn was ready. Brenda's friends were nowhere in sight, and Kam was at the bar with a short, chubby, baby-faced girl. It was time to strike. "I'ma tell you straight up, Brenda. I want you." Her face turned red, and she nervously looked away.

"Let's go," he said as he took her hand and helped her down from the high stool.

"What about my friends?" she asked as she looked around the club for them.

"Find 'em and tell 'em you're leaving."

She smiled up at him, "Okay."

"Go now. I'm gonna go find my man."

She hurried off in search of her friends, and Shawn found Kam at the end of the bar with his young lovely. He agreed to take a cab back to the hotel.

Brenda returned. "You ready?" Shawn asked.

"Yes," she replied. But was she really?

In the car, Shawn rubbed her thigh. He complimented her long blonde streaked hair and her soft, tanned skin. He even told her that she was his first and only choice in Florida. She was extremely flattered, as he knew she would be.

He parked and slid his arm around her neck. As they walked to his hotel, he poured on the charm. They kissed in the elevator. His warm mouth excited her.

He opened the door to his suite and let her walk in ahead of him. He wanted her to be impressed with its size and luxury. She was a bit shy so he eased her into the bedroom with sweet pecks on her face and lips. He gently lay her down on the bed and reached up under her mini skirt and pulled down her pink cotton panties. She had a tattoo of a kitten just at the edge of her pubic hairs. It excited him.

He undressed in seconds and slipped a condom over his penis so quickly that she didn't even see him do it. He rubbed his cock between her legs. The sensation radiated warmth and moisture from her. As innocent as she looked, she purred like a kitten, panted like a dog and begged him to stick it in.

Brenda moaned and raised her hips to meet his. For the first time in Shawn's sexual history, he didn't feel like coming.

"I wanna ride it," she said breathing heavily. He couldn't stop her in the midst of her heat so he lay on his back and closed his eyes. She hopped onto him and rode him ferociously, bouncing up and down, slamming her buttocks onto his thighs. Shawn opened his eyes to watch the show. Her breasts weren't very big, but her huge maroon nipples tempted him. He began to knead them with his fingers. And instinctively, he raised his hips towards her. He had to give her credit for all her effort. She managed to work him into a frenzy.

As he felt his excitement escalate, he pulled her off, laid her on her stomach and entered her from behind. He didn't want to see her face when he exploded. He wanted to imagine that Natalia's buttocks were slapping against him. He wanted to turn Brenda over and see Natalia's face. The more he thought about her, the more his passion rose until it erupted. He let out an exasperated sigh, rolled off Brenda and pulled off the condom. He went into the bathroom and flushed it.

Brenda wasn't finished, however, and she let him know it. She rushed into the bathroom behind him. "More," she pleaded. But for him, the thrill was gone.

The pitiful look in her eyes, however, made him say, "Aiight gimme a half hour."

He never before in his life needed a half hour to recuperate. But he now realized the difference between casual sex and lovemaking.

Before he met Natalia, he could knock a woman out with one powerful, blissful sexual blow and still keep going and going like the Energizer bunny. His stamina in the bedroom used to be relentless. Now with Brenda, he couldn't maintain a hard-on to save his life. Sex with Natalia was different because he had feelings for her, deep feelings. He respected her, and when he caressed her, his heart was really in it. He and Natalia were tuned into each other's inner soul, and, intuitively, they fulfilled each other's sexual deficit.

Shawn looked down at his flaccid member and wondered how this could happen to him of all people. Brenda wrapped her arms around him and laid her head on his smooth chest. He wanted to push her away, tell her to get dressed and get out. He needed, no wanted Natalia. But to spite her, he had to find a way to go another round with Brenda and enjoy it.

He kissed her forehead then slowly pushed her head downward. She objected by squirming under the pressure from his hand. "What's wrong?" he asked, confused at her resistance.

"Let's go to the bed," she said and tugged his hand. He stood at the edge of the bed waiting for her to get on her knees. "Can we do a sixty-nine?" she asked without looking into his face. *Sixty-nine? Is this bitch crazy?* Shawn sat down and shook his head. "Nah. I don't think so."

Brenda was shocked. "Why not?" she asked. Shawn wasn't up for explaining, and he didn't want to hurt her feelings either but she had to go. "I'ma take you home. I'm mad tired."

He got up and began dressing. It was too late — he had already hurt her feelings. She thought maybe she had gone too wild, and he thought she was a slut. Or maybe her body had repulsed him somehow. Whatever it was, she dressed knowing that she would never hear from him again.

Chapter Ten

❤

RETURN OF THE MACK

It was over. She thanked God that they were home.

Natalia had tan lines and her hair had lightened from the sun's continuous torture. Even though Mark told her that he loved the blonde highlights, she wasn't too pleased. She thought it made her hair look dusty. Mark brought her back to Brooklyn Heights. He didn't go in with her because he had an early meeting the next day. Secretly, he was happy that she chose to stay in Brooklyn a while longer.

When she entered her apartment, Renée was straightening up the living room. Natalia had asked her to housesit while she was away.

"Hey, you're home!" Renée shouted and rushed to hug her boss. As soon as the women finished embracing, the doorbell rang. Natalia assumed it was Mark and sighed as she opened the door.

"Hey-ee girl! Long time no see." Tracy beamed.

"Oh my God! Tracy!" The two beautiful women kissed each other's cheek and embraced. "I thought you moved to England!" Natalia cried as she wiped away lipstick from Tracy's cheek.

"I did. Don't you hear my accent?"

"Well, you do sound sophisticatedly British," Natalia giggled. "Come in, come in," Natalia urged as she took the heavy bag from Tracy.

"I'm so glad to see you. I've missed you," Tracy said as she ran her fingers through her naturally curly hair. Natalia loved her shiny, auburn coils.

"And I love the highlights in yours!"

"Oh, please. The sun did this to me," Natalia said as she lifted a bleached strand. "I'm going to have André fix this mess. I don't like it."

"Don't. I like the way it looks," Tracy smiled.

Natalia respected Tracy's opinions and, thus, had second thoughts about going to André.

Tracy was the only female that Natalia had ever called friend. A real friend.

They moved to the couch and sat facing each other. Renée came down the stairs lugging an electric blue gym bag. "Hi there," Renée said as she slung the bag over her shoulder.

"Renée, this is Tracy, a very dear, missed friend." Natalia patted Tracy's thigh. Tracy smiled a broad smile and reached out her hand. "Pleasure to meet you, Renée."

"Nice meeting you too. You're English?" Renee asked.

"No. I've just been living there for the past two years."

"Oh. I love the accent. Nat, I'm going to run. I'm worried about Poopsie. I'm scared that she could be starving to death."

Tracy raised an eyebrow, "Who's Poopsie? Please tell me that's not your baby's name," she laughed. So did Renée. "No, no. She's my cat. My neighbor was supposed to check on her from time to time, but I can't seem to get in touch with him. Oh, by the way Nat. You have a ten o'clock with Mr. Vanget next Wednesday. Please don't forget because he says he won't reschedule anymore. Okay? Well, bye for now," she waved at them and left.

Tracy removed her blue fox coat and laid it on the arm of the couch.

"I tried to call you, but your number was disconnected. And I didn't want to ask your dad because I didn't want to worry him. Why didn't you call me? I mean we're best friends, and I didn't even know where you were, Trace." Natalia's eyes narrowed.

"I know. I'm so sorry, Nat. It was a rushed decision." Tracy paused for effect and continued, "I don't know if you heard or not, but Steven is in jail. He tried to kill me. I don't know what I was thinking when I moved in with him." Natalia looked at her in horror. "Nat, you remember that guy he used to hang out with all the time? The light-skinned one?"

"Yeah...Charles?" Natalia recalled.

"Yes, that's right. Well, that ass wipe Steven accused me of fucking him. Can you believe it? After all the shit he put me through, he then accuses me of cheating on him! Then he beat the shit out of me in the damned street."

Natalia got up and changed the subject," Are you thirsty?" Steven was never good to Tracy, and Natalia didn't want her friend to dwell on him a second longer.

"No." Tracy hung her head, ashamed that she had let a man treat her so badly. She knew Natalia wouldn't say I told you so, but she was probably thinking it.

Natalia took a seat again and asked, "So how'd you know I was here?"

"Actually, I didn't. I visited my dad yesterday and he told me that you were living here again. So I checked out of the Marriott, dropped off most of my things at home and came here with only the barest necessities."

"Excuse me? And who said you could stay here?" Natalia jokingly asked. Tracy ignored her.

"So, fill me in on what's been going on in your life."

Tracy slid off the sofa and sat yoga style on the floor.

Natalia joined her. "No, you first."

"Okay, then." Tracy pushed her ringlets out of her eyes and settled into her yoga position. "I went to England with my Uncle Vaughn. At first, I stayed with him and his new wife. But then I met this nice girl named Sherrie, and she invited me to move into her flat in London. She got me a job working with her at the Rutherford Boutique. Her fiancé was this handsome black guy named Leonard. And, yes, Sherrie was white. Anyway, they'd always take me out with them. One night we all went to a pub and got very drunk. When we got back to the flat, I went straight into my room. But, Sherrie followed me and asked me to watch them have sex. Well, needless to say they didn't expect me to just watch...they begged me to join them. A ménage à trois. So I did. It was fun. But after a while, Leonard would come to see me when Sherrie wasn't home. I went along with it for a while until she caught us in the act. Of course she kicked me out and tried to have me fired, but it didn't work. Anyway, it wasn't so bad. We worked different schedules. But then I decided to move back in with my uncle. It was okay for a while, but I started to miss New York like crazy. So I saved my money, quit my job and came home. The end."

Natalia shook her head in disbelief. *Why is it she stirs up trouble wherever she goes?* But Tracy lived her life carefree. She did and said whatever she wanted, and Natalia admired her for it.

"My, my. Weren't you busy?" Natalia chuckled.

"You know me."

"So you had sex with the girl, too?" Natalia naively asked.

Tracy laughed hysterically at her friend. "I did say ménage à trois, didn't I?"

"Doesn't that mean three people having sex with each other?"

"Duh! Of course it does."

Natalia was flabbergasted. That could only mean that Tracy was bisexual. "How long have you liked w-women?"

"Oh, Nat. I'm not gay. I'm just kinky is all. And don't flatter yourself thinking that I've been secretly lusting after you!" she laughed.

"So tell me all about your adventures...if you've had any. I know how boring you and what's-his-face are."

"His name is Mark."

"I know. I'm just kidding."

"I don't know if I should tell you my story...you probably won't be able to handle it," she said, grinning.

Tracy tilted her head to the side, "You have something juicy to dish? You? Oh, do tell."

Natalia felt strangely proud, knowing that her story was going to knock Tracy's socks off.

For a half hour, she spilled all the details of her drama. At the conclusion, Tracy had to excuse herself to go to the bathroom.

"I can't believe it!" Tracy exclaimed as she walked out of the bathroom zipping up her jeans. "What a soap opera cliff hanger!" she sat on the couch. "You wanna know what I think?" Tracy asked.

"Not really," Natalia chuckled. "But go ahead. I don't think I'd be able to stop you anyway!"

"Nat, you have led such a tragically boring, conservative life for so long that I think you deserve a little excitement. I also think that you shouldn't jump into marriage right now. You're still young. You have time. If I were you, and I wish I was right about now, I'd keep em' both. Neither one has to know."

Natalia blushed. Tracy had just verbalized what she had been thinking all along.

"It won't work, Trace. Mark caught me once already. What makes you think he won't catch me again?"

"Honey, it was your first time — you're an amateur. You have to be trained by a pro before you can try it at home, sweetie," Tracy giggled.

"I can't do it," Natalia said, her face suddenly child-like and innocent. Then a radiant smile appeared. "I'm getting married in January." She paused then continued, "It's funny that you should reappear again — now of all times. You can be my maid of honor!"

"Same old Natalia." Tracy shook her head, "I wish I had your problem. If I had a sexy guy like Shawn, I'd have no trouble deciding."

"Of course you wouldn't. You're into criminals!" she laughed.

"Oh, please! He loves you and fucks the hell out of you, but you're going to marry good ol' safe Mark. You just finished saying that

Mark is hopeless in bed. Damn, you don't even have decent orgasms with him!" Tracy hopped up and headed for the kitchen. "He's corny, but he's got a big cock. That's the only thing that saves him in my book."

Natalia laughed. Everything Tracy said was true. But how could she cheat on Mark again? He was a good man, and he didn't deserve it.

Tracy stuck her head out of the kitchen. "I need to party. I know I'm asking the wrong person, but where's the party tonight?"

"Well, I know this one club where all the men are pimps and hustlers...your kind of crowd."

"Ha, ha, very funny. Seriously, Nat. I need to go out and mingle with my New Yorkers...I've missed them so."

"I am serious. Shawn took me on our first official date there. It's a flashy place, though. Or maybe you'd prefer the Nite Spot."

Tracy frowned. "The Nite Spot? Even I know that that club is so passé. I can't even believe it's still open! Are you sure those are the only clubs you know of?"

"Yes. I'm sorry that I'm not as hip as you, but I've sort of been caught up in a monogamous relationship."

"I see. Well, I don't want to go to the Nite Spot. Let's see how good you're boyfriend's club is." Tracy grinned, picked up her bag and brought it over to the couch. She took off her boots and socks and placed them near the bag. "I've got this really sexy dress I'd like to wear." She dug into the bag and pulled out a skimpy black tube dress. "Look at this Nat. Straight from Pa-ree, dahling."

Natalia admired the dress, "I see that you haven't changed one bit!" Natalia shook her head, and they laughed and laughed. It was just like old times again.

The group dispersed from the Delta terminal at JFK airport. Shawn and Tymeek took a cab together; Denise reluctantly shared one with Kam.

The ride home to Saint Albans took no time at all. In a hurry to start earning money again, Tymeek rushed into the house, gathered a few things and ran out again. He had to touch base with his workers then catch a shuttle to Atlanta. He was determined to open Wilsonridge as soon as possible. "I'll be back Sunday," Tymeek said, giving Shawn a pound and brotherly hug.

Shawn closed the front door after his brother and stood on the porch watching the colorful autumn leaves fall to the ground. He dialed Nut's number. "Yo, Ty is on his way. Everything aiight?" he asked.

"Yeah. So whut up, playa?" Nut sounded excited.

"Ain't nuttin'. I'm chillin'...bored as hell, though. So, what up for da night?"

"I don't know yet."

"What's up wit Spank and dem?"

"They here, chillin'. I dropped that shit off already and you know Spank ain't never got shit to do." Shawn could hear laughter in the background.

"Yo, let's go to the Stardome," Nut finally suggested.

Shawn thought about it for a second. "Yeah, we can do that. So y'all wanna meet there around twelve?"

"Nah, come get me from the crib. Spank can ride with Big Rob."

"I'ma be there like eleven-thirty, so be ready aiight?"

"Yeah, yeah," Nut chuckled then hung up. Shawn then called Aunt Freda to inquire about the money. They spoke for an hour discussing his plan to buy the condo, Shawn's love life and Tymeek's plans. When he got off the phone, he went through his closet and pulled together a killer outfit. He selected a pair of black slacks and an ice blue pullover. To top it all off, he chose a short brimmed black hat and a blue mink overcoat. He went to the bathroom and looked in the mirror. *How can she not want me?* he asked his reflection.

It was almost one o'clock when he pulled up in front of Nut's house.

"Niggah, I thought you said eleven-thirty."

"Just get in," Shawn chuckled.

"Damn, niggah! What the fuck were you doing?" Nut plopped down in the passenger's seat.

"I'm here, ain't I? And niggah respect my vehicle."

Nut laughed and Shawn drove off.

"I need some pussy tonight for real," Nut stated as he pulled out a cigarette. Shawn chuckled to himself — he was just thinking the exact same thing.

"You got condoms?" Shawn asked.

"Hell yes. I'm gon' get some ass tonight!"

"My sloppy seconds?" Shawn laughed.

"Whateva, niggah." Nut replied, knowing that there was some truth in what Shawn said. Shawn would always attract the pretty women like a magnet. The ones he didn't scoop who were hanging with the one he did would eventually notice Nut's hazel eyes (the only thing he had going for him) and give him some play. It wasn't that Nut was ugly, but his face didn't seem to be put together quite right. His lips were too thin, his forehead sloped downward, and his nose was so wide it took up most of his face.

"So I guess wifey don't mean shit no more, huh?" Nut asked.

"I can't wait forever, man. Anyway, she's marrying that white muthafucka. It's all good though." Shawn realized that his emotions were showing and quickly recovered. "A niggah definitely need some new pussy."

"So how was Florida?" Nut asked as he unzipped his black mink bomber jacket.

"I was with this Cuban girl, and I couldn't keep my dick hard for nuttin'. It was ill, yo. I couldn't keep my shit up. I bust only once. Can you believe that? You know my steez, son. She was young and pretty, too, nahmean? But I couldn't even blaze that right." He shook his head slowly. "But tonight...that shit ain't gon' happen."

Shawn parked in front of the club and searched for his human car alarm. He was nowhere in sight. "Where is that niggah? You see him?" he asked Nut. Nut stuck his head out the window and looked up and down the block. "Nah, I don't see him."

"I'ma park in the lot then. You wanna get out now?"

"Nah, I'll stay wit you," Nut said as he pulled out another cigarette.

Shawn parked the car, and they walked into the club without waiting on line or paying as usual. Shawn took his place at one of the VIP tables in the lounge as Nut scanned the crowd. "It's packed tonight."

Shawn took off his coat and laid it over the booth next to him. Nut took off his jacket and placed it on top of Shawn's coat. "Get that cat off my shit!" Shawn scolded.

"Fuck your squirrel coat, you fake ass pimp!" They laughed. "Service, please." Shawn snapped his fingers at the waitress as she hurried past their table. She paused and noticed who it was. "I'm sorry, Shawn. It's kind of busy tonight."

"It's okay. I was just fuckin' wit you. When you get a chance, can you bring two bottles of Cris?"

"Is that all?" she smiled.

"For now," he smiled back.

"Where that niggah Spank at?" Nut looked around.

"He probably ain't comin," Shawn replied as he removed his hat and placed it on the table.

Nut shrugged his shoulders. "Oh well, more Cris for me."

Twenty minutes later, Spank eased over to the table. "Whut up niggaz?" he shouted.

"Sit your Lurch ass down," Shawn chuckled.

"Where you was at? Smoking crack wit your moms again?" Nut

let out a hearty laugh.

"Nah, bitch. But your moms sure can toss a mean salad. I had that bitch wearing my shit like a moustache."

"Oh yeah, niggah? Well I had your moms licking the sweat from my balls cuz you know that bitch will do anything for a dollar," Nut howled.

"Both y'all corny muthafuckaz need to shut up." Shawn shook his head. The waitress returned with two bottles of Cristal and placed them on the table along with two glasses.

"We're going to need another glass," Shawn said, leaning back into his seat.

"Rob is coming. He's parking the car," Spank informed him.

"Okay, two more coming up," she smiled and left.

"I'ma go check on Rob," Spank said getting up from his chair. "Y'all want me to bring back some bitches?"

Natalia took so long to decide what she'd wear that they didn't leave until well after midnight. Tracy had assured her that they would be fashionably late. "Besides, after midnight is the best time to go clubbing. We'll make a grand entrance."

Natalia opted to call a car service instead of driving. She didn't want to worry about driving and parking or having her Navigator stolen.

The cab driver tooted his horn a couple of times before they realized he had arrived.

"All the way to Queens we go!" Tracy said enthusiastically as she tucked her lipstick into her purse.

"Natalia?" Tracy shook her arm.

"I'm sorry, what were you saying?"

"Oh, never mind. Hey, I think our driver needs some directions." Natalia instructed the driver on what exit to use and what street to take.

Finally, Tracy asked the inevitable, "So what if we run into Shawn?"

Natalia looked away. "I-I don't think he'll be there," she answered looking out the window.

"Now, you know that I know what you think I don't know," she gently nudged Natalia's chin and forced her to face her. "You're secretly dying inside aren't you? Wishing that he'll be there, aren't you?"

"Once again, Colombo, you've solved the mystery."

"Nat, it's okay. You're human. Stop limiting yourself. If you want him, have him. It's not the end of the world." She put her arm around her friend and rested her hand on her shoulder.

"It's just that I keep feeling so guilty about it. I really feel that Mark is a good man with good intentions..."

Tracy patted her shoulder and said, "We all cheat. It may not happen right now, it could even be years into a marriage or a relationship. And not because of anything our spouses, girlfriends or boyfriends do...it's just in our nature. We're primitive creatures. We derived from Neanderthals who copulated with everything in the cave. I'm talking, wild, pre-historic orgies. You can't be condemned for natural, biological urges. Gimme a break."

Natalia laughed loud, "It figures you'd come up with such an eloquent justification for infidelity."

"It's a fact," Tracy grinned.

"I'm not like you, Tracy. I'd be so guilt-ridden, I'd probably tell on myself!"

"Not if I can help it." Tracy snapped her fingers, and they laughed and laughed.

The vivid "Stardome" sign was a beacon in the middle of the dark, barren street.

"Yay! We've made it!" Tracy bounced up and down.

"How much?" Natalia asked.

"Twenty-four," the cab driver answered.

"My goodness. You'd think we left the state!" Tracy exclaimed.

Either they were really late or really early because there was no line at the door. Natalia and Tracy walked past the bouncers, and, as Tracy predicted, they immediately caused a stir. The bouncer's eyes widened and his jaw dropped. "Ladies, I can't take it. I have to let y'all in free," he said, smiling from ear to ear.

"Thank you," they both simpered. A tall man with two gold hoop earrings in his ear took Natalia's hand into his and asked, "Will you bless me with your phone number, please?" Natalia politely replied, "I'm engaged," and gently pulled her hand away. "He's a lucky man. A very lucky man."

When they entered the ballroom, heads turned. "I feel like an alien," Tracy giggled.

Natalia slipped off her coat. "I'm going to check our coats." Natalia waited for Tracy to take hers off.

"I'm going to find the bar. Meet me there."

Tracy squeezed her way through the crowd of scantily clad bodies and ended up at the bar. "You're best Cognac, please...on the rocks," she ordered.

"You thirsty, beautiful?" a masculine voice whispered in her ear.

"Why else would I be at the bar?" she answered sarcastically without turning around.

"I wasn't talking about a drink," he replied.

Tracy spun around on the barstool to face him. "That was really lame," she said with half a smile.

"What's your name, gorgeous?" he asked ignoring her snide comment.

"Tracy. And who might you be?" She looked him up and down and could tell by the way he hunched over that he was very tall. He had deep brown skin and was very attractive.

"Here you go miss," the bartender said as he placed her drink on the bar.

"My name is Spank," he finally answered.

"Are you a Little Rascal or what?" she giggled.

"Only if you want me to be," he retorted with a brilliant smile. "Me and my friends are up in the VIP lounge. I'd like to take you up wit me."

"Well, I have to wait for my girlfriend."

"Aiight," he said and waited with her at the bar. Spank was dressed in a dark brown sweater, brown slacks and a pair of brown alligator shoes.

"So are you a pimp or a hustler?" she asked with a harmonious giggle. He grinned and said, "Neither." Just then Natalia stepped between them.

"Okay, you lush, which poison did you order?"

Tracy gently nudged her arm to alert her of her faux pas. "Nat, this is Spanky."

Natalia looked over at him thinking how familiar the name sounded. Oh yeah, The Little Rascals. "Hello," she said reaching out her hand.

"I see beautiful birds flock together," he said, shaking her hand firmly, "And my name is just Spank. No 'y' at the end," he said with his eyes on Tracy. "I like your accent. Don't tell me you're just visiting."

"No. I'm here to stay." She smiled seductively at him.

"Good. So you ready?" He got off the stool and looked at Natalia again. *Damn she looks familiar,* he thought to himself.

"Go where?" Natalia asked.

"To the VIP lounge," Spank said as he held out his hand to Tracy. Tracy whispered into Natalia's ear, "He's so hot. Please just go up with us for a little while." Natalia rolled her eyes and sighed.

They climbed the steps to the VIP lounge. Spank had his arm around Tracy's waist and was whispering sweet nothings in her ear as she sipped her cognac and giggled. Natalia accidentally dropped her purse and bent down to pick it up. Spank pulled out a chair at the table for Tracy to sit down. Natalia stood up and straightened her dress. When she looked up again, her mouth fell open as she stared into Shawn's face. Shawn's eyes nearly popped out of his head. Surprised, they both blurted out each other's name at the same time. Nut leaned back in his chair, enjoying the moment.

Spank looked over at Shawn. "Y'all know each other?"

Shawn ignored him and just stared at Natalia. Tracy watched both of their reactions and smiled a huge smile, "So you must be the infamous Shawn. It's nice to meet you."

For a second, Shawn's concentration was broken. "How you doin'?" he said quickly as he got up from his chair and walked around the table to Natalia. He gently took her arm and guided her to an intimate corner of the room. "What are you doing here?" he asked.

"I brought my friend...I'm only here...she wanted to come," she stammered.

Shawn cupped her face with his hands. She was really there, and he could only believe that fate had intervened.

"What are you doing here? Never mind, you don't have to answer that," she said nervously.

"Believe it or not, I came here to get you out of my system. But, you see...fate wants us together. It brought you here to me," he whispered sweetly. He kissed her lips, parting them with his warm tongue and held onto her tightly. She couldn't fight his kiss. She didn't want to. She missed him so much.

"Come home with me," he ordered so sweetly it didn't seem like the command it was.

"I-I can't."

"You can. Even if I have to kidnap you again," he joked. She looked up into his face, and, right then, she let go of her guilt and rid herself of the good girl persona she had so desperately tried to maintain. She wanted to be with him tonight...and tomorrow. His kiss reminded her of what she had been missing.

"Come." He kissed her forehead and slid his arm around her waist. She didn't protest.

Before they reached the table, Shawn asked, "Will your friend be okay?" Natalia watched the happy expression on Tracy's face as she talked and laughed with Spank. "Well, I'd prefer it if we all left together."

"Maybe they're not ready to leave." Shawn grabbed his coat. "We about to leave, aiight, ma? Do you want to stay here wit my man,

Spank?" he asked Tracy.

"Sure, I'm fine." Tracy looked at Spank and asked, "Right?" Spank smiled at her and nodded. "No doubt."

Tracy got up, hugged Natalia and whispered in her ear, "Don't do anything I wouldn't do. In other words, do it all, girl!" They both giggled.

They were sitting in Shawn's car in the parking lot when Natalia lifted a heavy burden from her chest. "I still love you," she said, her voice almost a whisper.

"I know," he replied as he placed his hand on her thigh.

Shawn took her to the Waldorf Astoria in Manhattan. Of course he knew one of the hotel managers and, without a reservation, was given a luxury penthouse suite. They rushed into their room and disrobed immediately.

Shawn lay on top of her and explored her body with his fingertips as if he had never touched her before. Her skin was so soft and silky and between her legs was so hot and wet. He slid off the bed to his knees and pulled her hips toward him. He placed each leg gently around his neck so that she was wrapped around his face. Then he licked her inner thighs. Natalia was in heaven beneath his wet kisses and hot tongue. After teasing her for what felt like an eternity, he lapped at her wetness, sucking on her soft folds of skin, and kissing her pussy as if he was kissing her lips. His tongue flicked against her clit. She drew him closer to him. He continued licking her, faster and harder until she squirmed against his mouth and drowned him in an explosion of hot juices. After her first orgasm, she grabbed his head and pulled it toward her mouth. He licked his way up and kissed her hard and long. It felt like forever. Her body jerked underneath his as he sucked her tongue then her ripe nipples. She couldn't take it anymore.

"Give it to me...please," she begged. He slid his swollen cock into her hesitantly at first, teasing her by giving her only a little at a time. Unable to stand the teasing a second longer, she grabbed his buttocks, spread her legs wide and pulled him into her. Emotions so sorely neglected for much too long rushed at her all at once. Her mouth leaked syrupy sweet moans. "I missed you so much," she spoke in low, breathy gasps.

"Oh God, I missed you, too, Baby Girl," he managed to reply as he kissed her eyes, nose and lips. "I love you...I really do," he whispered. Another rush of emotion overwhelmed her, causing a deep yearning that pulled on her insides.

"It's okay...don't cry, I'm here. I'm here, baby girl." Shawn slowed his pace and rose up on his elbows. He wiped away her tears with his thumbs and gazed into her moist face.

"Its okay, Daddy's home now." He lovingly caressed her neck and face. "Close your eyes," he whispered. She closed them and he kissed each eyelid tenderly. The feelings she felt at that moment were unprecedented and unparalleled. She realized that nothing she ever felt with Mark compared with the feeling Shawn gave her.

Shawn continued to make slow, sensual, heart-wrenching, beautiful love to her over and over again until they both collapsed into a deep, peaceful sleep.

Shawn's pager vibrated its way right off the nightstand and into the garbage can below. The sound woke them up. Shawn checked the small screen then pressed a tiny button to check the time of the page. The page came in at nine-thirteen in the morning. The number belonged to Spank's cell phone. "I hope this niggah ain't do nuttin' stupid," Shawn thought aloud. For Spank to be calling him this early, it had to be important. Natalia fully woke up and rushed to the bathroom to brush her teeth with the complimentary toothbrush and toothpaste.

"What's wrong ma? Oh...your breath must be kicking," he laughed.

"Oh, be quiet!" she playfully hissed and slammed the bathroom door.

"I'd still kiss you, you know..." Shawn laughed and picked up his cell phone to call Spank.

"What!" he asked as soon as he heard Spank's voice.

"Kay told me you was here, player. You know I had to come handle my BI."

Shawn couldn't help but laugh at Spank's immature bragging. "Where's her friend?"

"Asleep. I blew her back out. You know how I do niggah," Spank chuckled.

"How y'all got here?" Shawn asked, scratching his calf.

"Rob dropped us."

"So what up?"

"Ain't nuttin'. "

Shawn got up, went into the bathroom and kissed Natalia on the neck.

"Ew! Now you brush your teeth, nasty," she giggled as he tickled her sides.

"Ay, Spank. I'ma holla at you later."

"Aiight."

Natalia handed Shawn a toothbrush with a glob of toothpaste on it.

"Damn! My breath is kickin'!" He looked at the big clump of toothpaste on the small toothbrush.

"Mm, hmm," she jokingly held her nose. After he finished in the bathroom, he came out naked dancing and singing "Sexual Healing."

"You are so silly," she giggled as she watched his penis bob up and down with each gyrating twist of his pelvis.

"Bend over," he pointed to the bed.

"No, I'm sore," she protested.

"I'll do it slow. It won't hurt." He turned her around and unhooked the clasp to her bra. His hot breath on her neck tickled and enticed her. She slid her panties down and assumed the position. Shawn did as he promised. He was very gentle.

Natalia's vagina was tender, and she wanted to kick herself for overdoing it. For a split second, Mark popped into her mind. She was forced to remember that they were meeting for lunch. "Shawn, I've got to go."

"Spend the day with me," he requested as he watched her pick up her clothes from the floor. She dressed in a hurry but had trouble putting on her boots.

"What's wrong?" he asked.

"I'm supposed to meet..." She let out an exasperated sigh and flopped onto his lap. "Even though...I've still got to marry him." She kept her eyes on Shawn's hand. "I know it seems strange, but I can't let him down. I just can't hurt him again." She nervously drew circles in his palm with her finger.

"What?!" he exclaimed as he shook his head and pulled his hand away. "So what was all that 'I love you shit' you was talkin' last night?"

Natalia stood up and retrieved her coat from the chair. "I don't expect you to understand."

"Damn right, I don't understand. And don't catch no attitude. How do you expect me to understand this shit? What am I supposed to do, huh?" Natalia ignored him, unlocked the door and opened it. He rushed to the door, and grabbed her.

"So what was this? You give me a goodbye-have-a-nice-life-fuck and leave?"

"Shawn, close the door," she demanded, unable to restrain herself any longer, a smile escaping her lips. "You know that I love you. But, I can't give up the life I had before you."

Shawn got on his knees and said, "Aiight I know what I gotta do...Will you marry me?"

"Yeah right. Where's the ring?"

"I'll get you one. Bigger and better than the one he gave you." He stood up and walked over to the bed and began putting on his clothes. Defeated for the moment, he asked, "So where you want me to drop you?"

"I can catch a cab, if it's a problem." She watched him slip his shirt over his head. What was she doing? How could she marry Mark knowing she loved Shawn as much as she did? How long would Shawn put up with being number two? She was back to square one.

"It's not a problem." He put on his coat and opened the door.

"You're sick of me aren't you?" she asked.

"I'm sick of your games, Natalia," he said and shut the door.

"I'm not playing games," she grabbed the lapel of his coat. "Shawn, I love you. God knows that you have a big chunk of my heart in your hands. But so does he. It's tearing me apart, but I have to do this. What you and I have wasn't planned, but what I have with Mark was. Please try to understand."

Inside, Shawn was fuming, but on the outside he was calm, cool and collected. He couldn't understand; he didn't want to. He wanted her all for himself. But the choice she presented to him boiled down to this: put up with her marrying Mark or give her up altogether. And giving her up was not an option.

"How many carats is the ring he gave you?" He inspected her hand. She didn't have it on because she was afraid to wear it to the club. "Five. Why?"

"Let's go." He took her arm and guided her down the hall.

"Why did you want to know?" she asked again.

"Don't worry about it."

In the car, she finally told Shawn that she had been staying in Brooklyn. He asked her where she'd be after she got married, and she couldn't answer him because she didn't yet know. He dropped her off in front of a tall building, gave her a quick peck on the cheek and left.

As she was checking her mailbox, someone yanked on her coat sleeve. It was Tracy, grinning like the cat that ate the gold fish. "So, how did it go?" she asked.

"I'm going to lose my mind, Tracy. I'm so confused...I feel like such a whore."

Instead of taking the elevator two flights up, they walked up the stairs to Natalia's apartment.

They took off their coats and went into the bedroom. Natalia sat on the bed, and Tracy sat in the boudoir chair next to the nightstand.

"Well?"

"I told him that I'm going to marry Mark. I think he's mad at me now."

"You think?" Tracy asked sarcastically.

"He doesn't have the right to be angry."

"Nat, it's not about that. You led him on. How can you have sex with him then tell him that? You want him to be happy for you and Mark and just say congratulations?"

"I don't know what the hell I want. I mean...I do...I just don't think I can have it all."

"Girl, please. Of course you can."

"How?" Natalia asked, really interested in the answer.

Tracy moved over to the bed and said, "Like Nike says, just do it!"

"Tracy! I can't be in two places at the same time."

"You don't have to be. Just be in two different places at two different times. Take your Ginseng and vitamins and go, girl!"

Tracy's answer wasn't practical, but it did make Natalia laugh. She was aware that she had to dig deep into her soul to answer her own questions. But each time she did, the answer was the same: she wanted both men. One without the other was like Kool-Aid without the sugar. Combined, they were the perfect man.

Natalia, bound by her naiveté and loyalty, came to the conclusion that she would marry Mark in January. That would be that. Besides, Shawn would stick around no matter what ...wouldn't he?

Chapter Eleven

❤

LET SLEEPING DOGS LIE

André put the finishing touches on Natalia's precious snow-white mink crown with organza veil before placing it on her exquisite swept-up hairdo.

"You look so beautiful," he tearfully admitted.

"Are you ready?" Tracy asked excitedly.

"Sort of." Natalia held back her tears as well. She didn't want to mess up André's masterful make-up job.

A knock on the door from the wedding coordinator announced that it was time.

Natalia looked at herself in the mirror one last time and took a deep breath. She was about to take the longest, most difficult walk of her life — down the isle. André escorted her from the room and took his place beside her outside the beautiful stained glass doors to the chapel. Two precious little girls in matching gowns held Natalia's lovely fur trimmed train. As the doors were opened, she was greeted with sighs and gasps. Mark's seven-year-old niece acted as flower girl. She stood in the doorway holding a basket of red rose petals mixed with artificial snow. As Natalia stepped into the chapel, the girl curtsied and began to walk slowly down the aisle, sprinkling handfuls of petals onto the white carpet as she went. The organist played the traditional bridal theme. André and Natalia began, feet in sync, to walk together down the aisle with the flower girls in tow. André stood proudly at Natalia's side as they stopped in front of the priest. Tracy was already waiting at the alter for them.

"Marriage is a sacred union..." the priest began as he opened his bible to a bookmarked page. Natalia glanced over at Mark and saw him smile. He looked so handsome in his black and white Armani tuxedo. She watched his posture and his expressions and thought of how much he must love her to have put up with all she had put him through...the humiliation and heartbreak. Mark reached down and took one of the baguette diamond wedding bands from the ring bearer's pillow. He gently slid it onto her ring finger and finished his vows. "Until death do us part."

She watched Mark's mouth move. She had been in her own little world and had missed his "I do."

The priest looked at her and posed the most important question of her life. "Will you, Natalia Marie Foles take Marco Antonio Delucchio as your lawful wedded husband, to love, honor and cherish in sickness and in health, to love and respect from this day forth, until death do you part?"

She looked into Mark's eyes and replied, "I do."

The priest asked her to recite vows similar to Mark's. After a sweet kiss, the newlyweds sprinted down the isle and out the church doors. As they waited on the chapel steps, photographers and guests snapped photos. Other guests blew bubbles from silver plated swan pipes. The delicate orbs floated up into the air and refracted the lights from the cameras and bright midday sun into thousands of tiny prisms.

Natalia looked at the mostly pale faces in the crowd and suddenly realized just how alone she was in the world. She had no family in the States, and her few living relatives were in Jamaica, England and Poland. To top it off, they were either too old to travel or held grudges against her dead father for having excluded them from his will. She had offered to fly them in for her wedding, but every last one of them declined. They made up excuses like children.

"Congratulations!" was shouted by all as the newly married couple got into a white stretch Jaguar limousine. They waved goodbye and blew kisses to everyone in the crowd. It was husband and wife, mister and misses, now.

The limo took them to a rented catering hall in New Jersey that looked like a castle. Inside the huge palace, their guests ate, danced and were treated like kings and queens. Before the midnight hour could arrive and turn their Jaguar into a pumpkin, Natalia and Mark escaped. They had been to so many exotic islands the past year that they decided to honeymoon in the good old U.S. of A. and spent a week at the traditional Niagara Falls.

Mark moved out of his apartment and into the house in Manorville. To give Mark a break with his daily long commute, Natalia agreed that every couple of months they would stay in

Brooklyn.

The first month of marriage was as blissful as a romance novel. She realized that having a warm body next to her every night, caressing hers, wasn't half bad.

And it was a wonderful relief to not miss Shawn as much as she used to. Just two weeks before her wedding, Shawn had made love to her. She pleaded with him to back off for a while so that Mark wouldn't get suspicious. But subconsciously, she had hoped that Shawn would tire of waiting around for her and give up, thus, making her decision for her. No such luck. Shawn came back into the picture sooner than she hoped.

He called her at home one day while Mark was at work. He had assured her that he was out of the drug game for good and that he had opened a car dealership and a large twenty-four hour laundromat in Queens. He charmed his way over to her house, and they ended up in such a powerful explosion of lust that Natalia couldn't have sex with Mark for a week. Mark believed her when she told him that since she stopped getting the Depo-Provera shots, her menstrual cycle was out of whack, and she was spotting all the time. It wasn't a complete lie. She hadn't had a shot in well over three months, but the spotting had already subsided.

Mark pulled into the driveway behind Natalia's Navigator. He grabbed his briefcase and a bunch of white and red roses bound with a white, satin ribbon and rushed into the house that was noisier than usual. He heard laughter coming from the kitchen and hesitantly headed that way.

"Hi." Natalia said, still laughing. "Hi," Tracy echoed. Mark kissed Natalia on the lips, then Tracy's cheek.

"For you." He pulled the flowers from behind his back.

"They're lovely. Just like my bridal bouquet." Natalia sniffed them then put them on the counter. She took a glass vase from one of the cupboards.

"It's just a little gift for saying 'I do' to me six months ago." He squeezed her in his arms. Tracy melted.

"Now the bad news...I have to go away for two weeks — the firm's annual Progressive Accounts Seminar. I'm required to attend every boring lecture and meeting." He took off his coat and loosened his tie. The brokerage firm of Weinstaub and Gloom were about to make Mark a partner. He had been on the go more than ever.

"Oh," Natalia said as she filled a vase with water. After arranging the roses, she carried the vase to the dining room and placed it in the center of the table. When Natalia returned to the kitchen, she rested her head on Mark's chest and asked. "Can't you bring your wife?" Mark kissed the top of her head.

"Yes, but there's really no need for both of us to suffer," he chuckled.

"Where is the seminar going to be held this year?"

"Los Angeles."

"Oh," she sighed. She really didn't care to go, but she had to make him believe that she did. She was glad when he insisted that she stay home.

"You girls can get back to your gossip now. I'm going upstairs to pack."

"Okay."

Tracy waited until he got all the way upstairs and said, "We should have a slumber party!" Natali's only thoughts were of two weeks with Shawn. She smiled, and Tracy understood. "You little devil," she whispered.

"It's party time!" Natalia said as she twirled around and shook her hips from side to side. Somehow she had become very good at being so bad.

By 6:00 a.m., Mark was dressed and ready to go. He moved Natalia's hair from her face and bent over to kiss her and whisper in her ear. "I've got to go now. The car service is here. I'll call you from the hotel. I love you."

"I love you more," she whispered.

As soon as he left the bedroom, she raised her head and looked at the clock. It was much too early for her to get up but she couldn't go back to sleep. So she got out of bed and padded downstairs. She went out onto the veranda and watched as Mark put his bags in the trunk. He looked in her direction, blew her a kiss and then got into the backseat of the car. She blew a kiss back at him and waved goodbye. He was gone! She couldn't wait to see Shawn's new condo and spend some time with him.

Natalia ran back upstairs and called him. His phone rang four times before he picked up. "Hi big Daddy," she said sweetly.

"Hey, Baby Girl."

"I'm coming over today."

Shawn checked his alarm clock. It was six-nineteen. "What are you doing up so early?"

"He just left. He's gone for two weeks."

"So come over now," he suggested, unable to hide his eagerness. He was going to have her for two whole weeks. The possibilities were endless.

"I can't come now."

"Why not?"

"Well for starters, Tracy is here."

"What up wit your girl? She homeless? Damn, she's like your fuckin' shadow."

Natalia giggled "She isn't homeless. We haven't seen each other in a while so I'm going to spend the day with her."

"Yo, she got my man Spank mad open," he chuckled. "So when are you comin' over?"

"Later tonight."

Tracy skipped into the room and plopped down on the bed next to her. "He left already?" Tracy asked, rubbing her eyes.

"Yep," Natalia said as she moved the receiver from her mouth.

"Who's that?" Tracy asked then figured it. "Good morning Shawn," she said loudly into the mouthpiece.

Natalia slapped her arm then rolled over onto her stomach with her feet up in the air, "So get ready for me," she whispered.

"No doubt. But I think I should be saying that to you," he chuckled. "Aiight. I'ma go back to sleep. I need all the rest I can get, right?"

"Uh huh."

"Tell me you love me," he ordered.

"I love you," she said checking over her shoulder to see if Tracy was eavesdropping, but she had left the room.

"I love you too, Baby Girl," he said and hung up.

Tracy came back into the room with a cup of coffee in her hand. "So you're going to go see him right now?" She rested her hip on the closet door.

"No. I told him I would be over later tonight. So that we can hang out." Tracy sat down next to her and took another sip of coffee. "Now I'm up."

"Well, I'm going back to sleep," Natalia rolled over onto her side and pulled the covers over her head.

"Alright then. I'm off to watch the telly," Tracy left the room.

"I'm off to watch the telly," Natalia mimicked her.

Natalia and Tracy spent half of the day shopping and the other half being pampered at the ritzy Madam Venus Schiorr Spa. They had manicures, pedicures and facials. Then they were wrapped, massaged and steamed. They left the spa with glowing skin and rested bodies.

Natalia took Tracy home then left for Queens with an overnight bag filled with goodies she had purchased at the Pink Pussycat Boutique. She got lost when she took the wrong exit off the Van

Wyck Expressway and had to call Shawn to help her find her way. When she finally pulled up in front of his townhouse, she was not in the best of moods. She had wasted nearly two hours!

He met her at the door wearing only his boxers. "Aw, my baby got lost." With one hand, he grabbed her bag, and with the other, he pulled her close and kissed her. He guided her into his apartment. It was the entire first floor.

He had decorated in an African motif. A black leather sofa with short wooden legs sat on one side of the living room. On it, she placed her purse as she checked out the rest of the room. The walls were covered with Afro-centric paintings of black women, children and strong tribesmen. A tall, carved mahogany statue of a naked woman with large pensile breasts, huge lips and a hoop in her nose practically blocked the hallway entrance. Shawn moved it out of the way and put it in a corner. Natalia took another look at the statue thinking that she was lucky to be the woman of the house and wondering what it would have been like if she had married Shawn instead of Mark. Would she sneak out to rendezvous with Mark? Would it have been as tantalizing?

Shawn led her down the long hall. "This is the kitchen," he said. She barely got a good look at the oak cupboards when he pulled her towards the master bedroom. "And this is the love suite." He picked her up and gently placed her on the bed.

"You have a one track mind!" she laughed. He just grinned and began to explore her curves.

"Wait. I've got to show you something," she said, removing his hands from her breasts. She reached for her bag.

"What is it?" he asked.

"You have to leave the room for a minute, and when I say come in, you come back, okay?"

He didn't need to see her in lingerie; he preferred her birthday suit. "Okay," he sulked and backed out of the love suite.

She pulled the door closed and emptied the bag on the floor. She had bought a pair of sexy red, spiked heel platform shoes and a red patent leather dominatrix outfit riddled with silver toned rivets and chains. The top of the camisole looked like harnesses for her breasts. She put her hair up under the matching cap and giggled as she recalled what prompted her to buy the get-up in the first place.

Tracy had dragged her into the Pink Pussycat mainly for laughs, or so Natalia thought. But in actuality, Tracy was there to stock up on the latest kink products. A salesperson told Natalia that she'd make a good dominatrix and showed her the red outfit. Naturally, she couldn't resist the temptation to be bad.

"Come innn," she called out after she fastened the last buckle on her shoes. Shawn wandered into the dark room and palmed the wall searching for the light switch. He found it and his mouth fell open when the lights flicked on.

"Spank me, baby. Spank me," he laughed.

She stood with her legs apart and pointed her finger to the ground in front of her. "Get on your knees, slave."

Shawn went over to her, took the cap off her head and tossed it aside. He pushed her down on the bed and went to his closet. From his robe's belt loops, he pulled out the satin sash. Then he took off his boxers and returned to the bed. With the sash, he tied Natalia's hands together above her head.

"I'm in charge," he said and unsnapped the crotch of her outfit.

"Yes master," she purred. He slid into her with powerful thrusts that made her body undulate. She wanted her fingers on his strong back, but she dared not ask him to stop to untie her. She rose up under him, working her pelvis and squeezing him inside her, reminding him why he was really her slave. Their body friction stimulated her in just the right place, and she came, screaming and finally whimpering. Hearing and seeing her ecstasy, he couldn't hold back and released his liquid warmth deep inside her. He untied her, and she wrapped her arms around his neck. They stared into each other's faces adoringly.

"Hold on," he said as he got up from the bed. She wondered what he was up to. He opened a dresser drawer and pulled out a small velvet pouch. He came over to the bed and put it on her stomach.

"What's this?" she asked.

"Open it and find out."

She unravelled the leather tie and put her hand inside the pouch. She could feel a soft velvety ring box. She pulled out the box and looked at it. *He couldn't possibly have bought me a ring,* she thought. She nervously looked at the box. "I can't..."

"Just open it," he insisted.

She finally opened it and found two silver keys. "Keys?" she asked.

"To here. That's how much I love you." He was completely serious about her. No other woman would ever get keys. Tymeek had a set but no one else would.

"Thank you, Shawn." She kissed his soft lips and hugged him like there was no tomorrow.

She woke up to a note on Shawn's pillow the next morning.

GOOD MORNING, BABY GIRL. I HAD TO GO TO THE LAUNDROMAT, BUT I'LL BE BACK IN A LITTLE WHILE WITH YOUR BREAKFAST. BIG DADDY.

She neatly folded the piece of paper and placed it on the dresser. She smiled to herself then frowned. *Why didn't I just wait? Now I'm stuck in a marriage,* she thought to herself and let out an exasperated sigh. "Oh well," she shrugged and went into the bathroom.

The steam filled the bathroom quickly and Natalia enjoyed the sauna effect. Shawn's bathroom was engaging. He had taken ideas from her bathroom and ran with them. A thirty-six inch television was built into one wall and a sunken roman-style hexagonal Jacuzzi sat in the midst of black and green marble. She opened the glass door to his cylindrical shower and stepped into the moist fog. She closed her eyes and let the powerful water massage her back. She piled her hair up on the top of her head and lunged forward, pressing her hands onto the smooth tile and arching her back to submit to the water's pulsations. She poured some of Shawn's aromatic tropical coconut shower gel into her hand and rubbed it up and down her arms. She was lost in a foggy gray dream of steam and scents that soothed her.

She soaped up twice and scrubbed her hair three times. Long enough, she thought. It was time to leave her wet paradise. She turned off the shower, shook her hair out and stepped out of the stall onto the dark green bath mat. She closed the door and checked to make sure it was snug.

When she turned around, she crashed into Tymeek. Shock and fear froze her in place as their eyes met. She stood face to face with her mortal enemy. She hurriedly covered her wet breasts with her right forearm and cupped her pubic bone with her left hand. Water dripped from her body. Her heart rate accelerated.

Tymeek's smile was eerie, and a pitch-black aura surrounded his face. He grabbed her behind the neck and she felt the rough skin of his hand. Even though he caressed her gently, she felt very threatened.

"So you really like my little brother, huh?" he asked, his voice husky. *What, a rhetorical question from a thug?* she thought.

"Well, I hope that's all it is. You just wanna be down wit a thug niggah. Get some real dick. That cracker can't give it to you like that, huh? That Mandingo shit," he chuckled. His face was too close to hers, his lips within kissing distance. The contact created a sexual tension between them. As he moved his hand to the side of her neck, his fingers roughly slid over her tender, moist skin.

"You better not be using him to get at me, you understand?" he said seriously. Oddly, his threat didn't register. All she could think about was the cinnamon scent coming from his mouth. *Big Red gum!* she remembered. Strange, but it made an impression on her. She had thought of him as a filthy, repulsive monster for so long that it never dawned on her that he was only a human being.

"So what's the deal with you and my brother anyway?" he asked calmly.

"I don't think that's any of your business," she boldly replied. Tymeek's chuckle made her nervous. Unconsciously, she shuddered and broadcasted to him that he made her nervous.

"You better not be playin' him. And you better not tell him that I was here neither cuz I'll fuckin' kill you with no problem. I don't trust your ass, no way," he stated blandly. He slid his fingers down her arm and skipped them across her stomach to where he finally rested his hand, enjoying her soft skin. His lips were so close to hers she thought he was going to kiss her. Instead, he nodded and said, "Nice." He approved, whatever that meant.

Natalia stood frozen still, wishing that the nightmare would be over and that he would leave. But it lingered for a few more minutes until Tymeek decided that he had done the damage necessary and left. As he reached the door, he turned to look at her and said, "I see how you got him. You better take care of him, too."

Before she could relax her arms and get dressed, Tymeek poked his head into the bathroom again and made her jump. "Don't forget what I said. This never happened, you understand?" She nodded quickly.

When she heard the door slam shut, she ran into the bedroom not bothering to stop and dry off. She grabbed her overnight bag, emptied it onto the floor and searched for her underwear. She dressed so quickly that she put her bra on inside out with the back strap twisted. She didn't care, though. She couldn't stay a second longer. *Where's my purse?* she frantically tried to remember. In it were her means of escape — car keys and cash. She scanned the room quickly but didn't see it. Then she dropped to her knees to look under the bed.

Suddenly, she heard the condo door open and close. She sprang to her feet, ran across the bedroom, slammed the door and pressed her back against it, hoping her 133 pounds would keep Tymeek from getting to her. She nervously awaited her fate as his footsteps grew louder. She bit her lip and dug in. She heard the doorknob turn, felt pressure from the other side and then a hard push. She couldn't hold it closed any longer and gave up. The door flew open.

"What are you doing Baby Girl?" Shawn asked and looked

around the room. She backed away from him, afraid that Tymeek was behind him. What if Shawn had sent Tymeek to scare her into staying? But then she remembered what Tymeek had said. If Shawn had sent Tymeek, then there would be no need for her to remain silent about his visit.

Shawn wore a confused expression as he looked at her curiously. "What happened?"

"I was, uh, just looking for my purse," she told him.

"It's in the living room," he reminded her.

"Oh, yeah," she smiled.

"Shawn, I've got to go home. I was going to stay, but I'm afraid that he'll check up on me," she lied, knowing full well that she had planned everything to a tee. If Mark asked why he couldn't reach her, she'd lie and say that she was at Tracy's. But most likely Mark wouldn't ask. She had regained his trust, and he promised not to return to his former suspicious and insecure ways.

Natalia continued to pick up her clothes and stuff them into her bag. She went to Shawn and reached up to put her arms around his neck.

He stroked her damp hair and sadly said, "I was all set to have you for two weeks." She looked up at him, and in his eyes, she saw the answer to her unasked question. Yes, he was worth the deception and the adultery. She stayed.

The apartment was dark. Natalia hadn't been back to Brooklyn in weeks. She flicked on the lights and saw Mark's CDs laying on the floor in front of the stereo system and a stack of Money magazines atop one of the speakers. The place looked lived in, and it annoyed her.

As she was tossing her purse on the sofa, her cell phone rang.

"Happy birthday to me!" André sang.

She laughed, "It's not your birthday yet, Andy. Tomorrow."

"So what! I can celebrate all week if I want to."

"That's true. So are you throwing another superb birthday bash?" she inquired. Every year, André threw himself a wild party at the China Club. Famous entertainers would attend and rock the house in his honor.

"You know it, honey," he replied. Natalia checked her watch. Tracy should be home soon. "You wanna hang out with me and Tracy tonight?"

"I can't. I've got a man, remember?" André's new significant other, Adonis, was super-sexy. His body was taut and packed with all kinds of bulges. He was a stripper at a men's club in the Village.

André met him through the owner who happened to be one of his clients.

"Well excuuuse me!" she drawled, imitating Steve Martin.

"That's right. I'm playing the man card just like you do with me," he chuckled.

"Touché. Well, I guess I'll see you tomorrow night, then."

"Alright, honey bunny. And bring lots of expensive presents, okay?"

"Oh, sure, sure," she laughed and hung up.

Tymeek pulled into his brother's used car lot. Shiny, slightly used Lexuses, Benzes, Escalades, Expeditions and Navigators surrounded him. He got out of the car and walked into the manager's office. Nut was sleeping on a small brown sofa.

"Get up! You fucking slacker!" Tymeek impersonated an anal retentive Caucasian. Nut jumped up and rubbed his eyes, "Whut up?"

Tymeek sat behind the big metal desk. "Where's the head niggah in charge?"

"I dunno," Nut shrugged.

"So what you doing sleeping in here?" Tymeek asked.

"That punk Mitch told me Shawn would be right back. I've been here since..." He checked his watch. "Shit, it's already one?" he asked surprised.

"Yo, I got here at eleven o'clock this morning. I can't believe this shit," Nut complained. Tymeek just laughed at him. He was meeting Shawn at one. Nut waiting on Shawn for over two hours was his own stupidity.

"What you on, niggah?" Tymeek asked, laughing.

"What?" Nut asked confused.

"Shawn don't come in here on the reg, stupid. Why didn't you call him first?" Tymeek explained.

Nut had, in fact, tried to call Shawn on his cell phone but kept getting his voice mail. He had left three messages, but Shawn hadn't called back. The manager, whom Shawn kept on after he bought the dealership, had told Nut that Shawn was coming in although he never did specify when. "So why you here?" Nut asked.

"Never mind that," Tymeek said as he got up from behind the desk. "I'ma go out front." He opened the door and Shawn waltzed in.

"Whut up my niggaz?" Shawn beamed.

"You ain't get my message?" Nut asked.

"I didn't check my voice mail, yet. My cell was dead, and I had to charge it for a while." He gave his brother a hug and a pat on the back.

"Aiight, let's go," Tymeek said.

"Hold up. I came to get a car," Nut protested.

"Oh, yeah. Come on." Shawn said and pulled Mitch to the side and told him to let Nut pick from a specific selection of cars. He told him to take the money Nut gave him and not to worry about the balance. Shawn gave Nut a pound and left with Tymeek.

"So how's business?" Tymeek asked, glancing first at Shawn, then into his rearview mirror.

"The laundromat is doing real good." He opened the car window and spit before continuing.

"The dealership is slow right now, but I'm gon' try to get an advertising spot in the paper."

Tymeek tried to keep his concerns to himself, but he had a bad feeling about the car dealership. The original owner had sold it so quickly and so cheaply that it raised his suspicions. But Shawn was so set on getting it that he knew there was nothing he could say to stop his little brother's impetuousness.

"So you close to your goal yet?" Shawn asked.

"I've got something coming up that will put me over the top," Tymeek replied. His time was running out on the property in Florida. The original developer who owned the property had told Gerald it would be fine with him to wait for the buyer Gerald had lined up. But in the ensuing months, he decided to move out of the country and wanted to close all of his business dealings before he left — forcing a deadline on Gerald's cousin. Tymeek had three hundred thousand dollars so far. But because his operations had expanded into Virginia and Atlanta, he had incurred unexpected overhead costs. And he had given Shawn almost two hundred thousand dollars from Aunt Freda's bank accounts. She had signed the checks to buy the car dealership for Shawn and, in fact, owned it. There was only a small amount of money left in the her accounts that Tymeek wanted to retain. He desperately needed to come up with the rest of the money before the two-month deadline expired.

"I've got these big time buyers in Maryland who want a load of nines, nahmean? Lou's cousin is gon' hook me up with a shipment."

"How much you gon' get?" Shawn asked.

"A quarter. Once I get that, I'm outta here." Tymeek slid his shades up to the top of his head, "I don't want no half cocked niggaz rolling wit me when I go up there, nahmean? So I'ma take Jake and

Big Stew wit me. I really didn't want to involve you, but I need you and Nut to go wit' me. I need loyalty surrounding me, nahmean?"

"Aiight," Shawn nodded.

When they returned from New Jersey, the bright summer sky had turned dark. Shawn had purchased eight cars at auction in Palisades. Tymeek dropped Shawn off at Lisa's house, as per his request, and went to the park. Natalia had gone to a party. Shawn had wanted to go with her but couldn't because she was taking Mark. The whole marriage thing was taking its toll on his patience, and he went back to his old mackadocious ways. Lisa was one of three women he had been seeing to pass the time until Natalia was available. Lisa was the closest he could find to Natalia. She owned her own beauty salon and her own house. She had long hair and was shapely — except for her breasts. Giving birth to two children had left her breasts shapeless and as flat as pancakes. He'd often avoid them when they had sex.

When he rang the doorbell, Lisa's eight-year-old son opened it. "Hey big man," Shawn said rubbing the boy's curly head. "Hi Shawn."

Shawn stepped inside, and the boy slammed the door behind him. Lisa met him in the hallway. "Hi. I didn't know you were coming." Her smile made her face even prettier.

"I stopped by to see if you can get a babysitter so we can go to the movies or get something to eat."

Lisa took his hands into hers and stared lovingly into his eyes. "We ate already, but a movie sounds good." She thought for a brief moment then said, "I think my mom is off tomorrow. I'll call and ask if I can drop them off." She hurried into one of the rooms off the narrow hallway. Shawn went into the living room and sat on the futon. Lisa's other son, Laton, who was five years old and his brother, Lamel, sat on the floor in front of the TV.

"What movie is this?" Shawn asked, leaning forward to watch over the boys' heads.

"'Spawn'," Laton answered without turning.

"That's an old movie," Shawn sneered.

"We know, but ain't nothin' else on," Lamel replied.

Lisa came into the room and announced that her mother was home and had agreed to watch the kids. The children didn't want to go and whined all the way to the car.

Instead of going to a movie, they ended up back at her house — where Shawn had planned to spend the evening all along. Lisa had a busy schedule, and there was very little time leftover for them to be alone. So any chance they found to be alone, sex was their first priority. They jumped into action as soon as they closed the front door. Lisa pulled him into the living room. She attempted to take her time opening her jeans, but Shawn grew impatient. He hooked his thumbs in her belt loops and yanked the jeans down. Then he pulled down his pants and boxers. His erect penis saluted her. Lisa got on her knees and licked the swollen tip. Fellatio was the one thing Lisa had over Natalia — she knew how to please him with her mouth. He pumped her mouth slowly, looking down at her bouncing curls. Natalia was the furthest thing from his mind.

Chapter Twelve

❤

BE CAREFUL WHAT U WISH 4

André and Adonis looked adorable in matching white outfits. Natalia watched them as they huddled in conversation at their table near the bar. She couldn't help but wonder how two such handsome men could be gay. *It should be a crime,* she thought to herself.

Tracy and Mark were on the dance floor, her husband moving quite rhythmically for a white guy. Tracy was backing her butt right onto his crotch. Natalia giggled at Mark's red cheeks. Tracy wasn't drunk but close to it.

Natalia approached André's table. A huge, transparent balloon filled with metallic gold stars and multi-colored glitter hung from the ceiling over his table. The sparkling golden script on the outside read: Happy birthday André, you old fart. Natalia had it and a huge rectangular cake with his picture in the frosting made especially for him. His gift was a sculpture they saw in a Soho gallery over which he salivated. She sat in the empty chair next to Adonis and tapped his shoulder.

"Hello love birds," she smiled.

Adonis moved closer to her and put his arm around her shoulder. "Are you enjoying yourself?" he asked.

"Oh, yes," she answered with a weak smile.

André sipped his drink and said, "Nat, would you please go and dance with your husband. Tracy looks like she's about to kill the poor man with her ass." Natalia laughed and turned to look at Mark and Tracy on the dance floor. Tracy's hips gyrated wildly, and Mark's face glistened with sweat as he tried to keep up.

"I'm glad they're having a good time," Natalia said turning back around.

"It's real cool how unaffected you are by that," Adonis said as he pointed to Mark and Tracy. He looked at André, "You should be more like her. More trusting." André sucked his teeth and sipped his drink again.

Mark finally broke free and approached the table gasping, "Water!"

Natalia, Adonis and André all burst out laughing. André waved his hand at the bartender. "Hey, Julius," André shouted. When Julius looked in his direction, he shouted to him to bring a bottle of spring water. Julius complied.

Mark grabbed the bottle and gulped until the water was gone. "She gave you a good workout, huh?" André grinned.

Mark nodded with a smile, "That girl can go." He looked at his bored wife. "You okay?"

"I'm fine. Are you okay?" she chortled.

Tracy staggered over and rested her elbows and weight on the table. "What happened to my dance partner?" she asked, not noticing Mark right next to her.

"Are you drunk, Tracy?" André asked, chuckling.

"No, I'm not drunk, Andy. I'm just tipsy."

"Yeah, uh-huh. You're about to tip right over," André laughed.

Mark put a chair behind her. "Have a seat Tracy," he said.

"I thought we were going to dance some more," she whined as she plopped into the chair.

"I'd like to dance with my wife now," he said holding out his hand to Natalia.

"Markie, I don't feel like dancing."

"Stop being so miserable and go dance with your husband," André chastised. Natalia rolled her eyes at him. She wasn't in the mood and only wished that there were some way to sneak over to Shawn's apartment. She had had sex with Mark before they came to the party and was left unsatisfied — again. With Shawn, satisfaction was guaranteed.

Mark had his orgasm and stayed inside of her. "Come on lady luck, Daddy wants a baby." Natalia wanted to puke. She had come to realize that her decision to marry him had been the wrong one. She loved him, but she wasn't in love with him. As he pumped away on top of her, she thought only of Shawn.

Tracy was indeed drunk. Her head twirls, endless giggling and slurred speech gave her away. Mark couldn't bear to watch her embarrass herself anymore, so he did the Boy Scout thing and offered to drive her home. "I'll be back, sweetie," he said as he kissed Natalia's lips.

This could be my chance, if only he wouldn't come back. "You don't have to come all the way back. I'll take a cab home," she said, looking into Tracy's face. "Get some coffee into her and make sure she's okay." If he stayed with Tracy, she could go to Shawn.

Mark thought about it for a moment then said, "I guess I could do that. But are you sure you'll be okay?"

"Of course," she said as she got up to help Tracy to her feet. Mark put Tracy's arm around his neck and supported her so she wouldn't tumble over.

"You're such a sweetheart, Mark," Tracy mumbled. Mark turned to Natalia and said, "I'll see you later. Call me if you need anything."

Natalia didn't even wait for them to disappear through the exit. She took out her cell phone and called Shawn. Adonis and André had gone to the dance floor, giving her the privacy she needed. Shawn's phone rang and rang. When she didn't get an answer at his apartment, she called his cell. She got his voicemail. I'll just go to his apartment and wait for him. She told her plans to André. All he did was shake his head, too busy enjoying his birthday party to lecture her — again. He just kissed her cheek and bid her goodbye.

When she got outside, she hailed a cab. The cab driver turned to her and asked, "Where to?"

"Flushing," she replied, rifling through her purse for the card with Shawn's address.

Mark managed to get Tracy into her apartment and onto the bed. He put on a fresh pot of coffee then went back into the bedroom, took Tracy's shoes off and put a trash basket by the bed. She had already thrown up once before they even got out of the China Club, and he wanted to be prepared in case she felt the need again. He left her to check on the coffee. When he returned to the bedroom, she was gone.

"Tracy?" he called out. He could hear water running in the bathroom.

"You okay?" he asked.

Tracy was hunched over the sink, toothbrush in hand. She turned around and said, "It's okay. I'm just brushing my teeth. I had a horrible taste in my mouth." She smiled a foamy smile. *Thank God she's sobering up,* Mark thought. "I made some coffee. Would you like a cup?" Unable to talk through the minty foam, she just nodded her head.

"Okay, I'll be in the kitchen."

Tracy finished brushing her teeth and blew into her hand to check her breath. She pulled a washcloth off the shelf, wet it with cold water and wiped her face clean. Then she opened her make-up and searched through it. She re-applied her make-up bag and lipstick and blotted her lips with a Kleenex before going into the kitchen.

Mark sipped a cup of coffee as he waited for her. When she walked in, he put his cup down on the counter and filled another to the brim for her. "Thanks," she said and brought the steaming cup to her lips.

"I didn't put cream or sugar in yours. It works faster if it's black." he said.

Tracy laughed, "OK. I know I kind of overdid it tonight."

Mark sipped more of his coffee but didn't finish it. He figured when his cup was empty, he'd go home. Tracy's eyes bored into his as she sipped sensuously from her cup. There was an uncomfortable silence. He nervously sipped his coffee again. Tracy took her cup to the breakfast nook and sat in a chair with white paint fashionably peeling from its frame. "Why don't you have a seat?" she asked, crossing her bare legs.

Mark sat down, avoiding eye contact.

"I can't thank you enough for bringing me home. That was really sweet of you." Mark's cup was empty now. He wanted to leave, but it seemed that she wanted company so he remained seated.

"You don't need to thank me," he smiled.

Tracy couldn't believe it, but she was attracted to him. His face was friendly. She could feel herself getting aroused thinking of what it would be like to cross the line and have sex with him. Natalia had said that he was boring in bed, but she also said that his cock was big and thick. *I bet I could train him to be good in bed,* Tracy thought to herself.

"I've got some great jazz CDs. Would you like to hear one or two? Or maybe we could watch a movie. This coffee has me wired," she said, grinning.

The coffee had him wide awake,too, and since his wife was still out partying, he figured he could hang out for another hour or so.

"Have you got Coltrain?" he asked.

"Yes. As a matter of fact, I do," she smiled.

Tracy casually led the way to her bedroom. She grabbed the remote from the top of her nightstand and pointed it at the compact CD player on the floor across the room. She pressed a disc number then pressed play. A mellow jazz melody filled the small room.

"That's cool," he said.

"Sit there." She threw several of her frilly decorative pillows from the bed onto the floor.

"I didn't know you were into jazz," he remarked.

"My dad got me hooked on it." She began moving her body to the horns blasting from the stereo. Mark tried to ignore her swaying hips. She slowly rubbed her hands up and down her thighs and closed her eyes as she listened to the music. Her slinky, silver satin dress shimmered under the soft white ceiling lights.

Mark felt himself getting turned on and decided it was time to go.

Tracy opened her eyes and took his hand. "Let's dance."

Mark pulled away. "N-no. I can't dance to jazz. I usually just listen and relax." He smiled then stood up. "I'm kind of sleepy, so I'm gonna go home now. Nat might call to see if you're alright."

Tracy looked disappointed. "Oh, OK. Let me walk you to your door." She followed him to his and Natalia's apartment.

"Thank you, again," she smiled.

"No problem," he said as he opened the apartment door. "Goodnight, Tracy."

Mark rushed into the bathroom and splashed cold water on his face. He was still hard. He undressed quickly and stepped into the shower, making the water as cold as he could stand. Tracy was a beautiful woman, and it was only natural for him to be tempted. He fantacized about shedding his inhibitions and throwing her down on the bed to finish what she connivingly had started. As a matter of fact, the thought had crossed his mind before tonight. Tracy was always so affectionate to him. He shook his body in the water. *Think football, Mark. Sweaty men. That should kill all sensation in your lower extremities.* It worked, and he finally became flaccid. As he lay on the couch watching a movie on Showtime, he checked the digital clock on the DVD unit. It was one o'clock in the morning. He yawned and waited for his wife.

Natalia opened the door to Shawn's apartment. It was dark and quiet. Too quiet. The house smelled light and pleasant — like cologne and bananas. She walked to the bedroom and turned on the lights. It was obvious that he wasn't home. She picked up his phone and dialed his cell number. This time, the voicemail didn't automatically answer — a female did after just one ring. The woman whispered, "Hello?"

Natalia thought she had dialed the wrong number so she hung up and dialed again.

"Hello?" The same woman answered again.

"Uh, hi, may I speak to Shawn please?" Natalia asked.

"Who are you?" the woman asked with more than a hint of attitude.

Natalia chuckled and asked, "Where's Shawn?"

The woman nastily replied, "My man is in the shower."

Natalia chuckled again. It was all she could do to restrain herself from saying something she might later regret.

"Can you please tell Shawn that Natalia called? And oh, please mention that I'm at his apartment waiting for him," Natalia said snidely before hanging up. A feeling of angst overcame her. What if Shawn had moved on? He certainly wouldn't appreciate what she said to his new woman. She wondered what she should do. Stay or leave?

Within ten minutes, Shawn called back. Apparently he had gotten her message.

Natalia nervously answered, "Hello?"

"You jealous?" Shawn asked. He didn't seem upset.

Natalia hesitantly asked, "Who was that?"

"It doesn't matter. I'm on my way." At least he cared enough to drop whatever he was doing and come to her. A doubtful triumph, for sure.

When Shawn arrived, he smelled like a fresh spring day — a dead give-away that he had just had sex with the other woman. She didn't want to be jealous but couldn't help it. She said nothing to him when he sat next to her on the couch. She didn't even look at him. He stared at her quietly, waiting for her to say something. The silent standoff went on for five more minutes before Natalia reached her boiling point.

"Were you fucking her when I called?" she asked as she looked down at her hands in her lap.

Shawn smiled to himself. She was jealous and it amused him. "Nah," he said blandly. He tipped her chin with his forefinger, forcing her to look at him. "How did it feel knowing that I was with another woman?" he asked seriously.

She saw where he was headed. "Point taken," she murmured.

"Humph. So how was the party?"

"Boring. I thought about you the whole time." Her hands went to his smooth cheeks. She pulled his face close to hers and kissed him. Thoughts of him with someone else ran across her mind, and she pulled back abruptly, afraid of tasting the other woman.

"What's wrong now?" he asked annoyed.

"Did you go down on..." she stopped herself. He probably wouldn't tell her the truth anyway. Besides, did she really want to know? Shawn chuckled and said, "Trust me you're the only one gettin' tongue."

That didn't help.

"Shawn, I can't keep yo-yoing like this. I feel that one day I'm just going to snap. I can't stand not knowing whom you're with or if you're wearing condoms...I have no say in the matter."

"That's right. Just like I can't tell you to divorce the white boy. Can I tell you not to fuck him? You don't know who he be fuckin, do you? Now you know how it feels!" He jumped up and went into the kitchen. Natalia sat quietly. Shawn was right. She didn't want to fight with him, though. She had come to make love to him, but it looked as if she was too late. Shawn came back with a can of soda in his hand. "I don't drink soda," she said, with a puzzled look on her face.

"So? It ain't for you," he snapped and swallowed a mouthful.

"If you're going to be rude, I'm leaving," she announced as she picked up her sequined purse. Shawn continued drinking his soda as Natalia got up and walked toward the door. Shawn paid her no attention and went into the kitchen again. Natalia looked back and saw that he had left the room.

How dare he! She let out a shrill sound then stomped into the kitchen. "Just because you already had pussy tonight doesn't mean you can treat me like shit and get away with it." She yelled and attempted to slap his face.

Shawn blocked the blow and twisted her hand behind her back. "Don't you ever raise your hand to me. You understand?" his voice so calm, it confused her.

"Let me go," she whined. He released her hand and grabbed her thick tresses, forcing her head towards his. He kissed her hard, knocking the wind out of her. She tried to push him away, but his tongue slithered into her mouth, igniting her loins. He grabbed her buttocks, lifted her from the tiled floor and dropped her onto the countertop. He reached under her dress and stuck his hand down her panties. He pulled his finger out of her, licked it, then slid the same finger into her mouth. She sampled her own juices, marveling at the taste. He removed a bread knife from the dish rack, sliced through the thin bands at the sides of her mesh bikini panties and watched as they slipped onto the counter. He pulled out his penis and rubbed it on her clitoris causing her to overheat. She panted uncontrollably waiting for him to enter her. He pulled her close to the edge of the counter and plunged in. After giving Lisa non-stop pelvis bucking, he didn't think he had any more steam left, but he did.

By the time they were finished, he could barely stand. It was five o'clock in the morning, and Natalia knew that she had stayed out way past her 'curfew.' She was quite sure that the party was over by now.

Even though he was exhausted, Shawn insisted on driving her home. When they pulled up in front of her building he kissed her passionately. He told her that he loved her, and her misplaced love was finding its way back to him.

She entered the apartment, trying to be as quiet as possible. Mark woke up anyway. He met her in the hall and followed her into the bedroom. He looked at the clock then at her. "What happened?"

"Nothing. Go back to sleep," she said as she laid her purse on the dresser. She went into the bathroom to shower before Mark could get a whiff of the sexual musk emanating from her body.

Mark came into the bathroom just as she was rubbing the bar of soap in her hands. "Can I join you?" he asked with a sleepy smile.

"I'm so sleepy. And so are you. I just want to wash off and jump into bed." She slowly turned away from him and hurriedly washed between her legs.

"Yeah, you're right. I was out cold before you came in. Hurry up so that I can snuggle up to that sexy body."

"Whew!" she muttered under her breath.

Chapter Thirteen

❤

BACKSTABBERS

Slowly but surely, Lisa began to realize that she wasn't the only object of Shawn's affections.

As she pulled into his used car lot, she saw through the showroom window that he was engaged in pleasurable conversation with a voluptuous young woman with the biggest ass she'd ever seen. Lisa approached cautiously since she wasn't sure what was going on and didn't want to make a fool of herself. The woman might be a customer.

Shawn noticed Lisa, and their eyes met. She stopped just inside the door and rested her back on the thick glass. Shawn's eyes returned to the woman in front of him, and he resumed giving her his undivided attention. Lisa's patience wore thin as the woman giggled and touched Shawn's chest and arm every time she made a point.

Lisa sighed loudly — loud enough to make her presence known. The woman turned around. Her pudgy pig nose and overbite put Lisa's mind at ease. Shawn had anticipated Lisa's reaction and told the woman, "Aiight, love, you can go speak to Jovan now. He's one of my best salesmen."

"Aiight, Shawn," she agreed, glaring at Lisa as she lumbered to the back of the showroom.

"What you doin' here?" Shawn asked.

"I can't come see you?" Lisa asked defensively.

"First of all, you're lucky that you caught up with me. Secondly, you should call me first. Don't be trying that checking up on a niggah bullshit."

"I'm not checking up on you. I was on my way to the mall and thought I'd stop in and say hello."

"Hold up," Shawn said, reaching into his pocket for his ringing phone. He pressed the answer button and asked, "What?" His annoyed expression softened as he heard Natalia's sweet voice.

"What's up Baby Girl?" he asked as he walked away from Lisa toward the open glass doors.

"Are you busy? Because I can call back." Natalia said with a hint of attitude.

"Nah, I'm not busy. Am I gonna see you today?"

"Yes, Daddy. How about now? Mark's flight doesn't get in until eleven-forty tonight," she paused. "And for some strange reason, he wants me to meet him at the airport. Do you want me to meet you or can you come get me?"

"I'm on my way," he said as he turned around. Lisa was right behind him.

"Who was that?" she asked.

"My business," he answered dryly. It didn't matter that she most likely overheard his conversation. Lisa was a cling-on, and he didn't have to worry about her cutting him off. The night Natalia called and Lisa answered the phone, Shawn all but told her to mind her own business — that she wasn't allowed to answer his phone or concern herself with his business. She meekly acquiesced. He had her hook, line and sinker.

"So some bitch calls, and you go running? You expect me to keep putting up with that?" her voice rose in anger.

"I gotta go," he said as he walked past her.

"You fuckin' punk!" she shouted after him.

He stopped dead in his tracks, turned to her, grabbed her arm, and forced her into his office. He slammed the door and pushed her up against it. "Do you realize where you at?" he asked heatedly.

"So fuckin' what? I'm not one of them little trifling hoes you be wit. You're not going to disrespect me!" she screamed.

"You disrespecting yourself right now. I told you before that my business is my business. You're not my mother or my wife. This is a place of business, aiight, so don't fuckin' start that pigeon shit, yellin' in front of my customers. If you're such a lady, act like one. You understand?"

Her eyes glazed over with a fresh coat of hurt, and she pursed her mouth into a tight pout.

"Relax," he told her, touching her cheek.

"Get off me," she said as she weakly hit him in his chest with a loosely balled fist. He chuckled, moved her away from the door and left the office. She watched through the glass as he drove off.

"Can I help you?" a short brown skinned salesman asked, pushing the office door wide open. Lisa shook her head and walked out. The salesman watched her leave, admiring her shape.

"That Casanova muthafucka got all the women," he whispered to himself.

Shawn pulled up in front of Natalia's building. He was dying to make love to her in the same bed where she slept with Mark. He wanted to mark his territory by leaving his semen all over Mark's side of the bed. Natalia belonged to Shawn. He wanted Mark to walk in on them while he lay on top of her, loving her the way Mark couldn't. He wanted Mark to give up and divorce Natalia.

He pulled out his cell phone and called, asking her, begging her, to let him come upstairs. But she refused, explaining that she wanted to go out and do more than the 'horizontal mambo', as she called it.

Natalia emerged from the building wearing tight, low rider capri length jeans, a matching halter top and the sneakers he bought her last year. Her long tresses were pulled back into a neat ponytail and she clutched a small Christian Dior handbag. Her pink tinted sunglasses also bore the CD logo. Shawn licked his lips as he watched her body. She opened the car door and plopped down in the seat. "Hi," she said cheerily.

"Hey, sexy." He leaned over to kiss her, but she grabbed his head with both her hands and kissed him hard.

"Mmn."

"So what's on the agenda?" he asked as he scanned her body.

"Well, I would like to start the day off by roller skating then —"

"Nah, nah Baby Girl. I don't roller-skate." He shook his head.

"Well I'll teach you then," she smiled as she placed her hand over his.

"I'm not gonna be looking like a clown falling on my ass," he laughed.

"I'm a good teacher."

"Uh huh. So where's this place at?"

"It's in New Jersey. Once we get to the Holland tunnel, I'll direct you better."

Shawn sighed, "I hope you don't get me lost."

The roller rink was practically empty with just a few children and adults skating in circles on the children's rink.

"Would you like to start on the kiddy rink?" Natalia asked, poking fun.

"Stop playin'. I used to skate when I was younger so I got some skills," he grinned.

At the skate center, they traded in their shoes for skates. Natalia laced hers all the way up and tied them tight. Shawn did only one criss cross then stuck the ends of the laces in the last holes at the top and then tied them tightly.

"You're going to fall and bust your ass," she giggled, looking at his skates.

"No I'm not. They tight." He double-checked the laces in both skates.

"Come on," she said as she grabbed his hand and pulled him onto the adult rink. They began to skate left foot first then sliding over the right. Drag and sweep. Shawn was doing quite well until Natalia quickened her pace to show off.

"Slow down!" he pleaded excitedly. She let his hand go and did a circle in front of him then began to skate backwards. "Show off," he chuckled. He stopped and rested and watched her swerve from right to left, backwards. Then she grabbed her right ankle and brought her leg up behind her and glided by him. "Damn," he whispered, impressed. She slowed down as she neared him again and stopped abruptly on her toes. "So you dragged me down here just so I could see you skate like a pro?" he inquired.

"Maybe," she grinned. "Come on. Try skating backwards with me." She took his hands into hers.

"Hello! No, you're not gon' make me fall."

"I'll skate in front of you and hold your hands...we'll go slowly. Come on, scaredy-cat."

She grabbed his hands, guided him into position and skated slowly, instructing him on his foot movements. He followed her instructions but lost his balance halfway around the rink and slipped. They toppled over, she landing on top of him. "I told you," he laughed loudly. Natalia looked into his young, handsome face wondering why she didn't remain single.

"What? Why you ice grillin' me?" he asked with a laugh and put his hands on her shoulders.

"This is why..." she pressed her lips against his. Their tongues did a ritual dance in each of their mouths. Shawn sucked on hers, sending tingles throughout her body.

"Excuse me! I have an eight year old here, so can you two please stop that." A heavyset white woman with a large fleshy mole on her cheek stood over them.

"Oh, we're sorry," Natalia apologized. They got up and brushed themselves off.

"Pardon us," Shawn said once on his feet.

"That is such inappropriate behavior. My son doesn't need to learn about sex on a roller rink," she snipped with an attitude.

"Ah fuck you, bitch," Shawn said under his breath.

"Shawn!" Natalia admonished and covered her mouth so he couldn't see her laughing.

"She just mad that she ain't gettin' none with her sloppy fat ass," he commented.

"That's not nice, Shawn," Natalia said, stifling another laugh.

"Let's get outta here." Shawn took her hand and they left the roller rink and the whispering behind.

They went to a matinee, kissed through the entire movie and missed all the good parts.

"I did everything you wanted, now you have to do what I want," Shawn told her as they left the theater.

"Oh noooo. I know what you want. I wanted us to just spend the day together having fun with our clothes on. I need to know that we can do that, too," she said seriously.

Shawn chuckled. "That just goes to show that you don't know me. I wasn't even thinking about sex. I want to take you to play pool."

"Oh..." she giggled, embarrassed.

"Now don't you feel stupid," he mocked, shaking his finger at her. She pushed his finger out of her face.

He took her to his friend's brand new pool hall in Corona, Queens. It still smelled of fresh paint. She had never been in a pool hall before and was under the impression that they were seedy and dark. This one was just the opposite. There was a snack counter, a video game center and lots of tufted leather benches to relax on. Hoop games and air hockey tables were toward the back of the hall behind many well-lit pool tables. The owner looked to be about sixteen years old. He stepped from behind the cash desk and slapped his hand into Shawn's. The two men hugged and patted each other's back. "Whut up, niggah?" he asked Shawn.

"Just living, man," Shawn answered, smiling. He took Natalia's hand and pulled her close to him. "This is wifey." He grinned at her and continued, "Nay-nay this is my man, Syrus."

"How you doing, ma?" Syrus smiled.

"Fine, thank you," she shyly replied. She wished that they would quit with the 'ma' reference. It was bad enough that they were so damn young.

"We need a table," Shawn informed Syrus.

"You play pool?" Syrus asked Natalia.

"No, but I learn quickly."

"I can't get my girl to play. She thinks it's stupid," he laughed. "Y'all can have table fourteen." He went behind the counter.

Shawn took her to the table and racked up the balls. "We're gonna play eight ball, okay? The object of the game is to knock all your balls in the pockets then hit the eight ball in afterwards. Because you're new at this, we won't call our shots."

He took two sticks from the wall behind the table, chalked both and handed her one. The balls were in a perfect triangle on the table. He took the white ball and placed it on the other side of the table.

"I'm gon' break. That's what this is called," he pulled back the stick then forced it forward, hitting the white ball. The white ball made a cracking sound when it hit the other balls which then rolled all over the table. A red ball with the number three went into a side pocket.

"I got the low balls," Shawn said.

"They didn't look that low to me," she replied with a laugh.

"Funny girl," he said as he shook his head and smiled.

Shawn was a good teacher. She was actually able to get in a few good shots — only three of her balls remained on the table. But he was already trying to sink the eight ball.

Maxwell crooned over the speaker system. Natalia swayed her hips from left to right and bounced her buttocks up and down as well.

"You can't dance," Shawn said.

"Oh yes I can."

"Don't worry. I'll teach you," he chuckled.

"Whatever," she giggled. "I can too dance," she pouted like a child. Time passed quickly. By the time they left the pool hall, it was already dark outside.

"Where to now?" she asked.

"To my place," he answered, holding the car door open for her. She looked at him apprehensively.

"I'm gonna cook something for us to eat. That's all," he assured her. She got in the car and reached over to push his door open. "That's why I love you," he smiled.

Mark called Natalia from the plane. The captain announced that the plane would be landing at JFK within fifteen minutes. She wasn't in so he left a message. "Hi. Where are you? I hope you're at the airport waiting for me. I miss you so much. The plane is due to arrive at JFK in about fifteen minutes. I hope you're there because I can't wait to see my beautiful wife."

The stewardess came over to remove his empty glass and asked if he would be needing anything else. He said no and jerked his shoulder, jolting his friend who had been resting his head there.

"Hey!" his friend said.

"Wake up, Stan. We're home," Mark said pointing his thumb toward the window.

"Thank God. I'm so freakin' tired." Stan tried to fix his wrinkled tie. "Do you have a car waiting for you?" he asked Mark.

"No, my wife is meeting me."

"You lucky bastard. My wife wishes I wouldn't come home much less pick me up!" he chuckled.

Mark shook his head. "How long have you been married?"

"Let's see. The dinosaurs weren't extinct yet because her family was at the wedding, so I would say over a billion years." They laughed loudly.

"How long for you?"

"A little over a year," Mark replied dreamily. He had no complaints.

"You're still on your honeymoon, for Chrissakes. Give it a couple more years," Stan scoffed.

Mark chuckled. "I don't think so."

"You're still learning, kid. Ah, to be young and dumb again," Stan said as he patted Mark's shoulder.

The plane landed, and as they taxied the runway, Mark thought of Rome. He had witnessed his colleagues in compromising positions. His boss, who has three children and has been married for twenty-two years, was with three women in one night. Mark was very uncomfortable with the whole thing, but he knew that if he were going to go all the way with the firm, he'd have to play ball. And temptation did have him by the balls, literally. One of the beautiful escorts hired by the brokerage firm performed oral sex on him. Since Natalia never did, he didn't feel too guilty about it. Besides, he didn't consider it cheating.

Stan passed him his carry-on luggage as they prepared to disembark. Mark went through customs and exited at the arrivals area before Stan. He saw lots of foreigners holding signs with impossibly complicated names, but he didn't see his wife. He pulled out his cell phone and called hers. Again, voicemail picked up.

He waited well over fifteen minutes, but there was still no sign of his wife. Frustrated, he called Tracy in the hope that she knew his wife's whereabouts.

The call was forwarded to Tracy's cellular. She answered the phone out of breath. "Hello?"

"Hi, Trace. Would you happen to know where my wife is?" Of course Tracy had an idea but would never say.

"No. What's wrong?" she asked, concerned.

"She was supposed to meet me up at the airport. I don't know what's going on. I told her I'd get in around eleven forty-five, and it's now ten after twelve. I don't see her anywhere."

Tracy assumed that Natalia was off with Shawn and had forgotten all about her loving husband. She remembered how he took the time to care for her after André's birthday party and offered to pick him up. "Which airport are you at?"

"JFK."

"Tell me which gate, and I'll meet you there in about fifteen minutes. Or is that too long to wait?"

Mark wanted his wife. *Why wasn't she here? Where the hell was she?* But, he didn't want to wait forever.

"Mark, is that okay with you?"

"I can just catch one of these cabs..."

"Don't waste your money. Have a seat and relax. Give me your cell number so that I can call you as soon as I get there."

Mark told her his number and took a seat.

Just as she promised, Tracy was there fifteen minutes later. Mark didn't know how she did it and didn't really care. He was just glad to be on his way home.

"How was the flight?" Tracy wanted to keep Mark's mind off Natalia.

"It was long. Too long," he sighed. He pulled out his phone again and dialed Natalia again. No dice. "I don't understand this shit. Where the hell is she?"

Natalia, you'd better get your ass home, wherever you are, Tracy thought. "Maybe her phone is off. Or she fell asleep."

"I can't imagine her forgetting about me like that." He shook his head.

"Listen to this." Tracy turned on the car's stereo system and stuck a CD into the slot. She turned up the volume. A jazz tune seeped through the speakers, easing Mark's tension.

"You sure know good jazz. I love this one."

"I heard it playing at the music store and knew I had to have it."

"You should take the Van Wyck."

"Okay." She stopped at the red light. Mark had fallen asleep. She sneaked a glance at him. His eyes were closed and his head lay on the headrest. He could pass for an even cuter version of JFK, Jr. As much as she tried not to be, she couldn't help but be attracted to him.

Mark was so chivalrous and sweet. Tracy envied that he adored his wife and admired the way he romanced her every chance he got. He was so loyal. Tracy wanted a man just like him. She would rather he be a dark skinned black man, but oddly enough, she didn't mind Mark's paleness.

He opened his eyes. "Was I snoring?" he asked as he caught her staring.

"Uh, a little," she answered nervously.

When they reached the building ten minutes later, Mark practically ran to his apartment. Tracy trailed behind him, keeping her fingers crossed, hoping that Natalia was in the bed sleeping.

Mark quickly turned the key and unlocked the door. "Natalia!" he shouted, checking the kitchen. Tracy went up the spiral steps to the loft. Empty. Mark rushed out of the bedroom, fuming. "She's not here. I can't believe this." He took off his coat and threw it on the couch. "Oh, God! What if something happened to her?"

Tracy performed, knowing damn well that Natalia was off somewhere with Shawn. "I don't want to think that," she said.

Mark picked up the phone and called the house in Manorville. No answer. "She could be in trouble. I should call the police."

Tracy took the phone from his hand and gently laid it back in the cradle. "Sit here and relax. We shouldn't think the worst. Let's not jump to conclusions." She picked up his coat and hung it in the closet. "Do you want a drink?" she asked.

"I could use one," he sighed, running his fingers through his dark curls.

Tracy went into the kitchen and searched the cupboards and fridge. She couldn't find anything with alcohol in it. She knew that Natalia didn't drink, but she figured since Mark did, there would be some sort of liquor around. But there was none. "I'm going down the hall to get my bottle of Grand Marnier."

"Wait," Mark said, getting up from the couch. "I have a bottle."

"But I didn't see it," Tracy said, surprised.

"I kind of keep it hidden," he smiled. He returned to the living room with a large, honey colored bottle and two glasses with ice. "Do you like yours on the rocks?" he asked.

"Sometimes," she replied and flipped her hair. He filled both glasses halfway and handed her a glass. "Sometimes I wish Natalia would loosen up and drink with me." He took a big gulp.

"I know what you mean. I get so tired of her passing judgement on me when I drink in front of her." Tracy sipped her drink, savoring the flavor. They laughed at their common bond. A few chuckles later, they had each downed three glasses of Grand Marnier and were starting on their fourth. Tracy had moved closer to Mark on the couch and with each giggle she slapped her hand down on his lap. Mark began to notice Tracy's exquisite beauty and felt drawn to her. She could feel the heat between them and kissed him. They moved quickly like two dogs in heat, ripping each other's clothes off. She licked her way down to his throbbing member and gently kissed the tip like she was licking a lollipop. Mark couldn't wait to be inside her. He pulled her face up to his and kissed her. They laid on the floor holding each other. When he entered her slippery middle, she moaned loudly and pulled him into her. Their bodies were covered in sweat as she pumped upwards and he pumped downwards. They bucked wildly until they came simultaneously, riding the high from the tingling sensations coursing through their bodies. Huffing and puffing, Mark rolled off her and onto the floor. They laid there looking up at the triangular shaped skylight. Guilt hadn't crossed Tracy's mind. She knew all about Natalia's extracurricular activities. Mark got up and held out his hand to her. She took it, and he pulled her to her feet. "I-I'm sorry that I took advant—"

"You didn't. I kissed you, Mark. I've been wanting that for a while now, and I don't regret doing it. It doesn't mean that I don't love Natalia because I do. But I'm a go-getter, and I just got what I wanted," she said bluntly, touching his strong chin with her fingers.

"I can't believe you're not taken. Any man would be lucky to have you."

"From your mouth to God's ears," she smiled.

"We'd better clean up before Natalia gets home." Mark looked around as if he was lost.

Tracy sucked her teeth and picked her shirt up off the carpet. For a moment, Natalia's disappearance hadn't bothered him. But now he was back to worrying about her. "Maybe André knows where she is." Mark carried his clothes into the bedroom. When he came back to the living room, Tracy was partially dressed and opening the door. "You can't leave like that," he said, shocked.

"I'm right down the hall. No one will see."

"You can't be too sure. Wait a minute." He went to the bedroom and took a pair of Natalia's jeans from the closet. "Here put these on."

Tracy was too tall, and the jeans reached only her mid-calf. Mark couldn't help but laugh. "Didn't you know that capri length is in style?" she asked and opened the door. "Thank you, Mark...for everything. And remember I'm just down the hall." She kissed him on the lips.

"Tracy...this can't happen again."

Tracy just grinned. "I understand you feel obligated to say that." She opened the door and sprinted down the hall.

Chapter Fourteen

❤

WHEN THE SHIT HITS THE FAN

"Oh, no!" Natalia jumped up.

"What's wrong?" Shawn jumped up with her and squinted. Natalia checked her watch. It was two o'clock in the morning. "Mark must've put out an APB on me by now."

Earlier, Shawn had fried chicken wings and baked a pan of macaroni just the way his Aunt had taught him. The food was very tasty and very filling. After eating, they watched a few of his movies, and before they knew it, fell asleep.

"I forgot to pick Mark up from the airport. He must think something happened to me. He's probably got the police scouring the whole of New York."

"What are you gonna tell him?" Shawn asked, hopefully wishing that this would be the last straw for Mark and he'd divorce her.

"I don't know. I don't know." Natalia was frantic.

"Calm down. You'll think of something."

"I've got to get to Long Island."

"Why?"

"He probably took a cab to Brooklyn, so I'll say that I stayed on Long Island...but fell asleep. It's worked before," she said hopefully.

"Come on, let's go," Shawn said wearily.

As soon as she arrived at the house, she ran to the phone in the kitchen and called Mark.

"Hello," he answered groggily.

"Honey, I'm so sorry...I fell asleep," she said in a sleepy voice.

"Nat, where are you?" he asked, now wide awake.

"I'm at the house."

Mark turned on the light and checked the caller ID screen. She was telling the truth.

"Did you wait long?"

"No." Mark didn't want her to know that Tracy picked him up so he didn't volunteer that information.

"I am so sorry that I wasn't there when you got in. Did you eat?" she asked.

"Uh, no...I ate on the plane. You know, first class always has something good on the menu," he chuckled nervously.

"I wish I could be there," she yawned.

"I do, too, sweetie. It's okay though. Go back to sleep. I'll see you in the morning." He couldn't bear talking to her after what he had done. Tracy's flesh flashed through his mind.

"Do you have the day off tomorrow?"

"Yeah," he replied unenthused.

"Well, goodnight, Markie. I love you," she said sweetly.

"Goodnight, Nat...I love you more."

Tymeek picked up Nut at Shawn's house. Big Stew and Jake were already in the white van that Denise rented with yet another fake driver's license and credit card. The pickup was to take place at Tony's firing range in Riverhead.

Tymeek parked on a dirt road fronted by an electronic steel gate. Shawn got out of the van first follwed by his brother.

Tymeek walked around to the back of the van, slid the door open and said, "Stew, I want you wit' me. Nut and Jake, you two stay here with the van. Be ready for anything."

Stew's big feet dented the moist dirt when he hopped out the van. Stew, Shawn and his brother walked up to the wired gate and were greeted by a tall, well-built, red bearded guard in brown army fatigues. Two black leather gun holsters with forty-four handles sticking out of them were strapped around his shoulders.

"I'm here to see Tony," Tymeek said as he looked past red beard and into the vast lot.

Red beard pulled a walkie talkie from his back pocket and grumbled into it, "I got some guys up here say they here to see you." He moved his thumb from a button on the walkie-talkie and asked, "What's your name?"

Tymeek sucked his teeth and answered, "He knew I was comin'. Tell him the only black muhfucka he was supposed to meet wit today is here." Stew chuckled. The guard cracked a half smile and pressed the button again and repeated Tymeek's words verbatim. They could hear the static filled laughter coming from the black box. Then the laughter stopped abruptly and the voice commanded, "Let em' in."

The guard opened the gate wide and looked at the van before leading them into an aluminum barn-like structure. They walked the length of it until they reached a back room. Bulletproof partitions fronted a courtyard filled with animal and human forms painted on paper targets. The guard stopped at one of the partitions and whispered to a compact, muscular man wearing brown tinted glasses and slicked back hair.

Tymeek scanned the environment. Two thick-necked men built like body builders stood guard at the last two firing booths. It didn't appear as if they were practicing. Instead, it seemed as if they were waiting for something. Tymeek had a feeling about Tony. He knew that Lou was under the impression that Tymeek had rolled over on him to get his appeal. He remembered how underhanded Lou had been and was sure that it ran in the family. Tymeek had only met Tony once before, a while back when Lou had a large pick-up to make. Tymeek could tell then what a racist prick Tony was. Tony was a hothead who loved trouble and always came prepared for it. Tymeek wasn't afraid of dying and Tony knew it. It made Tony dangerous to deal with.

After a brief conversation with Tony, the red bearded guard motioned for Tymeek to approach. Tymeek turned to Stew and Shawn and whispered, "I got a bad feelin' so stay over here and watch everything and everyone."

"How ya doin', Meek? It's been a long time." Tony said as he patted Tymeek's shoulder.

"Yeah," Tymeek said dryly. Tony's chubby fingers on his shoulder were unsettling, and he casually shrugged them off. The phony smile on Tony's face became a sly grin.

"I've got a truck waitin' for ya. So you got what I asked for?" Tony asked.

Tymeek wasn't distracted for a minute as to the location of the red bearded guard and the two Mr. Universe wannabes.

"I wanna see the truck," Tymeek demanded. Tony looked over at Red. "He wants to see the truck, Danny. Show him the truck."

"Come with me," Danny instructed and waited for Tymeek to follow him behind a huge curtain.

Tymeek didn't move. "I want you there with me, Tony, when I see the truck."

"Come on, guy, don't you trust me?" He held his arms out to the side. They slapped his thighs as he let them fall. "I'm a business man, Tymeek. I don't give a shit about you, but I do care about money. You got it, we do business. That's it," he smiled and stuck a cigarette in his mouth.

"Why don't you lead the way?" Tymeek asked, waiting for him to move.

"Pal, just go and look at the shit. If you're happy with what I got, we can close the deal."

"We have no deal if you don't go ahead of me...pal," Tymeek paused for effect.

Tony took a drag from his cigarette and swallowed the smoke. "Okey dokey."

Tony walked slowly toward the curtain. As soon as he was within a few inches of it, however, he stopped short. It was then that Tymeek's suspicions were confirmed. Tony was stalling. If he stepped behind the curtain, he was as good as dead.

Tony realized that by hesitating, he had tipped Tymeek off. He shouted to the red bearded guard, "Danny, don't fire yet!" and ran behind the curtain.

Tymeek snatched the gun from his waistband and followed Tony. Tony pulled a gun from his jacket but tripped. The gun fell from his hand and slid across the floor. As he tried to recover it, Tymeek jumped him and pressed the barrel of his own gun to Tony's temple. Danny pointed his gun at Tymeek.

"I'll blow a hole in your fuckin' head, Tony! You better tell that redneck muthafucka to back the fuck off," Tymeek shouted. The bodybuilders stood idly by in the last booths. Shawn and Stew moved in on them as soon as they saw the look on Tymeek's face.

Tony bolted, and Tymeek pursued. Shots were fired, and the bodybuilders fell dead in a heap. What Shawn didn't expect were the three big men charging in from the opposite direction. Big Stew emptied his clip at them. Shawn's perfect aim hit one in the eye. Nut heard the shots and jumped out of the van firing. Jake grabbed an automatic rifle and ran out after Nut. By the time they reached the firing range, bodies were strewn across the floor.

Tymeek cocked his gun at Tony's sweaty forehead and slowly slid the barrel from his brow to his cheek to his ear. Danny's finger tapped the trigger of his gun, his face red and dripping with sweat, shooting the niggah dead the only thought on his mind. Tymeek grew tired of the stand off and quickly unloaded a bullet into Tony's ear. Tony's twitching body dropped across Tymeek's knee to the floor. Danny fired and unwittingly finished off Tony. Luckily, Tony's excess fat shielded Tymeek from the deadly rounds. Shawn spun around and shot Danny in the neck and back. He fell flat to the floor but attempted to get another round off. Tymeek shot him in the chest and he dropped face first.

"The Wild, Wild West!" Stew yelled. "Let's see what's behind the Wizard's curtain!" he shouted as he ripped it down.

They all laughed, knowing that they had not only cheated death but won the spoils of war as well.

Tymeek searched everywhere but came up empty. "Where the fuck they at, you fuck!" Tymeek shot Tony's dead carcass. Blood splattered all over his sneakers.

"Shit. Don't tell me we went through all this shit for nothin'!" Jake shouted.

"Damn!" Shawn cursed, kicking the dust off his Timberland boots. His foot hit a piece of metal sticking up from the floor. He took a closer look and realized it was a latch to an opening in the floor. "Yo, I found something!" he shouted.

Tymeek ran over to where Shawn was standing, and together, they lifted a hidden plate in the floor. Steps led down to a small room. Tymeek went first and found stacks of wooden crates. He opened one; it was filled to the top with rifles and handguns.

"Jackpot!"

Happy birthday, Baby Girl. I got you something special to make sure that you slip away to see me tonight."

"I don't know," Natalia said as she peeked out of the bathroom into her bedroom. She wanted to be sure that Mark was downstairs with the other guests. There wasn't anyone in the hallway so she left the bathroom and sat on the bed. Putting the phone back to her ear, she whispered, "I can't make it tonight. Mark threw me a big party, and he's expecting me to stay home..."

"Tell him you're going to stay at a friend's house." Shawn desperately wanted to give her the engagement ring he just bought. His ring was much bigger than the one Mark had given her. And he wanted her right now more than ever.

"I can't use Tracy because she's spending the night here."

"Damn. Can't I give you your gift on your birthday? That's fucked up."

"I promise I'll see you tomorrow. Trust me, Daddy. I'd much rather be with you right now." She heard footsteps and hurried Shawn off the phone.

When the receiver hit the base, Mark was in the room. "I didn't hear the phone ring. Who was that?"

There wasn't enough time for Natalia to come up with a good lie. "Wrong number," she smiled as she hopped off the bed and hugged him. "Thank you so much for this party. It was so sweet of you."

Mark didn't fall for the sweetness in her voice. She was definitely hiding something. He pushed her away and looked into her eyes. "Do I make you happy? Or do I still bore you?" He caught her off guard and she stared at him blankly.

"The truth please...I can take it," he insisted.

"Mark, where's this coming from?"

"I need to know. Humor me." He cupped her face with his hands.

"Y-Yes. I'm happy," she tried to smile.

"That's not what I asked you." He walked out of the room.

She followed him and stopped him in the hall. "What about me? Do I make you happy?"

Without hesitation, he answered, "Sometimes."

She followed him down the stairs. Tracy was waiting at the bottom. "Hey, birthday girl. Where have you been hiding?"

"Mark, can I talk to you?" Natalia asked, ignoring Tracy. Mark turned around to face her and waited for her to speak. Tracy watched them and waited. "In private," Natalia said, through gritted teeth. She grabbed his hand and led him back upstairs. She closed the doors to their bedroom and sat on the bed. "Mark, what you said...it means that you don't love me anymore?"

Mark sighed and said, "I just want to have sex with my wife. Every time I touch you, you're either too tired or menstruating. There's always an excuse." He folded his arms. Natalia had been avoiding having sex with him for so long that he was becoming suspicious. *Good thing I still have that private investigator's number,* he thought. The mysterious phone call pushed him over the edge. *Time to call my spy.*

Natalia hadn't been having sex at all, not with anyone, for the past month. What she shared with Shawn had become more meaningful without sex, and spending quality time with Mark was simple, enjoyable fun. The truth was that she hadn't been in the mood for sex, especially not with Mark.

"Mark, I just haven't been aroused...it's not that you don't turn me on. I don't know. Maybe it's turning thirty that's making me feel differently."

Mark wasn't amused nor was he buying her excuse. "Hey, it's a party and the guest of honor should be partying," he said, effectively ending their conversation. He waited for her to meet him at the top of the stairs.

Natalia sensed that Mark had become suspicious of her. As she went back to the party, she decided to avoid Shawn for a while.

Natalia poured herself a glass of punch.

"What's going on, honey bunny?" André whispered in her ear.

"Oh, Andy..." Natalia sighed.

Tracy joined them with an empty glass in her hand. "I need a refill."

"I can't believe you're drinking a non-alcoholic beverage," André chided.

"Who says there's no alcohol in it?" Tracy grinned.

"There can't be." Natalia looked into her glass. "I don't taste any."

"God, I'm just kidding." Tracy poured herself some more punch and rested the glass on the table.

"So...what's going on with you and Mark tonight? You guys don't look like the happy couple we all know and love."

Natalia glanceded at André.

"You're too damn nosy, Tracy. Besides I asked first." André and Tracy simultaneously turned to Natalia.

"Well?" Tracy pushed.

"I think that Mark suspects that I'm cheating on him because I haven't been giving him any...um, any...uh, you know."

Tracy's smile widened as she imagined how to take advantage of the situation. "How long has it been?"

"A little over a month."

"Mmn. That poor man." Tracy shook her head and continued, "I bet Shawn is getting his share and then some."

Natalia pushed Tracy hard. "It's not like that. We haven't had sex either."

"Really?" André asked surprised.

"We're becoming close friends. He respects me enough not to pressure me. Besides, I like watching him squirm," she replied.

"How ironic. Married and celibate," Tracy giggled.

"Hush, he's coming," André warned.

Mark broke through their circle. "A conspiracy?" he asked with a faint smile.

Tracy looked seductively into his eyes. "Maybe," she grinned. She was hitting on him right in front of his wife. He felt the urge to grab her and ravish her, but instead, he moved his eyes from her deep v-neck to Natalia's face.

"I don't recall giving the birthday girl a kiss," he announced and stepped closer to Natalia. He kissed her sensuously on the mouth, hoping the kiss would deter Tracy from coming on to him again.

"Wow!" Natalia exclaimed.

"Can we go upstairs, now? I have something to give you," he whispered in her ear, licking her lobes and caressing her neck.

"Okay," she answered breathlessly, aroused that he had kissed her that way with so many people around. André had left the kitchen, but Tracy lingered, pretending to search for another glass.

She became turned on watching their kiss and imagined them making love. They were both so beautiful.

Even with the loud music playing downstairs, Tracy was able to hear Natalia moan and Mark grunt through the bedroom doors. She heard faint thumping and slapping noises. She sucked on her middle finger, preparing to satisfy herself in the powder room. She used the sounds of their sex as an aphrodisiac. When she was done, she rejoined the party with a pink glow on her face.

Mark and Natalia returned to the mix a while later. No one missed them. The party was lively and singles were hooking up left and right. Tracy had many admirers and gave her card to a few. In the wee hours of the morning, the party finally died down as everyone slowly filed out to their cars.

The last thank you was said, and Natalia was off to bed. Mark gathered up the gifts and put them in the living room. Tracy stayed up to help him even after he insisted that the maid was coming in the morning to clean up.

As he was tying closed a trash bag, Tracy made her move. She pulled her dress up over her head, dropped it to the kitchen floor and stood naked behind him. She slid her hand around his chest then down to his crotch, gently rubbing it until the soft lump became a solid mound of manhood.

"Stop," he whispered, breathing heavily, trying to move her hand away. It felt so good, but he couldn't have sex with Tracy when Natalia was right upstairs. He grabbed her hand and turned around. "We can't," he whispered with regret when he saw her beautiful naked body.

"Oh yes we can, Mark. She's asleep." Tracy persisted, moving her hand into the waistband of his pants. "We can."

"No, Tracy. No..."

Tracy grabbed his head and forced a kiss onto his lips. He kissed back eagerly. She had him.

He wrestled with temptation and finally ran upstairs. He had to get away from her; he couldn't resist her. Running seemed to be the only answer. He quietly closed the bedroom door and went into the bathroom. Tracy boldly opened the bedroom door, crept past her sleeping friend and went in after him.

"What are you doing?" he hissed, astounded.

"I told you that I'm a go-getter," she whispered into his ear.

Mark grabbed her by the hand, checked on Natalia, then escorted Tracy out the room. He pulled her down the hall to one of the guest bedrooms.

"You're crazy, you know that?"

Tracy just smiled, rubbing her erect nipples. She lay on the bed spread eagle.

"I am very, very flattered," Mark said, watching as Tracy's hands roamed her body. "I want to...God, I want to...but I can't." He walked out of the room.

"What?" Tracy asked in disbelief. She sat up and shook her head.

Mark returned to his bathroom and rinsed his face with cold water. He slipped under the covers and snuggled up to his wife. He gazed at her angelic face in the dim light and hoped that she revered him in the same way.

In the morning, Natalia helped Tracy load her wheeled travel suitcase into the trunk.

"This thing is heavy," she exclaimed, closing the trunk.

"Thanks, Nat."

"Well, I'll see you when you get back. Maybe you'll get lucky in the city of love." Natalia giggled.

"Oui, oui!" Tracy smiled and got in her car. She rolled down the window and said, "You sure you don't want to come? I hear French men are incredible in bed."

Natalia's eyebrows jumped. "I've got to be at the opening of the Foles Wing at the Sydney Rehabilitation Center on Monday."

"Oh, right. Well, I'm off. Come here."

Natalia moved closer to the car. "What?" she asked.

"Closer," Tracy instructed. Natalia put her head all the way in the window.

"Is this close enough?" she laughed.

Tracy grabbed her face and kissed her on the lips, "I'll see you in three weeks!" She waved at a stunned Natalia and drove off. Natalia dismissed the kiss as a joke and went back into the house.

Lottie busily moved from room to room, dusting and sanitizing. The phone rang, and she answered it. "Mrs. Delucchio," she called to Natalia who was sitting at the dining room table, sipping a cup of tea. Still not used to her married name, Natalia did not respond. The maid brought the phone to her. "A call for you, Mrs. Delucchio."

"Oh, I'm sorry. I didn't even hear it ring. Thank you." She put the receiver to her ear. "Hello?"

"I want to see you today, no excuses."

"Shawn? You shouldn't call me here!" she hissed in a low voice.

"Just get your ass over here," he commanded.

"Yes, master. Give me two hours."

"One and a half," he said and hung up.

Natalia was more excited than usual to see him. Perhaps it was because Shawn had become more than a lover — he had proven himself to be husband material. But perhaps, she was just horny.

Watching his wife's half-naked body bounce up and down on the screen made Mark angry as hell.

The morning after Natalia's party, Mark had rehired the private investigator to follow Natalia but never expected results so quickly. After just two weeks of surveillance, the detective had gathered evidence of Natalia's extracurricular activities and had dropped off the videotape Mark just watched. Embarrassed that his wife had been seen in all her glory, Mark rushed him out of the house with yet another large pay off.

Once he was alone, Mark's heart sank way down to the pit of his stomach. He couldn't believe that Natalia hadn't ended her affair with Shawn. He was furious.

The tape was three hours long. He watched as Natalia and Shawn had sex on a couch and on the floor. At the end of the tape, Mark was shocked by Shawn's sensual marriage proposal and Natalia's response. As she remained perched on Shawn's lap with her legs wrapped around his back, her lover looked deeply into her eyes and said, "I know that I can't have you right now. But I'm gonna ask anyway..." He slid his pinkie finger in and out of his mouth. Then he took her ring finger into his mouth and slid the diamond ring onto it using his teeth. "Marry me, Baby Girl." Natalia was all choked up but still managed to say, "If I could...I would marry you right now."

A single tear rolled down Mark's cheek. He hadn't been an angel, but he didn't plan on cheating on her again. It hurt him to the core to hear her admit to loving someone else — a murderer at that.

Earlier, Natalia had called to say she'd be home late. She claimed to be with André. Mark didn't question her. Then the detective called.

The television screen went blue; the tape had stopped. Mark's eyes were bloodshot from too many hours staring and crying at disturbing images. The chest of his silk robe was wet from angry tears. Feeling vindictive, he thought of Tracy. She seemed to want him more than his own wife.

He heard a car in the driveway and looked at his watch. It was after midnight. There was no question in his mind that Natalia had been with Shawn. Mark paced the floor waiting for her to come in, and startled her as she stepped through the door.

"Oh, hi. What are you doing up so late?" she smiled nervously.

"Where did you and André go tonight?"
"Nowhere special. We just hung out." She tried to slip past him and up the stairs. Mark smelled a fruity aroma as she neared him.
He grabbed her arm. "I want to show you something."
"I'm tired. Can't it wait until tomorrow?" she asked.
"You're tired, huh?" he scoffed.
She didn't like Mark's tone. "Excuse me? Is something wrong?" she asked.
"Come with me." He took her arm and guided her to the TV room.
Mark sat Natalia down on the couch and stood in front of her. She wondered what he was up to and tried to look around him. He pressed play on the VCR remote then sat next to her. The videotape began to play. It showed her talking to Shawn outside his townhouse.
"Explain this to me," Mark calmly asked.
"H-how did you get this?"
"What were you doing? Tell me what you were doing with him," Mark requested agitatedly.
"Well, w-we, we just talked..." she stammered.
"That's it, right? Just talking. Talking about this and that, right? Okay." He blew hard and shook his head. He fast-forwarded to the part where Shawn proposed. Natalia was horrified at the sight of her atop Shawn's lap. She turned away from the screen.
"That doesn't look like talking, does it? Stop lying to me!" He forced her to look at the screen.
"Now I see why you couldn't perform your wifely duties with me. You were too busy fucking some lowlife drug dealer!" he shouted. The veins in his neck bulged and pulsed with every word.
"You had me followed? I can't believe you would violate my privacy like that."
"Violate? Violate!?" he shouted at her with a look of disbelief. He hopped off the couch, grabbed her and threw her down on the floor, hiking up her skirt to find that she wasn't wearing underwear.
"You fucking slut!" he shouted, staring at her neatly trimmed pubic hair. He couldn't concentrate. Blood from his brain rushed to his cock. Rage fueled his hormones and excited him. He couldn't help himself.
Mark untied his robe and exposed his rock-hard penis. She realized what he wanted but was too guilt ridden, too horrified to even contemplate having sex with him.
"Leave me alone!" Natalia cried and attempted to get up.
An animalistic urge overcame Mark. He pushed his wife down, grabbed her arms and pinned them over her head. His fingers dug

into the soft flesh of her wrists with such force that he cut off her circulation. He was tired of being a sucker. With a vengeance, he thrust himself into her. She pleaded for him to stop, but he commenced to rape her anyway. He closed his eyes to shield himself from the pain, shock and fear in her eyes. He pounded into her until he exploded.

When he pulled out, he swatted the sweat from his forehead into her face. Looking into her tear-filled eyes, he spat, "Now you've been violated." And left the room.

Natalia couldn't move. She remained on the floor, shocked by what had just happened. *Who was that man? Mark would never...*it was too insane to be true. She pulled her skirt down and curled into a fetal position.

Mark stuffed a few shirts and some underwear in a small bag and took four of his suits from the closet. He went outside and tossed everything onto the back seat of his car. When he went back into the house for the last time, he saw that Natalia was still on the floor, curled up like a baby. He looked down at her, regretting what he had done, then shaking it off. She deserved it. He stepped over her, took the tape from the VCR, looked at her one last time and left.

Natalia rolled onto her back and slowly sat up. She was in pain. Her wrists were bruised, and she hurt down below. It hadn't been a dream. Mark had really raped her. She stood up and made her way to the bedroom. The closet doors and dresser drawers were wide open. Mark had left her.

Of all the emotions she could have felt, guilt was the one that consumed her. She never imagined that losing Mark would affect her so much, but she took some comfort knowing that she wouldn't have to pretend anymore. She finally admitted to herself that her marriage had been a sham.

She went downstairs and nibbled on party leftovers, but nothing went down easily. Appropriately, it was raining. Natalia opened the kitchen door and went outside onto the deck. It was raining so hard that a misty gray fog had rolled in. The sound of the heavy drops hitting the wood soothed her.

Wet and cold, she went back inside and picked up the phone.

"Frenzi," a woman with a thick French accent answered.

"Tracy, please."

"One moment."

Tracy came on the line. "Hello, how may I help you?"

"Hi, Trace. It's me..." Natalia sobbed. She didn't want to cry but she couldn't help it. She poured her heart out to Tracy and told her all that had happened.

"I hate to say it...but I told you so. You should've covered your tracks better."

"I don't need to be chastised right now, Tracy."

"Hey, I told you not to marry him." Tracy was quite pleased to hear that Natalia's perfect life wasn't so perfect anymore. Tracy had once been jealous of Natalia but over time realized that what ticked her off was Natalia's spoiled ways. She had a perfectly wonderful man but wasn't satisfied. Tracy knew that if she were with Mark, she wouldn't cheat on him.

"Do you know where he is?" Tracy asked.

"No, and there's no telling what he might do."

"Hmmm, yes. I wonder what he might do. Poor guy must be so hurt..."

Natalia couldn't understand her best friend's attitude. "Where is all this coming from?"

"Look, he's a good guy. I feel sorry for him," Tracy replied blandly. A silence followed as Natalia sorted out her thoughts. "Nat?"

"What?"

"I'm sorry. I'm sure you feel bad enough. I know what we can do. Let's go away."

"Where to?"

"Anywhere but here."

"I think I should speak with Mark, first."

"Well, call him so that I can make reservations. By the way, where do you feel like going?"

"It really doesn't matter...I'll talk to you later. I'm coming out to Brooklyn."

"Why don't you meet me here?" Tracy suggested. Natalia thought it over before responding. "Sure. Is it raining there?"

"Yes, really hard, too. So I'll see you later?"

"OK."

The slippery roads were no match for the Navigator's four-wheel drive capability. The thick fog had cleared once she reached Manhattan.

She searched Sixty-Seventh Street for a parking garage and found one three blocks away from Frenzi. The boutique didn't look like much from the street, but once inside, it was a different story. Modern furniture and Plexiglas mannequins filled with water and tiny tropical fish served as backdrops for gorgeous designer clothing.

A woman with a pixie hair cut and a sparkling sequined halter top jumped out of nowhere. "Ello, iz a gloomy day, no?"

"Why yes, it is. Hi, I'm Natalia," she said, searching for Tracy.

"My name iz Patrizia." Her wide smile took up the whole bottom half of her face.

"I'm here to see Tracy."

"Oh, wait one minette," she said and scurried to the back room.

As she waited, a beaded Krizia sandal caught her attention.

"I like that one, too. Would you like a pair?" Tracy said and hugged her.

"They are cute..." Natalia grinned and hugged back.

"Done," Tracy said and turned to Patricia. "Can you get me a size seven in these?"

The doors opened and a young version of James Dean hurried into the boutique. He was clutching a white paper bag. "Damn, I'm soaked," he whined.

"Ricky, you should've taken my umbrella," Tracy laughed. He ran to the back, dripping water everywhere. "Here, sit down," she directed Natalia to a Plexiglas bench. "Did you call him yet?"

"No. I don't think he'll talk to me." She looked down at her wet toes.

"You'll never know if you don't call," Tracy said, fixing the shoe display. "Why don't you call him now?"

Natalia shook her head. "Not yet. And stop pressuring me."

"I just want this to be over for you. It's better to just go ahead and get things like this over and done with. Ya, know?" Tracy sat next to her.

"I guess." Natalia stared into space. Patricia returned with the sandals, and Natalia slipped her feet out of her shoes and into the sandals. "I like, I like," she giggled.

"Take them, they're yours." Tracy walked behind the counter. Natalia dug in her purse and pulled out her wallet. "How much?"

"Zero dollars. I'm giving them to you."

"Tracy...thank you."

"Here, now call him." Tracy handed her the phone.

"You don't give up do you?" Natalia snatched the phone from her friend's hand and dialed.

It took several attempts to reach him. Just as she anticipated, Mark slammed the phone down when she did finally get through.

To cheer her up, Tracy took her to a comedy club, The Chuckle Wagon. It was a tiny bar and grill that showcased up-and-coming comedians of all races. Tracy made sure to get a table right in front. Although none of the comedians picked on them as she had hoped, a couple of young men at the table next to theirs did. One of their group had just turned twenty-one, and his friends harassed Tracy by asking her to give the birthday boy a lap dance. Her attire, or lack thereof, led them to believe that she was a stripper. As tall as she was, she should have known better than to wear a micro mini with four inch spiked heels. Natalia couldn't help but laugh at their presumption. Tracy wasn't the least bit insulted. She even fueled the fire by winking, licking her lips seductively and blowing kisses at them.

When they returned to Brooklyn, the rain had eased up a bit. Tracy asked Natalia to spend the night at her apartment, but Natalia preferred to be alone. She kicked off her shoes and went straight to the bedroom. She flopped down on the bed and wondered where Mark was staying. He had stopped subletting his old apartment a long time ago, and she couldn't imagine him shacking up with somebody else already. She called his cell again. After hanging up on her twice, Mark finally let her get a word out.

"Please..." she hesitated as she realized that he was on the line. There was a painful silence between them. Mark let loose a long drawn out sigh and asked, "What's the use calling me, Natalia? What's done is done. It's over now. Most definitely over," he declared dryly.

"I feel the need to explain myself."

"What is there to explain? You're a whore!" he yelled.

"Mark, I know you're angry with me. But please put your anger aside and let's talk...in person."

"I don't think you want to do that," Mark sounded irritated.

"Mark, like it or not, we're married. We need to talk so we can figure out what to do next."

"I already know what to do. Ever hear of divorce?" he asked sarcastically.

"Mark, please. Can we talk in person? I really want to get this whole thing over with. Please. Where are you? I'll come to you if you want."

Mark's anger came and went. What he and Tracy had done in no way evened the score, but it did earn her the right to see him face to face and explain why she hurt him. "I'll meet you in front of the Catholic church on Clinton Street in twenty minutes."

He must be somewhere in Brooklyn, but where? Natalia wondered. "Okay. Twenty minutes." She was anxious to see him — to apologize, to say goodbye and to find out how he planned on taking his revenge. Would he take half of her wealth?

Natalia stood in the rain on the church steps. Her hair was soaked and sticking to her head and face. She checked her watch. Mark was more than ten minutes late. She didn't believe he wouldn't show up so she remained where she was hoping that sooner or later he'd come.

Another ten minutes later went by before he appeared. "I was going to leave you out here, but I just couldn't do it," he said, his love for her still apparent.

"I'm glad you didn't." She looked into his sad eyes.

"Mark, I love you, and I care about you...but I'm not in love with you." Her words cut into his heart.

"I kind of figured that out after seeing the video." He used sarcasm as a shield.

"I married you for the wrong reason."

"What reason was that?" he asked.

"I felt like I had to. I couldn't...I didn't want to let you down. And you were my security blanket. Safe. I knew what to expect. I knew what I had in you. I felt like I owed you. I was stupid, I know." The burden lifted from her heavy heart and released her.

"Really. Well, I was stupid for not seeing you for what you are, a..."

"Mark, please. I understand that you're angry, but I've had enough of the name-calling," Natalia cut him off before he could call her another demeaning name.

He cupped her cheek with one hand, moving the wet hair from her face, and shook his head. "Why is it that we can never have what we truly want? No matter how much of a good thing you think you have..." He looked at her long and hard. She waited to hear the rest of his sentence, but he didn't finish. He just left her standing on the steps in the rain.

Chapter Fifteen

❤

BETWEEN A ROCK AND A HARD PLACE

"I wanna see some dirty southern ass!" Nut chuckled.

"We here for business, so act like it," Tymeek said sternly. Luck had been on their side. They made it all the way to Georgia without any state trooper interference. Interstate 20 took them directly to the convenience station where they were scheduled to meet Boone, the man with whom they were about to make a major deal.

"Damn, it's mad quiet out here," Nut observed.

"That's why I like it," Tymeek said as he pumped gas. The air was remarkably refreshing.

Shawn missed his woman. In order to make a quick call to her, he decided to go into the mini-mart for privacy. "I'ma get a soda," he announced.

"Bring me a Pepsi," Nut shouted.

Shawn walked with a suave bop to the mini-mart. Before he reached the door, Big Stew also yelled out, "Bring me a forty ounce Pepsi!"

Shawn laughed and went into the store. He made his way to the back and searched the refrigerators for a six pack of Pepsi. When he found it, he decided to buy two.

As he waited on the long line to pay, he pulled out his cell phone. Natalia knew he was going to Georgia, but he had led her to believe that his grandfather had died and he was going to the funeral. Shawn's grandfather had died — five years ago. But it was a plausible story none-the-less.

"Hey Baby Girl," he said sweetly.

"Hi big Daddy." He could hear the smile in her voice. "I miss you," she cooed.

"Me too," he whispered as he moved with the line. He noticed that the woman in front of him was eavesdropping. "I miss that sweet pussy," he said loud enough for her to hear.

"Ooh, you're so nasty," Natalia laughed.

Shawn watched as the eavesdropper shook her head and squeezed closer to the customer in front of her.

"Have you reached Decatur yet?" Natalia asked.

"Nah, but we mad close."

"Uh...okay. What?" she wasn't sure what he had meant.

"Oh, I forgot that I was talking to the grammar queen. I said, we really close...aiight?"

"Aiight, yo," she laughed.

"So what's up wit dude? Has he been tryin' to get at you or what?"

"Who, Mark? No. I haven't seen him. But I do have a meeting with him and his lawyer tomorrow. God only knows what they're going to ask for. But enough about me. I want to offer my condolences."

"Thanks," he replied, not feeling too good that he once again had to lie to her.

"I can't wait to see you again. When are you coming back?" she asked with the anticipation of a child.

He paid for the six packs as he cradled the phone between his ear and shoulder. "Maybe tomorrow. I got a business to run, nah-mean?" He put a twenty on the counter.

"Good. I want to see you as soon as you get back. Do you understand me?" she teased.

"Aiight ma," he laughed.

"I love you...and I don't care who's listening. You'd better say it back to me."

"I love you," he replied as the smiling clerk handed him his change. He quickly clipped the phone onto his belt and went back to the van. Stew and Nut were both resting against the side of it. Stew kept wiping droplets of sweat from his brow and nose with a handkerchief. And Nut stretched like a cat and pressed his butt up against the van.

"Here." Shawn handed one of the six packs to Nut. "You want one?" he asked Tymeek whose feet dangled out of the driver's side door.

"Hell yeah, niggah!" he chuckled and snatched a cold can. He gulped the soda, and, as if he were in a television commercial, let out a satisfied "Aaah".

"I just called Boone. He's comin' to meet us and guide us the rest of the way," Tymeek said and reached for another can of Pepsi.

"Damn, how long is it gonna take for him to get here?" Shawn asked.

"About an hour."

Shawn shook his head and wiped the sweat from his forehead with the back of his hand. "What we supposed to do for an hour?"

"Wait." Tymeek crumpled his empty can with one hand.

Whut up niggah?" Boone said as he and Tymeek briefly embraced.

"Ain't nuttin,' " Tymeek replied.

"I got a shack down dere in da woods." Boone pointed towards the cluster of trees.

"This is some jungle type shit," Nut chuckled.

"Ay, Shawn, whut up, baby?"

"Sup," Shawn replied as he pounded his closed fist onto Boone's. Boone took them through the woods and down a crude path to the broken down shack. Two big country boys were waiting for them.

"So what you got?" Boone asked as he pushed open the screen door.

"A hundred like you wanted," Tymeek replied, waiting outside the shabby screen door and watching as Big Stew effortlessly dragged two crates of guns down the hill. When he reached the shack, Tymeek took one from him and dragged it inside.

Sitting on a card table in front of Boone was a big black canvas bag. Tymeek pushed the crate with his foot until it was in front of Boone's. Boone handed Tymeek the black bag then glanced over at one of the guards standing watch by a dusty window. Their eyes met, and Boone nodded toward the crate. The guard went to it and pried the lid off with a crowbar. Both he and Boone reached in and began their inspection. Tymeek looked to Shawn who had pulled out a money-counting machine from a faded duffel bag Nut brought to the table. Shawn helped Tymeek pull out the rubber banded stacks of money. Tymeek removed two rubber bands from one stack and placed it into the machine. The machine immediately began flicking through each bill.

"Damn, niggah! You ain't no joke, you got yo' own money machine and shit," Boone chuckled.

"Ya know how we do," Tymeek smiled and continued stuffing stack after stack into the machine. The count amounted to what he had been expecting, and Boone had what he wanted. The transaction was complete.

"Aiight man, we out. One," Tymeek said as Boone gave him a pound. They were two of a kind — all business and no play. The men parted ways with their entourages lagging behind as they hiked back up the hill to the path.

The back of the van was now empty, and Big Stew stretched out. He made himself comfortable and fell asleep. Nut was wide awake and wired. Visions of tax-free dollars floated in his head.

Shawn admitted that he was hungry so Tymeek took them all to a small diner on the outskirts of town. They ate heartily and joked. For once, even Tymeek was in good spirits and told a couple of his own jokes.

It was pitch dark, but Tymeek still found his way back to the main road, Old Wesley Chapel. Luckily for them, it was the wee hours of the morning, and their van seemed to be the only vehicle on the road. Tymeek kept dozing, and the van swerved from time to time. They all dozed off right along with him. It just so happened that Shawn opened his eyes just as Tymeek was about to slam into the back of a state highway patrol car.

"Wake up!" he shouted. But it was too late. The van rammed right into the rear of a patrol car, jerking everyone forward. Nut's head hit the back of the driver's seat. Shawn's long arms saved his head from cracking into the windshield. Big Stew's heavy body barely moved. The State trooper stumbled out of the car disoriented. He lumbered towards the driver's side of the van with gun drawn, blood dripping down to the tip of his nose from a gash in his forehead.

"Get out of the vehicle now!" he shouted at Tymeek.

"Aiight, aiight. Don't shoot," Tymeek stalled, sliding his hand behind him. Pulling his gun from the band of his pants, he eased it slowly onto his lap. Nut and Big Stew were busy stashing the money inside their pants and socks. Shawn calmly waited for the fireworks. He knew what his brother was up to. He also knew that he would burn in hell for not stopping him.

"I said get out, now!" the trooper shouted again. He seemed to have trouble aiming the barrel of his gun directly at Tymeek.

"Chill man, I'm coming. Just don't shoot." Tymeek said. Then in the blink of an eye, he shot the trooper in the bridge of the nose. The trooper's gun went off into the air as he fell back.

"You fuckin' crazy!" Nut shouted.

"Shut da fuck up!" Tymeek yelled. "Stew, come help me get him in the car.

"WH-what? Niggah you crazy," Big Stew stuttered.

"Come on!" Tymeek yelled and hopped out of the van. He dragged the trooper's limp body back to his patrol car. Big Stew hesitantly followed and helped him stuff the body behind the steering wheel. Tymeek pulled off his T-shirt and used it to clean the door handle and the window he touched. Then he popped the trunk and found a plastic container with spare gasoline. A rusted funnel lay next to it. He opened the container and poured gas on the front seat and on the body.

"Stew, give me your lighter." Tymeek flicked on the lighter and threw it onto the state trooper's lap. He closed the door using his T-shirt. The inside of the car was engulfed in flames by the time they got back to the van. Tymeek floored the gas pedal, and the van sped off down the road. No one spoke a word all the way back to New York.

Natalia and Mark sat across from one another in the deposition room at Trunkett and Stenger law offices. Mark avoided eye contact with Natalia as their lawyers spewed legal jargon.

His lawyer slid a folder over to her lawyer. "I believe you'll find the figures accurate and our request reasonable, if not fair," he smiled.

Natalia's lawyer skimmed the contents of the folder, her face serious. "This is not reasonable and you know it," she announced and directed Natalia's attention to a paragraph that read: I, Natalia Foles, agree to a monthly stipend of 8,000.00 dollars as per request of the aforementioned, in order for the aforementioned to maintain the lifestyle said person is accustomed to.

"So this is payback? This is how you're going to punish me?" Natalia yelled. Mark looked away from her angry glare. "Answer me, you money hungry bastard! This is ridiculous! I will not pay you alimony. Hell no!" she shouted.

"Well, then, I suppose we'll just have to take our claim to the judge and air all of your dirty laundry in court for the news reporters and gossip columnists. Hell, we'll put you on the cover of the Post. Hmmm, esteemed, altruistic motivational speaker involved with murderous drug king pin. Now that's a headline," Mark's lawyer smugly chuckled.

Natalia's lawyer recommended Natalia calm down, and she did for the moment.

Mark whispered into his lawyer's ear. The lawyer then said, "My client is willing to knock it down a thousand a month, but that will be our final offer."

Natalia tried to bite her tongue, but she just couldn't. He had money of his own. It wasn't like he was broke. "You fuckin' prick!" she yelled, jumping to her feet. Her lawyer realized that Natalia might just leap across the table, so she escorted her into the hallway.

"Look, your outbursts don't help. Do you understand me?" she asked an irate Natalia.

"I'm sorry, but he's being an asshole. I can't believe he wants alimony...I can't believe it," she spoke as if her lawyer wasn't standing right there in front of her.

"Listen to me. They have the upper hand. We take this issue to court, they'll probably be awarded more than what they're offering us now." She smoothed back her hair and said, "But you're my client, and it's your call. Do you want to accept their offer?"

"Should I?" Natalia asked.

"I just told you. They have the upper hand. Unfortunately, I don't think we have much choice in the matter."

"Damn it!" Natalia stomped her right foot onto the carpet.

"Ready to go back in?" her lawyer took her hand.

"Yes," Natalia answered without emotion. She felt drained. Mark had beaten her and was sticking it to her good.

Natalia and her lawyer reentered the deposition room to find the two men laughing, at her expense, no doubt. It burned her up to see him enjoying the moment, but she kept her mouth shut. At her lawyer's insistence, she signed the documents.

She stormed out of the building and to the corner of Lexington and Thirty-sixth Street to catch a cab.

Her cell phone rang as the driver headed toward the BQE. It was Tracy.

"Damn it! I told you to meet me at the travel agency at two-thirty didn't I?"

"Oh, Tracy, I'm sorry. Are you there now?"

"No, I left. I just told Margolis to book us on a flight to Spain next week. She's going to call me around four to let me know the details."

"Spain?"

"Well, you know how badly I want to discover my roots...besides you didn't show up, so you can't get mad at me. You should have been there to pick a destination together. Now you're stuck with me on my cathartic adventure to find Tracy senior." All Tracy knew about her mother was that when she was two years old, she fled to her native country after committing grand larceny. She had embezzled money from the Windham Modeling agency where she worked as a bookkeeper and had wired funds to her deceased mother's bank account in Spain. She did call Tracy every year on her birthday and sent beaded jewelry she designed herself. Tracy had only one photo of her mother. In it, her mother held her in her arms and was wearing what Tracy called a 'hooker poncho' because it seemed to be the only thing she was wearing. Her bare legs were short but sexy. And her bold blue eye shadow and bright red lips made her seem whorish. Tracy didn't feel any anger towards her mother. In fact, she longed to see her again and ask her face-to-face why she did what she had done.

"Do you even know how to locate your mother when we get there?"

"I'm not at liberty to answer that question over public air waves."

"Alright, Tracy. I'll stop by your place later."

"Well, why didn't you show? And what happened at the meeting?"

"I'll tell you when I see you, okay?"

"Oh, don't tell me. You're with him aren't you?"

"No, I'm not. I'll speak to you later. Buh-bye."

In spite of the stench of week-old garbage and the sound of shrill sirens, New York never looked so good.

Big Stew ditched the van, and through one of Shawn's chop shop hook-ups, replaced it with a burgundy Buick with a new identity. Nut was relieved when Shawn took the keys from Tymeek and ordered him to chill out in the backseat. Minutes later, Tymeek was asleep.

"Yo, how we know they ain't gon' trace that trooper back to us?" Nut asked as he fidgeted in his seat.

"Nut, we burned him up. Ain't gon' be no fingerprints and you know there wasn't no witnesses."

"Your brother is out there, yo. That niggah just don't give a fuck!" Shawn drove to his brother's house and dropped him off. When Tymeek was safe in his bed and sleeping like a newborn, Shawn looked down at him in astonishment. *How could he kill a cop just like that and then sleep like ain't nuttin' go down. This muthafucka is cold blooded.* But, in reality, it wasn't anything new to Shawn. He had witnessed his brother's wrath before. But this last episode bothered his conscience badly.

Shawn locked the front door and got in his car. He thought about Tymeek as he drove. This killing had to be his last one. Shawn wanted Tymeek to buy the land in Florida, build his condos and settle down. Live for a change and enjoy life.

Shawn had not slept for a full twenty-four hours. As badly as he wanted to see his Natalia and make love to her, she would have to wait until he caught up on his sleep. He parked the car in his garage and dashed inside to shower before crashing. But the warm steam and the fragrance of his exotic coconut soap aroused his senses, heightened them, and invigorated him. As he stepped from the shower, he was no longer tired.

Still wet, he grabbed a towel from the rack and headed for his bedroom. He quickly blotted his back and buttocks before flopping down on the bed. It was just after ten. He dialed Natalia's number, and when she answered, her soft, kitten-like hello was so sexy, he immediately became erect.

"Hi Big Daddy!" she exclaimed.

"Hey Baby Girl. Did you miss Big Daddy?"

"Yes I did..." her voice became sexier by the second.

"How much?"

"A whole lot."

"So come over and prove it to me," he said seductively.

"I'm packing."

"Packing?" His body sprang up, and his dick lost steam.

"I'm sorry. I'd lose my head if it weren't attached," she giggled.

"Yeah, and?" He wanted her to get to the part about why she was packing.

"Tracy and I are going to Spain. We're leaving Thursday, and I just wanted to make sure I had everything I need. I'm going to be pretty busy the next couple of days."

"Can I come with you?"

"Ordinarily, I wouldn't mind, but Tracy's going to find her mother, and I think she would rather it be just the two of us. You understand, don't you?"

"Yeah I understand. Y'all are going to get some international dick," he sarcastically remarked.

Natalia giggled so hard, she snorted.

"Damn, you got dolphins over there?" he chuckled.

"Ha, ha...you're hilarious."

"There you go with those big words again."

"You really should be a comedian, Shawn."

"I know. I got mad jokes. But listen, I wanna see my Baby Girl anyway. So wassup?"

"Now, you know I'm coming Daddy."

"Multiple times, baby. Ya know how Big Poppa do."

The air conditioner's cool breeze dried their sweat as they lay holding each other. Shawn and Natalia were on another planet where no one but the two of them existed. They had made love for two hours. He had kissed every part of her honey skin, and her lips and tongue had ventured to previously unexplored parts of his muscular body. Even though they had been on the trip before — many times — this trip felt as if it were their first. *What is it about Shawn Wilson?* she asked herself. Why is he the only man ever to be able to open her up and make her feel — really feel — love, heart first? She looked into his young face and realized that whatever it was, it couldn't be dissected. He would remain an mystery, her splendid enigma.

As usual, he could have gone another round, but he saw her contentment as she lay within the security of his powerful arms.

"Shawn, I've never been so at peace..." Her fingers fluttered from his nose to his lips, finally landing on his dimpled chin. "I can't remember ever being with a man who made me feel as if nothing else matters but the two of us and the moment. You are my comfort zone." She didn't care if he sensed her vulnerability. He was The One. She could feel it.

"You must be The One for me, too. I've never just cuddled before," he chuckled, his breath gently tickling her face. She smiled at him, and he at her, and all was right with the world.

They slept for hours and wouldn't have awakened if the phone hadn't rung. Shawn didn't answer it, but Natalia jumped up and reached for the phone, forgetting that she wasn't home. "Nah, boo, let it ring."

"Oh. I'm sorry, I thought I was home," she mumbled sleepily, and laid her head back down on his chest.

The house phone stopped ringing but then his cell phone began. "Shit." He gently lifted Natalia's head and placed it on the pillow. He grabbed the phone from his dresser and answered, "What?"

"What da fuck took you so long?" Tymeek yelled, "Derrick and em' got robbed."

"Fuck!" Shawn shouted. Natalia jumped up again, this time more coherent. She watched Shawn's expression and knew instantly that something was wrong.

"They got it all. That's fucking up my count, yo." Tymeek shouted into the phone. "Can you believe this shit?"

"Damn! So what we gon' do?"

"Hector said it was them niggaz from Snyder. I got some shit for 'em though. But now I gotta get them things from the basement. Ya know what I'm talkin' about, right?"

"Yeah." Shawn answered. Tymeek was referring to the remaining crates they had found at Tony's artillery range. Tymeek had stashed them inside the basement of a boarded up building that belonged to another one of his associates.

"Come meet me at da house," Tymeek ordered before hanging up.

Shawn knew that his brother wouldn't want to know that he was laid up with his nemesis and didn't want to leave. He knew that Tymeek saw the land deal slipping through his fingers and would do anything to keep it in his grasp. Shawn had to go. He turned to look at what he would be leaving behind. She stared at him, confused.

"Baby Girl, I gotta run take care of something. Will you wait for me?"

"I've got to run some errands tomorrow morning."

"So what that mean? I'm not gon' see you until you come back from Spain?"

"I didn't say that, did I? I can come by tomorrow night." She swung her feet off the bed and onto the floor. He walked over to her just as she stood up and grabbed her naked body, pulling it to him. Their skin felt nice and cool against each another.

"Damn, I wanted to lay with you until the sun came up," he whispered.

"Me, too," she whispered into his chest.

"I love you," he said and kissed the top of her head.

"I love you more." She wrapped her arms around his waist and sighed as she squeezed.

Tymeek was puffing on a blunt when Shawn walked in. He was surrounded by an entourage of people he considered associates. He never called them friends. Most of them worked for him, and the rest had been in his circle ever since he entered the drug game. Upon seeing his brother smoking, Shawn knew that there would be a body count before the night was over.

"Those muthafuckaz don't know!" Tymeek shouted as he paced.

Shawn made his way through the circle of bodies around his brother. Tymeek looked up and saw him. For a brief moment, the red beams of murder piercing his vision disappeared and he grabbed his little brother and hugged him. But just as quickly as he grabbed him, he pushed him away.

"We goin' to Flatbush. Its war, nahmean?" Tymeek's eyes lit up, bloodshed red again.

"Ty, lemme holla at you for a minute," Shawn said, putting his arm around his brother's shoulder and guiding him to a quiet corner of the room.

"What?" Tymeek asked as he sucked more smoke from the blunt.

"You know I'm down to get these niggaz...but they just did that shit. Think, man. They gon' be waitin' for us to retaliate. You headed straight into an ambush."

Tymeek was so angered by the news of the robbery, he hadn't

thought things through. His only interest had been revenge. Now, as Shawn's arm rested on his shoulder, he recognized the truth. If he went out on this rampage, it would be another gamble with the law, and he might be caught. But something had to be done.

"Shawn, if we don't go for those muthafuckaz tonight, they gon' think a niggah gettin' soft. We know where they at wit my shit. I wanna get em' now before they move. Look, I got all those vests from Tony's range so we ain't gotta worry. I don't care if they know that we on our way, they dying tonight, yo."

Shawn watched the expression change on his brother's face. It was out of his hands now. All he could do was ask, "So where's my vest?"

They couldn't sneak onto Snyder Avenue even if they wanted to. The caravan of jeeps and cars was too obvious. Shots rang out all along the streets. Shadows jumped from behind cars, and jeeps and dashed behind buildings, cars and even innocent crackhead bystanders. One of the robbery accomplices jumped into a Yukon and attempted to speed off. But Tymeek's crew mowed the truck with bullets and it rammed into a rundown, two-family house. The engine fluids leaked, ignited, and finally exploded. The blast shattered glass and splattered bodies. With police car sirens nearing the scene, everyone scattered like roaches. All that was left for the police to sift through were dead bodies and debris.

Instead of going back to Queens, Tymeek drove north to Scarsdale. His hideaway apartment was as large as a house. The roomy duplex was decorated just as lavishly as his home in Queens, but since it was too far from all of his businesses, Tymeek used to sublet it to his cousin-in-law. She had moved to Maryland, but left the place spotlessly intact.

Shawn and Tymeek were alone in the hideaway. The other crew members also knew to go anywhere but their homes.

Once again, Tymeek had cheated the law. And even though he didn't retrieve his money, he felt victorious. His reputation remained intact. But the score had not been settled, and he still needed to come up with more cash. The land deal deadline was looming, and he wouldn't let it slip through his fingers.

Tracy stopped in front of what appeared to be a huge, gorgeous, painted billboard of a starlit sky. But it wasn't a painting at all. It was actually the night sky of Valencia.

The city was more spectacular than either Tracy or Natalia had dreamed. As she stepped out of the car, Tracy breathed in the sweet, moist air and would have sworn she tasted roses.

The Astoria Palace Hotel looked its name with marble pillars and huge crystal Chandeliers. Their room had a terrace overlooking the entire city of Valencia. The view was breathtaking.

Natalia opened the glass paned doors to the terrace and leaned over the flowerpots hanging from the carved stone rail. "This place is overwhelming," she said, exhilarated.

"Just like its people. Ahem," Tracy said and patted herself on the shoulder. She put her arm around Natalia's neck, resting her temple against Natalia's as they watched the people scurry beneath them.

"Oh, Tracy, this is so nice. Thank you for making the arrangements."

"Anything for my best girlfriend," she smiled and went back inside the suite. "Let's unpack and go to the cocktail lounge," Tracy yelled to Natalia who was still out on the terrace.

"For what? So you can drink yourself silly?"

Tracy had already helped herself to a tiny bottle of Bacardi rum.

"Here we go again," Natalia mumbled under her breath.

"What?" Tracy held her hands up. "Puhlease, it was right here in the room. That means we can drink it. Besides, maybe we won't have to leave the room," she giggled and began sucking on the short neck of the small bottle.

"Tracy you shouldn't be drinking while we're here on a quest to reunite you with your mom." Natalia snatched the empty bottle from Tracy's fingers.

"I should meet her drunk. Show her what kind of life she made for me. A life without a mother...a fucked up little girl without any maternal guidance," she said with contempt.

Natalia saw that Tracy was fighting back tears so she went to her friend and hugged her.

"I'm alright," she sniffled and pulled away from Natalia's tight hug. "Okay, I know what we should do. Let's take one of those sightseeing boat rides."

"I don't think they'll be running now. Remember we're in a different time zone. It's past ten," Natalia replied.

Tracy smiled a drunken, goofy smile and began to unpack her suitcase. "Where's my red dress? I know I packed it. You know I don't leave home without my fuck-me-now dress!"

"I'm going to take a quick shower, or do you want to take one first?" Natalia asked as she pulled her T-shirt over her head.

"No. You go ahead. I'll take one later." Natalia looked at her in disbelief.

"What? I don't feel dirty," Tracy said, tugging a red piece of cloth from the bottom of her suitcase.

"Whatever you say," Natalia waved her hand and headed for the bathroom.

When she got out of the shower, Natalia saw that Tracy's suitcase was still on top of the bed where she had left it. Clothes were strewn all over the bedspread. *I can't believe she left me,* Natalia thought as she put lotion on her body. She hung her garment bag on the hook on the back of the closet door and unzipped the bag. She flipped through the various outfits she had brought but couldn't decide what to wear.

Forty minutes later, she finally made up her mind. Another hour passed before she was dressed and ready to go. She had selected a pale pink linen dress and pink sandals. After applying a matching shade of pink lip gloss, she grabbed the room key and stuffed it into a small, pink beaded purse.

It wasn't difficult to find Tracy. She was in the cocktail lounge causing a stir. As usual, admirers flanked her, her red dress her calling card.

Natalia sighed as she approached the group of men. Their hands clung to bottles of champagne as they gathered like fans around Tracy, the superstar. One of the men leaned over the table and whispered into Tracy's ear. She seemed to enjoy the attention, but Natalia was appalled at their groping. She quickly slipped in between them and whispered into her friend's ear, "Let's get out of here." Tracy just giggled and took a sip from her nearly empty champagne glass.

"Let's go," Natalia demanded loudly.

"Go where?" Tracy giggled more. She was getting on Natalia's last nerve. *Why does she always feel compelled do this to herself? She's worth more than this,* Natalia said to herself. But it seemed that Tracy wanted, no, needed to self-destruct.

"I love you, Tracy, but I'm not going to watch you fuck yourself over!" she said dryly before storming off.

Tracy was shocked at Natalia's outburst and ran after her friend. "Nat, look, I'm not doing anything illegal. I'm just having a drink and learning about my people."

"Your people?" Natalia asked with a hint of sarcasm.

"Okay, so I wasn't born here, but I'm a direct product of Spain. Nat, I know you can't understand where I'm coming from. I'm sure you think that if anyone should be fucked up, it should be you...but I just don't have the strength that you do. I'm sorry, but I can't control myself the way you do..." she sighed and slapped her hands against her milky thighs.

"I don't think like that. I just don't want to see you hurt yourself." Just then, Natalia felt a sharp pain in her abdomen. "Ow!" she cried as she doubled over.

"What's wrong?" Tracy tried to help her friend straighten up.

"I don't know. I just felt a sharp pain right here," she pointed to where it hurt.

"Is it bad?"

"No, it's going away," she said as she stood up straight. "It's probably the salmon I ate on the plane. Lord, could you imagine? I come all the way to Spain to have my stomach pumped." They laughed.

"Alright. I'll come back to the room with you...and Nat, I'm sorry." Tracy opened her arms.

"Hey! People might think we're lesbians," Natalia laughed, pushing Tracy's arms down. "It's okay if you want to stay down here. I don't mean to be a wet blanket, but it was a long plane ride, and I'm tired." Natalia glanced down at Tracy's stomach. The red material of her dress was stretched almost to the point of transparency. "Tracy you're getting fat," she chuckled.

"That's just my beer belly. I think it's sexy." She patted her stomach, "Well, I do want to finish my drink..."

"Are you okay being down here alone?" Natalia asked.

Tracy twisted her mouth to the side and said, "You know I'll be fine and not alone! Go get some rest."

"Do you have enough mace?" Natalia asked before stepping into the elevator.

"I hope I won't need it, girl," Tracy waved.

When she awoke, Natalia looked out the French doors to the terrace. The panorama was as beautiful as a postcard. The sun shone brightly, and a slight breeze gently billowed the sheer white curtains. When she rolled over, she saw that Tracy's suitcase was still where it had been the night before. Tracy hadn't slept in her bed.

Her mouth felt as dry as if she were stranded in the Mojave Desert and the taste in her mouth was unbearable. She felt nauseous and ran into the bathroom. She bent over the porcelain bowl, prepared to vomit but nothing came up. To get rid of the horrible taste in her mouth, she started to brush her teeth. But as she did, a wave of nausea came over her again, and she barely managed to swing her head over the toilet again before everything she had consumed the day before came up. She flushed the toilet, gargled with mouthwash and brushed her teeth — twice.

After cleaning up after herself as best she could, she sprayed her Calyx fragrance to mask the distinctive foul odor. Natalia was now certain that she had food poisoning and was grateful that she had gotten it all out of her system.

Tracy was very nervous. They were on their way to Ibiza where her mother lived. Tracy's father had given her all the information he had about the woman he still loved. She was a designer of dolls, jewelry and accessories and sold her creations mainly to hotel gift shops.

Natalia had never seen this side of Tracy before. "She's probably got a new life by now. New kids..." Tracy smiled nervously again. She wouldn't admit it, but she was afraid that her mother would reject her.

"Don't think like that, Tracy." Natalia took her hand and smiled. "I'm sure she's going to be thrilled to see you."

The car dropped them off at the El Corsario Hotel.

Tracy spotted a van parked at the side of the building. "That's her name on the van!" she said excitedly. They ran to it. Tracy peeked in the window, but the van was empty.

"She'll probably be out any minute now," Natalia offered.

"What if she doesn't make the rounds herself?" Tracy asked.

"Then we will pay the driver to take us to her wherever she is." Natalia dug into her purse and grabbed a handful of peseta.

"No, I'll pay. It's my mother," Tracy said and crossed her fingers as she leaned against the passenger door and waited. They both kept their eyes glued to the service entrance. Minutes later, a woman emerged from the building with a heavyset, long haired man wearing a sweat soaked wife beater.

"Toma," the woman said to the man, slapping keys into his hand. When she looked ahead and saw Tracy, she dropped the small box she was carrying under her arm. Beaded necklaces, earrings, bangles, hand painted dolls, and toys crashed to the ground.

"Tracy?" she asked, astounded.

"Mom..." Tracy whispered with tears in her eyes. At first, they stood just staring at each another. Then Tracy ran to her mother and hugged her with her long arms.

After the woman returned the hug, she gently pried Tracy away and stepped back. Tears fell from her eyes onto the flowers on her T-shirt. "Ay, Dios mio!" she cried as she stroked Tracy's face with her small hands. "How?" she managed to say in English.

"I've always wanted to see you. I know I shouldn't have come, but

I had to. I had to see you in person. I love you," Tracy gushed.

Their reunion was a thousand times better than anything Tracy could have imagined. Natalia and the long haired man waited to be introduced.

"I love you, too. I hope your father told you that. I have pictures of you. And cards you made for me...I kept everything."

Realizing that they were in public view, Tracy wiped the tears from her face. She looked over at Natalia and motioned for her to come forward. "Mom, do you remember the Foles'? The people Daddy worked for?"

"Ah, yes. Don't tell me this is little Natty," she laughed. "I used to call you that."

"Really?" Natalia blushed.

"Yes. You and Tracy used to fight all the time over a little wooden pony I had made for her," she chuckled. "And you're still friends to this day...that is so beautiful."

Tracy's mother looked like an older, tanner version of Tracy. Poor Tracy would constantly go to tanning salons and to the beach to make her skin darker, but she would always just end up bright red. Her mother's body was fuller than Tracy's and much shorter, but it was apparent where Tracy got her shape.

The long haired man had gone to sit in the van. Tracy's mother still hadn't introduced him. She dug into her knapsack for a piece of paper and a pen and wrote her information down for Tracy. "I have more hotels to go to this afternoon, but this is my home address, and I want you to come to my house tonight for dinner." She handed the card to Tracy. "You are so beautiful," she said as she caressed her daughter's face. "Mi niña, muy bonita...muy bonita," she smiled.

Tracy was in heaven. She finally found the woman who given birth to her, the woman she had dreamt about, the woman she wanted in her life more than any other.

Tymeek chose an abandoned lot behind Shawn's used car lot to do his deal. He was uncomfortable not knowing the customer, but money was money, and right now, he needed it badly. He did, however, trust his hook-up.

A green and yellow plastic tarp hung from the chain link fence, effectively concealing the abandoned lot. It was private property, but the developer was forced to postpone construction until the building permits were issued. So the site was unguarded. It was easy to cut through the flimsy padlocks with a bolt cutter.

Tymeek stashed the crates between the corner bodega and a

burned out, abandoned building, through an underpass and down a flight of concrete steps on the far side of the lot. He shoved metal garbage cans in front of the crates to hide them from view.

He heard a car system pumping hip hop music just as he finished his preparations. A new Expedition zoomed by with Nut behind the wheel, blasting his new stereo system. Shawn sat in the passenger side. "Whut up, niggah?" Shawn shouted to Tymeek and hopped out.

"I gotta do some things before we go back there, aiight?" Tymeek said.

"Aiight. You got everything?"

"No doubt. Stew and 'em is on their way." Tymeek rushed off to his jeep.

"I'ma go inside and check up on shit," Shawn yelled after him. He went inside and opened the door to his office.

The manager was in, his feet up on Shawn's desk, chatting on the phone. When he saw Shawn, he jumped up. "Alright then, I'll call you back on that," he said and quickly hung up.

"What the fuck..." Shawn asked, bewildered.

"I'm sorry, man. I was just in here to find something and, uh, my girl beeped me."

"But why you calling her from in here? You got your own damn office," Shawn said, inspecting his desk.

The manager brushed off the desk where his feet had been and eased his way past Shawn to the door. "I'm sorry boss."

"Just keep your ass in your own office!"

The manager nodded and pulled the door closed. Shawn sat in his chair and picked up the phone. Natalia was supposed to have returned from Spain two days ago. She hadn't called him since before she left, and now he was worried. He tried not to think of the plane crashing, but he couldn't help himself.

He called her house then the condo then her cell. He left a message for her on the cell phone. "Baby Girl, you better have a good excuse for being MIA. I'm at the car dealership takin' care of some things, so call here and leave a message if I don't answer my cell. Oh and...I love you. You heard me, I said I love you."

Nut burst into the office and shouted, "They here, let's go!"

Shawn didn't like the look of things as soon as he walked into the abandoned lot. There were two men with Tymeek, grinning as they listened. None of the crew knew much about K-money except that he was the new kid on the block. He had been selling guns for a couple of months, but in the Bronx, he was already making some noise as a hustler. K-money's wide smile disturbed Shawn. Nobody in their right mind would come to a deal without an entourage.

Shawn approached them. "So where the rest of your niggaz at?" he asked him casually. Both men chuckled and looked at one another.

"That's what your man just asked me. They on their way. They ain't business oriented like me."

Shawn looked over at Nut who just shrugged.

"Let's go," Tymeek said, turning to lead the way.

"Why we can't do it out here?" K-money asked.

"I'm sayin' no disrespect, but I don't know you, nahmean. You could be on some grimy type shit. There could be eagles on the roof, nahmean?" Tymeek waved a pointed finger up in the air.

"I ain't never deal wit you before and my manz and dem ain't here yet so I'd rather we did it out here. You feel me?" K-money looked Tymeek straight in the eye.

Shawn cracked his knuckles and waited for Tymeek's outburst. It didn't come.

"True. I can understand that," Tymeek said.

Shawn couldn't believe his ears. Ty must be desperate.

"Aiight y'all. Wait here," Tymeek told them before looking up to the rooftops surrounding the lot. Then he disappeared into the underpass.

"I hear y'all niggaz got the five boroughs on lock," K-money said, watching Nut from the corner of his eye. Shawn didn't respond. Just then, the gate shook and startled everyone. Shawn reached around for his gun and was ready to squeeze until he saw Big Stew trying to squeeze his huge body through the opening in the fence. Three men followed him, one with a straw cap, one with a white du-rag tied tightly around his head, and another with a 'blow out' that looked like a short, shiny afro.

"Whut up?" Big Stew asked as he briefly hugged Shawn. "Where my niggah, Ty?"

"Down there," Shawn pointed to the underpass. He could see Tymeek's shiny bald head bobbing up and down as he dragged the crates to the top of the stairs.

"Ay, yo K, come here," Tymeek's waving hand was all they could see. K-money cautiously approached. Tymeek opened a crate.

"Damn!" K-money exclaimed as his eyes grew wide. Big Stew and Shawn were behind him now, waiting to see the money. He turned around and called to his friend. His friend moved slowly and pulled out a plastic bag from the front of his pants and passed it to K-money.

"Open it up," Shawn commanded. He didn't trust these guys one bit. The vibes he got were disturbing, but what disturbed him the most was how Tymeek didn't seem to be his usual sharp self. Ordinarily, he would have never compromised for anyone, especially a first-timer.

K-money gladly opened the plastic bag.

"Count it," Tymeek said, covering the crate.

K-money counted aloud, and when he was done, even though Shawn's hand was out, he made an extra effort to step down one step to place the bag in Tymeek's hand. K-money asked, "Um, how can we get out of here wit these?" He seemed nervous.

"That's not my problem. Our transaction is complete." Tymeek pushed the crate with his foot and called to Shawn. "If you want, you can tell him to get the car and pull up in front of the building right there." He pointed towards the burnt out building with boarded windows and blackened brick.

"Aiight," K-money said, looking upwards.

Shawn followed his eyes and saw a flicker of light. "Fuck! It's a set up!" he shouted turning to Tymeek.

But it was too late. The gate clanged as it was kicked open, and the tarp fell to the ground. A dozen men in navy blue parkas rushed them. Big Stew went for his gun and busted off shots to keep them at bay. The FBI agents fired back. K-money and his partner dove into a patch of brown grass. The others followed Big Stew's lead and began firing. The man in the straw hat ducked down and tried to reach for his gun, but a bullet pierced his thigh and sent him crashing into a pile of cardboard boxes.

Tymeek started to run but tripped over the crate. As he got back on his feet, he remembered that his little brother was still out there. When he reached the top of the stairs, his heart pounded in of his chest. Shawn lay on the ground, his hand dangling over the top step. "NO, NO, NO!!" he shouted.

Tracy was so caught up in catching up with her mother that she begged Natalia to stay a couple of days longer. Natalia agreed. Tracy was so happy. For the first time in a long time, Tracy didn't drink any alcohol. Natalia looked at her best friend as she talked with her mother. She had a wide smile on her face while she looked through a scrapbook filled with photos. Natalia smiled, too. All her friend needed was her mother's love.

The taxicab smelled of a mixture of curry and dirty gym socks. Natalia rolled down the window and took a breath of fresh air.

Tracy had taken her own cab because she wanted to go straight home. "No stops!" she said and snickered at Natalia because she knew that Natalia was planning a detour to see Shawn.

Natalia checked her messages, knowing that Shawn must have been worried about her. She had promised to call him when she got back. After hearing Shawn's deep voice say 'I love you' for the second time, she grinned. She couldn't wait to see him. She called the dealership and was told that Shawn wasn't available at the moment. The person insisted she called back. Impatient, she dialed his cell phone. There was no answer so she decided to surprise him.

It didn't take any time at all to get there. When the taxi pulled up to Shawn's dealership, Natalia noticed there was a lot of commotion going on both inside and outside. Something wasn't right. Cars were parked at odd angles in the front lot. "Doesn't he know Buick's aren't in anymore?" she giggled to herself.

She dragged her suitcases through the glass doors and left them near the entrance. Men in gray and blue suits, wearing sunglasses and carrying walkie-talkies scurried about. She approached Shawn's office and opened the door. A white man with a blue T-shirt was slamming the manager of the car lot into the corner.

"Well, well, well," he said as he released the manager, "Aaah, yes, lookie here. I see my luck has taken a turn for the better."

"Wha..." she started to say when he grabbed her. "Have a seat," he pushed her down onto the sofa.

"Get your hands off me!" she yelled and smacked his hand from her arm, "What the hell is going on?"

"I know all about you and your boyfriend, Ms. Foles," his smirk confident and demeaning at the same time. "My name is Bailey Strect, FBI." He quickly flashed his credentials in front of her face.

"I beg your pardon?"

"Just sit down and be quiet for now."

"Don't talk to me that way." Natalia pulled out her cell phone and began to walk toward the door.

"Oh, no you don't," he lunged at her, knocking the phone out of her hand.

"Are you crazy?" she asked as she struggled to get away from him.

"Let's go. I see I'm going to have to restrain you," he chuckled as he cuffed her and took her outside to a black car parked on the corner.

"Now, you just sit here and relax." He pushed her head down and shoved her into the car.

"I want my lawyer. You can't do this, damn it!" she screamed.

He rolled the window down a couple of inches and slammed the car door shut, "Just stay put."

Natalia watched him sprint down the block. What was she doing sitting in the back of a FBI agent's car, handcuffed? What kind of mess did Shawn get into this time? "Why me?" she sighed.

Shawn, wake up, yo. Come on P.B. You ain't dead," Tymeek sobbed.

Shawn's back was soaked in blood. Tymeek had dragged him to the bottom of the stairs. As he shook Shawn's limp body, he heard footsteps. It sounded like someone was dragging their feet as they ran.

With all his strength, Tymeek hauled his brother's body over his shoulder and ran to the back door of the bodega. He burst into the store, knocking over boxes. "Don't fucking say nothing. Don't you tell 'em shit and you'll live. You hear me?" he shouted at the shocked clerk. The clerk nodded. Tymeek limped cautiously out the front door. As he surveyed the street, he noticed a car double parked across from the bodega with a woman in it. His eyes locked with Natalia's and for a brief moment the world froze.

"Shawwwn! No, God, please no!" Natalia screamed, tears pouring down her face. She couldn't believe what she was seeing. Shawn was covered in blood. She grabbed at the door handle but couldn't get out. So she watched Shawn until he and Tymeek vanished around a corner.

Tymeek's knees were just about to give out when a car pulled up next to him. He turned to see Nut behind the wheel.

"Hurry up, man. Get in!" Nut shouted.

Tymeek gathered his last bit of strength and ran to the car. He lifted Shawn onto the back seat and then slid in front. He lowered his head as Nut raced to La Guardia hospital. When they reached the hospital, they both knew that they had to discreetly drop Shawn off. They wouldn't be able to stay to find out what happened.

Nut helped Tymeek carry Shawn into the Emergency Room. Then Tymeek ran to the triage nurse's station. The on-duty nurse rounded up two of her colleagues. They rushed Shawn into an operating room. Before they could be questioned, Nut and Tymeek ran out of the hospital.

By the time they reached Newark Airport, Tymeek desperately wanted to call his aunt and mother and tell them about Shawn. But he couldn't. He assumed that both their phones had been tapped. He convinced Nut that they had to leave the country and go far, far away. Nut protested but realized that they were wanted men — by the FBI, no less. They would be lucky if they could even board a plane without being captured.

Tymeek purchased two tickets to Atlanta, where he planned to acquire phony passports. While setting up shop in Georgia, he had heard about Amsterdam. Rocky told him that they loved black people there, and the women take good care of black men. He said that mostly everything was legal and had assured that if he ever needed to disappear, Amsterdam was the place to go.

Tymeek and Nut got lucky. They made their flight to Atlanta just in time. They rushed onboard, all the while checking over their shoulders. Their paranoia didn't subside until the plane lifted off.

As he looked out over the clouds, Tymeek thought of Shawn. *What if they didn't get Shawn to the hospital in time? What if Shawn was gone? How could this have happened? It was that fuckin' snitchin' hoe. I told him not to fuck wit her. Shit!*

He turned to Nut who seemed to be in pain. "What's wrong wit you? You hit?"

"Nah. I think I broke my finger trying to hotwire that fuckin' car." He showed Tymeek his crooked index finger.

"Yup, something is wrong wit it," Tymeek replied wearily. "That bitch gon' get it now. Definitely," Tymeek mumbled through gritted teeth.

"What bitch?"

"That bitch Shawn was fuckin' wit. That bitch set us up," he spat, "I told him to leave her ass alone." He pounded his fist on the armrest.

"How you know?"

"I saw her sitting in the Fed's car all comfortable and shit." He rubbed his hand over his face then sighed. "Damn, my little bro," he rubbed his eyes, trying to keep himself from crying.

"He's gonna be aiight, Ty. He's gotta be," Nut said, his voice trembling with anger.

"A hit is out on that bitch as soon as we get off this fuckin' plane. That bitch is gonna get hers. She long overdue."

Chapter Sixteen

❤

BABY BOOM

You do realize that taking my client into custody without any substantial evidence implicating her in any of your alleged assailant's criminal activities is an infringement upon her rights?" Susan Beyard's words were sharp and confident as she sat with her knees pressed together with a pad on her lap.

She whispered something to Natalia and Natalia whispered back. "I also understand there was a degree of unnecessary force used by agent Strect. I don't believe that I'd have a problem bringing a suit against him. My client is a well-respected, law-abiding citizen. There was no need for handcuffing her and shoving her around like a common criminal." She moved some loose strands of hair behind her ear.

"Ms. Beyard, I don't want things to get blown out of proportion. We believed that Ms. Foles had pertinent information that would have helped our case against the Wilson brothers. We have her on tape with one of 'em, so we presumed that she knew about his dealings."

"Well I don't't!" Natalia shouted. She jumped up and said, "Susan, please get me out of here."

"We're leaving," Susan said then turned to face the two men. "Let me reiterate, gentleman. I reserve the right to bring the civil rights infringement into court if you so much as look in my client's direction." Susan grabbed her briefcase from the floor and ushered Natalia out of the office.

My head is spinning," Natalia sobbed into Tracy's bosom. "I'm being punished."

"Where's Andy?" Tracy asked, stroking Natalia's hair

"I called him over an hour ago." Natalia's sobs got louder.

"I don't know if he's dead...I miss him so much. He's dead...I don't, oh, please no..."

"It's okay. Think positive, Nat. Think positive..." Tracy gently moved Natalia's wet face from her chest. "Lay down, I'm going to get you some tea."

She rested her head on a soft pillow. Her eyes burned, her heart ached, and her body felt lifeless. The vision of Shawn's bloody body kept flashing before her eyes, scaring her each time. "Please don't let him die. Pleassse." She called his house just to hear his voice on the outgoing message on his answering machine.

"Oh, Shawn," she moaned.

Tracy returned with a flowered teacup and matching saucer on a wooden tray. "Sit up, sweetie."

Natalia sat up and rested her head against the headboard behind her. Tracy placed the tray over her lap, and Natalia took a sip of tea. "Can you call Andy again, please?" she asked as she placed the cup back onto the saucer.

"Nat, I called him well over an hour ago, and he said he was on his way." She patted Natalia's hand. "Don't worry. He's coming all the way from Manhattan, so it's going to take him a while to get out here."

"I've got to know what happened to Shawn." She took another sip of tea. "I can't drink anymore. Here," she said as she handed the tray back to Tracy.

"I know this is driving you crazy. I wish I could tell you where he is...that he's alright..." She took the tray and left the room again. *Where could I call?* Natalia thought. *Who would know where to find him?*

His head felt heavy and his body numb. He tried to get up, but his body didn't respond to his brain's command. He opened his eyes and saw a hairy white face staring down at him.

"Hello, Mr. Wilson. You're at La Guardia Hospital. I am Dr. Letto. Can you hear me? Raise a finger on your left hand if you can hear me."

Shawn raised the index finger on his left hand. I can move, he thought. He continued to move his left hand slowly up to touch his face, but a metal cage of some sort blocked his progress. He felt along the cold bars and realized that they went down to his neck. He tried to move his right hand but couldn't. He tried to move his legs, but he couldn't.

"What's wrong wit me? I can't feel my legs!" Shawn cried out.

"Please relax, Mr. Wilson. You've been shot. One of the bullets penetrated your spinal column and is lodged in the spinal ganglion. You are paralyzed from the waist down as well as partially paralyzed on your right side. We've removed the bullet from your neck and repaired most of that damage, but at this time, we cannot dislodge the bullet in your Lumbarsacral spine. We are afraid that our interference might make matters worse."

Shawn stared up at the white ceiling wishing he was dead. To him, being paralyzed was a prolonged death he'd rather not endure. He heard other voices.

"Go ahead. He's awake now. But try not to upset him. He may also be a little incoherent from the medications."

"Thanks, doctor. This won't take long."

"Hey, Shawn. I see you're up and at 'em." Another white face appeared over him. "Look, I just want to know if you can remember what happened."

Shawn did remember. But he knew that if he told this man, he'd probably spend the rest of his shattered life in a minimum security prison. "Huh?" he played dumb.

"Do you remember what happened to you? How did you get here?"

"What happened to me?" Shawn asked.

"Do you know your name?"

"Wha-what's going on?" Shawn pretended to be disoriented. "Do I know you?"

Frustrated, the man shook his head. "Hurry up and get better. I'll be back to talk to you again."

A nurse came in and announced that he had two more visitors. Shawn expected more white faces. Instead, his mother and aunt came into the room with tears streaming down their faces.

"Stretch? Baby can you hear me?"

"Aunt Free!" Shawn managed to smile.

"I'm here too, Shawn."

"Mom?" Shawn asked in surprise.

"Yes, baby. I'm here."

"Ma, I'm paralyzed."

"We know. But they said it could be temporary. They have a specialist coming in to see you tomorrow. He's supposed to be real good with this kind of injury."

"Aunt Free, did Ty do a Whodini or did they bag him?"

"Whodini, baby. But don't worry about him. You stay strong and beat this thing. I know both my babies are gonna be alright. Don't you worry." She maneuvered her face over his and carefully planted a kiss on his forehead. His mother brought his left hand to her lips and kissed it. Shawn gently rubbed his knuckles against her cheek. He could feel moisture on her cheeks.

"Ma, don't cry. It's gonna be aiight. You know I'ma bounce back," he attempted to chuckle, but he didn't believe what he had just said.

"Stretch, they said you can't eat solids just yet. I was all set to feed you too." His aunt lifted a large black plastic bag into his view.

"Macaroni and cheese?" he grinned.

"You know it."

His mother smiled a weak smile and leaned over to look into his face. "I'm praying for you. I've accepted the lord's wrath. But I also know that he's going to forgive you and Tymeek. I know he's going to give you both second chances...he understands." Another tear slid down her cheek.

"I'm sorry, Ma." He squeezed her trembling hand.

"No, baby. I'm sorry." She broke down and Freda had to take her out of the room to comfort her. He tried to turn his head to see into the hall but the apparatus connected to his head and neck was too heavy. He could hear his Aunt Freda crying. He didn't want to hear anything anymore. As much as he tried to clear his mind of all thoughts, one persisted. Natalia...

André stayed with Natalia for two weeks, and Tracy replaced him when he went back to his salons. She arrived with a bouquet of fresh flowers.

"Honey! I'm hooome," she shouted after opening the front door with her key. Natalia ran down the stairs and hugged her.

"I'm so glad you came back! Being here all alone last night was hell."

"Cheer up, girlfriend," Tracy said as she handed her the flowers.

"Awww, that was so sweet of you!" Natalia raced into the kitchen to put them in a vase. Tracy followed.

"Andy baked this lasagna," she took a half empty pan out of the fridge.

Tracy looked down and giggled. "Damn, Nat! You must've been starving!"

"It's sooo good. Girl, you've got to taste it."

"You're kidding me, right. You ate half this huge pan of pasta at one sitting?"

"I know, I can't believe it myself!"

"That's so unlike you! But I have to admit, I've been eating up a storm lately, too..." Tracy covered her mouth as if she had said a curse.

"What?" Natalia asked, curious.

"Never mind." Tracy sat at the table and tapped her fingertips on the wood.

"OK, what's going on? Come on and tell me." Natalia sat across from her.

"Haven't you noticed anything?"

"Like what?"

"Let's just say I haven't seen my friend in like five...maybe six months."

"Well, I haven't seen mine in about a month and a half, but that's what happens with stress." Natalia shrugged and continued, "And don't you take the Pill? I remember how great it was when I was on Depo..."

"But, I'm not under stress...and I stopped taking those pills once I discovered ribbed condoms, girl!" she slapped her hand down on the table and laughed. "Look at this damn bulge." she giggled nervously, rubbing her stomach. Then she became serious again. "Nat...I'm pregnant."

Natalia's eyes widened, "Oh, Tracy...what have you done?"

"Well, I didn't do it by myself, you know," Tracy chuckled.

"Who's the Daddy?" Natalia asked mimicking a thick southern accent.

"You don't know him. He was a one-night stand during one of my vodka episodes. I really needed what he was selling at the time," she lowered her eyes to her fidgeting hands. "And I don't want to hear anything from you about safe sex or any of that shit. The condom broke, so don't think I didn't try to protect myself. It doesn't matter, anyway. I'm going to have the baby. I need someone to love. And someone to love me back...forever," she smiled dreamily.

"Tracy, Tracy, Tracy..."

"What, Nat? I don't need to hear any of your holier than thou speeches that you keep tucked away in that head of yours. Just knit your Godchild some booties and prepare for my baby shower. I'm going to need a lot of stuff!"

Natalia laughed. Maybe a baby would change Tracy's life for the better.

They ate lasagna, watched movies, reminisced about the good ol' days and snacked on Ritz crackers and rocky road ice cream until they couldn't stay awake a minute longer. Tracy slipped under the thin covers on the right side of the bed, and Natalia slept on the left.

She didn't want to sleep alone again. The night before, nightmares kept her awake. She ended up in the TV room watching late night television until she dozed off sitting up. Tonight, she turned on her side with her back facing Tracy and snuggled with a pink satin neck roll. Tracy had plumped up an extra pillow and placed it between her thighs. "Goodnight mommy-to-be." Natalia sang.

"Alright, already," Tracy snapped.

Even with Tracy next to her, Natalia barely slept. Images of Shawn played over and over again her mind. She woke up in the middle of the night sweating profusely, her hair damp and skin hot. She went into the bathroom, closed the door and turned on the faucet. She splashed cold water on her face which made her have to pee. As she began to pull her panties down, she heard a weird noise. It sounded like an arrow whizzing through the air.

"What the hell is that?" she whispered to herself. When she opened the door, she saw a dark figure retreating from the bed. Tracy's hair was matted with blood.

Natalia screamed and surprised the intruder. He tripped, but held onto one of the bedposts to stop himself from falling to the floor. He righted himself and began to shoot. Without thinking, she grabbed the cordless phone from the nightstand and hurled it at him. He blocked it, but by the time he looked up again, she was already running for the door. He pounced on her and they struggled. Natalia kicked her foot backwards repeatedly until she connected with his testicles. He groaned and released the gun. It knocked Natalia on the head before hitting the floor. She kicked back once more to push him off of her and scrambled for the gun. He grabbed her ankles, and she kicked at his face with her bare feet. She reached the gun and rolled over onto her back, aiming it at him but fumbling with it. She pressed her finger against the trigger, but nothing happened. The safety lock was jammed. "Nooo!" she yelled.

"You stupid bitch! You're dead now!" he shouted.

Natalia threw the gun down the hall. Her assailant jumped on top of her as she tried to get up from the floor. He grabbed a clump of her hair and slammed her head against the wall. He banged and banged until he heard a cracking sound. He untangled his hand from her frizzy mane and dropped her bloody head onto the floor. He rolled her over and began squeezing her neck with his gloved hands but suddenly stopped as a sharp object burrowed its way into his ear. Blood spurted everywhere as the bullet exited through the other ear.

André dropped the gun, rushed over to Natalia and dropped to his knees. "Nat, please wake up. Please..." He caressed her red face and slid two fingers down to her neck. He couldn't feel a pulse.

He ran into the bedroom to get the phone. Then he saw the bloody curls surrounding Tracy's pale face. "Aaaaaahhhhhhhh!" he screamed, his body shaking as he cried. He ran out of the room, stepping over the intruder's body, and into Natalia's study. He grabbed the phone he found there, unknowingly smearing it with Natalia's blood. He could hardly remember what to dial.

Freda slowly pushed the wheelchair up to the automatic doors. Shawn's body looked frozen as if he was a mannequin. His expression was blank. His eyes didn't blink, his nose didn't twitch and his lips were sealed together.

When the doors opened wide to accommodate his wheelchair, he finally made a sound. A sigh. Freda slid her fingers through his tiny curls to his forehead trying to comfort him.

His body wasn't responding to physical therapy or the experimental drug treatments as his doctors had hoped. The authorities had given up getting information from him, and since they had nothing on him, he was a free man. But free from what? Certainly not paralysis.

He believed that everyone around him took pity on him, knowing that he could no longer do any harm. His mother visited him daily and read scriptures from the Bible as she massaged his legs and limp arm. Each time she left, he wished she wouldn't return. In her way, she said 'I told you so' every chance she got. Every day, she reminded him of why he was in the hospital. And although she knew that he had developed a life outside of crime, she reminded him that he hadn't gotten out completely and that was why he found himself in the condition he now was in.

As he rolled up and down ramps in his wheelchair to the small blue and white ambulette waiting for him, he thought of Natalia. Would she be able to love him now? He was no longer a man. He could no longer function. Would she want a cripple?

Freda snapped one of the back wheels into a buckle and locked the brakes on the wheelchair.

"We're going to 203-143 116th Avenue," she said in a strained voice.

"Aunt Free..." Shawn protested, his eyes remaining fixed on his thighs. "Are they sure, Aunt Free? I mean, did they tell you if there was a chance of me going back to normal?"

"You've got to continue therapy then we'll see." She put her hand over her trembling chin. She wanted to cry again. She cried when they called her and told her to come pick him up. She cried when the therapist warned her not to give him false hope. She was tired of crying, but her nephew was never going to be the same, and she knew it would kill him when he came to the realization.

"I'm saying, I could work out every day if I have to," he slid his hand down to his crotch and apprehensively squeezed. He felt a little something, but the feeling was so slight, he wondered if he had imagined it.

The sound of the motorized ramp annoyed him. There was no way he could go through life having to depend on others to take him where he wanted to go and to push him around.

Freda watched as the driver rolled her nephew down the ramp. She tried to smile. "Well baby, are you ready to be pampered?" Shawn didn't answer.

He looked around at all the perfect little houses on the street and watched the cars pass by. Everyone seemed to be going on with their busy little lives. Walking and driving. Things he wished he could do again.

"Thank you," Freda said to the driver as he slid the ambulette doors back into place. "No problem," he replied.

She was ready to grab the wheelchair handles, but Shawn said, "No, Aunt Free." He put his hand on the wheel and began to roll slowly forward. Freda watched her once strapping nephew struggle with his new legs...wheels.

"Baby, it's got a motor. Just flip the switch."

"Nah, this chair ain't gon' blow me up," he chuckled as he tried to roll forward again. The chair barely moved. It was harder than he thought. When he realized that he was getting nowhere fast he blew hard and rubbed his face with his hand. It was his first day as a handicapped person out in the real world, and already he was frustrated. Freda saw that he couldn't move the chair by himself so she turned the wheelchair motor on and placed his hand on the flexible joystick. He steered the chair to the front door. She had convinced him to stay with her since her house was ground level. And if anyone could take care of him without complaining, it was she. She had taken a month's vacation from work to take care of him and even outfitted her house with accessories for the handicapped.

"Welcome home, Stretch," Freda's longtime boyfriend Clarence greeted him as he held the door wide open.

"Wassup Big Clare," he smiled as Clarence patted his shoulder.

"There's a game on. You wanna watch it with me? I got some Heinekens in the fridge and some popcorn on the table. We good to go!" he chuckled.

"Who's playing?" Shawn asked as Clarence wheeled him into the living room. He backed the wheelchair up to the couch. "The Jets and The Rams."

"I know we kickin' they ass," Shawn chuckled.

"Not even, man. The Rams scored two touchdowns. And we just fumbled on the first down."

"We gon' come for em', don't worry."

Freda came into the room with a frosty bottle of beer in her hand.

"Here baby," she said as she handed it to Shawn.

"Thanks, Auntie Free," he grinned.

"Ooh, I ain't heard that in years," she laughed.

"Where's mine?" Clarence asked with his arms up in the air.

"In the fridge, niggah." She sucked her teeth and walked out of the room. Clarence shook his head and laughed. Shawn laughed at him, not with him. He thought Clarence and Freda had a great relationship. They had been together for thirteen years.

Shawn put the bottle to his lips and sipped. It had been a long time since he drank beer. Living the life, he was used to Remy Martin, Cristal and Dom Perignon. Nothing but the best. But as he sipped his regular beer, he realized he would from now on be just another regular guy.

The game was disappointing. At halftime, the Rams were up by seven.

"You getting sleepy now, Stretch?" Clarence asked. He had watched Shawn's head droop every now and again during the game.

"Yeah, I'm kind of tired."

"Alright then. Let me get you to your room." Clarence got up from the couch and rolled Shawn down the hall into a spotless room. The bed was made up with huge pillows. Clarence slipped one arm behind Shawn's back and the other under his thighs. He tried to lift, but Shawn was too heavy.

"Hold up," Shawn said, trying to push himself upward from the wheelchair with his good arm.

"Let me try again." Clarence crouched down like an umpire, raised up a bit then slid his arms under Shawn again. He bounced up with all his might, but Shawn's weight overpowered his underdeveloped arms.

He dropped Shawn on the bed. "Sorry 'bout that."

"It's aiight," Shawn looked down at his feet. He wanted the socks off but wouldn't dare ask Clarence to take them off. "Could you tell Aunt Free to come in here, please?"

"Okay, Stretch." Clarence pushed the wheelchair to the bottom of the bed and left the room. Then Freda walked in with a smile, but Shawn could see the worry and pity hidden in her eyes. "You hungry, baby?"

"No thanks. Um, Aunt Free, I can't sleep wit socks on."

"Oh." She quickly slipped them off his feet. He shook his head at the sight of his ashy feet. "I can't take this. What I'ma do when I gotta go to the bathroom?" he asked.

"Baby, I got you this gadget that helps you get in and out of your wheelchair. Oh, damn, I left it in the hall closet. I'll be right back." She rushed out of the room and returned lugging a tubular metal contraption that resembled a walker. "See. It's also going to help you strengthen your weak arm. The doctors say that if you use your arm as much as you can every day, you should get back most of the feeling in it." She seemed enthused, but Shawn could only stare at the silver monstrosity.

Shawn shook his head in despair.

"Don't worry, baby. You'll get the hang of it. Before you know it, you'll be in and out of the bed with no problem." She rubbed her hand over his head.

"Freda! The phone!" Clarence called out.

"Who is it?" she shouted.

"They won't say, but it's long distance."

"Hold on baby. I'll be right back." She rushed out of the room.

Within a few minutes, she was back in the room with a smile on her face. She whispered in his ear, "That was a woman named, Selvanna...or Sevlanka. Shit, whatever the hell she wants to call herself. Anyway, she called to relay a coded message from Ty-Ty. He's sending somebody over here to get you so that he can talk to you."

Shawn's expression didn't change. He was glad to hear that Tymeek was alright, but angry at him because he was the reason Shawn was paralyzed in the first place.

"Okay?" she whispered.

"Yeah," he answered dryly.

Her body ached, especially her buttocks. Her head throbbed as if a symphony of drums was playing between her ears. It was difficult to open her eyes. When she finally did open them, something blocked her right eye. She tried to move, but her body refused to cooperate with her brain, and she collapsed back onto the firm bed.

"She's awake, she's awake!" she heard André screeching off in the distance. Then the pitter-patter of shoes became louder.

"Hello, Ms. Foles," said a smiling blonde haired woman in green scrubs. "We're so glad you're awake."

Natalia tried to ask what was going on, but the tube that was pumping her lungs with oxygen and the mask covering her mouth and nose prevented her. Her eyes began to tear up as she saw André.

"Hi honey bunny. Why'd you leave me like that? I missed you." The bandages, tubes and mask made her attempt to smile seem like a cry for help.

"Oh, you must be so uncomfortable. As soon as we can determine whether or not all of your bodily functions are operating properly, we'll get rid of this cumbersome stuff," the blonde haired woman said.

Natalia was tired again and closed her eyes. She tried to fight it, but the medication won. She was out again.

The next time she opened her eyes, her face felt a lot lighter, and her right eye was no longer covered. Slowly, she moved her hand up to her face. She felt indentations in the skin around her eye and gasped. She continued to explore. The right side was swollen, especially at her hairline. She moved her hand higher to the top of her head and felt a soft, silky material with an elastic edge. She tugged but the elastic snapped back and stung. "OUCH!" she heard herself squeal, but her voice was hoarse. She didn't sound like herself. Pushing her body back, she tried to lift herself up on her arms

"Hold on, Ms. Foles," she heard someone say. She turned in the direction of the voice and saw an Asian woman hurrying towards her.

"Lay back. Let me show you how to use the remote for the bed," she said as she gently pushed on Natalia's shoulders. The nurse unhooked the white remote from the side of the bed rail and said, "You push the red button for help or if you're in pain. This white button operates the bed. Follow the graphics on this card which shows all the positions you might want," she said as she handed Natalia a 5" x 7" laminated card. "This tan button turns the television on. And these buttons with arrows change the channels." The nurse pressed a button on the bed's remote, and the head of the bed began to rise.

"Is this high enough for you?"

Natalia shook her head. The nurse adjusted the position until she was sitting upright.

"I bet your mouth is real dry." Natalia nodded. "I've got just the thing for you," she smiled. She left Natalia's bedside for a moment and returned with a yellow pitcher, matching cup and a straw. The nurse filled the cup halfway with ice chips and brought it to Natalia's lips. She tilted the cup and a couple of ice chips slid onto Natalia's tongue.

"More," Natalia muttered. The nurse tipped the cup again. "Thank you."

"You're welcome." The nurse put the cup down on the bed stand.

"What's wrong with me?" Natalia asked with ice chips in her mouth.

"You should ask your doctor. She'll be here in a few minutes."

Natalia watched as the nurse carefully removed the tape securing the I.V. in her left arm. Some of her blood had mixed with the clear liquid in the skinny tube. The nurse flushed out the tube then reattached it so the drip would go a bit faster. "Okay, there you go. I'll be back soon."

"Okay." Natalia reached for the TV remote. Her stomach felt bloated, and it was difficult for her to lean forward. She felt uncomfortable, as if she had eaten an entire cheesecake. Finally, she slid her hand over her belly. "Oh, my, God!" she exclaimed as she looked down. Her stomach was swollen yet perfectly round. She had either gained ten pounds, or she was pregnant. She stared at her belly in awe. God had such bad timing. Shawn. As far as she knew, he was dead. She remembered seeing all the blood as Tymeek carried him away and...

"TRACY!" she screamed hysterically. The bloodcurdling scream alerted the entire hospital staff on the fifth floor. Three nurses and a doctor rushed into the room.

"What happened?" the doctor asked, glancing at the heart monitor. One of the nurses grabbed Natalia's wrist and took her pulse.

"Tracy..." Natalia began to tremble. "Where is she?"

"Calm down, Ms. Foles. Just relax." The doctor began to read her chart. Natalia eased back into the pillows and put her hand over her forehead. She continued to cry as she looked up at the cracked white paint on the ceiling. After an hour, she fell into a deep sleep, the kind that only happens after suffering a long, hard cry.

Natalia spoke before she opened her eyes. "What's wrong with me... besides the obvious?" She opened her eyes and glanced down at her belly.

Her doctor smiled and replied, "You've been in a coma, Ms. Foles, due to cerebral hemorrhaging, caused by a concussion you sustained five months ago."

"Five months? Are you kidding me? I've been asleep for five months?"

"Yes, you have. Hence the six month old, miracle fetus growing inside of you," she pointed enthusiastically at Natalia's abdomen. Natalia lifted the hospital gown to look.

"Is the baby going to be...normal?" she asked, tracing her fingers down the light brown line running from her navel.

"Don't worry. We've been taking excellent care of you. You are going to have a healthy baby." The doctor checked each apparatus that Natalia was hooked up to. She found the baby's heart monitor and turned up the volume to let Natalia listen.

"Ooh, my God. I can't believe it. I'm having a baby." The doctor smiled at her then consulted her chart.

"When will I be able to leave, doctor?" Natalia asked as she covered herself with the sheets.

"Well, now that you're awake, we need to be sure that you're body can function without help."

"Where is Tracy?"

"I'm sorry to be the bearer of such awful news," the doctor sighed, "but she didn't make it."

Natalia hunched her shoulders and wrapped her arms around herself. She fought back the urge to scream. Tears welled up in her eyes, but she managed to control herself. "The baby?"

The doctor glanced at the floor.

"No...No, NO!" She fell back on the bed.

"Please, Ms. Foles. Try and relax. Your baby needs you to regain your strength. We have to concentrate on the baby's health, okay?" Natalia sighed heavily. She wished she was having a bad dream.

"Your friend's baby..."

Just then a nurse raced in and grabbed the doctor's arm. "It's Mrs. Guitierrez. She's back and worse than ever." They both ran out of the room.

"No, don't leave. Wait, doctor, waaait!" Natalia shouted after her.

The doctor called out, "I'll be back." She stopped a nurse in the hall and instructed her to give Natalia a mild sedative. The nurse injected Natalia and waited for the drug to take effect. Minutes later, Natalia was asleep.

Outside, the sky was a murky gray. The chilled, foggy mist tickled Shawn's nose as he watched the empty street. His eyes narrowed when a silver Ford Excursion pulled up in front of the house. Freda rolled him to the monstrous vehicle.

"It's good to see you, man," Big Stew said leaning over to hug an apathetic Shawn. "How you doin' Miss Freda?" Big Stew kissed her cheek.

"I'm okay, Stewey," she smiled and went to get Shawn's bags.

"You ready to take this long ass trip?" Big Stew asked. Shawn raised and dropped his shoulders. Big Stew scooped him up, put him in the front seat and stuck the wheelchair in the back. Freda handed over one of Shawn's bags and rolled the other closer to the curb. Big Stew tossed the bags in the back with Shawn's chair.

"You take good care of my baby, you hear me?" Freda whispered to Big Stew.

"I will," he smiled then kissed her cheek again. She waved good-bye to Shawn. He flashed a smile and waved back.

Shawn sighed as he looked over at Big Stew's tree trunk thighs. Envy gripped him, and he wished he could be the driver instead of the passenger. He wished a lot of things.

"So they ain't get you, huh?" Shawn mumbled.

"Nah," Big Stew said as he turned the key in the ignition. "This is so fucked up, yo. Man, I'm sorry—"

"Where's Ty?" Shawn cut him off.

"Far from here. And we gon' hafta take the indirect route, so it's gon be a lonnng ride, nahmean?"

"Yeah aiight," Shawn muttered.

They drove to D.C., and after being dropped off at the airport by one of Big Stew's little brothers, they boarded a plane to Mexico. A petite Mexican man met them at the airport and drove them in a dusty four door pickup truck to a port town on the outskirts of Puerto Vallarta. Big Stew sat in the back with the wheel chair. Shawn slept on and off throughout the trip.

They ended up at a small house near the water. When they approached, a dark figure stepped out onto the porch. Tymeek.

He approached his brother and flung his arms around him. Tymeek let go after a few seconds and stepped back. Shawn's eyes glistened.

"Look at me man..." Shawn's lips quivered with a mixture of anger and angst.

"I know man, I know...I'm sorry, baby bro. I wish it was me instead of you..." Tymeek pretended to shade his eyes from the sun, trying to hold back tears. Shawn looked past him at the old house. Tymeek wheeled him inside.

"I had to let you know that," Tymeek said as he sat in a wicker chair across from Shawn. "I didn't give a shit about the risks, ya know? I had to see you, bro. You ain't deserve this." He rested his forehead against tented fingers. "Damn. It wasn't supposed to go like this!" He was on the verge of breaking down.

Shawn saw it coming and felt obligated to say something so Tymeek would know that he wasn't blame. "It's not your fault, Ty. What's done is done." He looked around and said, "So, this is where you at?"

"Nah, I'm staying in Holland for now. I'm not gon' be able to live in the states no more. It's cool there, though. But I'm thinking of moving to France or some shit like that. They love a bald black niggah, nahmean," he chuckled but in a quiet, unnerving way.

"Where's Nut?" Shawn asked.

"He's holdin' it down out there for me. We got a little something happening in Amsterdam right now, nahmean?" he chuckled yet another misplaced chuckle and looked at his little brother's sad face.

"I came all this way, risking my ass, 'cause I got some good news. I'm gettin' some money together so you can come and get this operation out in Holland that will make you better. I've been keepin' on top of your doctor reports, and what they afraid to do here, you can have done in Holland, no problem. I hooked up wit this Dutch nurse, and she told me about this new operation. So you gon' be aiight. I promise. You feel me?" Shawn didn't seem enthused. Tymeek noticed.

"I have one more thing to tell you, Shawn. I took care of that bitch for snitchin'. She a fuckin' Super bitch and shit cause' somehow she took my man out before he could finish the contract. She must have nine lives, but she in a coma so that's almost as good."

"What bitch?"

"You ain't know?"

"Know what?"

"She the one that set us up. I told you about that bitch. I told you."

"Who?"

"Your girl. The one I told you not to fuck wit from get go."

"Fuck!" Shawn shouted, slamming his fists down on the armrests of his wheelchair, finding strength he didn't know he had.

Tymeek sucked his teeth, "Aw come on, man. Fuck that bitch! She the reason you in that fuckin' chair. Fuck her!"

"She's in a coma?"

"Last I heard. She could be dead by now. I hope they pulled the plug on her ass. But, yo, don't worry bout' that. I need to know if you gonna come wit me or what."

"How do you know it was her?" Shawn couldn't believe Natalia would sell him out.

"Trust me man, I know. I saw her there myself in one of the Feds' cars."

Shawn looked into his lap. Had he really been so blinded by love? He had refused to believe that she was only out to get Tymeek. He didn't listen and now look at him. He couldn't believe it. It was all her fault. He was in a wheelchair because of the one woman he had fallen in love with.

"I'ma have to make some special arrangements."

"What?" Shawn asked in a daze.

"You comin' wit us right?"

"Yeah," his voice seemed thinner than air, yet his heart was heavy. There had to be some sort of explanation. "Do you know what hospital she's in?" he asked.

"Nah," Tymeek answered, watching him ruefully. "Fuck her man. Do you hear me? Forget that bitch. I told you not to let pussy rule you, didn't I?" His voice raised a few octaves before he caught what he was saying and doing to his broken-hearted sibling. The worst thing he could ever do. Kick a man when he's already down.

"Man, I'm sorry. I hate this shit. I fucked up...I hate that it went down like this, ya know?" he lifted himself from the chair and palmed the top of Shawn's head. "It's gon' be aiight though."

Shawn's mirthless gaze told Tymeek that he had it bad. So bad that he probably didn't believe one word of what he just heard. Tymeek positioned himself over Shawn, resting his right arm on the motorized console of the wheelchair. Leaning in so that his mouth reached Shawn's ear, he said, "I feel you man. I know your heart is fuckin' wit you right now, but she deserved it. I did it because I love you. I don't give a fuck about her."

"I know," Shawn sighed.

Tymeek sat down and slid his fingers in between one another. Resting his elbows at angles to his knees, he said, "You can't leave right away. Maybe in, like, a couple of weeks I can arrange everything. Aiight?"

"Yeah," he replied and tried to operate the electronic joystick on his wheelchair. He bumped into the wicker chair, ran over Tymeek's foot and backed into a wall.

"You need driving lessons, man!" Tymeek laughed.

For the first time since he lost his legs, the ability to become erect, and his woman, Shawn laughed.

Natalia opened her eyes and followed the bright light to the window. Her body felt even weaker than before. She eased up onto her elbows and scanned the room. On the bedside tray next to her, she saw a steaming mound of pale yellow scrambled eggs. Her mouth watered when she spotted a small container of orange juice with sweat dripping down the sides. She was hungry, starving. She couldn't remember her last meal but was certain it came via plastic tubes.

Weakly, she sat up and scooted towards the tray. She opened the little packets of salt and pepper and sprinkled some of each onto her eggs. Eagerly, she stuffed a forkful into her mouth. Then just as quickly, spit the horrible tasting slop back onto the plate. "Ughhh!" She peeled the foil cover off the orange juice container, tilted her head and swallowed it all. "Eeew! Even the damn orange juice is insipid!" She slammed the container down onto the tray, but it bounced onto the floor and skid under the bed.

She pushed the tray away from the bed and slowly lifted her body from the bed and stood up. For a moment, she felt woozy, as though she was going to faint. She held onto the wheeled tray for support. When her lightheadedness subsided, she let go of the tray and tried to take a step. The cold tiles made her shudder. With curled toes, she limped on the heels of her bare feet towards the door, dragging the IV with her. She pressed the alert button several times and the doctor instantaneously showed.

"Look at that! You couldn't wait for us to unhook you, could you?"

Natalia looked around and noticed that she was free from all the machines.

"I need to stretch my legs," she smiled.

A heavyset nurse with mousy brown hair rushed in. "Is everything alright?"

"Yes, nurse. I'll handle it from here," the doctor replied. "Ms. Foles, I saw the alert while I was at the nurse's station. I came to find out what you needed. I assumed that you were still upset about our earlier conversation."

She took Natalia's arm and led her to the padded wooden chair next to the bed. "Sit down." Natalia was apprehensive, squatting to sit but not quite making contact with the chair.

"You see, I didn't have the chance to explain about your friend's baby." Natalia froze

"What is it?" she asked.

"I actually have good news." The doctor gently pushed on Natalia's shoulders, forcing her buttocks to sink down.

"G-good news? Tell me, please."

"You asked me about the baby—"

"Yes, the baby. Is it...alive?"

"Yes."

"Oh, thank God! Thank you God, thank you."

"But—"

"But?"

"It's alright, Ms. Foles. The baby is in an incubator, on a respirator. An emergency C-section was performed immediately upon Ms. Drelpher's arrival in ER. She was thirty-one and a half weeks pregnant." She took Natalia's hand, pressed two fingers against her wrist and glanced at her watch.

"The specialists are hopeful that she will be able to come off the respirator in another month or so. The baby barely weighed four pounds after she was removed from the womb. But now she is fourteen pounds, two ounces. I just saw her this morning, and she's already gained another 3 ounces in the past three weeks. She's really progressed...very alert," she smiled and continued, "Her father is in with her now. He's been here all day. He's devastated. I feel so sorry for him."

"The father?" Natalia asked. She seemed confused for a moment but then a weak smile formed on her face. She could meet him and perhaps they could console one another over their common bond. "May I see the baby please? I am the godmother."

"I don't think that would be wise. Besides, only parents are allowed in ICU."

"Well, can I at least speak with the father and watch the baby through the glass window? Is there a window?"

"Well, yes, there is. This is against my better judgement, but I guess it wouldn't hurt if you watched the baby from outside. I'll take you upstairs myself." She looked around briefly. "Wait here. I'll get a wheelchair."

The father. Who is the father? She hoped that he was a decent man. She looked down at the hospital gown she was wearing. "I can't meet him like this," she thought aloud. She looked around the room and noticed one of the closet doors was ajar. Just barely visible was her satin robe. "Oh, Andy, what would I do without you?" she said to herself.

"Talking to ourselves, are we?" The doctor laughed.

"Oh..." Natalia blushed and said, "I know you're very busy, but can you wait a couple of minutes for me to change?"

"Sure. I'll take a minute and check on my other patients. I'll be back for you."

"Okay. Oh and thank you doctor, doctor...?"

"Levin. And you're welcome. I'll be back in about fifteen minutes, okay?"

"Okay."

Natalia went to the closet and opened it all the way. Not only did André bring her robe, but he also brought three of her silk nightgowns. She slid her robe and a rose-colored nightgown off their hangers. She lifted the bottom hem of the gown and yanked a loose thread. Then she searched the overnight bag Andy had packed for some deodorant. She found a bottle of body wash, toothpaste, a blue and yellow travel toothbrush, and a pair of pink fuzzy slippers. Carrying everything in her arms, she made her way to the bed where she dropped her bundle. She smoothed out the robe and gown, picked up her toiletry items and padded to the bathroom. It smelled as bad as she did — a horrid mixture of Ben Gay and Listerine.

She placed the toothpaste and toothbrush on the sink and wheeled her IV back to the closet. She dug down deeper into the bag and pulled out a plastic bristled hairbrush. She was dying to detach her IV but did not dare to attempt it. She resigned herself to the fact that she would have to lug it back to the bathroom.

After fighting to remove her hospital gown, she stepped into the shower and basked in the warm water. It was so refreshing, she almost forgot that she had only a limited amount of time until her doctor returned. She washed herself as quickly as she could with a thin hospital washcloth. And while still in the shower stall, she grabbed the toothpaste and toothbrush and brushed her teeth. When she was just about finished, she heard a knock on the bathroom door. "Yes?"

"It's Dr. Levin. Are you ready?"

"Just a minute, please."

"Okay. I'll be at the nurses' station."

"Thank you!" Natalia grabbed the hospital gown from the sink and threw it on the floor to use as a mat. She dried off, covered herself with her nightgown, slipped her damp feet into her soft pink slippers and left the bathroom. She closed the door to her room and drew the curtain around her bed. She slipped the gown over her head, careful not to tangle with the IV. Putting on her robe was more problematic. After much wiggling and maneuvering, she finally got it on without popping out her IV. She fought the matted tangles in her hair with the brush and returned to the bathroom again to see if she looked halfway decent. She parted her hair down the middle with her pinkie fingernail. Brushing her hair downward, she noticed her eyebrows had grown in. It made her look angry. "Ugh, I look like a werewolf," she whined. She wet her fingers and pressed them against each brow in an attempt to smooth them out. "Oh, well. That's as good as it's going to get," she said to her reflection.

She waddled down the hall to the nurse's station. "The doctor will be right back for you, Ms. Foles. Please have a seat in the wheelchair," one of the nurses informed her. She cautiously lowered herself into the wheelchair and waited for Dr. Levin to return.

"So what took you so long?"

Dr. Levin chuckled and grabbed the wheelchair handles, "You look very nice."

"Thanks. I didn't want to meet my goddaughter in that hospital get-up. It might scare her."

When the elevator stopped, Dr. Levin wheeled Natalia at a steady pace down twisting corridors until they reached the Pediatric Intensive Care Unit.

She pressed a large, round button on the wall next to the two big doors, and they slowly swung open. The doctor then wheeled Natalia over to the nursery. "There she is. The one with the pink stork that says Baby Girl Drelpher. Can you see her?"

"Yes," Natalia's voice cracked. She saw the baby's pale little feet and hands were moving. And even though she couldn't see the baby's face, she did see curls. The baby's hair was even curlier than her mother's.

"I know she's just as beautiful as Tracy was," she said dreamily.

"She is. I wish I could bring you in to see her up close."

"Oh, that would've been great. Where's her father?"

"I don't see him. Maybe he finally decided to take a break," Dr. Levin said, her eyes scanning the room. "Okay then. I better get you back to your room before the hospital administrator has my head."

"Thank you so much for doing this for me."

"You're very welcome. I'm just sorry I couldn't do more." She began pushing Natalia away from the glass. Natalia took one last glimpse at Tracy Junior. She was so happy that her friend's baby was doing well.

When they reached the Unit's doors, they opened automatically. And in came...

"Mark?" Natalia asked flabbergasted.

"Uh, Natalia?"

"Hello, sir. I just brought Ms. Foles to see your beautiful little girl. She says she's the godmother."

"Um, I—" Mark stammered.

"You're the father?" Natalia's eyes widened.

"I was coming to see you...I had no idea..."

"You're the father?" her lips trembled.

"Nurse, is she going back to her room now?"

"Yes, she is. And I'm Dr. Levin," she said and looked down at Natalia. "Are you okay?" she asked, placing her hands on Natalia's stiffened shoulders. Natalia stared blankly at Mark.

"Uh, Nat, I'll be down to see you in few minutes okay?"

Natalia was too shocked to answer. "Let me take her back to her room." Dr. Levin banged the button and the doors reopened. Mark watched them leave and rubbed his hand over his face.

Chapter Seventeen

❤

NEVER SAY NEVER

"I'm gonna miss you, Stretch," Freda whispered in Shawn's ear. He turned his face towards hers and planted a kiss on her cheek.

"Why you rushing me off? You still got me for a couple more weeks," he chuckled.

"Mmm hmn. Anyway, guess what's for dinner?"

"I don't know...ummm...macaroni?" he asked hopefully.

"Yup. Let me get you a big ol' plateful." She pinched his cheek and left him in the living room in front of the television.

What Tymeek had told him never left his thoughts. How Shawn wished he could talk to Natalia and hear her explanation! She couldn't have turned him in! He had given her his heart. He missed her so much — her Calyx perfumed neck, her raspberry sweet skin, her girlish giggles, her high-pitched moans. Everything. But now she was his nemesis. He hated what she had done to him.

He looked down at his lap and squeezed his lifeless crotch. *A twinge?* Maybe he imagined it. He flipped through channels angrily, aimlessly. Nothing was interesting enough to replace thoughts of Natalia's betrayal. For a brief moment, he envisioned his hands gripping her throat and hearing her muted gasps as he squeezed the life out of her. But even after he took his revenge, he ended up kissing her limp body, caressing it, reviving it. Again, he thought he felt a twinge.

"Here you go, sweetie." Freda placed a folding table and a plate in front of Shawn and served him a heaping helping of baked macaroni along with three fried chicken legs. "I'll be back with some soda." She hurried off and returned with a tall glass of Pepsi on the rocks. "You all set?" she smiled.

"Auntie Free, you're the greatest."

"Thanks, Ralph!" she giggled on her way out.

Shawn ate like he hadn't eaten in days. When he finished, 'Blade' was on pay-per-view. He was grateful that Freda had bootleg cable. He could watch whatever he wanted with no problem. He moved the tray to the side of his wheelchair. "Aw, yeah this my movie right here," he smiled to himself. Techno beats blasted from the television speakers as he turned up the volume. The doorbell rang. Shawn ignored it, knowing his Aunt would answer it. The doorbell rang again. Shawn looked behind him. "Aunt Free?"

"I'm coming." Freda whizzed by and opened the door. "Oh hi, Lisa"

"Hi, Miss Freda."

"Come in. Is it still raining out there?"

"Yeah. It's getting heavier now." Lisa shook her umbrella outside the screen door.

"Stretch, it's Lisa," Freda called out.

"Shit," Shawn grumbled.

"You want anything to drink, Lisa?"

"No, thank you." Freda took Lisa's coat and umbrella and hung them on the coat stand in the hallway.

"I cooked, so if you're hungry, let me know."

"Okay, thanks." Lisa slinked into the living room. "Hey baby."

"Wassup?" he murmured. She pulled the wheelchair back and began to turn it around to face her.

"What you doing?" he asked, aggravated.

"Shawn, I never did anything wrong to you, did I? So why you acting all stink?"

"I'm not in the mood for company, that's all." He tapped his finger against the joystick, pushed it and pulled it back. "Move," he said as he tried to spin his chair back around to face the television.

"Why do you have to act like this? You are so damn evil." Lisa plopped onto the couch. He ignored her and instead watched Wesley Snipes swing a sword and rip vampires into bursts of red clouds.

"Shawn, I know you're angry because of what's happened. I know that. But you can't be mean to the people who care about you," she said as she clamped her hands together and crossed her legs. Shawn chuckled at the charred corpse roasting on the television screen.

"Shawn? Fuck that damn movie. You have company!" Lisa shouted with attitude.

"Look, yo, I'm paying for this movie, so I wanna see it," he lied.

"So, I'll reimburse you."

"Nah, that's aiight."

She jumped up from the couch, squeezed in between the wheelchair and the TV.

"What the fuck is wrong wit you?" He tried to push her out of the way.

"Let it out, baby. Just let it out," she grabbed his face and looked at him lovingly. "Don't keep it inside...let all the anger out."

"What are you my psychiatrist?"

She slowly squatted in front of him, placing her palms on his thighs and resting the side of her face in his lap. "I miss you so much. Lahmel and Lamont ask about you a lot."

He could only look down at her. He wasn't a man anymore. What used to make him a man, defined his manhood and instigated his conceit, was now gone. *What does she want with me now? Why did she come? Women are nothing but sneaky, underhanded manipulators with ulterior motives.* He watched her neck pulse to the rhythm of his building anger.

"Why are you here, Lisa?"

"Because I miss you."

"Like I said, I'm not in the mood for company."

"Are you sure?" She lifted her face from his lap and smiled a devilish grin.

"Yeah." His eyes skipped over her mussed hair back to the TV screen. Lisa's hands slowly slid up his thighs and began massaging his flaccid penis.

"Don't!" He slapped his hand down on hers.

"Maybe you just need the right stimu..."

"I don't need shit! What I do need is to be alone. That's what the fuck I need."

"Fine! Just remember that God don't like ugly, and you're being very ugly right now. You keep it up, you'll never get better." She snatched her hand from under his and sprang to her feet. "Don't take that shit out on me 'cause you can't get it up," she muttered as she left.

The door slammed, and Freda rushed into the hallway. "What the hell?" She ran to the living room. "You alright?"

"Yeah," Shawn answered.

"What did you do to that sweet girl?" She slid her right arm across his chest as her left massaged the top of his head. She rested her chin amidst the tiny curls.

"I don't feel like seeing nobody."

Freda sighed and withdrew her hand and arm from around him. She backed up the wheelchair. "Aw, come on Aunt Free..."

"I want to say something to you, baby, and I want you to listen." She took the remote from his hand and turned off the television. She turned the wheelchair around so that Shawn was facing her and then sat down on the edge of the couch. "Shawn, you know you are my baby, and I love you...I love you like you are my own son. Hell, you are mine!"

Shawn smiled a big, bright smile.

"Stretch, you know I understand that you and Ty-Ty got into that...that lifestyle thinking only about the money. Maybe the both of you didn't ever weigh the consequences. I know deep down y'all are good at heart," she sighed, then looked him straight in the eyes. "But baby, you knew damn well that your days were numbered. Now I hate that my baby is hurt. If I could give you my legs, I would. But even though you're in that wheelchair, sweetie, you can thank the Lord that you are still here on this earth. You can't take out your anger on other people just because fate dealt you this bad hand."

Shawn sat solemnly silent. Perhaps what bothered him most wasn't the wheelchair or his legs. Maybe it was his bitterness. He trusted a woman, gave his heart, and she tore it up, chewed it, spit it out and handed it back to him in bloody pieces. Maybe it was the death of his manhood. Maybe it was all of the above.

"Aunt Free, I'm miserable right now. I've got all this time to feel sorry for myself, nahmean? I can't stop asking...why me?"

She stood and pulled his head to her stomach. "I know sweetie, I know. But if you keep your wits about you and don't give in to self-pity, you'll be alright. You come from a stronnng family, so I know you're strong. And it's that strength that will get you through this."

Shawn felt foolish to have to be consoled by his Aunt as if he were six years old again. He remembered that on his sixth birthday, his mother got him a big cake with Spiderman's picture on it and Happy Birthday Shawn in big red and blue letters. Everyone sang Happy Birthday, and he blew out the candles. But then right after, his cousin Jahmil plunged his hands into the cake and tore Spiderman's spider suit to pieces. Shawn screamed, and they fought and Jahmil ended up with a split lip. They both got spankings. Shawn ran into his room wailing because his birthday had been ruined. Seconds later the door opened, and instead of his mother, his Aunt Freda appeared. She pulled his wet face into her stomach, just as she was doing right now. The memory made him laugh out loud.

"What's so funny?" She backed away to see his face. He smiled and shook his head. She was glad that he laughed and even happier to see him smile. He wore it so well.

"I was just thinking about when me and Jahmil got into a fight on my sixth birthday. You remember?"

Freda laughed wildly. "Man, you beat that poor boy's butt. You know, Rita was mad at you for busting her baby's mouth. That's why you're mother spanked you. She didn't want Rita to think that you were spoiled."

"How come you were always there for me and Ty? Even more than Ma?"

"Because before your mother spit y'all out, I was there rubbing that big ol' belly. You must've had a big ol' head because my sister's belly turned the corner before she did when she was pregnant with you." She giggled, "I had to baby-sit y'all all the time, and it was heaven for me, you know, because I didn't have my two brats until way after you're hot ass momma!"

Shawn laughed so hard, he could have sworn that he felt a pang between his legs. "Ma got the best sister in the world. I hope she know that." He smiled at his favorite aunt. She had helped him forget his troubles, even if it was only just for a few minutes.

He fell asleep in the wheelchair after catching the end of 'Blade'. His chest hurt from the pressure of his chin resting on it. It was ten-fifteen. He flicked on his wheelchair motor and tried to make a U-turn but failed, bumping into the television and nearly knocking it off the stand. "Fuck," he mumbled under his breath. The phone rang. He guided his chair to the phone and picked it up. "Yeah?" He was noticeably frustrated.

"Hallo, I speak wit Shawn? Is Svelanka."

"Svel who?"

"I am relaying message for you. The woman...you-know-who is inside Saint Paolo Hospital. Somebody who loves you want me to let you know that."

At first, Shawn thought the call was a joke. Then the name Svelanka rang a bell. He remembered she called him for Tymeek once before. Tymeek was letting him know where Natalia was.

"Aiight thanks."

"Okay, bye-bye."

He now knew where she was. But what good did it do him? He couldn't wheel his way into the hospital and say, "Here I am. Look what you've done to me." But, oh, how he wanted to!

"I guess Mr. Hardcore has a heart after all," he chuckled. The wheels in his head were turning faster than those of an Amtrak train. With Spank dead and Nut in Holland, who would take him out to Long Island? He didn't want to involve Aunt Freda, and he couldn't very well drive himself. As he thought about it, one other candidate came to mind ...Clarence. *And he's off tomorrow.*

Natalia clenched her hand so hard that her long nails dug into her flesh. She had to know if she was dreaming or not. There was no physical pain. Just a heartache that numbed her completely. A look of bewilderment remained on her face.

"Are you alright?" Dr. Levin asked. Natalia didn't hear her. "Ms. Foles?"

"Y-yes?"

"Are you alright?"

"No," tears filled her eyes again.

"Are you in pain?"

"Dr. Levin...the kind of pain I'm in...there is no medication for. You can't help me." She lifted her weak body from the wheelchair and trudged to her bed.

"Are you sure?" Dr. Levin asked.

"I suppose I could use something."

"What's that?"

"I'm getting a headache. Can you give me something for it?"

"I'll send the nurse back with Tylenol."

"Thank you, doctor." Natalia smiled a weak smile and lowered herself into the chair. She grabbed the phone on the table next to her and called André.

"Andy, please?"

"Hello?"

"I-I can't believe what's going on in my life. I'm being punished," Natalia cried.

"Whoa, slow down, princess. Oh, honey bunny, are you crying?" André asked.

She tried not to break down on the phone because she knew if she did, André wouldn't be able to understand what she would be saying. But she lost her composure anyway and wept loudly. Her nose ran, her lips quivered and her eyes burned. She dropped the receiver.

"Natalia! Natalia!" André screamed into the phone.

She wiped her face with the sleeve of her robe and picked up the receiver. "I'm...I'm sorry," she exhaled loudly.

"What's going on? Never mind, I'm on my way. Hang up and try to relax. Do not move from that hospital bed, do you hear me?"

"Andy..."

"Andy nothing. Stay in that bed. I'm on my way."

She heard a click then a dial tone. She loved André. He was so dependable. He was the only person she had on her side. *Shawn is dead. Tracy is dead. Damn near every one I love is dead.*

Tracy had betrayed her. How could she have? And Mark. Why her best friend? A baby. A baby without a mother and a vindictive father. Natalia felt dead inside. What was it about her life that attracted death? Then, like a ton of bricks falling on her head, it dawned on her that the baby forming in her womb could be Mark's. She wondered if he had noticed her round stomach or her maternal glow. She remembered how badly he had wanted a child with her. He would be just as vengeful with a baby as he had been during the divorce. She knew he'd demand joint custody. Perhaps even full custody. She had to hide her plump belly from him and keep her baby a secret.

She tried to cross her legs but the mound under her robe wouldn't let her. Even after she struggled and wiggled enough to where her calf finally slid into place over her right knee, she was still uncomfortable.

Then she noticed it. Her engagement ring. "How could I not remember?" she thought. It was so beautiful. But what amazed her even more was that it was still on her finger. Her swollen finger was her built-in anti-theft device while she was in the coma.

She remembered when Shawn proposed to her and the comfort of his arms clasped around her. She remembered the moistness and the friction as she sat on his lap. She remembered the warmth he gushed into her just minutes before he slid the ring onto her finger with his mouth. She twisted the ring around her finger. "Oh, Shawn..." she sighed.

"Eh-hem," Mark cleared his throat.

Natalia looked up and caught him adjusting his tie. He took a deep breath, "Nat, before you go ballistic, please just let me explain."

Natalia glared at him with murder in her eyes. For a few of seconds, Mark waited, watching her lips, expecting her to say more. She didn't.

"First off, she pursued me. I know, I know, that's not an excuse. I'm just telling you everything. The whole story." He ran his fingers through his hair. "I wanted to get even. So the last time she tried to seduce me, I took the bait. But then I began to really like her. She paid attention to me. I mean, she really paid attention."

As her anger built, Natalia balled her fists and her eyes became glassy. She was so angry, but why? She didn't want him anymore. Besides, while he was tiptoeing around with Tracy, she was busy breaking headboards with Shawn. How could she be angry?

"Nat, I hadn't expected this to happen the way it did...I can't believe it," he winced. He walked towards her. She could feel his eyes affixed to her belly. She unsuccessfully attempted to hide her condition with the drape of her robe. He stopped in front of her and slowly moved his hand towards her stomach.

"Don't touch me!" she snapped.

"I'm sorry," he straightened up and stepped back. "You seem to have gained a lot of weight. Or maybe you're pregnant." His sarcastic words angered her more. She wanted to pick up the phone and throw it at him. Maybe knock out his front teeth and wipe that dumb smirk off his fucking face. Bastard!

"Well?" he tapped his right foot. *How dare he?!? Tapping his damn foot like I owe him something. He's such a prick!* she thought.

"Well what?" she asked, disgusted.

"It could be mine, couldn't it? I mean, I know that you've been in here for, like, five months. I came and saw you right after André called me and told me about you and Tra..." He dropped his arms and looked out into the hallway.

"So you're a father. Congratulations, Daddy. So you and Tracy...Tracy and you..." she sniffled and tried to hold back the tears. But they came dancing down her cheeks anyway. "I hate you!" she sobbed.

"Nat, you ripped my heart right out of my chest. How can you sit there and act as if you're innocent?" he said through gritted teeth. He looked at the wet robe flowing over her tummy. "Look, we shouldn't rehash what's in the past. We can't change what we've done. We can only learn from our mistakes and avoid making others."

"What? Are you a fucking fortune cookie?" she muttered.

"No, I'm not. I understand you're angry. You shouldn't get upset — not while you're pregnant. I don't mean to upset you, but I remember what I did to you before I left the house." A shadow of shame swallowed his face. He rocked back and forth as if someone had hold of his hips, pushing and pulling. "I've never done anything like that in my life. God knows, I regret it. I'm so, so sorry for hurting you Natalia. I couldn't believe you didn't call 911...that the police didn't come for me. I don't know what came over me that night. I was like a mad man."

Natalia could not forget what he had done, but she had tried. Her guilt made her believe that she had prompted his outrage and that, somehow, she had asked for it. Besides, at the time, he was her husband. What jury would have convicted him? A jury would not have believed her husband raped her after she had just come home from making love with another man. "I don't want to talk about that."

"Okay, we won't. But the fact still remains that...I might have sired your child."

"Sired? Oh give me a break," she let out a sarcastic chuckle.

"I could be the father, and you know it."

"What is it with you, huh? One child isn't enough? Will it make you feel like a big man knowing that you sired both Tracy's baby and mine?" He was making her sick.

"It's not like that. I just want to know. I'm entitled to know. Right now, you hate me so I'm not going to get into it with you about my paternal rights. But as soon as you've calmed down, we really need to discuss this matter further. I'm entitled to know, Nat."

"You're not entitled to my body! This baby is in me, not in you. Trust me, the way Shawn and I went at it, it's got to be his baby. Lady luck never seemed to be on your side any way." She knew her words would slash through him. Words were as lethal as any weapon when it came to the male ego.

Mark was hurt, and though he desperately wished it didn't show, her victory danced in his eyes. For a moment he couldn't say anything. She struggled to unhitch her knee from her calf and stood up.

"Have a nice life, Mark," she waddled towards the bathroom.

"Nat, wait. We need to..."

"Just go Mark. When I come out, I don't want to see you. Go back to your baby," she slammed the bathroom door.

She flushed the toilet and opened the door slowly. He was gone. She couldn't deal with her demons right then. She was weary and just wanted to lay down. She wriggled onto her side, took the extra blanket from the foot of the bed and put it under her belly. With palms together as if in prayer, she slid her hands under the side of her face. Still not comfortable, she grabbed a pillow and shoved it between her thighs. She was asleep in minutes.

She woke up to white lilies and a single yellow and orange bird of paradise. A flower arrangement had been placed on her bedside table. She smiled then frowned. If they were from Mark, she was prepared to throw the vase across the room. Tentatively, she took the card from the flowers and turned it over. HONEY BUNNY PLEASE GET BETTER SO THAT I CAN STOP WORRYING! U GIVING ME WRINKLES GIRL! LUV ANDY. Natalia laughed.

"Finally! Sleeping beauty is awake!" André glided over and cautiously hugged her. "Woo girl, soon I won't be able to fit my arms around you," he laughed.

"That's not nice. Don't make fun of the fat girl," she smiled.

"Okay, now tell me what had you so frantic earlier."

"You should sit down."

"Uh, oh. I feel a panic attack coming on...No wait it's a heart attack," he waved his right hand around, eventually pressing it under his left breast.

"Well you're in the right place to have one," she chuckled and began twisting her engagement ring around her finger. "Earlier today, I found out who the father of Tracy's child is."

"Who is it?" André asked, acting like a kernel of popcorn about to burst. His fidgeting distracted her.

"Well?" he asked loudly.

"Shhh! We're in a hospital, you know."

"Yeah, a hospital not a library. So spill it already."

"Mark," Natalia exhaled. André put the back of his hand up to his forehead and fell back into the chair.

"Oh no, he didn't. No, no, no. You didn't just say that...no it can't be!"

"Heard it from the proud poppa himself."

"Are you kidding me?"

"Nope."

"How? I mean..."

"They did it. The nasty...and you know what really hurts is that she lied to me. Right to my face, she lied to me. She sat across from me in my kitchen and told me that I didn't know the father. We laughed and talked, and she never said another word about it. I thought we were best friends," she shook her head.

André pushed up out of the chair and hugged her. "Tracy's gone, Nat. Nothing can bring her back. Don't let this taint your memories of her. I know it's going to be hard, but she's dead and that poor baby is left without a mother."

"It's so ironic," she said as she fought back more tears.

"What is?"

"Her daughter will grow up without a mother just like she did." They hugged each other tightly. Natalia pulled away from André's arms and scooted back towards the middle of the bed. Her feet dangled from the side, making her seem like a little girl whose feet were too short to reach the ground. André watched her little feet shake restlessly.

"You're making me dizzy, girl," he smiled, hoping a little levity would lighten the mood.

"Andy, I need to get out of here. I want to go home." Home where both good and bad memories awaited.

"Well, the doctor says you might be released Friday."

"That's three days away! I want to go home now."

"Nat, they just want to make sure that you and the baby are okay. Be patient."

"And to top it all off, I think Mark is going to demand a paternity test. I can't deal with that. And there is a slight chance that he could be the father. And I know that low down son of a bitch will fight me every step of the way just to make my life hell if he is the father. He practically threatened me when he was in here earlier."

"Wait a cotton pickin' minute. Did I hear you right? How in the hell could he be the Daddy?"

"That's another twisted story. Let's just say Mark has an evil twin, and he's taken over Marks' life."

"Damn girl! Your life is like a soap opera during sweeps week."

"Well, life is stranger than fiction...unfortunately mine plays out like an Edgar Allen Poe tale...unrelentingly bleak."

Shawn tried to go up the steep ramp to the handicap entrance of the hospital, but the motor sputtered then stopped.

"It's either too steep for the chair's motor or you've got a cheap ass chair, Stretch." Clarence chuckled and grabbed the handles of Shawn's chair and pushed him up the ramp.

"I hate this shit, man," Shawn sighed.

"May I help you?" the woman sitting behind the front desk asked. Clarence looked down at Shawn. "We're here to visit Natalia Foles. Which room is she in please?" Shawn spoke as properly as he could. The woman tapped at the computer keyboard. She glanced at the monitor and said, "I'm sorry. Ms. Foles left the hospital already."

"But she's in a coma. How can she leave the hospital?"

"I'm sorry, sir, but that's what my computer shows."

"Oh, nah, your computer is wrong."

"Sir, our system is updated every hour. And it shows here that Ms. Foles checked out yesterday at 1pm."

"But she's supposed to be in a coma! How the hell she..."

"Thank you, Miss. This is just a big misunderstanding. We'll go clear it up. Come on, Shawn. It's alright. We'll find out what's going on," Clarence interjected.

They weren't home for more than a couple of minutes before Shawn called Natalia's home number. He got a recording saying the number was disconnected. Then he called information. The operator gave him the phone numbers for seven different N. Foles from all five boroughs except one, which she told him was unlisted. He called all seven. One was a foreigner, two were men, one was an elderly woman, and one he assumed was a dyke because she sounded more like a man than he did. He dialed the next to last one and it was also disconnected. He then called a live operator and asked her to call the unlisted number and tell the person his name and phone number and say it's an emergency. "Sir, she says to hang up, and she'll call you right back."

Ecstatic, Natalia hurriedly wrote down the phone number and dialed it. A recording came on; Private calls are not accepted at this number. Please hang up and dial star eighty-two. She did as the recording directed, and the phone only rang once before Shawn answered. He didn't speak a word. He waited to hear if the voice belonged to Natalia.

"Hello?" Natalia breathed heavily with excitement. Hearing her voice for the first time in such a long time knocked the air right out of him.

"Shawn?"

"All I want to say to you...I just can't believe you used me. The one fuckin' time I trust a bitch and this is what I get?" He huffed after he caught his breath

"Shawn? What are you saying?"

"Don't act like you don't know. Ty told me you set us up. Now I'm a fuckin' cripple because of you! Are you happy, bitch?" He slammed the phone down.

With the receiver still glued to her ear, she waited. She waited for the alarm clock to go off to wake her from this nightmare. She waited for Shawn to pick up his receiver again and say, "April Fools!" She waited, but nothing happened. She felt like the beams holding up her life had come crumbling down. He hated her and she didn't know why. What was he babbling about? Why did he say those mean things to her? Did he track her down just to hurt her feelings? Her hand weakened and trembled with the receiver still in it. Slowly she slid it back onto its base. She had no clue as to where he was. She didn't even have the chance to tell him about the baby.

Shawn's eyes glassed over as anger ripped through him. But he was angry with himself. He wanted to hate Natalia, but he just couldn't. He tried to rid himself of the love inside his heart for her. It kept pushing it's way back in. How could he have been so stupid? 'I saw her in the Fed's car'. Tymeek's words echoed in his head. He didn't get the chance to say everything he wanted. He looked at the caller ID box. Her new unlisted number stared back at him. He picked up the phone and dialed it.

Natalia sank back into the bed, grabbed a pillow, stuffed it under her neck and stared at the phone, willing it to ring. When it did, she nearly fell out of the bed. She grabbed the phone and panted, "H-hello?"

"You know what's so fucked up? I wanted to marry you. I changed just for you. But all along, you knew you were just out to get my brother. You fuckin' played me!"

"Shawn, I swear I don't know what you're talking about. Please just tell me where you are."

"Shit! You still tryna use me for the Feds, huh? Fuck y'all, aiight. I don't know where he is, so fuck y'all!"

"Shawn, no!" But it was too late. He had hung up on her again. Natalia pressed buttons on her phone to view the caller ID and read the name on the screen. "Freda Thompson," she read aloud. She got out the phone book and started on her homework assignment for the day — to find an address for Freda Thompson. After ten minutes, her diligence paid off when she matched the number she had dialed to one of the Freda Thompsons in the phone book.

Baby, since we're here alone...do you want me to try again?"

"You know, you and that one-track mind is gon' get you in trouble," Shawn chuckled.

Lisa unzipped her jeans and pulled them down. She stood there wearing only her panties. She grabbed a bottle of lotion from the nightstand and slipped under the covers with him. He watched the sheets ruffle as she tried to pull his boxer shorts down. He couldn't feel her hands as she smoothed the thick white cream over his thighs. When she reached his sleeping member and it didn't respond, it made him feel so inadequate that he grabbed her hand.

"Pull em' back up," he ordered.

"Baby, if you'd just let me do it I bet you it'll get hard," she smiled.

"Nah, that's aiight." He hated not being the man he used to be, but, apparently, Lisa didn't mind. She still cared about him. Shawn still thought about Natalia but wished that love would leave him alone.

"Baby don't you have therapy today?"

"Tomorrow."

"What did they say the last time?"

"So far, the only thing that's improved is my right arm. I have full use of my right arm again. But the rest...never mind what they said. I'm hungry."

"So?"

"So go get me something to eat," he slapped her butt.

"Yes sir," she giggled and jumped out of bed. She bent over and picked up her jeans then turned around to look at him. "Did that do anything for you?"

"I don't think you'd be able to handle me if it did...cuz a niggah is ready to bang, bang, bang!" He pumped his fist with each bang. He sat up in bed and grabbed his calves, pushing and scooting. Lisa pushed the chair up to the bed and helped him into it.

Aromas from the kitchen danced under his nose, and he couldn't wait to eat. "I hope you in there putting love in that chicken," he shouted to Lisa.

"I am honey, I am," she yelled back. She was a good woman. So why didn't he want her, desire her, or love her? Why wasn't she in his every thought? He looked at the caller ID box. He wanted to call Natalia back. He wanted to hear her voice. He wanted to see her one last time.

"Heeere's Lisa!" she waltzed into the room with a mountain of cubed cornbread. "Taste it," she shoved a piece into his mouth.

He bit off a piece and chewed. "Damn girl, you can shabibble!"

"You know that's right," she smiled.

"What is that sweetness?"

"I put honey in it."

"So wassup wit the chicken?"

"It's almost finished baking and the macaroni is almost done, too."

"Now, you know, can't nobody make macaroni like Aunt Free."

"Whatever," she waved her hand and placed the bowl in his lap. "Let me go check on my chicken."

"Yeah, go do that, cuz a niggah is starving!" He laughed then stuck the rest of the cornbread into his mouth. The doorbell rang. "Can you get that before you go check your food, Aunt Jemima?"

"I got your Aunt Jemima," she laughed and went to the front door. She opened it and the smile on her face disappeared.

"Hello, are you Freda Thompson?" Natalia asked.

"No, and she's not here."

"Is Shawn here?" Natalia's feet felt like they were stuck in cement. Her nerves and the excess weight she carried were starting to take their toll. Her swollen belly peeked out of the chinchilla swing coat she wore.

Lisa put her hand on her hip and snarled, "Why?"

"Is he here?" Natalia asked again.

"Ay, yo, hurry up and close the door! You lettin' in all that cold air," Shawn called out.

"Shawn!" Natalia's face lit up. She pushed Lisa out of the way and wobbled past her.

"Excuse me? Hel-lo? Where are you..."

"Shawn?" Natalia shouted, ignoring Lisa.

Lisa grabbed Natalia's hand.

Natalia yanked her hand away and yelled, "Don't touch me!"

Shawn heard her voice, but he didn't believe it was really her. Could it be? "Natalia?" he called out. He rolled out into the hallway, and there she was.

"H-how did you...what are you doing here?"

"I had to see you. We need to talk," Natalia hid her stomach with her bag.

"Who is this, Shawn?" Lisa's hand slapped her thigh.

"Go home. I'll call you later."

"NO! Tell me who she is," Lisa shouted.

"Just go home. I'll call you later."

"Ugh!" she growled and stomped off down the hallway with her fists at her temples.

"What are you doing here?" Shawn asked still in shock.

"So that's why you cursed me out over the phone, huh? Because of her?"

"What? All I wanna hear from you is the reason you did it. That's all I wanna know...why?"

Lisa stomped past them with her coat and purse dragging on the floor.

"I'ma call you later, aiight?"

"Fuck you, Shawn!" she cursed and slammed the door behind her.

"So you love her now? Is that it?" Natalia asked.

"Don't come in here talking that stupid shit. LOOK AT ME!" he shouted so loudly that Natalia nearly fell over. She did and realized that he was in a wheelchair.

"Oh, Shawn..." she gasped. He rolled into the living room, leaving her sniffling in the hallway. She followed him. "Shawn, I think I understand why you're so angry, but you've got it all wrong."

"I wish I never met you," his voice wavered with resentment. He stared at the blank television screen trying not to look at her reflection in it. Her perfume tickled his nose. It was the sweet smell that he missed so much. He wanted her in his arms. He struggled with memories of them together.

"Shawn, I didn't do what you think I did. I got your message on my voicemail when I flew back in from Spain. I took a cab straight to the dealership, and a FBI agent handcuffed me and shoved me into his car...," she tried to stop herself from crying as she spoke. "I s-saw you...your brother...he had you over his shoulder and your back was covered with blood...I thought you were dead!" She took a deep breath to keep herself from crying. The wheelchair spun around, and Shawn stared into her eyes to determine if her crying was real or all an act.

"I screamed your name..." she couldn't finish and her knees buckled. Shawn quickly moved his chair and caught her as she collapsed in his lap.

"What's wrong with you?" he asked, brushing her hair away from her face. She struggled to stand.

"I'm okay," she fixed her coat to hide her belly.

"No, you're not okay. What's wrong with you?"

"Why do you care? You hate me, don't you?"

"When Ty told me you set him up, I had every reason to believe him. I blamed you for everything."

"How could you blame me? How could you even think I'd do that?"

"Look at me!"

Natalia looked away. It hurt her to see him in that wheelchair. It hurt her even more knowing he blamed her.

"See, you can't even look at me."

"Shawn, that's not why...listen I have something to tell you. Before I do, tell me if you still love me. I need to know if this changes everything."

"If what changes everything?"

"Do you believe me when I say that I had nothing to do with what happened?" Shawn lifted his hand and took hers. He looked up into her eyes and stared into them a while longer. "Yes," he sighed, putting her hand against his cheek.

"And do you love me, Shawn? I mean really love me?"

"I was mad tight, you know? But even still, I never stopped loving you. I couldn't."

"So now do you want to tell me about the woman who just left?"

"She's a sweet girl...but I don't love her. In fact, she's always pushing herself on me, no matter what I say. She pities me 'cause I'm a cripple."

"Don't say that."

"Are you blind?" he dropped her hand.

"No, Shawn, I'm not blind. What I am is optimistic. I know doctors who can help you."

"Don't worry about me. I don't know why you're pretending to care anyway. You know that you don't want me any more. I can't give you what I used to."

"Is that what you think? That all I want from you is sex? I just want you."

"But I can't be the way I was...we can't have kids and shit. We can't do shit!" he pounded his fist on his thigh.

"Oh, but you can, Daddy. Trust me, you can," she smiled at him. Shawn shook his head and looked down into his lap.

"No, Nay-nay...I can't."

"Well, maybe this will make you feel better." She opened her coat wide. Her belly bulged as if she had a basketball under her sweater.

"I'm pregnant," she beamed.

Shawn's jaw dropped. He rolled closer to her and palmed her basketball with both his hands. "Oh, Baby Girl..." his eyes smiled as he rubbed her tummy.

"Are you really happy Daddy?" She put her hands over his.

"I'm gon' be your baby's Daddy," he laughed.

"Are you happy?" she repeated. He looked into her face. She actually was glowing.

"Hell, yeah! I'm glad you are pregnant cuz I was thinking to myself damn, my baby got mad fat!"

Natalia laughed so hard it made her have to pee. Shawn's laugh trailed off and his face turned serious, "Nay...I've got to go far away in order to get my health taken care of, nahmean?" he whispered.

"Why are you whispering, nahmean?" she mocked.

"Because these walls have ears."

"Oh. So how long will you be gone?" she whispered.

"I don't know."

"But I can get you help right here."

"Ty already set it up for me."

"Oh," she sighed and grabbed the arm of the couch. "Oh God, my back is killing me."

"So how many months are you?"

"Five and a half."

"Only three and a half to go."

"Only?" she scoffed.

"You know what I mean," he chuckled. "I love you, Baby Girl. But soon I won't be able to call you that no more."

"Why not Daddy?"

"See, you won't be able to call me that no more either 'cause I'm gonna have a real Baby Girl calling me Daddy."

"Or a baby boy."

"True," he smiled. "True."

Chapter Eighteen

❤

MIRACLE IN BROOKLYN

The bathroom seemed so far away, and her slippers were nowhere to be found. She tiptoed down the hall without them. After flushing the toilet, a sharp pain dug into her side. "Oh, no!" she whined. It was time.

Because Shawn was out of the country, André had become her Lamaze coach. After all the classes they attended together, no number of diagrams, lectures or practice sessions could have prepared her for the excruciating pain she now felt.

Natalia grabbed the sink and braced herself. If only she could reach the phone before another streak of lightning hit! She palmed the walls and made it to the bed, grabbing the phone as she crumpled onto it. She called André, and he assured her that he would teleport himself to Brooklyn if he had to. She tried to lay back, but another contraction stabbed at her. "Owww!" she cried out. The second pang lasted longer than the first. She instinctively knew that baby was ready to make his debut.

She couldn't keep still. She wanted to stand. She wanted to lay down. She didn't know what to do with herself. Then it dawned on her to get dressed. As she attempted to put on one of her maternity dresses, another contraction overwhelmed her, and she ripped the dress. She had to find another one. Finally, she pulled out something easier to slip on, a denim farmer's dress that made her look like a chubby kindergartner. Then she searched for her Nike slip-ons. As she slipped her right foot in, another contraction attacked. This one nearly made her pass out. She had no choice but to get herself to the hospital. She couldn't wait for André any longer. She called down to the lobby and told the doorman to get her a cab.

"Ms. Foles, stop flopping around like a fish. You keep that up, and you're not going to have any energy left to push."

"But it hurts!"

The nurse stuck a gloved finger into Natalia's vagina to determine how far she had dilated. "Oh, please, you're barely three centimeters," she said.

"That can't be."

"Just relax." The nurse attached the fetal monitor to the strap around Natalia's pregnant belly and turned up the volume. "Listen to the baby's heartbeat and relax."

Relax? Natalia wanted to punch her in the face.

The nurse opened the door, and André rushed in. "Okay, okay... coach is here."

"Oh, thank God! Andy, please get Dr. Summers in here."

"Okay, but how do you feel?"

"Like shit! Now go!"

"Mommita, it'll be okay. You're gonna get through this."

"Andeeee, please get the doc..." she convulsed and inadvertently vomited.

"Ew! Oh honey," André ran into the bathroom and soaked several paper towels with warm water. He wiped her mouth clean. "I'll be right back."

"I need a doctor in here! It's like the Exorcist up in here! She just threw up, and she's in a lot of pain," André shouted.

A short woman in green scrubs put her hand on his shoulder, "Sir, please calm down. That's all very normal for a first time mother. Who's her doctor?"

"Doctor Summers."

"Okay, Nurse Cavin, please page Dr. Summers and have an orderly clean up the room. I'll come in to check on her, sir."

"Thank you so much." He ran back to Natalia. She was biting her lip so hard it hurt, but at least the pain distracted her for a nanosecond.

"Oh, honey bunny...okay, okay...the doctor is coming. I brought your focus item," he searched the suitcase he had brought with Natalia's things. He pulled out a tarnished gold frame with a picture of Natalia at three years old with her parents in Jamaica. They were surrounded by vibrant green grass and trimmed bushes and standing by a horse.

"Oh, Andy, you're such a sweetie."

"Now focus on this image." He held it up in front of her and took her hand. "Squeeze my hand when another one comes...but please don't break my fingers, OK?" he giggled.

She managed a smile and then focused on the photo. Her mother was so beautiful. She had a deep Jamaican tan and sparkling blue eyes. Her father was tall and thin. Her mother seemed so small next to him. He was dressed to the nines. *Must be what made mommy go gaga over him,* she thought to herself and giggled out loud.

"What's so funny?" André asked.

"Nothing...ohhhhh, arrrrrgh!" She squeezed Andre's hand so hard he shrieked.

"Ow! Watch that!" he squealed.

"How're we doing in here?" Dr. Summers asked with a smile.

"I'm dying," Natalia said dramatically. The doctor rolled a stool over and sat between her legs. After probing Natalia with gloved fingers, she exclaimed, "Wow, you're dilated nine centimeters. We've got to get you into the delivery room." She left to find an orderly.

"See, I told that stupid nurse...arrrghhh!"

Oh, Natalia, he's so beautiful." Renée smiled down at the tiny baby boy. He grabbed the finger she offered. "And what a grip! You're a strong boy, aren't you? Yes you are. Hey, bright eyes." she spoke in an annoying squeaky pitch. Natalia believed that she could see in her son's expression just the tiniest bit of annoyance. He seemed to screw up his face to tell Renée to leave him the hell alone and let him catch up on his sleep.

Natalia picked up her bundle of joy from the bassinet. "Isn't he gorgeous?" She nuzzled his nose with hers. "And look at all this hair!" She twirled one of his dark curls around her finger. "He needs a tan though," she giggled and lifted her shirt. The baby's mouth eagerly latched onto the taupe nipple on her engorged breast. "Ow, junior! Calm down, chubbiekins." She began to rock back and forth in a comfortable white frilly padded rocker that André had given her as a gift.

"He looks older than seven weeks. He's going to be tall. Wow...you're a mommy," Renée beamed.

"I know. I can't believe it myself." Shawn Jr. was practically pale. His eyes were bright and his chubby cheeks were ripe for pinching. When Natalia saw her baby for the first time, she honestly couldn't tell who he looked like. But now, she thought he resembled her. With Shawn light-skinned and Mark white, she had no idea who Shawn Jr.'s father was. She wanted and prayed for him to be Shawn's son.

She hadn't heard from Shawn since before he left. She loved him, yearned for him. And she hadn't called Mark. She hoped he had forgotten about her and her baby. But she expected him to come calling any day now. Tracy's baby hadn't made it.

"Does he sleep through the night?"

"No, and it's driving me bananas. He refuses to sleep. He wants to party all night," Natalia laughed. "Just like his mommy."

Renée chuckled, "Well, I guess I should find a way to postpone you're meeting with the Dell representative."

"Yes, please. I'm going to be unavailable for a while. Mr. Green can step in for me. I'll call him. Uh oh. Looks like Grumpy Gus might not want anymore milky."

The doorbell rang. Then there was a rapping on the door. "Who could that be? Charles didn't call to announce anyone," Natalia said with a worried look on her face. Again, more knocking.

"Could you get that for me, Renée?" Natalia asked as she rubbed Shawn Jr.'s tiny head. She watched his angelic face while he slept with her nipple still lodged in his little mouth. She gently pulled it out, pulled down her shirt and looked hard and long at her baby to see if she could discern who his father is. She looked up from his peaceful face and her eyes locked with those of one of his possible creators. "Shawn!" she shrieked excitedly. He walked stiffly towards her.

"Oh, Shawn...you can walk!"

"How's my Baby Girl?" he smiled. He bent over and looked at the precious newborn in her arms. He looked at the woman who had given him this miracle. "He's beautiful, just like his mother." He kissed her on the lips.

"I missed you." She took her hand from the baby's head and touched his cheek, "I missed you so much." He put his hand over hers and placed a gentle kiss on it. Then he looked at Junior with a proud smile.

"He's a junior. His name is Shawn Wilson Junior," she said proudly.

"No doubt. That's my boy," he grinned, "Lemme hold him." He slipped one hand under the baby's head and another under his flat bottom. "Oh, he's a big boy."

"Yes, he is. He's greedy, too," she laughed.

"Yeah, that's my little man. He's gonna play football."

"Oh, no he won't. I don't want my baby getting hurt," she shook her head. She watched him with Junior cuddled up to his chest. She watched how he rocked him in his arms and how his big strong hand cupped the baby's head.

Renée interrupted the moment. "Okay, Natalia. I'll see myself out.

I'll call you tomorrow."

"Oh, I'm so rude...I'm sorry Renée. This is Shawn Senior."

"Hi, it's nice to meet you." Renée smiled.

"Same here," Shawn looked up briefly.

"Okay, I'm off," Renée waved.

"Thanks for stopping by," Natalia waved back. Renée smiled at the happy family then closed the door behind her.

"Baby Girl...I can't believe it. I've got a son," he said, amazed.

"I know, Daddy," she smiled. Then she had an epiphany. Shawn was walking. If he could walk then he could make love to her again.

"How's my other Big Daddy?"

"He's making a recovery. He's not himself just yet, but he's almost there," he grinned mischievously.

"Hmmm. Did he also have to undergo therapy?"

"There you go. You don't trust me?" Shawn asked.

"Well, you were around all those buxom blonde bombshells. I'm sure he didn't need much help around those Dutch sexpots," Natalia pouted and folded her arms.

Shawn got up and placed the baby in the bassinet. He stood a moment longer over the bassinet then moved the couch. "C'mere."

"No," she playfully pouted.

"Stop playing. Trust me. Mr. Hand was the only one helping out," he chuckled and patted his right thigh, "C'mere."

She swayed her hips as she walked over to the couch and straddled him.

"Nasty girl," he chuckled and shook his head. Her arms went around his neck, and she rested her cheek on his forehead. "I missed you so much."

"Baby Girl, while I was away, I concentrated so hard on being able to come home and give it to you right," he grinned.

"Oh Shawn. You don't have to worry about that. I can wait as long as it takes...we can do other things," she gave him a mischievous look.

"Oh yeah? So let's get started." He squeezed her swollen breasts.

"Ow! Shawn! Don't do that! They're full of milk and very sore."

"I'm sorry, mommy," he rubbed her sore breast gently and felt a wet spot.

"See? Look what you did."

Shawn examined the wet spot on her T-shirt and said, "Mmm, milk. Now all I need are some Oreo's, and I'll be straight." They both laughed.

Shawn wheeled the bassinet into the bedroom, went back to the living room, took her hand and led her into the bedroom. They lay down on the bed and cuddled. One big happy family slept.

lthough the FBI had confiscated his used car lot, Shawn managed to hold onto the Laundromat since it was in his aunt's name. His fiancée was rich, but he didn't want to be a kept man. He wanted to have his own. So every day, he woke up at four-thirty in the morning and drove to Queens to open up Bubblin' Brite.

Living in Brooklyn cramped his style. It wasn't so much that he lived far from his business as much as the fact that he missed the familiarity of his Queens neighborhood. Getting up at four in the morning and lugging himself half asleep to the laundromat pissed him off, but he wanted to run his business properly. Shawn had a family now, and he felt his life was finally meaningful. He loved watching the baby's cheeks cave in and out as he sucked Natalia dry. It gave him a warm fuzzy feeling inside. They weren't legal yet, but they were working on it. Shawn wanted a huge wedding so that all of his family could attend. Natalia happily agreed.

The phone rang repeatedly. Natalia jumped up and grabbed it. "Yes?" she huffed.

"Good Morning, Ms. Foles. There's a Mr. Delucchio here to see you."

"Who is this?" Natalia inquired.

"George, Ma'am." He couldn't have known that she had told Charles not to allow Mark into the building. The moment she feared had arrived. Mark would try and stake his claim on her baby.

She looked at the alarm clock. It was only eight-seventeen. She wanted to fire George for interrupting her very much needed sleep. And she wanted to kick Mark's ass for just being alive. But no matter what, she would have to deal with him sooner or later. It would be better to get it over with now, before the law butt in.

"Let him up," she heard herself say. "Damn him," she mumbled.

She ran to the bathroom, gargled with mint mouthwash and splashed cold water on her face. While applying lip gloss, she heard the doorbell ring. After running the brush through her hair, she grabbed her silk robe and slipped into her fuzzy slippers. At the door, she asked, "Who is it?"

"Ahem, me of course." He sounded so pleased with himself. She plastered a smile on her face and opened the door.

"Good Morning," he said with an evil grin.

"Good Morning," she said through her frozen smile.

"Did you miss me?" he chuckled.

"Please, come in," she stepped aside. She watched him survey the condo with eager eyes. "Looking for something in particular?" she asked.

"Still sarcastic as ever. Ahhh, I do miss that." He grinned then asked, "Can I see my baby?" Natalia wanted to slap the grin from his face. She wished he would just disappear. Any love she ever felt for him was completely gone. How strange. Could she change her feelings that easily? Did she ever love him? Does she really love Shawn?

"Well?" His arrogant tone annoyed the hell out of her.

"I'll go get him."

"Him? Wow, it's a boy?"

"I'll be right back," she rolled her eyes at him. He twisted his hands in anticipation. Deep down, he wanted the baby to be his. He didn't care that the mother would hate him. In fact, he'd come to resent her, which made their feelings mutual.

"He's still sleeping so please keep your voice down," she whispered and rolled the bassinet slowly toward him. Mark peered in at the baby's small button nose and pink cheeks. "Oh, he's...he's so handsome."

"Thank you," she smirked.

"Emily says that the sooner we get the paternity test done, the better it will be for everyone involved. So when can I set it up?"

"Hold on. First of all, who the hell is Emily?"

"Oh, she's my wife." His smile suggested that he had hoped that Natalia would be upset and surprised.

"Your wife?" Natalia pretended not to be perturbed. "Married. So you've remarried already?"

"Yeah, we just came back from our blissful nuptials in Hawaii."

"Congratulations," she pursed her lips. "How nice."

"Can I pick him up?"

"I'd rather you didn't. He'll wake up. He's a light sleeper."

"Uh, right," he shot her a look that said *I know you don't want me to touch him.* The look also said *Bitch.* "Look, I don't want to be a nuisance, but I'd really like to get this paternity test over with. Can we agree on a date?"

"Do what you have to. Set a date and let me know."

"I'm going to need your new phone number."

"Sure. Wait here I'll get a pen and paper," she sighed. She went into the kitchen and wrote down her number on a pink Post-it. She returned to the hallway and handed Mark the slip of paper.

"Okay. Thanks. I'll give you a call tomorrow."

"Great," she said trying to fake an enthusiasm she didn't feel.

"You know, Natalia. I'm not going to hide the fact that I'm really rooting for myself to be the father. I just hope things work out for all of us, and we can all get along."

"You're the wrong color to be quoting Rodney King," her voice wavered with hatred. "But thank you for telling me that you've remarried. I believe that remaining single was a condition of your alimony agreement."

Mark remained smug. "Your anger can't be good for the baby, Nat. You should really watch it. It suggests that this environment might be unhealthy for him," he threatened.

"Mark, Mark, Mark. Like I told you before, Shawn Jr. — oh that's his name by the way — is Shawn's child. I mean, we all know what bad swimmers your little soldiers were," she smiled snidely.

"We'll soon find out, won't we?"

"I guess," she said and walked over to the door to open it. "Okay, buh-bye."

"I'll call you tomorrow. Let's not drag this out. Let's all be mature adults in this matter."

"Whatever," she grumbled.

"Oh, and if the baby is my son, I think I have just cause to demand reinstatement of my alimony. To care for the child and all."

Natalia slammed the door behind him and woke the baby. He started to cry. Natalia wanted to do the same.

Shawn arrived home to the smell of burning rice.

"Baby Girl?" He rushed into the kitchen. A steaming pot of burnt rice sat in the sink. He walked over to it and covered the pot. When he turned around, he found Natalia standing in front of the refrigerator.

"The only thing I could salvage were the Cornish hens," she sighed and ran her fingers through her hair.

"Awww, Baby Girl. You tried to cook for Daddy?" He squeezed her in his arms and kissed the top of her head, her forehead, her nose then her lips. They kissed and kissed until Natalia's anxiety faded. She felt so secure in his arms. When he squeezed her close to him, she felt electricity, the kind only sexual excitement could elicit. And Shawn's member was waking up, too. In fact, he felt buff. She grinned and moved her hand down to grab the prize.

"Baby, I'm sorry but..."

"Don't worry Daddy. It's okay," she kissed his chest.

"But you know how I do." He rubbed her back.

"Oh, I know. And we'll get back to that old way again soon. But, I think for now, we should take it easy. I don't wanna break it," she giggled.

"Well, we better get it on now while my lil' man is still a baby. Cuz when he gets to the terrible two's, we ain't never gon' be able to do it," he laughed.

Natalia sighed loudly. She had to let him know that he might not be the father, but she didn't know how. She tried to gather her thoughts.

"What you thinking about, Ma?"

She sighed a long drawn out sigh and said, "Shawn…I have something to tell you."

"What?" he asked. She could feel his chest muscles flex and tighten as he adjusted himself under her.

"Well, remember the day we went to Atlantic City?"

"Yeah. What about it?"

"When I went home that night…Mark was watching a videotape of us."

"What? How the fuck did he get a tape of us?"

"He hired a private detective to follow me. The same way one who followed you and got all that information about you. He had photos of you and police files…Anyway, that night, when I came home, Mark was watching us make love on your couch and he saw you propose to me. He was so angry, he lost it. He…he…he raped me."

Shawn sprang up and grabbed her face. "He raped you? Why didn't you tell me? Why didn't you get that niggah arrested?"

"Oh, please. Do you think that would have happened? He was my husband at the time. I came home after midnight. I was having an affair. I felt guilty. I didn't th…"

"Baby, he raped you. He has to pay for that."

"Shawn, I don't want to think about it anymore. What's past is past."

"No, it's not." Shawn got up and paced back and forth.

"Shawn, please don't be angry. I don't want you to do anything stupid." Shawn looked up from the floor, his eyes blazing with anger.

"I am telling you this because Junior may be his child."

"Oh, hell no!" he shook his head violently. He let out a low growl and plopped down on the couch. With wrists resting on his knees, he closed his eyes tightly and shook his head as if to clear it.

Natalia got down on her knees, crawled over to him and took his hand in hers. "Shawn, I wish this wasn't happening. But he came by earlier and…"

"He was here?"

"Yes. Early this morning, he came by to announce that he's going to set up a paternity test. If I didn't agree to it, I knew he would have taken me to court to mandate the test. Daddy, I'm scared that he's going to try and take the baby away."

It was all too much for Shawn to handle. Why hadn't she told him what Mark had done before now? This was his fault. Mark wanted to hurt her because she loved somebody else. He sat quietly with his face in his hands. Natalia watched as his strong chest heaved with exaggerated breaths.

"Shawn? Talk to me."

"So when are the tests?"

"He's going to call me."

Shawn said emphatically, "He ain't taking the baby, period."

"Well, if I know him, and I do, he's going to be devious, and use everything about your past to make us out to be unfit parents."

Shawn tipped her chin with his forefinger and when her teary eyes met his, he said, "I'm real sorry that I've caused you all this trouble. I know before you met me you didn't have all this shit to deal with in your life. I came into it and messed everything up."

"No, Shawn. You breathed life into my life, and I'm happy. I made the choice to have you in my life. I'm glad I made that choice. Everything that's happened has proven that our love is real. We may be different, but we compliment one another like peanut butter and jelly," she smiled.

"But all of this is my fault. He only wants to hurt you because you chose me over him."

"I know he's still angry at me for that. He's still trying to punish me. But he will not take my baby. I will fight him with everything I've got."

Susan Beyard hand delivered the test results to Natalia at home. She walked into the bedroom with a serious look on her face, Natalia knew she wasn't about to hear what she had hoped to hear.

"Susie, you don't look like you're bringing good news."

"Please have a seat, Natalia."

Natalia eased back in her rocking chair. Susan sat beside her and sighed. "Unfortunately, it seems they have cornered us again. Mark's lawyer happens to be a formidable opponent, not wet behind the ears as I had hoped." She crossed her legs. "He's already requested a custody hearing. Mark wants full custody."

Natalia gasped. How could it be? How the hell could Mark be her baby's father? That must be what Susan is saying. Was this some sort of cruel joke?

Susan tapped her thigh with a white envelope. "The results aren't what I am worried about. Yes, he has rights. But I am more concerned about the custody hearing. You know that Shawn's history of criminal activity will be the main focus throughout. We have to eliminate him from your...family equation."

"What?"

"It would only be until the custody suit is over."

"This is so wrong, Susan. Mark's only doing this out of spite. He doesn't care about Junior."

"I know it. You know it. But the judge doesn't. He bases his rulings on evidence and proof. Unfortunately, Mark is holding all the cards. All his lawyer needs to do is subpoena Shawn's criminal records. That's all. And your baby will go directly into Mark's happy two parent home. I know you don't want that. So to give us something to work with, you and Shawn need to separate. We will claim that after learning Junior's paternity, he left you. With Shawn out of the picture, you have a much better chance of keeping your son. Judges usually award custody to the mother."

"I'll do whatever I have to," Natalia sobbed. A tear fell onto Junior's plump cheek. She wiped it away with her pinkie finger and smiled at him. There was no way Mark and his bimbo du jour would get their hands on her baby.

"I hate to drop bad news and run, but I've got another meeting," Susan grinned.

"Let me walk you out."

"No, no. I'm fine. You just keep that precious little boy safe."

"Oh, I will. Thanks Susan...for everything."

"I'm just so sorry I couldn't bring you good news," Susan said as she prepared to leave. When she turned to open the door, Shawn was standing there. "Oh, hi. You scared me," she clutched her chest. Shawn flashed a phony smile and stepped aside. The heavy plastic bag in his hand grazed his leg. "Goodnight," she said and hurried down the hall.

"Hi," Natalia said sadly.

"Hi," he said as he dropped the plastic bag to the floor and leaned against the wall. "I heard what she said. I heard what you said, too."

Her eyes said that she was sorry, but she couldn't say the words. In fact, she didn't know what to say. All she knew was that Junior was her first priority. Even her love for Shawn had to take a back seat. "I have to..."

"I agree with you. You have to do whatever you got to."

"It's the only way. Susan said just until the custody hearing decision is in. Then if you still want to marry me..."

"Do you think any of this changes how I feel about you?"

"Well, I thought that, since Junior's not your baby, you wouldn't ...I mean, biologically, he's Mark's son, and I know how much you hate him."

"You think I could hate your baby? That baby is still mine. I couldn't care less what the test says. I love you, and I can love our baby no matter what," he spoke emphatically, his arms moving with each sentence.

"God, how I love you," she smiled.

Shawn took the baby from her arms. "I love you, lil' man. As far as I'm concerned, you're still my little running back." He chuckled and said, "Oh, and I love you too Baby Girl." Natalia playfully punched him in his side. "Hey I'm holding the baby. Be careful!" he scolded. "Damn, does he ever stay awake for more than five minutes?" he laughed.

"Hey!" she playfully scolded.

Shawn put Junior back in his bassinet. "You know that we have to make a girl now, right?"

"Whoa, big fella. That won't be for at least two or three years. I'm not ready to do that again anytime soon," she laughed. The phone rang. Shawn took it from its base and passed to her.

"Hello?" Natalia answered.

"Hi Nat. I take it you've heard the news."

"Yes, Mark, I've heard," she answered with hostility in her voice. Shawn shook his head and rolled the bassinet into the bedroom. He couldn't stand to listen to her talk to that punk. He realized Mark was attempting to ruin her life because of him. It wasn't fair. He sat down on the bed and looked at Junior's buttocks perched in the air. His pale little calves were exposed from under his gown. Shawn pulled a receiving blanket from the hall closet and covered his son, then sat on the bed and tried not to imagine what Mark was saying.

"Well, the hearing date is in two weeks. You'll receive an official summons tomorrow. I hate that we have to do things this way, but I know that I can provide the baby with stability. Children need that as well as consistency. And, to be blunt, your current living arrangements may not be all that stable or consistent. In fact, you're endangering Marco Jr. by keeping th-that murderer around. I can't believe you'd even consider having that man live in your house under the same roof with our child."

Natalia had never been passive in her life. But there she sat, quietly, without screaming or spouting insults. She just listened. She let him go off on a tangent about how society had been negatively affected by women like her who choose sex and men over their own children. How those neglected, unloved children become the undesirables and serial killers of the world. She swallowed hard and bit her lip to keep from defending herself. She waited for a break in his ramblings before attempting to respond.

"So you see, my wife and I are much better suited parents. She's an administrator for the Board of Education. She has a lot of experience with children. You'd never have to worry about Marco." He took a breath and paused — finally.

Natalia inhaled and exhaled slowly, licked her lips and said, "Mark, there is no reason for this custody suit. We can come to a fair arrangement on our own. Don't you think that taking a child from its mother for the sole purpose of revenge is wrong? I don't deserve that. I would never put my child in any danger. Never. So why don't you call off the bloodhounds, and, like you said to me before, let's handle this like mature adults."

"That's just it, Nat. The man, if I can even call him that, that teenager is not mature. Have you forgotten that he's a murdering drug dealer! Need I say more?"

"Mark, this is so unnecessary. I'm trying to be cordial. I'm trying to keep the peace. But if you keep backing me into a corner, I'm going to come out fighting."

"I see. So now you're violent just like him."

"Would you shut up about him! Thanks to you, he's left me. Isn't that what you wanted? Aren't you happy now?

"Really?"

"Yes, really."

"It doesn't change anything, Nat. Your judgment has been off for so long that I wouldn't be surprised if you took him back tomorrow. I still want my son." She heard a click as he hung up on her.

"Ugh! I just want to kill that man!" she shouted.

Shawn reappeared carrying a duffel bag. "I'll be by my Aunt Freda's house." He kissed her lips and turned to leave.

"Shawn, wait." She threw her arms around his neck and put her head on his chest. "I hope you're not angry."

"Baby Girl, I understand. Stop thinking I'm mad. I know this is how we gotta do it." He wrapped his arms around her and squeezed. "Its gon' be okay. I love you," he whispered.

"I love you more," she whispered back.

"I know." The embrace ended, and she watched her man leave.

She paced all night with the baby. When the alarm rang only two hours after she fell asleep, she nearly threw it. She looked at the bright red numbers. It was six-thirty. She got up, pumped her breasts for more than ten minutes, trying to fill at least four bottles for when André came over to babysit. She had to be in court at eight-thirty.

She turned on the television and caught the weather report on Good Day New York. It was going be hot but not humid. By the time she finished her orange juice and croissant, it was nearly eight o'clock.

Getting dressed was easy. She wanted to dress as homely as possible. She selected the first maternity dress she had purchased, an ankle length crepe silk floral print. It was loose on her. Over it, she threw on a dusty rose silk blazer. She pulled her hair back and twisted it into a neat bun. She didn't put on any make up, just some pink lip gloss. She grabbed the Winnie the Pooh knapsack she used when she took Junior to his doctor appointments and stuffed her wallet and extra breast pads into it. The doorbell rang. She kissed the baby and rushed to the door.

"Hi. Bye." She pecked André's cheek.

"But, honey bunny, you know I'm new to this. Does the baby come with instructions? Pamphlets or something?" André asked.

She laughed and said, "As a matter-of-fact, I did leave instructions on the fridge. Hopefully. I'll be back soon very soon. I can't stand to be away from my baby for more than an hour. Family court is only a five minute cab ride from here. I'll be back before he wakes up." She smiled then said, "Wish me luck."

"Good luck. God got your back. Don't worry," André smiled.

Natalia ran to the elevator and pressed the button but decided to take the stairs instead. As she walked towards the Exit sign, she heard a door being unlocked. André stuck his head out into the hallway and shouted, "Nat, before you go, you've got a call."

"Take a message Andy."

"No, this is an important call." His eyes widened and his eyebrows danced as he ran towards her. He put the cordless phone to her ear.

"Yes?" she said wearily.

"Good luck mommy. I love you."

"Oh, thank you, Daddy. I love you more."

"Okay, enough with the mushy stuff. Get your ass to court." André yanked the phone from her ear and pushed her. "Go girl, go!"

By the time she hailed a gypsy cab, it was eight-forty. When it pulled up to the Family Court building, she stuffed a ten dollar bill into the little plastic pocket in the window partition and didn't wait for change. She quickly got out of the cramped cab and ran up the steps of the court building. She looked for the information desk. When she found it, she asked for Room 330, Part B.

"Down the hall to your left. Take the elevator to the third floor," the guard replied.

"Thank you."

Natalia walked into the dimly lit courtroom and saw Susan sitting in front. "Good morning," she whispered as she sat down.

"Good morning, Natalia."

Natalia looked around but didn't see Mark or his attorney. "I hope they don't show up. I hope he's really thought about this and just drops this whole thing," Natalia said wistfully.

"Wouldn't that be nice?" Susan smiled. But then the doors opened, and in came Mark, his attorney and a dark haired woman with a heavily made up face.

"No such luck," Susan sighed.

"Damn," Natalia sighed, too.

Chapter Nineteen

❤

FINALE?

Mark strolled into the courtroom with confidence. He took the Tammy Faye look-a-like's hand and squeezed it gently. She smiled at him and gently kissed his cheek. To Natalia, it seemed as if they had rehearsed. After they took their seats, Mark glanced over at Natalia. She rolled her eyes and flared her nostrils. It was pure reflex on her part. The last thing she wanted was to show him that he had gotten to her. She looked away before she became angrier than she already was and began to flip through the paperwork Susan was arranging.

"So how does this work?" Natalia asked.

"Well, they go first. They play their hand and then I see what cards I can use."

"Oh boy. I guess I should prepare myself for fireworks?"

"Maybe, maybe not. Like I told you before, judges do not like to take children away from their biological mothers. They would only consider it under extreme circumstances," Susan replied.

"Anything like mine?"

"It's highly unlikely." Susan adjusted her glasses on her nose.

Just then, a tall man with long, blonde-tipped dreadlocks stood at the front of the courtroom and announced, "All rise. The honorable judge Marsha Graham presiding."

An old woman in a flowing black robe sat behind the judicial bench. After the bailiff told them to be seated, Mark's wife looked over at Natalia. She stared as if she had never seen a black woman before. Natalia felt her stare and turned just in time to catch her before she turned her head.

The judge addressed the court then gave Mark's attorney the opportunity to plead his case.

"Good Morning, your honor. We're here to establish a healthy environment for a newborn who we feel is in imminent danger." The attorney flipped open a yellow folder on the council table in front of him. He pulled out a few papers and said, "May I approach, your honor?"

"Yes," the judge answered as she perched a pair of reading glasses on the bridge of her nose. Mark's attorney handed her several sheets of papers which she thoroughly read. She looked at the court reporter and announced, "The court acknowledges the submission of paternity results concerning the paternity of Shawn A. Wilson, Junior. Let the records show that Marco Delucchio is legally declared the father, ninety-nine point nine, nine percent."

The attorney returned to his place at the table. "Your honor, my client is asking for full custody of the child based on evidence which I would also like to submit." His assistant handed him a blue folder. He, in turn, brought it to the Judge. She opened the folder and looked through its contents.

"You have in front of you, Judge Graham, rap sheets and incriminating photographs of Ms. Foles' fiancé, Shawn Wilson. What this evidence indicates is that Ms. Foles' home is an unfit living aenvironment for an adult let alone an infant. We also believe Ms. Foles should be tested for substance abuse as well."

"Pure conjecture your honor!" Susan said as she jumped to her feet.

"Counselor, I have in front of me records and photographs of your client's fiancé. Apparently, he is a drug dealer with a rap sheet a mile long. On it, I see a manslaughter charge that was plea bargained down to a mere slap on the wrist and a narcotics and illegal arms case that is still pending." Judge Graham sighed, took off her glasses and laid them down on the desk. "I hardly think that this is the type of person that should be raising a child. Ms. Foles, please stand." Natalia stood up nervously and grabbed onto the extra material of her dress.

"Apparently, Ms. Foles, you are not using proper judgement here. We are talking about your child. You should not have a criminal anywhere near him." Natalia looked away from the judge's condescending stare. She glanced over at Mark and could see him nodding in agreement. He even had the audacity to shake his finger in her direction as if he were chastising her. It set her off. "You're only doing this to hurt me. You don't even care about my baby!" Natalia cried.

Susan popped up and grabbed Natalia by her shoulders to try to calm her down. Natalia trembled with anger and her nostrils flared like a bull being teased by a Matador's red cape.

"Ms. Foles, it is clear to me that you may not be using your best judgement. Additionally, your demeanor suggests that you may be under the influence of..."

"Your honor!" Susan replied as calmly as she could. "Ms. Foles' relationship with Mr. Wilson is over. She does not intend to marry him." Susan tried to clean up the mess that Natalia had created.

"I hate you, Mark!" Natalia jumped out of her seat and spat. She turned to the judge, and with sad eyes, said, "Your honor, he's only doing this to punish me. You can't let him win. He's just being vindictive. He's mad because I chose someone else over him."

"You chose a criminal which to me is proof enough that your state of mind is not up to par right now. Perhaps you need counseling."

Susan unsuccessfully tried again to push Natalia back down in her chair. At her wit's end, she admonished through clenched teeth, "Sit down, Natalia!"

"NO! Don't you see him over there, gloating? This is his plan! He couldn't wait to stick it to me." Natalia stomped her feet, "Please don't take my baby. He's only using my baby to punish me. Don't you see that?" She jumped up and down, waving her hands. She glared at Mark and shouted, "YOU SON OF A BITCH! I HATE YOU! I HATE YOU!"

Susan plopped down in her chair in defeat. Natalia had completely ruined any chance of winning this battle.

"Sit down, Ms. Foles!" The judge was very annoyed.

Mark threw gasoline onto the fire by shaking his head and saying, "Tsk, tsk. You're making a spectacle of yourself. How could you take drugs knowing you have a child to take care of?" That was the straw that broke the camel's back.

"Arrrgh! I hate you!" Natalia screamed as she squeezed past Susan and tried to attack Mark. Mark's attorney grabbed her flailing arms, and the bailiff ran over. He grabbed her and lifted her a few inches from the ground. He carried her out of the courtroom screaming.

"My goodness, that woman is unstable. Counselor, your client is hereby ordered to undergo drug testing as well as a psychiatric evaluation. Custodial rights of Shawn Wilson Junior shall be remanded to Marco Delucchio until the results of the so ordered tests and evaluation come back," Judge Graham ruled.

"Your honor, we're talking about a newborn here. Ms. Foles is breast feeding the child. Please show some compassion. Mr. Delucchio cannot breast feed."

Susan looked over at Mark and shot daggers at him with her eyes.

"Ms. Beyard, more damage will be done to the child should he remain with Ms. Foles. He can switch to formula. It is just as healthy. All of my children were raised on formula, and they grew up just fine." The judge looked over at Mark's attorney and said, "To enforce this order, your client shall be accompanied by a representative from social services when he picks up the child from Ms. Foles' residence. I also stipulate that a police officer accompany Mr. Delucchio as well. I am concerned that both father and child may be in physical danger. These orders are active immediately."

"Your honor, my client is upset," Susan continued. "The unfounded accusations made against her character and her lifestyle pushed her over the edge. How can you take the child away from his mother? At least allow her visitation. I'll even take supervised visitation. Please reconsider your honor..."

Mark's attorney shook his head and interrupted, "Your honor, after that incorrigible display, there is no way my client will agree to unsupervised visits by Ms. Foles."

The judge agreed. "I'm sorry, counselor. Your client must be professionally evaluated before I'll consider her capable of motherhood. She must comply with my order, also effective immediately. I will not allow visitation." She banged her gavel and said, "Court is dismissed." In frustration, Susan slammed her hand down on the table.

Mark's expression was devoid of compassion. He actually smiled when he embraced his attorney. And then he hugged and kissed his wife. Susan watched in disgust. How could a man be so evil?

She sighed and grabbed her briefcase. Mark's attorney approached her with an outstretched hand. She just looked down at it, scoffed at his gesture and walked out of the courtroom. Natalia ran to her.

"P-please tell me that the judge changed her mind."

"I'm sorry, Natalia. She has awarded Mark temporary custody. The order is effective immediately. Visitation is disallowed pending the outcome of your drug tests and psychiatric evaluations."

"NO!" Natalia screamed as she dropped to her knees. Susan helped her up. "This can't be happening," she sobbed.

Just then Mark and his wife approached. "I'll be by later for my son," he said without remorse.

Natalia was about to run after him, but Susan grabbed her arm and yanked her back. "Don't you dare give him any more ammunition," she said angrily.

"I can't...I can't let him take my baby," Natalia wailed like a wounded animal.

"Natalia, let me get back to my office to arrange for the tests and the psyche evaluation. You go home and give that baby all the love you can until that bastard comes. Okay?" Susan said.

Natalia slung the Winnie the Pooh bag over her shoulder. She had no more fight left in her. She looked at Susan with watery eyes, turned and left the courthouse.

She slammed the door so hard that the noise frightened Junior, and he began to cry. Natalia ran to him. André was sitting in the rocker, rocking back and forth with Junior in his arms.

"Oh, no," he gasped as he saw the look on Natalia's face.

Natalia took Junior from André and snuggled him to her bosom.

"He just ate," André said softly.

"I want him to remember my heartbeat, Andy," she said weakly. "Mommy loves you sooo much." She rubbed her cheek against his. She patted his back, and he burped.

"Oh, that's two. He burped for me earlier," André said.

"Andy, the judge actually gave Mark full custody. I won't even be able to see my baby until I take some stupid drug tests...Oh, and get this. I have to undergo a psychiatric evaluation, too! He's so fucking vindictive. He practically laughed at me in the courtroom."

"I can't believe him. He's a real piece of work," André commiserated. "Shit, Nat, who wouldn't need a psychiatrist after dealing with his ass!"

Natalia took Junior into the bedroom, laid down on the bed with him and cuddled close him to her chest. She looked into his innocent eyes. Then he gave her a gift. Junior smiled and showed her his shiny pink gums. Natalia began to cry again. "Thank you, my little honey bunny." She kissed his button nose.

André rushed into the room with the phone in his hand. "I didn't hear the phone ring," she said softly.

"I was on the other line. Here," he tried to give her the phone. She pushed it away. "It's Shawn." André placed the phone on her shoulder and fixed it so that the receiver was by her ear.

"Daddy, he's taking Junior today."

"Damn!"

"You should've seen him in court. He was awful. He wants me to suffer, Shawn. He doesn't care about the baby. He's coming for Junior later today. What am I gonna do?"

"Don't worry, Baby Girl. We'll figure something out. I know I'm not supposed to be over there, but you need me right now."

"The cops will be here with him."

"Say word. He's a punk. I don't care about the cops. I'm still coming."

"You can't be here. If they see you here, I'll never get custody. I want you here so badly but it's not a good idea."

"I know mommy, I know. Aiight, what if I hide when they get there? I want to be there for you. Let me come over."

Natalia looked at her cooing baby boy. "Daddy, he just smiled at me. Junior smiled for his mommy. He knows that mommy is sad. He smiled to tell me everything is going to be alright."

"Baby Girl, I'm coming, okay?"

"Okay. I love you Shawn."

"I love you a helluva lot more," he said. "Are you smiling for me right now?"

"Yes, Daddy."

"Good. You know Daddy is going to fix this, right?"

"Yes..." she sniffled.

"Don't cry mommy. I'm on my way."

André could see the conversation was over even though Natalia's ear and shoulder still cradled the receiver. He took the phone from her and lay behind her, wrapping his right arm around her waist. "I never thought y'all would make it through all that y'all have gone through and still be together," he said, rubbing her arm. "I guess it was more than passion. You two really love each another. I wish so much that we could live happily ever after."

"Junior's smile told me it's going to be okay, and I believe him." She caressed her baby's head. He yawned. "Okay, okay Junior we'll shut up now so that you can take your nap." She covered him with a blanket and put him in his bassinet.

"Should I go or do you want me to stay until he gets here?"

"Shhh. He's falling asleep," she whispered. "Hmmm hmmm hmmm, hmmm hmmm," she hummed a melodious tune to lull Junior to sleep.

"But..." André tried to finish. Natalia shooed him out of the room, never missing a hum.

André decided to take the garbage to the incinerator. He unlocked the door and reached for the knob, but it turned before he could touch it. The door opened, and André assumed a ninja stance. "Hi-Yah!" he shouted. Shawn laughed at André's peculiar position.

"Oh, it's you. You scared the hell outta me. I thought I was gonna have to get buck wild up in here," he laughed.

"My bad," Shawn laughed.

"She's in bed resting. This is so fucked up." André let out an exasperated sigh.

"I know man." Shawn put his keys back in his pocket.

"I guess now that you're here, I can leave. Take good care of her for me. Tell her she can call me for anything, okay?"

"Aiight, man. Thanks." André grabbed his satchel and the garbage bag and left. Shawn went into the bedroom. Natalia had cried so much, the pillowcase was soaked through.

"We're going to get him back. Some way, somehow." He scooped her up in his arms and pulled her head to his chest. "It's gonna be okay. I'm gonna make it okay." He stroked her hair.

"I don't know what I'd do if he kept my baby," she sniffled.

"He won't."

"I hate him so much. I just...I just want to kill him."

Shawn had thought the same thing many times on his way over. In fact, he had come up with several murder scenarios. But then, he began to plot alternatives to killing Mark.

"Baby Girl, I've got a plan B. I hope you agree to it. It'll be the only way for you, me and junior to be together without ever having to worry about that white boy."

"How Shawn?"

"Aiight, listen. I'm sure he won't be home all day every day. So when he's gone to work, and Junior is with the babysitter, I'll go over, tie up the babysitter, make sure she's in a safe place and take Junior. I'll burn the house down and leave another baby's corpse in Junior's place. I can get a body from my man who works at the Bronx morgue. And while they're investigating the fire, you and I can be on a plane to Amsterdam. They can't come for us over there. So whatchu think?"

Natalia was stunned. "Uh, you really thought this through didn't you?" she asked, astounded.

"I just want you to be happy."

"But his wife, she might be home and..."

"Well then, she'll get tied up, too. Listen, I don't plan on hurting anybody. I just want to get Junior back. Besides, that fuckin' cracker deserves to come home to a burned up house. Look what he's doing to you."

"But, Shawn, that seems so extreme."

"I've already set some things in motion. I've got his address, and I got somebody who'll stake out his house. Like I said, my man already got me a body so all you have to do is say okay."

"Shawn this is all so, so..."

"Remember that nobody will get hurt."

Natalia looked into his eyes and caressed his face with her left hand, "You'd do all of that for me?"

"And Junior," he smiled.

"Hmmm, Amsterdam. I guess I'd look good in clogs," she smiled. "Oh, but I'll have to sell my businesses. I can't sell this building, though. This was Daddy's first venture. I know what I'll do. I'll give it to Andy. I'll have everything transferred into European accounts and..."

"So does this mean your down with it?"

"Ya iz good," she said in a Dutch accent and laughed. Shawn grabbed her face and planted a wet, sloppy kiss on her lips.

The heavy pounding on the door could only be Mark. Only he would be so inconsiderate. Shawn quickly hid out on the terrace. While she waited, Natalia packed all of Junior's clothes, diapers, rattles and blankets and had even pumped two bottles of breast milk. She rolled the bassinet into the living room and opened the door very slowly.

"Good evening, ma'am," the social worker said with her hands on her hips.

"Yeah, yeah," Natalia said blandly and flung the door open. She went to her baby and peered into the bassinet. "Mommy loves you, Shawn, Jr. You're going bye-bye for a little while. It's going to be okay," she spoke softly. Mark rode in on his high horse, eyes darting back and forth surveying the room. The police officer remained at the threshhold.

"Do you have somewhere for the baby to sleep or do you need the bassinet?" she asked as calmly as she could.

"I have a nursery all set up at my new house."

"Oh, how convenient," she grumbled under her breath. The social worker reached into the bassinet and picked up Junior.

"I want to hold him," Mark took the baby from her.

"There are two bottles of breast milk in the bag. It's best if you wean him off of it by alternating with the formula. You have to refrigerate the bottles. They'll last only a day or two," Natalia said as she stroked Junior's soft curly hair.

"Thanks," he managed to say before snatching the bag from her hand.

She looked over at the officer. "Did you see that? He's holding my son, and he just snatched the bag from me. I hope you saw that."

"Sorry ma'am, I didn't. Do you have everything, sir?"

"I guess so," Mark replied as he looked at Natalia. She was quietly drowning in tears. As one slid down her honey-glazed cheek, he looked away. He saw how badly he was hurting her — he had wanted to, but now he felt miserable. Still, he had to finish what he started.

As they all turned to leave, Natalia said, "Wait. Please." Mark turned around. "Can I hold him one last time?" Mark looked at the social worker then at Natalia then back at the social worker. The social worker nodded.

"Okay," he said. Natalia took Junior in her arms and kissed his forehead. She rocked him back and forth and held him up in front of her. "I love you, honey bunny." She snuggled him up to her chest and rubbed the back of her fingers across his plump cheeks.

"Okay, let's go, big boy," Mark said and took Junior from her. He couldn't stand to watch the emotional goodbye any longer.

"Goodnight," the social worker and policeman said. Mark looked at her with a hint of pity. "Nat..."

"Just go," she said weakly as she crumbled to the floor. She slammed the door behind them with her foot and sobbed uncontrollably. Shawn ran to her, dropped to his knees and held her in his arms. "It's not over Baby Girl. He didn't win. Remember we got plan B."

Just as she planned, Natalia had her accountant transfer funds into an international web account. She was willing to turn over the Madison Avenue McDonald's and the Brooklyn building to André, but he convinced her that it wasn't necessary. He would oversee their operations along with her business manager to make sure all revenues went directly into her new account. She sold her other McDonald's to Gavin Pert who owned a chain of franchises. Within three days, all of her business transactions were taken care of.

Shawn had already recruited an accomplice and told Tymeek about his plan. He also told Tymeek that he and Natalia were getting married at the justice of the peace that week. Although Tymeek still harbored bad feelings towards Natalia, he agreed to help make his brother's move to Amsterdam easier. He also promised to stay away from Shawn until Shawn told Natalia that they would be living near his brother.

Mark had bought a brownstone in Cobble Hill, Brooklyn and that was how he met Emily. She worked part-time as a realtor. They went out on a couple of dates, and Mark could see that she was the type of woman his mother had always wanted for him. She didn't mind cooking and was supportive. When he asked her to quit the real estate job so that she could devote more time to helping him with Junior, she eagerly obliged. She was the typical Italian wife, the type who would eventually bore him. Unlike his ex-wife, Emily had no opinions of her own. She was too agreeable, almost to the point where she seemed to do things only to make him happy.

Mark had a master plan. Quite proud of himself, he strategically avoided sex on their honeymoon, claiming food poisoning. And since they had been home, he continued to find one excuse or another not to consummate their marriage. Junior provided the final, perfect excuse. Mark had it all planned out. The marriage would never be consummated. And after he was given sole, complete custody of his son, he would have the marriage annulled. He only married Emily to get custody. She provided him with what the court would assume was the perfect household in which to raise a child. So far, his plan was working out just fine. He hired a nanny to help with Junior, specifically because Emily had no children nor maternal instincts.

"Cecilia, I bought two boxes of Enfamil yesterday. They're in the bottom cupboard," Mark said as he rested his briefcase on the floor and tucked his shirt into his pants.

"Okay, Sir. I'll prepare more bottles. Junior is a very healthy eater."

"I know. It seems like he's getting bigger by the minute," he chuckled and walked to the door.

Emily ambushed him with a hug. "Have a good day, honey." She acted like June Cleaver every morning. In the beginning it was sweet, but now it was just annoying.

"Thanks," he said as he tried to dodge her kiss.

"I'm going to take the baby to the park today. He needs to get out."

"No."

"No? Why not, Marco?" she asked with a hand on her hip.

He hated when she called him Marco. If it weren't for Junior, she'd be long gone. He hoped that he could put up with her long enough to gain full custody. "I don't want him outside just yet. He's a newborn, and very susceptible to germs. You can go out if you'd like. That's why I hired Cecilia...to free up your time."

"Alright, if you say so. I won't take him anywhere."

"And can you start calling him by his name. Stop referring to him as the baby and him."

"Marco, there's no need to get huffy."

"And, for God's sake, call me Mark. Why did you start calling me Marco anyway?"

"I'm Italian, what can I tell you? Don't worry, baby, I won't say it again," she smiled sensuously. She slipped her arm around his waist and whispered, "So are you a little less stressed now? Can we start our honeymoon when you get home tonight?"

"We'll see." He removed her hand from his waist and left.

Emily walked into the kitchen where Cecilia was warming a bottle of formula. "I can see that damn brat is going to be a thorn in my side," she muttered to herself. Cecilia looked at her in disbelief. "What are you looking at?" Emily spat and searched the cupboards. "Where are the cups? Oh, never mind. Make me some coffee." She waved her hand at Cecilia.

"Mrs. Delucchio, I'm a nanny not your servant."

"You're job is whatever I say it is. Capisci?"

"I'll quit right now. Then what would you do?" Cecilia snapped back.

"Are you threatening me? I can have your ass back on a raft to Cuba in no time."

"I will feel sorry for Junior, but I will not take this from anyone!" Cecilia threw the dishtowel down on the table and slammed the bottle down.

Emily grabbed her arm as she tried to walk off. "Oh, no you don't. You were hired to do a job, and you're going to do it!"

"I don't have to do anything. Take your hands off me!" she tried to pry Emily's hand from her arm.

During the commotion, neither woman realized that two strangers had slipped inside the house. Both wore ski masks and entered through the side door that led up from the empty apartment Mark hadn't yet rented. One crept into the nursery, and the other lugged two hefty laundry bags and rope into the bedroom.

Cecilia hadn't been able to remove Emily's hand from her arm. "You will not leave, damn it!" Emily shouted.

"You're a crazy woman. Leave me alone." Cecilia finally broke free and ran into the hallway. She abruptly stopped as she heard a noise coming from the bedroom. She turned around slowly with fear in her eyes and whispered, "Someone is here."

Emily tiptoed towards Cecilia. In their fear, both women forgot their fight and huddled together, listening. They heard Junior's faint coos.

"Oh, no. They got the baby," Cecilia whispered, her hands instinctively reaching up to cover her mouth.

An eerie creak sounded behind them. Before they could turn around, a cloth was thrust over each of their faces. They struggled but couldn't get free. Then they felt a rope looping around and around them, squeezing their bodies together. Cloths were stuffed into their mouths to muffled their cries for help. They were dragged to somewhere in the townhouse and left alone. The next thing they heard was furniture being moved.

Shawn had Junior. He ran down to the empty apartment where an elderly woman waited. She took Junior from his arms and out to a car idling on the corner. She quickly strapped him into a car seat and drove off. Shawn went back to the nursery to start the fire. His accomplice had already placed the baby corpse in the crib.

"Aiight, man. I'm gon' blaze the place so go start the car," Shawn instructed. Before Shawn struck the match, he grabbed clothes and blankets and threw them over the infant's stiff body. He lit the match and threw it in the crib. Then he went to the bedroom and lit another match.

As soon as Mark opened the door, he inhaled thick smoke. He waved it from his face and ran into the bedroom. "NO!" he screamed then jumped on Shawn's back and tried to rip off the ski mask. Shawn flipped him over onto the floor. Mark scrambled to his feet and began swinging. He connected twice with Shawn's chest. Shawn stumbled backwards trying to bob and weave out of the way. Mark looked around the fire-engulfed room for something to use as a weapon. He ran into the kitchen and grabbed a long serrated knife. Shawn tried to escape, but Mark attacked him and sliced into his shoulder with the knife. Shawn swung around and began to pummel Mark with his gloved fists. Mark jabbed at him and nicked his chest. Enraged, Shawn wrestled Mark to the ground, managed to get hold of the knife and rammed it into his stomach. Mark's eyes closed tightly, his teeth clenched in pain. He rolled to one side and began to hyperventilate. Shawn watched him gasp for air. He didn't mean to hurt Mark, but it was too late.

Shawn ran into the kitchen and pulled off his gloves. He threw them on the stove where a pot of boiling water had evaporated, the baby bottle inside melted and burned into a black glob. The gloves fell into the burner's flame and caught fire instantly. He ran out the open front door, pushing past a neighbor who saw the smoke pouring out the window and came to investigate. She screamed when Shawn ran to the waiting car on the other side of the street. As they sped off, he heard sirens in the distance.

"You ain't see that niggah going in the house?" Shawn asked, winded.

"Who? I had to move the car because a woman came out, and I ain't want her getting suspicious with me in this mask. I ain't let her see my face though."

"Fuck it. What's done is done."

All went as planned. Shawn and his accomplice met the elderly woman at her house, paid her and picked up Junior. They left and were on their way to Newark airport. Junior slept through the whole ride.

"Aiight, you know what to do. Thanks, man." Shawn gave the man a pound, a wad of cash and rushed to the international departure lounge. He looked around, searching for the love of his life, and spotted her sitting cross-legged, shaking her foot nervously. "Surprise," he grinned.

"Oh, Junior, mommy missed you." Natalia's face lit up as ahe cuddled her son and kissed his tiny forehead. She sighed and looked into Shawn's eyes, her fear plainly evident.

"Are you having second thoughts?" he asked her.

"Can't they have us extradited? I thought they could do that for Federal crimes. This is a federal crime," she whispered.

"Don't worry. They can't come for us there. They don't have any jurisdiction in Amsterdam 'cause it's an arbitrary country. Besides who's gonna know he's still alive. As far as they gon' know, Junior died in the fire," Shawn assured her.

"How do you know all of this?"

"I just do," he smiled. She wasn't worried anymore. She was about to embark on a wonderful new life with her brand new husband and son. "I love you," she put her arm around him and her son.

"I love you...like you wouldn't believe. Trust me." He kissed the top of her head. Over the loudspeaker came the announcement: PASSENGERS FOR FLIGHT 1133 BOUND FOR AMSTERDAM PLEASE BEGIN BOARDING NOW.

"That's us. Come on let's go," Shawn said as he grabbed the Louis Vuitton bag from the chair with his free hand. Natalia was so happy that Junior was back that she kept her eyes glued to him. She kept making funny faces at him and talking to him in baby babble.

"So, what we gon' name my little girl?" Shawn asked with a chuckle.

Natalia looked up at him with her mouth twisted to the side. "Now, you know that's a long time from now," she laughed before turning just in time to see men clad in blue with guns drawn, blocking their path to the departure terminal.

"Freeze!" They shouted in unison.

"What the fuck?" Shawn asked incredulously.

"Don't move!" one shouted and inched closer, his gun pointed directly at Shawn. Shawn looked at Natalia then back at the officer.

"What's going on?" Natalia asked nervously.

"Put your hands up, ma'am." Natalia raised her arms in the air slowly as a look of panic flashed across her face.

"What's the problem, officers?" Shawn asked nonchalantly.

"Sir, I'm coming over to take the baby...no sudden moves, you understand?"

"But what's all this for? We didn't do anything."

The wheels in his head were spinning. *What could have gone wrong with his plan? Who snitched? Had they been followed all the way to the airport? Did his accomplices get picked up? Did they give him up? How the hell could the cops know?*

The officer approached slowly. From the corner of his eye, Shawn could see the look of sheer horror on Natalia's face. It broke his heart. This shouldn't be happening to her. She didn't deserve this. With his free arm he grabbed Natalia in a headlock. "How did you know I kidnapped this woman and her son? It don't matter cuz now I'm just gonna snap her neck if you don't let me get outta here!" Shawn shouted.

Natalia started to cry. She knew what Shawn was doing. The cops looked at each other then one said, "Release the woman and child to our officer."

"NO!" Shawn shouted as he tightened his arm around Natalia's neck. He jerked Junior in his arm to keep him from sliding down.

"Don't do this," Natalia whispered.

"Let me outta here, and I won't hurt 'em!" Shawn shouted.

"Now you know that we can't do that. Be smart. You can't make it out of here alive. Look around you!" the agent shouted back.

Shawn looked at Natalia's scared face. He released her and pushed her to the floor in front of him. "Take the baby and run," he whispered.

Shawn was about to hand her Junior and the Louis Vuitton bag slung over his shoulder when he heard a cracking sound. A rookie with a nervous trigger finger saw Shawn move and assumed he was reaching for a gun. The FBI agent squeezed his trigger over and over again. The shots surprised everyone. Bullets whizzed through the air and struck Shawn in his torso and thighs. No longer able to stand, he dropped Junior on his head and fell to the floor.

Natalia watched as a puddle of blood seeped through the blue and green rabbits on Junior's receiving blanket. Her eyes grew wide, and her body shook uncontrollably but no tears came. Her jaw dropped, and her eyes rolled back in her head. Her breathing slowed and everything stood still. Voices were muffled, and colors blended and blurred into gray. Before she fainted, she heard a sound like a ticking clock. Maybe it was telling her that she had no time left. Maybe she was drifting up to heaven — or careening down to hell.

The blood. The screaming. It was all so surreal. Natalia knew that she wasn't dead because she could still hear and feel. Hands grabbed at her. A cold gust of air washed over her. *Why am I not dead?* she thought. She was tired of being the sole survivor.

She closed her eyes, hoping for peace.

LIFE IS A GIFT. NOT A GIVEN.

— NURIT FOLKES